"THERE'S NOTHING HERE TO SCARE A MARINE ..."

"Get it out, get it out! No! I'm not going!" Magnan yelped. Then he fell to his knees and looked up at Retief in desperation. Behind him, Red was doggedly trying to creep uphill. "Feller's gotta do what a feller's gotta do," he explained.

Magnan scrambled up beside Retief. "Hurry!" he urged. "We have to do as it says! Otherwise ..."

"Mr. Retief," Bill blurted, "don't you hear it too?"

"I didn't hear anything to scare a Marine, Bill."

"Yes, Mother, I'm coming," Magnan added in a conversational tone. "Coming Sergeant?"

Alone now, Retief was scanning the crest of the slope above when the Voice spoke quite clearly, impinging not on his ears but thrusting in among his thoughts.

... THERE'S A GOOD FELLOW! I WAS BEGINNING TO THINK YOU'D NEVER LOWER THAT IMPRESSIVE SHIELD OF YOURS! NOW, IF YOU'LL JUST COME ALONG WITH THE OTHERS, I WANT TO EXPLAIN CERTAIN MATTERS TO YOU BEFORE DISASTER OVERTAKES US ALL ...

Retief heard a sound from ahead, and turned quickly to see a carpet of wriggling foot-long creatures with large glowing eyes advancing toward him in an undulating wave; then a silent impact behind his eyes, and blackness closed in.

KEITH LAUMER
REWARD FOR
RETIEF

BAEN
BOOKS

REWARD FOR RETIEF

Copyright © 1989 by Keith Laumer

A Baen Book

Baen Publishing Enterprises
260 Fifth Avenue
New York, N.Y. 10001

First Baen printing, February 1989

ISBN: 0-671-69804-4

Cover art by Gary Ruddell

Printed in the United States of America

Distributed by
SIMON & SCHUSTER
1230 Avenue of the Americas
New York, N.Y. 10020

INTRODUCTION

1

Second Secretary Jame Retief of the Terran Embassy to Sardon was just finishing his after-dinner brandy in the transport's Junior Officers' Mess when his chief, First Secretary Ben Magnan, hurried up and took a seat opposite him.

"Retief," he began excitedly, "there's something they're not telling us!" He glanced around as if to ferret out spies, then resumed: "It's widely known that Goldblatt's Other World, more formally known as Sardon, and listed in the handbook as U-784-a, called Spookworld by the vulgar, has not been visited by Terrans since its discovery, two centuries ago. Yet on the occasion of the Becentennial of discovery a full diplomatic mission is dispatched here to normalize relations. Who, may one inquire, has laid the groundwork for our establishment of an Embassy of Terra? How is it we've been alerted to keep an eye open for distressed Terran spacemen said to be marooned here? And who, *who* is the author of the rumors which have given rise to the place's unsavory reputation? What are we to do? Simply to leap into troubled waters unprepared is hardly a strategy worthy of the *Corps Diplomatique*! And, we'll be there—or here—very soon now, I believe." He consulted a well-worn schedule, and frowned. "You'd best finish your drink—or better, dump it in the potted jelly-flowers just there."

Retief nodded, and took another sip.

"Still," Magnan went on in a more confident tone, "rumors *do* arise spontaneously. And as for these rumors in particular—dragons, plagues of stinging nits, magic spells, trolls, enchantments—only a small child—or a Spaceman—could take such nonsense seriously." He nodded, as if satisfied with his argument.

"Rumors usually have some slight basis in fact," Retief pointed out. "Sardon is probably a little strange—but so are most places."

Magnan gave him a stricken look. "That's hardly comforting, Jim," he carped.

HAVE NO FEAR, BEN, a silent Voice spoke suddenly inside each man's skull. I ASSURE YOU THINGS HERE ON ZANNY-DU ARE QUITE PEACEFUL FOR THE MOMENT, THOUGH I CONFESS THERE ARE TROUBLEMAKERS ABOUT. IT WAS I WHO AGREED TO RECEIVE A MISSION FROM TERRA. JUST RELAX, AND LEAVE GREAT AFFAIRS TO THE GREAT.

Magnan, confused by the Voice, stared, open-mouthed, at Retief. "Jim!" he gasped, "it's all very well to jape with *me*; *I* understand your curiously warped sense of the facetious—but for Heaven's sake don't let Ambassador Shortfall overhear any such vainglorious remarks! But—" he paused uncertainly. "I was looking right at you and your lips didn't so much as twitch. How—?" He seemed to collect himself with an effort. "Atmosphere in ten minutes," he announced briskly after a glance at his thumb-chron.

"Make that maybe twenty seconds," Gus, the table-attendant corrected tonelessly. "I been feeling the vibes for a couple seconds now. We're already into maybe point six microbars gas. Feel that?" he queried as the aging vessel jolted abruptly, rattling the tableware. "Old Cap never could hit a ETA," he added. "See? What'd I tell ya?" he went on complacently as the first near-supersonic whisper of atmospheric friction started up. "I wouldn't bet two demi-guck this tub'll hang together for another class one pilot error, neither," he commented with apparent indifference, watching Magnan closely for his reaction. "Flunked her mid-cruise, you know," he went on. "If they didn't owe me six months back wages, I'd of jumped her at Furthuron."

"That will do, my man," Magnan said testily. "Surely you have duties elsewhere."

"I can take a hint," Gus acknowledged. "I been reading up on this here Spookworld, too," he ploughed on relentlessly. He absentmindedly pulled out a chair and nearly sat in it, but Magnan's sudden attack of black-lung caused him to shift in mid-squat and mime correcting the placement of the chair. "Course," he remarked, "if you don't wanna hear about how they got a lot of dead guys down there, zombies-like, maybe, and some kinda monsters,—bugs is bad, too, I hear. I guess I better get back to work. . . ."

"By all means," Magnan said coldly. "And I remind you, sir, that the planet about which we are about to enter landing orbit is listed in the Handbook as U-784-a, and correctly referred to as Sardon, or less formally, Goldblatt's Other World, after its intrepid discoverer."

"Which he ain't been heard from since," Gus commented gloomily. "Maybe we'd be better off if she did break up; get it over with fast, you know." He grabbed for support as the old ship bucked again and began a slow rotation.

"Do you mean to suggest," Magnan demanded, "that this vessel is unspaceworthy?"

"Naw, it ain't that," Gus corrected. "She's OK in space, it's getting her down that's tricky. How's about a

shot of the good stuff fer you, Mr. Magnan? You don't
look so good."

"I'm very well, thank you, Gus," Magnan replied
faintly. "Heavens, Retief," he addressed the younger
man. "Do you suppose . . . that is—"

"Never suppose," Retief suggested. "I doubt very
much that we'll encounter any zombies down below."

"Well!" Magnan came back tartly. "Of course not!
What do you take me for? I was concerned about the
condition of this infernal vessel to which we've en-
trusted our lives! It's disgraceful! 'Flunked his semi-
annual,' I've been informed by a Usually Reliable
Source."

"Yes, I heard him," Retief concurred. "It was something about the logs being in arrears, I understand."

"Well, what a relief!" Magnan exclaimed. He shot
Gus a pained look. "Very bad form," he stated, "starting rumors about unspaceworthiness, to say nothing of
zombies inhabiting the wilderness below us."

"Never started no rumors," Gus objected. "Figgered
you gents wouldn't blab none." With that reproof he
abruptly resumed his duties in response to a *"Hsst!
garcon!"* from the next table. Magnan leaned toward
Retief and said earnestly:

"One hardly knows *what* to think. The Post Report said
nothing of Carribean superstition on GOW. Pardon my
use of the acronym, Jim; I'm upset, is all."

"No sweat, sir," Retief reassured his chief. "After all,
our Confidential Terran Source didn't mention Papa
Dumballa."

"Oh, you mean George, the janitor back at Sector
HQ. Well, George is all very well, but he's hardly as
prestigious as, say, 'a Highly-Placed Official,' for example, meaning the janitor in the local Foreign Office."

"Still," Retief reminded the nervous Magnan. "The
Press flacks, for all their prestige, get their dope the
same way *we* do, in the Press kits the Information
Agency cooks up."

"Based on reliable rumors," Magnan nodded. "I still feel there are some aspects of the situation which will remain obscure even to TIA until the Mission has actually arrived and presented credentials."

"And perhaps taken a walk around the block," Retief added. "If there really is a monster called Worm down there, maybe seeing it will confirm its existence."

" 'Monster,' pah!" Magnan scoffed. "Really, Retief, if you're nervous, perhaps we could arrange to get the nod as ship's complement, and remain aboard for the nonce."

"I'll pass, Ben," Retief dismissed the suggestion. "If there really *are* zombies down there, I'd hate to miss meeting them."

Magnan stared from Retief to the cloud-streaked disc of Goldblatt's Other World slowly swelling on the wall-screen beside him.

"It looks pleasant enough," he remarked hopefully, "but do you really think there might be something to this zombie talk?"

"If so," Retief told him, "Captain Goldblatt didn't mention it in his Report of Discovery. He reported 'no intelligent life' but plenty of gnats."

"Then," Magnan demanded earnestly, his eyes on Retief's, "to whom is this Mission accredited? Surely Sector hasn't established diplomatic relations with an uninhabited jungleworld?" He dropped his eyes and began fiddling with his teaspoon. "I had it in confidence from Bob Trenchfoot, who was in the Advance Party, that the climate is salubrious in the extreme. They were able to procure adequate quarters for both the chancery and the Residence in the city Zanny-du. So, you see, there *must* be autocthonous inhabitants!"

"Flawless reasoning, sir," Retief agreed. "That could explain the disappearances, too."

"What disappearances?" Magnan yelped.

"Just reliable rumors, Ben," Retief soothed. "From time to time, it seems, the Monitor Service has detected a tramp freighter making an unauthorized call at Zanny-du; such vessels have apparently never reappeared to be chastised."

"No matter," Magnan dismissed the subject, "an accredited Terran Diplomatic Mission is hardly to be compared to some illicit merchantman."

"I almost forgot!" Gus interrupted, arriving at a trot, "they say they got like mind-readers and all down there—a guy's got no secrets! I'm staying aboard, personal! Good luck, fellows, if yer still going down there." He fixed his gaze on Magnan. "You got guts, Ben, for a bureaucrat," he said. "I'll say that fer ya."

"By the way," Magnan said to Retief, ignoring the cheeky fellow, "I was about to mention that I'm Duty Officer today, and my duties require that I remain at my station, monitoring the B & F read-out. Just in case of last-minute budget changes, you know," he added comfortably.

"You're going to stay on this tub, alone?" Gus queried, miming a degree of amazement that would explain, nay, excuse his gaffe, as he sat in the extra chair. " 'Cept for me, I mean, and I'll be holed up in the cold storage vault, with a hand-blaster and a supply of refills."

"Alone?" Magnan echoed. "Hardly, Gus. I'm sure Mr. Retief will wish to be at my side. A blaster?" he went on. "Whatever for?"

"For them damn caterpillars down there," Gus stated firmly. "I heard about how they got ways to drive a feller off his jets and then eat him after. Not Mrs. Gunderson's boy Gus; no sirree!" He rose. "So long, gents," he muttered. "What beats me," he added over his shoulder, "is how they know all this stuff about Spookworld which nobody ain't been there in two hunnert years. Well, good luck and all, but. . . ." Gus' voice trailed off as he departed.

"Remember, Retief," Magnan said in a voice with a distinct tendency to tremor, "stay close, and ignore Gus's silly rumors."

"As you wish, sir," Retief said. "Of course, that will involve your coming down to the surface, since I'm the only licensed atmosphere pilot aboard, and I have to accompany the landing dinghy."

"That's the most ridiculous thing I ever heard of!" Magnan declared. He then added, "Not counting iceberg census on Icebox Nine, of course, or the Goodies for Undesirables Program in general. In fact," he pressed on, warming to his topic, "galactic diplomacy itself—"

Retief's hand covered his chief's mouth at that point. Magnan sputtered and mimed resistance until released. Retief wiped the spit off his palm on a worn table napkin.

"Thank you, Jim," Magnan managed at last. "I don't know what got into me."

PRAY BE REASSURED, BEN, a silent voice said faintly, like a shout heard at a distance. Magnan stared at Retief in amazement.

"Did you hear that?" he whimpered. "Now I'm hearing voices!"

JUST THE ONE, the Voice corrected.

"One is infernally-well enough!" Magnan yipped, clapping his hands over his ears.

"Easy, sir," Retief urged. "Just play it cool. I'm sure there's an explanation."

"Then you heard, too!" Magnan almost sobbed in relief. "What about you, Gus?" He turned a sharp look on the waiter, who had hurried back.

"Not me, Mr. Magnan!" Gus objected. "I don't even know no big words like that 'reassured'; me, I got my ammo to see to. Ta, gents, and watch yer step down there."

2

After the usual last-minute delays while various staff members went off to ascertain that something vital to the Mission had not been overlooked, then the ritual of rank-determined seat-selection in the cramped shut-

tle, the bumpy ride down through a turbulent, layered
atmosphere, debarkation on the wind-swept ramp, and
a grit-in-the-eyes ride to the terminal where tiny gnat-
like insects swarmed, the diplomats alighted from the
converted golf cart and found themselves herded to a
primitive baggage-claim carousel, all the while closely
surrounded by a surprisingly large number of larva-like
locals, none of whom seemed to be aware of the courte-
sies due the Terran Mission. The tiny insectoids swarmed
everywhere. With an effort, Magnan refrained from
batting at them.

"Pity regs don't permit one to swat the pesky things,"
he muttered, fanning fruitlessly at the nuisance. "But at
least they don't seem to bite."

"They couldn't handle our alien protoplasm," Retief
pointed out.

"Let's be duly grateful for small mercies," Magnan
mumbled, waving the midges away from his face.

3

"It's amazing," Magnan stated, sounding Amazed (21-b).
"This structure is, except for its shabbiness, a near-
perfect duplicate of the Old Terminal at Marsport, the
one they restored, you'll recall. Except, of course, that
there's no one in sight except these rather reprehensible-
looking locals. Still, at least I don't see any zombies,"
Magnan added in a whisper to Retief, as they dumped
their hand-baggage on the conveyer belt in the huge
and curiously fragile-looking terminal building. "Heavens!" he went on, "for a time, when the shuttle was
bouncing about, I feared we'd never again put foot on
Terra Firma, so to speak. Still, we're here now—and
to think we were concerned about the place being
unpopulated." He fanned listlessly at the swarming nits,
and cast a disapproving glance on the caterpillar-like
creature, clad only in a complicated harness of crudely
decorated straps, which was grappling with his three-
suiter. Other, similar beings swarmed the area, some,

their official straps adorned with bangles and quill-paint waited behind the counters marked, in Standard: 'CUSTOMS,' 'IMMIGRATION,' and 'HEALTH.' These latter shuffled papers busily, but without apparent purpose.

"They've adopted civilized ways to the extent of taking care to discommode visitors to the fullest, with technicalities," Magnan muttered, "but it appears the actual nature of the routine is lost on them. They think it's a religious ritual, I do believe. Look at that fellow, arranging my toilet articles in some arcane pattern! Adulterating the pure faith with heathen superstition! Unspeakable!"

"Hey, pal," the porter interrupted Magnan's indignant remark, in a voice like air escaping from a leaky bladder, "there's another Terry custom us boys picked up." He was holding out four callussed, olive-green palms, making his meaning clear.

"No fair," Magnan muttered, reluctantly placing a base-metal demi-cred chip in each. "Back home, they only have two, and usually only stick out one! Uncouth, I call it!"

"Still, they're quick studies," Retief pointed out, greasing four palms of his own.

"Hey!" Magnan's recipient growled. "What are you, some kinda cheapie? Six bits, after I maybe sprained a moobie-bone?" He threw the coins aside contemptuously. "Oh, I musta dropped that, pal," he exclaimed, as if in ignorance of his opening remarks, ducking to retrieve the cash. "That's OK," he continued, "you can gimme a guck, and I'll forgit how you threw the coppers at me."

"I saw that!" Magnan gasped. More baggage-smashers were gathering.

"Better stay clear, Mr. Magnan," Retief suggested.

"Here, you!" Magnan barked at his assigned porter, who had completed his devotions and was sampling his client's facial creams with a blunt forefinger.

"Needs salt," the impudent fellow commented, as he tossed the near-empty jar in atop Magnan's newly-tailored extra-super-top-formal dickey-suit.

"Look what he did!" Magnan moaned, leaping to rescue the pristine cellulon garment from the oozing yellowish medicament. "You ought to be horse-whipped!" Magnan declared, facing the upraised visage of the unabashed local.

"Why?" the lout demanded. "I ain't no editor."

" 'Editor'?" Magnan echoed. "Whatever connection does redaction have to the brutalization of my effects?"

"Don't ast, Ben," suggested Hy Felix, the dour Press Attache. "You oughta see what some o' them boys done to some o' my most artistic prose."

"That's not the same!" Magnan insisted. "Personal effects and lit'ry effects are quite different entities! But in any case, the cheeky fellow surely deserves chastisement of the most explicit sort! Perhaps you should sock him on the nasal orifice, Retief," he concluded, and offered his place to his junior.

"Oh, going to do mayhem to the person of an official of a friendly power in the performance o' his duties and all, hey?" the 'pillar' challenged loudly, attracting more locals to press in against the periphery of the crowd now surrounding the personnel of the beleaguered Terran Mission.

"Well," Magnan said, eyeing Retief expectantly, as the latter made no move. "What are you—I mean for what are you. . . ." His tone changed from snappish to apprehensive as his voice trailed off.

"*Mister* Retief!" he spoke up with renewed vigor, speaking now to be overheard. "*Must* I warn you again to respect local customs? Why, if this pious gentlebeing wishes to sample my expensive and hard-to-find-on-a-frontier-world skin-food, can we deny him that portion of his ritual?"

"That's more like it, chum," the pushy fellow commented, tossing aside an empty container labeled *Span-ish Mane.*

"He'll find it difficult to devour his next stolen fruit," Magnan confided to Retief, "with hair growing luxuri-antly from his esophagus. Serve the rascal right, too."

The local quickly recovered the pilatory container, sniffed it suspiciously, swallowed nervously, then squinted at the fine print on the inconspicuous label on the back of the jar.

" 'Goose-poop oil'!" he yelled and thrust the offending pot at a gape-jawed fellow union member. "This here two-laiged foreigner done pizent me!" He paused to run a finger down his throat, apparently to determine whether his esophogeal tissues had yet sprouted a pelt, but gagged instead.

"That's it, Meyer, bring it up!" his side-kick encour-aged, while the ring of profit- or revenge-seeking locals closed ever tighter about the Terrans. Ten feet from Magnan and Retief, His Excellency the Terran Ambas-sador Extraordinary and Minister Plenipotentiary, Clyde Shortfall, was clutching at the arm of his Military Atta-che, Colonel Fred Underknuckle. "Do something, Fred!" he whimpered. "These savages are on the point of rending me—us, that is, limb from limb! Now, what about that unsavory chap over there behind whatshisname, large chap, Retief, I believe he's called? One can't help wondering what the fellow—the local, that is, not whatsis—is about to do with that length of metal bar-stock he's hefting."

"Prolly just locking the gate, sir," Fred reassured his superior sagely. "That's what it is, you know, a locking-bar."

"But, for Heaven's sake, man!" the AE and MP ob-jected, "that would mean we're penned in here in Immigration for the night, which I understand is seven-teen hours long, without so much as a folding chair for me to rest on—with no adequate provision for the basic necessities for my staff, that is! As you know, Fred, I never rest until I've seen my people cared for," he added for any celestial scorekeepers who might be listening in. "Demmed outrage," he muttered. "Why don't you stop him, Fred?"

"Well, Mr. A.," Underknuckle responded hesitantly, "if Yer Ex is sure you wanta start something—"

"Who in the world said anything about 'starting' anything, Colonel?" Shortfall yelped. "Just don't stand there like a spineless oaf and allow us to be held in durance overnight, when a word—"

"Doubt if words'll help now, Chief," Fred countered ruefully as he watched the local tentatively prod Retief with the bar, then jab energetically when the six-foot-three Terran failed to budge. Instead, Retief turned casually, plucked the four-foot length of one-inch steel from the 'pillar's' grasp, bent it double, and carefully arranged it as an ornament on the extended neck of the former owner.

"Here, you!" the porter barked in his coarsely accented Standard, "this here's gubment property, and you went and ruint it!" He tried to pull it off his neck, but Retief grasped both ends of the bar in one hand and squeezed them together, locking it in place.

"Why, Retief, whatever—?" Magnan began as he turned in time to see the disgruntled fellow point and begin yelling:

"Looky, fellers, what this here Terry done gone and went and did! Stop 'em, before they make a break fer it!"

"Fred!" Shortfall's short, fat voice snapped. "I call upon you to take appropriate action!"

"I don't guess you wanta tell me what the appropriate action *is*," Fred predicted gloomily. Then, "sure not, chief, that's *my* job and am *I* glad the monkey's on *my* back! Lessee," he went on with less enthusiasm, as reality caught up with point-making: "This local crumbum assaults one of our boys, which the local lodges a beef and yells for mob action. I guess our best move is to get off a fast Note apologizing for the whole thing."

He looked expectantly to His Ex. "So the ball's in your court, Mr. Ambassador, sir," he concluded. His gaze went to the gaggle of admin staff huddled in the lee of the Great Man. "Where's Miss Furkle?" he demanded. "Get Furkie," he ordered a chinless code-clerk. "Tell her to bring her field-kit, on the double."

"Whatever, Fred, do you imagine Euphronia Furkle can do in this exigency?" the Ambassadorial voice rumbled, in a tone only a hesitating suicide would find encouraging.

"Well, sir, to take down the Note and all," the colonel prompted his chief. "You know, I said about getting off a fast apology and all."

"Your fatuous proposal was duly noted, Fred," Shortfall assured his military advisor. "But may I enquire as to precisely what it is for which you propose I offer expressions of regret and pleas for forgiveness?"

"Sure, go ahead," Fred acceded cheerfully.

"Oh, sir," Magnan cut in diffidently. "I wonder, as the locals are about to attack us in force, hadn't we better *do* something, instead of standing around jawing?"

" 'Jawing,' Magnan?" Shortfall yelped. "As it happens, I am taking counsel of my military expert as to precisely the appropriate steps to be taken to rectify the unfortunate situation into which *your* isolationism has plunged us! As for yourself, I assign you personal responsibility for ensuring that Mr. Whatsis—Retief—is guilty of no furthur provocative acts!"

"Gee, sir," Magnan whined, "all he did was not get skulled with a locking-bar. *That* would have been an Interplanetary Incident; and besides, it would probably have set off this mob, which is at the point of exploding in a frenzy of xenophobia!"

" 'Xenophobia,' Ben?" Shortfall echoed sadly. " 'Mob'? Really, you must do something to curb or at least conceal your Isolationism, before I'm forced to take official notice." He turned and spoke quietly to Euphronia Furkle, who had belatedly taken her position to his left and slightly to the rear. She nodded emphatically, shot Magnan a scathing glance, and muttered a note into her recorder.

"Sir," Magnan spoke up desperately, "am I to understand that avoiding being brained is 'Isolationism'? Excuse the expression."

"No, Ben," the AE and MP replied in a melancholy tone. "It's calling—and thinking of—this carefree throng as a 'mob.' "

"But, sir," Magnan struggled on like a fly with five legs mired in flypaper, "this throng is gathered awfully close around us, and they're shaking cargo-hooks and things at us, and shooting us dirty looks and yelling unflattering epithets—so one can't help feeling somewhat threatened."

" 'Epithets,' Ben?" His Ex demanded. "I wasn't aware you'd audited the language, or even that the language of this mystery world was known."

"They're speaking a rather old-fashioned dialect of Standard, sir," Magnan gasped out, shying as a well-aimed dungtray whizzed past his head. "Didn't you notice, sir, when you were meeting with the delegation who accepted your credentials?"

"Never listen to the admin chaps," Shortfall admitted. "Sign-language works better, and there's less chance of committing myself to some unwise position by inadvertance, like the time on Raunch 41 when Stan Hairshirt unwittingly obligated the Corps to lift in two hundred shiploads of custom-made plastic joss-houses under the impression he was accepting an invitation to tea."

"A tragic end to a great career," Magnan murmured.

"And *I'm* not interested in ending *my* career," Shortfall barked, "here in this damned terminal, surrounded by a yelling, ah, throng, before I've even had a chance to have my Exequatur framed!"

"Sure not, sir," Magnan chirped. "Still, one has to do *some*thing, before it's too late!"

"Too late for what, Magnan?" His Ex challenged, turning his back on the spectacle of his plump Commercial attache, Herb Lunchwell, being pitched headfirst over the Health counter. "Ben," he said sharply, "tell Herb he's not maintaining the dignity expected of a senior staff officer of this Mission (horsing about with the locals in that fashion)," he added as if explaining to himself and thus to the Galactic press just why he had ignored his colleague's plight.

"None of us are, sir," Magnan pled desperately. "We're all being herded like cattle toward the baggage delivery chutes."

"Then *do* something, Ben! That's an order!"

"What am I to do, Mr. Ambassador?"

"Your demand for instruction in detail in lieu of prompt response will be reflected in the Initiative column of your next ER, Ben, I trust you realize," Shortfall pointed out mournfully. "Very well, if you irresponsibly insist on specific instruction before carrying out the simple task with which I have charged you . . ."

"Yes, sir?" Magnan prompted eagerly.

"Magnan," Shortfall said sternly, his eye holding Magnan's, "take the necessary action. At once!"

"You call that specific, sir?" Magnan whimpered. "I was hoping maybe you'd give me a secret call-sign for summoning a squadron of Peace Enforcers or something."

"Am I to understand, Ben," the AE and MP purred, "that you decline to carry out your precisely stated instructions, and instead propose openly provocative overreaction?"

"Good lord, no, Mr. Ambluster," Magnan gobbled. "I mean 'Mr. Ambassador,' " he amended lamely. "I better get on with it, sir, now that I have your official OK."

"Just what you imply by the barbaric expression 'OK,' I am unsure, Mr. Magnan," the Great Man intoned as cordially as Rameses II agreeing to be relocated above the dam.

Magnan was craning his neck, searching the surrounding crowd of scared-looking Terries and loot-
smelling locals for Retief, whom he found standing beside
him.

"You heard His Excellency's guidance!" Magnan
blurted. "We're to, uh, how did he put it . . .? 'Take
the necessary action'?"

"I hope Miss Furkle caught that on her recorder,"
Hy Felix, the sour-faced Press Attache muttered. "Otherwise, I wouldn't be surprised if old Shorty tried to
disclaim responsibility."

So saying, he caught a close-pressing porter by his
badge-strap and jerked him away from the Felix lug-
gage, lying open on the Customs Inspection counter.

"No looting, you," he barked. "The idea is, you're
suppose to be checking to see if I'm smuggling any
snarf-weed or boo-boo caps into this hellhole. Keep the
fingers off my comix, which they're valuable classics for
personal use. Look at that, Ben," he addressed his
colleague, " 'Famous Funnies, Volume one, Number
One,' in mint condition, lucky it's in a glassine bag and
all, otherwise it'd prolly be finger-marked and on the
way to being a Category B item."

"Easy, Hy," Ben counselled. "He's probably just a
lover of literature."

"That caterpillar?" Hy scoffed. "All he knows is it
looks like somebody might pay a guck or two fert."

"Hy," Magnan remonstrated. "That came close to
being a prejudicial remark."

"Whattaya talking, 'pre-judgement'? I waited and
judged the bum *after* he done it."

"And I doubt," Magnan persisted, "the epithet 'pillar' would be found acceptable to the adjudication board
of the Interplanetary Tribunal for the Correction of
History."

"You threatening to report me to ITCH?" Hy scoffed.
"You're a wimp, Ben, but you were never nasty about
it before."

Magnan's retort was obscured as he was knocked flat
by a bigger-than-average local whose abrupt arrival also
threw Hy Felix back against the Immunization desk.
The feisty Press man helped Magnan to his feet, then
stepped up onto the adjacent counter and uttered a
yell.

"Mr. Ambassador?" he bawled. "I protest! This here
autocthone or whatever you wanna call it assaulted me
and Ben. That's OK with the Department, maybe, but
the Agency don't have to put up with the rough stuff.
So what I say is, let's take the necessary action pronto!"

"And precisely what action, pray," His Ex demanded
loudly, "would the Agency consider necessary in this
situation?"

"First," Hy responded gamely, "I got to get this
mug's name, rank, and cereal number."

"That's 'serial' number, Hy," Magnan corrected.

"Never knew my diction was sharp enough you could
tell the difference," Hy shrugged off the comment.

"It's the difference between 'serry' and 'seery,' "
Magnan pointed out. "As representatives of Terran culture, we must always be on our toes, class-wise, Hy."

"You tryna impress those doo-dahs with yer class?"
Hy scoffed. "Which they got none at all. Look at that
fellow tryna feel up Furkie."

"Just the old personal search, bud," the offending
security pillar corrected, releasing the indignant secretary.

"Anyways," he went on, "any interesting topography
that dame ever had is buried under six inches of adi-
pose. She wintered well, I'll say that for her, even if I
had the glands for it," he added out-of-context.

"Well," Miss Furkle snarled, aiming a dagger-like
glare at Magnan. "Are you going to let that outrage
pass, without appropriate response?"

"But," Magnan temporized, "what . . .?"

"I'll show you, Ben Magnan, you spineless worm!"
Without hesitation Miss Furkle hoisted her considerable bulk onto the HEALTH counter, grabbed up some-

one's metal-framed briefcase, spurned with her foot the
excited official which approached her as if to interfere,
then, with a full one-hundred and eighty-degree wind-up,
slammed the heavy case against the pushy fellow's blunt
cranium, bouncing him backward, giving two of his
associates room to advance on the irate lady Terry. She
accorded each a hearty blow on the top of his head, and
they too fell back.

"Next!" Miss Furkle yelled. "Come on, Ben," she
added, "get up here and give a girl a hand." She yelped
as an Immigration clerical type eased in from behind
and grabbed her ankle. She executed a less-than-nimble
soft-shoe and fell backward, squarely on top of the
cheeky fellow. An avalanche of locals closed over the
struggling antagonist, through which Miss Furkle rose,
still swinging. Retief caught one by his straps and tossed
him into the path of the most aggressive looking of
those still crowding forward, then stepped up on the
counter and cleared away those who obscured his view
of Miss Furkle, now back on her feet and laying about
her effectively with her improvised bludgeon. Dodging
the murderous swipes, Retief offered a hand and helped
her up beside him. The nearest locals, all of whom had
felt the weight of Miss Furkle's wrath, were moving
back out of range now. The uproar subsided gradually,
though purposeful activity was now seen at the fringes
of the mob, as the group of the new arrivals began
noisily shaping up the throng.

Magnan tugged at Retief's coat tail. "Heavens!" he
yelped, eyeing Furkie disapprovingly. "And we were
talking about class!"

"Not much class, maybe," Retief conceded, "but not
without a certain style."

4

The choleric voice of His Excellency, the Terran AE
and MP, became audible above the muttering of the
frustrated Zanny-duers.

"Retief! I saw that! You laid violent hands on a number of local citizens! Have you taken leave of your senses?"

Retief stepped down beside the Chief of Mission.

"Skip all that, Mr. Ambassador," he suggested. "Get everyone over to the side of the counter, fast. Charlie," he addressed a code-clerk, "give me a hand with the customs counter. We'll have to swing it around to the side."

"What for?" Charlie inquired, but he pitched in, and a moment later the two counters formed a twenty-foot L. Retief dispatched his helper to urge the Terrans to climb over the barrier, while he moved over to shift the Health unit into place to convert the L into a U. He enlisted Magnan and Hy Felix to assist in herding the Terrans around and over the counters, then shoved the Baggage section into place, completing the square, with the Terrans inside, and the clamoring locals outside. Those of the latter which attempted to climb the modest barrier were quickly dumped back outside by Retief, over the objections of Ambassador Shortfall, who had reluctantly joined those inside, after having been tripped and frisked by a briskly efficient fellow in Security straps and badges.

"What in the world do you think you're doing, Mr. Retief?" the Chief of Mission demanded, attempting in vain to distract the latter from the chore of repelling would-be borders. "You're interfering with the official function of host officials!" he complained. "*What* are you doing? I demand to know!"

"I'm forting-up, sir," Retief told him. "Before they get coordinated and suffocate the lot of us."

"But this is a peaceful world! A *friendly* world. The world, in fact, to which I am accredited as Terra's representative! Am I to report to Sector that you've converted it into an armed camp?"

"Unarmed," Retief corrected.

"As well it should be!" Shortfall snarled. "We're just among our friends we haven't met yet, just like it says in the Manual! The locals are a bit boisterous in their enthusiasm of their welcome, perhaps, but there's not a weapon in sight!"

"Have you noted the shredding-hooks on their ventral surfaces?" Retief inquired. "They don't need skinning-knives."

"Skinning-knives?" Shortfall whimpered. "You've gone mad, Retief! Report yourself under arrest in quarters, at once."

"I've always wondered how you did that," Retief remarked, fending off a thicker-than-usual pillar which had gotten its forward half up onto the counter directly behind the Ambassador, who turned in time to catch a glimpse of the underside of the creature's torso as it slithered back.

"Great Scott!" he yelled. "Do you mean those rows of great, curved, ivory-like claws tucked under there are for—?"

"Exactly, sir," Retief confirmed. "Now, if you'll be so kind, sir, as to give the order to get everybody inside, we can buy a little time."

"To be sure," Shortfall agreed. "And by then no doubt the authorities will have arrived to quell the enthusiasm of the, ah, throng." He broke off to bark a command at Colonel Underknuckle, who began hastily shooing the laggards within the improvised barricade.

"Retief," Fred called over his shoulder as he prodded Herb Lunchwell, the last straggler, back over the counter. "I say," he went on, "I do believe your tactical scheme is in error. I was thinking of Major Dade and his command, who were wiped out by someone called Seminoles in ancient times; it's generally felt some of the soldiers might have survived had they scattered in the woods; instead they built a triangular breastwork of pine-logs, so concentrating themselves as to give the savages an easy target."

"You may be right, Fred," Retief conceded. "But we don't seem to have any woods available, and with our people scattered and being cut out and surrounded one by one, we didn't stand a chance. Now they'll have to come to us, and perhaps we can discourage them if we concentrate all able-bodied men, plus Miss Furkle, at whatever point they start over the counter."

"Possibly, Jim," the military attache conceded dubiously. "At least, it gives one a breather. There were three of the beggars attempting to steal my insignae of rank, simultaneously. Outrageous!" He waved aside the persistent gnats and returned to his traffic-copping.

Retief muttered 'excuse me,' and stepped around the indignant bird-colonel to seize by its straps a 'pillar' which was struggling to retain a grip on Nat Sitzfleisch, the Econ officer, as it withdrew across the barrier. When Retief hauled its forequarters back atop the counter, it dropped Herb and devoted all its energies to resisting Retief's efforts and to yelling "Help! I'm being savaged by this foreigner!"

Retief lifted the creature's front half and threw it back across the barricade, and at once was confronted by another eager intruder. Behind him, Magnan wailed.

"Gracious, where are the police?"

"Right here, chum," a raspy pillar voice responded. Magnan whirled to see a local, differing from the rest of the throng only in the large brass badge on a brass chain draped around its upper torso.

"You got some kinda beef, outlander?" the cop inquired in a tone of Mild Curiosity, a feeble 31-c, Magnan judged.

"I should think, sir," he yelped over the din, "that would be obvious."

"Well, it ain't," the cop replied. "I see this here throng of folks eager to get through the routines and get going on their holiday junkets, which they're stalled by you foreigners tryna play fort with official property here, which I got to write you a citation. Which one is the wise guy?"

"*That* one," Magnan supplied quickly, pointing at

Retief, just as the latter threw back yet another enthusiastic invader. "I *told* him—that is I *would* have told
him if I'd had the chance—not to do it."

"Oh, you were in on it, too," the cop muttered,
before mumbling into his note-taking device, which at
once said *urch*! and disgorged a ticket in triplicate, the
yellow copy of which the cop handed over without
apparent rancor.

Hy Felix pushed through, scenting a story.

"What we got to do, Ben . . ." he pontificated. "We
got to like suck up to the friendlies, which we're
outnumbered ten to one."

"B-but how can you tell which are which?" Magnan
wailed. "They never seem to change the scowl on their
faces," he went on, "so one can hardly know if they're
being affable or insufferable!"

"They'll catch on to the system in a few months," Hy
guessed. "Look at the Grobies out on Smurch Nine-
teen: they got faces like a slab o' rock, but they worked
out the system with the cheek-tendrils, so they could
do a Phony Sincere Smile to Allay Apprehensions of
Inferior Species (679-A through W) with the best of
'em. Too bad they developed a 41 (Fearsome Grimace
Designed to Avert Attack) that you couldn't tell from
their 679, and used it on the next boatload o' Bogan
tourists come along, which the Grobies went extinct all
of a sudden. Take this fellow, now," he indicated the
cop. "I'll show you how to sweeten him up." He scuttled around to what he judged was the policeman's
front side.

"Hi, there, officer," he began heartily. Then in an
aside to Magnan, "They like it when you call 'em 'officer,' on account of they're enlisted personnel and nacherly
it makes 'em feel good when the civilians think they're
officers and gentlemen and all—"

"That's enough out of you, fellow!" the cop told Hy,
and handed over a citation. "I know you fast-talking
types; think you can pull the blaff-shag over a fellow's

oculars with a little sweet-talk. Well, yer dealing with
Chief Smeer of the Zanny-du National Secret Police—
that's 'ZNSP,' for anybody wants to try to pronounce
it—which I'm taking the lot of youse in."

"Chief!" Shortfall cut in sharply. "I must remind you
that my staff and I enjoy diplomatic immunity!"

"Whatta I care what yer personal tastes is?" Chief
Smeer inquired indifferently, with a yawn which exposed rows of curved yellow fangs. "Me, I like a good
girlie show."

"Most unusual dentition for a harmless herbivore,"
young Marvin Lacklustre commented. "Like it said in
the Post Report they were," he added.

"To perdition with the Post Report, Marvin!" His Ex
yelled. "That's not all it left out! I shall personally lay
the matter before the Deputy Undersecretary upon my
return!"

"You ain't hardly here, yet, pal," the chief reminded
him. "So yakking about yer 'return' is a little previous,
which you might not make it."

"Do you imply, Chief," Shortfall yelled, "that some
doubt exists as to our return home, in due course?"

"I can't say about that, Cap'n," Smeer told him.
"Depends on what kinda impression you make on our
Diety and Chief of State, the great Worm."

"Did you say 'worm'?" Hy jeered. "You take orders
from a worm?"

"You got something against beings which they're lucky
to be kinda long and narrow and ambulate close to the
ground-like?" the chief demanded in a tone like a
trimming-knife paring away fat.

"Gracious, no!" Clyde Shortfall arrived in time to
reject the suggestion. "Why, when I was out on
Furthuron, I grew to love both Hither and Nether
Furthuronians, affectionately known as Creepies and
Crawlies, respectively."

"It was the other way around, Mr. Ambassador," Hy
Felix corrected, a provocation which his chief ignored

for the present, though in response to his lifted eyebrow, Miss Furkle, in a lull in her onslaught, confirmed the remark had been duly recorded in the record, signalling this intelligence by forming an *O* with her thumb and forefinger, and making a flicking motion toward her chief.

"Looky there!" the porter with the improvised necktorc rasped. "They're giving the signal for the massacres," a pronouncement which netted a renewed surge of fist-shaking and "Terry-go-home's" from the throng.

"Holy Moses, Ben," Hy Felix blurted. "Didja hear that? Now they're talking mass murder. Oh, boy," he muttered as he groped among the slung camera-bags he considered essential to the image of a newshawk. "Where's my mini-swift?" he inquired in a tone of One Aggrieved by Treachery in the Ranks (1241-m). "Ben, do you suppose one of these light-tentacled baggage-smashers has purloined my sender, which it's Agency property?"

"There it is, right next to your first-aid kit, Hy," Magnan told him. Hy grabbed the prodigal unit and began transmitting in his best classic Ed Murrow style:

"*This* is Zanny-du! Disaster is about to overtake the Terran Mission, dispatched here to cement relations with the putative inhabitants of this mystery world, never officially explored since reported two centuries ago by the redoubtable Captain Goldblatt, which we're surrounded by a blood-thirsty throng." Hy paused to glance at his Chief for approval of his tactful choice of collective nouns, then hurried on. "Not to say 'merry mob,' which His Ex, Ambassador Shortfall is taking this like a trouper. Faced with the imminent demise of his entire staff, hisself, and Terran policy at this end of the Galaxy, the veteran diplomatic pro would appear to the uninitiated to be as totally unconcerned as if he didn't have a clue to what's going on. Folks, is that some kinda cool, or what?" Hy concluded his dispatch and

turned in time to fend off a grab by an acquisitive
Customs being intent on lifting his telephoto equipment.

"Leave yer meat-hooks offa my stuff," Hy commanded.

"Hyman," Ambassador Shortfall cautioned. "Do mind
your tone, lest these simple people misinterpret your
enthusiasm as hostility."

"Enthusiasm?" Hy echoed. "Which this crudbum is
tryna swipe my Mark 19, which I've signed fer it, and
besides I'll need it to record those close-ups of the
inoffensive ladies and gents of the Embassy staff being
throttled, or gutted, or otherwise unlawfully kilt in the
preformance of our duties and all!"

"Surely you exaggerate, Hyman," Shortfall expostu-
lated mildly. "Where's that Retief fellow? I understood
he was sometimes rather effective in pacifying throngs
of this sort, correcting misunderstandings and all that."

"He's right here, sir," Magnan supplied, indicating
his subordinate who had now grabbed two pillars at
once; he hauled them close and threw them down
across the counter on their backs, and planted a foot on
each one. He glanced up and caught Magnan's eye.

"Ben," he said, "if you'll use your umbrella to poke
the yellow spot on each of these fellows. . . ." He indicated with his chin a sallow patch at the center of the
ranked shredding hooks.

"What's that?" Magnan yelped. "Poke them with my
umbrella, you say?" He clutched his rolled brolly to
him as if to protect it from involvement in such goings-on.

"Hurry, sir," Retief urged, "before it dawns on them
that I can't hold both of them down with a foot each and
have anything left to stand on."

As one hypnotized, Magnan extended his weapon
and in gingerly fashion poked one supine pillar, as
directed. The creature responded by rolling up into a
two-foot sphere, which Retief sent rolling with a well-
placed kick. Astonished, Magnan poked the other and
looked about for new targets, as Retief sent the second
tightly-curled pillar after its partner.

"Capital, Jim!" Magnan cried. "Do arrange some more. Heavens, I'd no idea I was so formidable a warrior, actually!"

"Did you say 'warrior,' or 'worrier,' Ben?" Felix inquired in his cynical fashion.

"I realize, Hy," Magnan replied loftily, "that by your remark you intend to reflect discredit on the latter activity. However, the role of constructive worrying in the successful conduct of interplanetary affairs is not in so cavalier a fashion to be dismissed."

"Well, par *me*, sir," Felix returned, still playing to a hypothetical grandstand. "If that's how it is, you better get busy worrying our way out of this one; it was bad enough having his Ex's 'throng' warming up to dismember us, but now you got the cops on our back, too. So worry good, Ben. I'm pulling for you."

"Your remarks, Hyman," the Ambassador put in, "are uncalled-for. This is not a matter for constructive or even creative worrying. This is a time for prompt, effective *action*! Ben already has his instructions, you may inform the Agency, should you survive this affair."

"Yeah, Boss," Hy acknowledged. "I heard the instructions: 'take the necessary action,' you said. What's that supposed to mean?"

"Calmly, Hyman," Shortfall admonished the agitated newsman. "Rest assured that the Department requires no action of Agency personnel at this time."

"'Terran Information Agency slandered by Ambassador Clyde Shortfall with dying breath,' " Felix intoned, as if dictating a fast-breaking headline over the din of the city-room at Sector.

"Take no hasty action, despatch-wise, Hy," Shortfall advised. "Lest I be forced to reflect your negative attitudes on your upcoming ER. And what do you mean, 'dying breath'?"

"Well, Mr. Ambluster," Hy responded apologetically, "it ain't likely yer Ex will be doing a whole lot more breathing after that fella behind you knocks yer brains out. Right, chief?"

"It appears also that certain succinct comments in the Reverence for Superiors column would not be amiss," Shortfall came back smartly, ignoring Hy's remark except to step aside in time to see yet another locking-bar impact on the Customs Counter beside him.

"Still on the old ER gambit, eh, Mr. Ambluster?" Felix challenged, "which I guess I saved yer skull that time."

"Oh, Hy," Magnan interjected sweetly. "Would you just take my brolly and poke that fellow Retief is holding upside down? Right on that saffron-hued spot. My hands are occupied keeping the looters out of our baggage."

Felix complied, and exclaimed happily when the object of his thrust promptly curled up and was sent rolling along the baggage chute by another of Retief's well-placed kicks.

"Wow!" Hy yelped. "Where'd you learn that one, Ben?" He leaped at another exposed Zotz-patch, then another.

"Retief tipped me off," Magnan explained. "I understand he picked it up from some illicit publication or other, actually quite contrary to the Manual."

"Good thing!" Hy returned. "Prolly the *Journal of Isolationism Today*, a yellow sheet if there ever was one, but handy sometimes." He lent substance to the latter comment by dispatching two pillars in quick succession.

"—and do like me!" Hy finished sending yet another tightly-curled local off to the baggage carousel.

"Gentlemen!" Shortfall's voice sounded, almost lost against the general outcry. "Let us not escalate this trifling incident into a pitched battle! Nice work, Ben," he added in a lower tone. "Keep 'em back, but don't do anything that could be interpreted as overreaction, or even aggression on our part."

"Who's to interpret?" Felix demanded, poking on with undiminished enthusiasm. " 'Enbattled Terrans Defend Position Against All Odds,' " he quoted from his soon-to-be-filed Pulitzer Prize-winning story.

Having, with Hy's help, cleared the route to the ramp doors, Retief caught Magnan's eye. "Time to evacuate all personnel, sir," he suggested. "Get 'em together and lead 'em in a rush and you'll make it." He pivoted one counter aside, to open a lane to the rear.

Magnan looked dubious, but complied, herding his charges through the improvised opening in the enclosing barrier and across the littered floor to the portal normally used by the baggage carts, and out onto the dusty tarmac, where a fitful wind blew grit into their faces.

"It seems to me," Magnan commented, waving away an insistent cloud of gnats, "that these confounded midges are as excited by this outrage as are we ourselves."

After sending off a final determined pillar, Retief joined the rest, followed at once by Chief Smeer, who pointed at him accusingly and yelled.

"This here one's the ringleader! I seen him! Grab him, boys, which after a couple years in a Zanny-du jail waiting to be squashed, he'll show a little restraint before he goes using them tactics he got outa that there bootleg book Ben Magnan was bragging about!"

His troops, hardly distinguishable from the noisy local trash element from which they had been recruited, moved up purposefully, while Shortfall bustled over to confront the chief.

"See here, Chief," His Ex barked. "The principle of diplomatic immunity, once breached, will lose all force, an eventuality with which I do not intend to have my name associated! It's your clear duty to restrain this, ah, throng and to escort me and my people in safety to our quarters!"

"Oh, yeah?" Smeer riposted. "Who's gonna make me?"

I AM, a silent voice cut across the ramp. Smeer responded by becoming interested, quite suddenly, in the ceiling structure far above. He gazed up at it apparently lost in awe, while the Terrans stared at each other in astonishment.

"There!" Magnan exclaimed. "It's that Voice again! You heard it, too, didn't you, Hy?" he appealed to the saturnine Agency rep.

"No comment, Ben," Hy replied stonily.

"We all heard it, Mr. Magnan," Marvin Lacklustre confirmed. "It said, 'I am,' in an archaic dialect of Standard, but it was clear enough!"

"This is no time for wool-gathering, Chief!" Shortfall rebuked the musing cop.

Chief Smeer returned his attention to the crisis at hand, assumed a more conciliatory, or at least less aggressive expression and made 'all right, folks, take it easy' gestures.

"Am I to understand, Chief," Shortfall demanded, "that you are now ready to provide an appropriate escort for my Mission to the quarters I am assured have been reserved for us in the city?"

"Well, yeah, OK, I guess," Smeer muttered, as if wishing to avoid overhearing what he was saying. "Come on, I got a couple paddy wagons'll save youse the walk. It's only a couple miles, but I guess you boys are tired, after starting a riot and all—"

"It was hardly us, or we, who precipitated the disorder!" Shortfall challenged, and the two went off together, disputing technicalities, while the other cops directed the staff toward a row of delapidated vehicles with faded logos reading 'SALVAGED BY HONG KONG SANITARY DEPARTMENT,' or 'EX-BOLIVIAN HOME DEFENSE FORCES,' and even 'GIFT OF THE GROACIAN AUTONOMY TO THE PEOPLE OF FUST,' into which the Terrans were unceremoniously hustled.

5

Magnan peered anxiously out the smeared window of the rude van into which the Terrans had been thrust by the cops, as it bumped over a cobbled street like the bottom of a narrow ravine. He winced at each jolt, but exclaimed, "Why, it's quite charming! Looks exactly like the Place de l'Opera as painted by Pissaro or somebody! All these messy facades, mere blobs of color, and windows that aren't square and don't line up! The only thing is," he added, "they look the same close up. They really *are* just sort of slopped together!"

"Doubtless an optical illusion, Ben," Stan Bracegirdle, the Assistant Cultural Attache remarked. "I was Art and Revolution critic for the Activist Press for years, you know," he went on, redundantly, as it happened, since he had individually informed everyone on the staff of his impressive artistic credentials at first meeting.

"Yes, I know, Stan," Magnan muttered. "But I hardly see what that has to do with the fact that this city appears to have been designed to be viewed from a distance, a sort of Impressionist Architecture, if you will. But what are all those cables strung between the buildings?"

"You imply that such an architecture is in some way objectionable?" Stan inquired sternly.

"I *said* it was charming," Magnan reminded the attache. "It's just that it looks like it might all fall down. Look at that roofline! It sags like wet cardboard!"

"A most sensitive assessment I'm sure, of a remarkable subtlety of line," Stan dismissed the remark.

"And we're supposed to be assigned apartments in one of these collapsing structures!" Magnan blurted. But he made no further protest when the vehicle halted and a surly cop thrust his head and forequarters inside and told him bluntly that he "and the trouble-maker" were to enter a particularly shabby structure, where, on the second floor, he showed them to a suite featuring an uneven floor and walls covered in scabrous lichen-like encrustations in shades of puce, magenta, and cyrhotic yellow.

"My word, Retief," Magnan muttered indignantly when they were alone. "This is appalling! But after that boisterous reception at the port, I suppose I should have expected that we would be spared nothing."

"Still, the A/C works," Retief pointed out. He sat on the bed. "And the mattress isn't bad."

"Retief!" Magnan protested. "Don't go being cheerful about this disaster! And after we were promised the Imperial Suite, too," he carped.

"Maybe the emperor was the one they hanged; drew, and quartered," Retief suggested.

Chapter One

1

An hour later, Retief and Magnan had settled into their spartan quarters, and adjusted to the lack of anything resembling a bathroom, or even a chair.

"We must remember to call it Zanny-du, like the indiginees," Magnan remarked, adjusting the lie of his Top Three Grader lapels. "Now, we'd best hurry along to Staff Meeting. His Ex no doubt has some choice bits of gossip—useful tips from the Classified Report—that is."

2

It was a greenish dusk when the two newly-arrived diplomats emerged from the building via the irregularly-shaped pedestrian exit, pointed out earlier by their local guide/guard, to emerge on the city's main avenue. Main or otherwise, it was the only route to the lofty, shedding, wattle-and-daub structure across the way bearing the newly-installed brass plate lettered 'Embassy of Terra.'

"B-but Retief—" Magnan stammered, eyeing their proposed route, a springy plank of goomwood some twenty-seven inches wide and three inches thick, "it's nothing but an oversized two-by-four!"

"It's quite broad by local standards, sir," Retief reassured him, as he stepped out on the narrow bridge. It bounced alarmingly as the two Terrans proceeded along it, fifty feet above the ground, which was invisible in the black shadows below.

"Great heavens, Retief!" Magnan blurted when he reached the intersection with Embassy Drive, an unplaned two-by-six. He froze in place, his arms windmilling, unable to advance the first step. "Why in the worlds," he demanded of an unheeding cosmos, "did Ambassador Shortfall select *this* Acrobat's nightmare as the address for his Mission? No mere human could be expected to cross this thing, without even a handrail." He peered anxiously down past his feet and shuddered. "At least the gnats aren't so bad here," he offered.

"There wasn't much choice," Retief reminded his supervisor. "All the other main streets are narrower."

"Doubtless all sorts of dreadful creatures lurk down in those lightless depths," Magnan told Retief. "What if one should lose one's footing and fall amongst them?"

"Don't worry," Retief comforted his supervisor. "You'd no doubt be killed by the fall. But we only have this short stretch to cross to make it to Staff Meeting on time." He preceeded his chief out onto the final narrow stretch of timber, well-worn, presumably by the multiple feet of generations of Zanny-duers.

"Wait!" Magnan called. "Don't leave me here!" As if goaded by the concept of being alone on the swaying foot-path, he took a hesitant step. "Look there, Retief!" he cried, pointing to the entry to the Embassy, below and to the left, just ahead, opening on a relatively broad ledge where a crowd of elongated locals had gathered, some armed, all shouting and shaking half a dozen fists each, while others busied themselves with prybars levering open the folding metal gate.

"The Embassy is under attack!" Magnan yelled, in his excitement hurrying past Retief to the point opposite and above the wide doorway and its besieging mob, crowding onto the porch-like entry slab.

"Here, now, you in the yellow headdress!" he shouted over the din, addressing a noisy fellow who seemed to be the prime agitator.

Having thus captured the attention of the locals, Magnan retreated along the plank as the focus of the angry mob shifted instantly from the intransigent gate to himself. Rocks arced toward him, a few chipping wood near his feet.

"Get Terry!" the cry went up. And "there's two of 'em!"

"Rush 'em!" the boss troublemaker commanded, and his minions obediently crept forward, first crowding, then crawling atop each other, forming a mound directly below the point where Magnan crouched, babbling.

"Retief! *Do* something!" he yelped. "Remember, as Ambassador Straphanger so stirringly put it when the avalanche cut off the rescue party: 'Do something, even if it's the wrong thing!', an exhortation to the implementation of which his whole career bore witness! However, in this instance I feel you should improve upon His Excellency's example at least to the extent that you avoid availing yourself of his alternative!"

"Good thinking, Mr. Magnan," Retief congratulated his supervisor. "Any ideas as to what might not be the wrong thing?"

"Just get me inside, intact, instantly," Magnan specified. "And yourself, as well, of course, if you can manage it," he conceded generously.

"Incisive instruction, indeed, Mr. Magnan," Retief commented. He backed off a few steps, then, taking a running start, jumped over the fringe of the mob to impact feet-first atop the heap of eager rioters on the porch; the mound promptly dissolved, its individual numbers making all possible haste to withdraw to a more statesmanlike distance from the rude tactics so unexpectedly employed by the foreign barbarian. Yellow-headdress bustled forward like a ten-foot inchworm completing his circuit.

"Who," he demanded with an accent even worse than that of Chief Smeer and his SWAT team, "are you, fellow? And why? Can't you see that by your careless mode of perambulation, you've injured a number of public-spirited citizens, to say very little of busting up this traditional eating-pyramid formation!"

"I noticed, Mr. Loudmouth," Retief conceded. " 'Retief' is the handle. Par me if I don't offer to shake manipulatory members."

"Come down at once, sir," Loudmouth yelled to the Terran standing atop half a dozen stunned rioters who were writhing feebly as they attempted to disentangle their elongated bodies each from the other.

"Done busted Roy's cranial plumes, too," the leader noted aggrievedly, just as Retief launched himself at him, slamming the excited fellow backward, sending the yellow headdress rolling in the gutter. Its owner turned back upon himself to scramble frantically after the badge of office, snatching it up, dripping gutter-goo just as one of his retreating underlings was about to trample it.

Retief stepped over a laggard rioter which snapped green teeth an inch short of his ankle, and used his key to open the folding gate just wide enough to slip inside, slamming it on the elongated neck of Loudmouth, who, after a quick recovery, had thrust his upper end, bearing various sense organs, through the opening. The trapped alien yelled and whipped his orange-and-black bristled length against the frail-looking barrier.

The gate bulged inward as the crowd, noting their chief's discomfiture, heaped themselves against it, and, incidentally, against their trapped leader, who redoubled his efforts as well as his vocalizations.

Retief went across to the closed door to the Guard Room just as it burst outward, and a resentful-looking Marine Guard sergeant burst out, power pistol in hand.

"Let me to 'em!" the excited lad yelled. "Oh, hi, Mr. Retief," he added, attempting to peer over Retief's shoulder. "Where *are* the crud-bums? Two of 'em come under the gate and conned me into the hut and slammed the door. Les and Dick are due here to relieve me any second, and if they woulda found me locked in—!" He left the rest to his hearer's imagination. As his eye fell on the first invaders just slithering under the bulging gate, he loosed off a burst of needles which chipped the hard, red, unpolished stone floor and sent the pillars scrambling back to the safety of numbers. Retief took the sergeant's arm gently and said, "No more shooting at this point in the negotiations, Bill. It's still early in the day. Let Mr. Magnan and me try the verbal approach."

"Verbal, schmerbal," Bill responded carelessly, and attempted to throw off Retief's restraining grip.

"Here, Mr. Retief," he said, surprised at his failure to shrug off the latter's seemingly casual hold. "You got a pretty good grip on you, for a civilian."

"I wasn't always a civilian," Retief reminded him.

"Yeah," Bill offered. "I seen you at the last Armed Forces Day shindig, all tricked out like a Battle Commander, medals and orders and all. Some kind a reservist on some backwater world, I heard."

"Sergeant!" Magnan's strained voice cut in abruptly from the gate, through which he had at last struggled. "Our Mister Retief's rank is quite legitimate, I assure you; and as you know a Battle Commander outranks a Fleet Admiral-General. Commander Retief is General-in-Chief of the Armed Forces of his native world, Northroyal, on detached duty to the Corps Diplomatique Terrestrienne."

"Oh, par me, General," Bill said more quietly, to Retief. "But are we just gonna stand here and let them savages cut us up for bait? Is that how they win wars out on Northroyal?"

"Hardly, Bill," Retief soothed the excited non-com. "But I might point out that no war, in fact, exists here on Sardon."

"And," Magnan put in, "it is precisely to the contravention of such an eventuality that our efforts are dedicated."

"I'm glad you made it inside, sir," Retief told Magnan.

"While they were busy with the gate, I jumped down like you," Magnan explained. "Tight squeeze, and I had to step on the yellow headdress while that noisy fellow was wearing it. But then I can always point out that his head had no business being in a position to be stepped on."

"I heard that, Terry!" Loudmouth yelled from his awkward position pinned in the gate. " 'A technical defense is the last refuge of the scoundrel,' just like your own CDT Handbook says!"

"The wretch is too cheeky by half," Magnan huffed, "but still, let us not precipitate formal hostilities unduly."

"There ain't nothing formal about a good hose-down with a particle gun," Bill objected. He made another, less casual attempt to free his arm, which Retief released, at the same moment plucking the potent handgun from the sergeant's grip. He checked the charge indicator and handed it back. "Don't fire until you see the yellow of their eyes," he advised. At that moment, Loudmouth, who had succeeded in forcing entry in advance of the main body, jittered to a stop before Retief.

"Your name?" he demanded in his squeaky voice, which had been slightly bent by the gate.

Magnan stepped forward. "*I* am Consul General Magnan," he advised the nosy local. "First Secretary of

Embassy of Terra, and Budget and Fiscal Officer to the Terran Mission to Sardon," he elucidated. "May I inquire to what we are indebted for the honor of this delegation's informal visit?"

"Sure, go ahead and inquire," the Sardoner agreed. "But don't wait around for an answer; I got nothing to say, except 'Terry Go Home.'"

"Your manner, sir," Magnan countered stiffly, "is hardly that which one expects from a representative of the government to which I am accredited, and which has issued to me an Exequatur confirming the acceptance of my credentials. Now do step aside and permit me, and my colleague, Mr. Retief, to proceed without further boisterousness."

"Boysters will be boysters," the local dismissed Magnan's plea. "Retief, eh? I heard o' that one from Chief Smeer; hows come he's threatening I and my boys with that weapon?"

"You err, sir," Magnan countered icily. "We are diplomats, and having disavowed the use of force, are of course unarmed."

"Oh, yeah? Then I guess my name ain't Smudge, which I'm Chief of Metropolitan Police."

"Curious," Magnan observed. "This morning at the post, we met one Chief Smeer who claimed chiefship of the same organization. However, not having the honor of your acquaintance, sir, or Chief," he amplified, "I can hardly be in a position to confirm your personal appelation."

"Oh, well, OK, 'Deppity Chief Smudge,'" the local amended.

"Oh, he's Smudge, all right," Bill spoke up. "I seen the sucker before when we done the familiarization course."

"In that connection, sir," Smudge spoke up briskly. "You're unner arrest; or what I'm tryna say, this Retief is unner arrest." He turned his gaze—an eye like a badly fried egg—toward Retief. "You gonna come quiet, or what?"

"I must protest, Mr. Smudge!" Magnan yelped. "Mr. Retief enjoys diplomatic immunity! Especially right here in the Embassy lobby!"

"Whatta I care what he enjoys? Myself I like a quiet dinner with a pal," Smudge rebuked Magnan. "All I know is I got orders to pick him up. So let's not get ourselfs no Interfering With a Officer in the Preformance of His Duty rap and all, OK?" He reached for Retief, who somehow wasn't quite there anymore, having stepped aside.

"That won't be convenient, chief," Retief told the exasperated cop. "You can go now, and don't forget your subordinates."

The cop uttered a yelp and charged, only to rebound from Retief's fist; he made another try, and somehow his face impacted Retief's knee. Behind him, the overstressed gate fell with a *crash*! and the entire mob was through and advancing at full charge, but at an abrupt *Blap*! from the direction of the little group of Terrans the main body changed direction and went pouring back out through the entry over the ruined gate and off along the ledge; from the two-by-fours crisscrossing the abyss, an indifferent populace hardly glanced up at them passing in full cry. Only Smudge and another laggard remained behind, still intent on reaching the Terrans.

"OK, that's *another* felony rap, pal," Chief Smudge squeaked. "Killing my boys in the line o' duty!"

"Whom are you addressing, sir?" Magnan demanded. "You appear to direct that ridiculous charge at me and my subordinate with a fine impartiality!"

"Gee, thanks," Smudge replied. "I been working on the old impartiality in my spare time; glad it shows."

"Actually, as you see, Chief," Magnan persisted, "I, myself am and have been unarmed."

"Right!" Smudge agreed promptly. "That'd leave this

Retief here as the felon, unless ya wanna count old Bill, which he's a nice-looking kid. *He* never slaughtered no cops."

"I hardly think—" Magnan started, but was cut off by Smudge.

"Yeah, I noticed," the chief concurred. "So I'll just put the cuffs on this crinimal here, and get going; you're cutting inta my alky break." He turned briskly to Retief, but instead encountered the hard hand of the Marine guard.

"Don't go off half-cocked, Bub," Bill advised the local. "I done the shooting, which I aimed over their heads and din't kill no cops which that's a arrow I could correct. So you can leave Mr. Retief out of it. Fact is, he told me not to shoot, but when I seen fifty o' your hookbellies coming at us, I loosed one off. And I still got the weapon . . ." He patted the holstered power gun. "So don't tempt me."

The chief abruptly became interested in adjusting his harness, which had been wrenched somewhat awry by the sergeant's grip.

"Nobly spoken, Sergeant," Magnan commended the lad. "Now just hold the chief here whilst Mr. Retief and I repair to our offices to set in motion the wheels of process to restore a modicum of order to this developing chaos," Magnan ordered crisply, and set off toward the elevator bank, casting a haughty look on the discomfited Smudge as he passed.

"Hey, don't go casting no haughty looks on me!" the cop objected. "And tell this here gorilla to aim that thing at his foot!"

"That cut it," Bill commented, and grabbing the offensive fellow by one of his multiple arms, he swung him around and released him into the path of his own advancing minions, who carelessly knocked him down *en passant.*

"You seen that!" Smudge squeaked, when he had regained half a dozen of his feet. "The Terry rent-a-cop laid hands on me; Hunk and Dopey seen it too; right, Dopey?"

"I din't see nothing except you stepped on my favorite foot," Dopey replied resentfully, miming dire distress as he limped away.

"That leaves you and me, Constable Hunk," Smudge told his lone remaining subordinate. "Now, you gonna put the cuffs on this here killer, or what?"

"I don't see no dead bodies laying around, Chief," Hunk demurred. "Who'd the sucker kill, anyways?"

"It hardly behooves you, Detective Hunk," Smudge objected, "to raise these fine technical distinctions at this here juncture."

"What juncture?" the promotee demanded, looking around confusedly. "I don't see no juncture."

3

In the conference room on the third floor of the Chancery, twelve senior Embassy Officers sat at the long table, listening to the shouting from the street, and awaiting the arrival of the Chief of Mission. Beyond the high, draped windows, the view was of deteriorated facades elaborately woven of twigs, vines and plastic gribble-grub bags, and linked by cables along which local pedestrians crept in their deliberate way; when two met, one simply swung to the underside of the narrow cable. The rickety structures were interspersed with tall, palmlike whicky trees overgrown with glowering goobloom vines, all silhouetted against a twilight sky of palest lavender in which hung the oversized crescent moon, nicknamed Loony by an irreverent code-clerk. The cries of the mob gathered in the gloaming had fallen into a chant:

"Give us Retief!"

"What's that they're yelling?" Major Tremblechin of the Military Attache's office inquired rhetorically, cupping his hand to his ear. "Retief? That's that rather insubordinate chap who made all the fuss at the port, isn't it? What in the worlds would they want with *him?*"

"Perhaps to assist in one of their colorful tar-and-feather, or, rather resin-and-leaf-litter ceremonies I read about," Art Proudflesh, the Cultural Attache suggested indifferently. "Still, I doubt he'll cooperate. The crude fellow has no appreciation of cultural phenomena at all."

The door banged open and the AE & MP entered, slammed an elaborately strapped and bulging briefcase down before his throne-like chair at the head of the table, and barked:

"Gentlemen! In the name of interspecies amity I have endured insult, injury, ritual defilement and gross discourtesy with a Smile, Saintly (107-B), thereby impressing on these rascally locals the loving kindness and empathic understanding of noble Terra . . ."

As he paused to permit his audience fully to savor Terran loving kindness and empathy, Hy Felix, the Information Agency man spoke up predictably:

"—and convinced 'em we're chicken."

"We, Hy, are hardly, as you so crudely put it, 'chicken,' " Shortfall reproved the impudent fellow, "indeed uncommon toughness of moral fiber is required to endure patiently, nay, cheerfully while one's inferiors arrogantly assume every prerogative of mastery, brush aside one's most cherished traditions, and impose the most demeaning of conditions as the price of accepting Terran largesse!"

"Makes ya wonder why we don't put these crumbums in their place and get the heck out of here," Hy mused aloud.

"It induces no such speculations in me, Hy," Shortfall snapped. "I am here to implement Terran policy, a policy which has traditionally been based on the hallowed principle of reverse inferiority."

"Anyways," Hy grumped, "I never said we're chicken. I said you make 'em *think* we're chicken."

"Patience, Hy," the Ambassador reminded his PR man, "is a virtue one has to home in diplomacy. We shall reap the rewards of virtue in due course. In the meantime—" he paused to exchange his residual 107 for a well-practised 921 (This Is It), about an m, Hy reckoned. Before he could speak, Colonel Underknuckle, the Military Attache, rose and cleared his throat portentously.

"Let's get tough with these infernal caterpillars *now!*" he proposed crisply. "We got plenty small arms and ammo in the lockup; from these windows we can blanket the plaza . . ."

Shortfall cut off the intemperate officer: "Imagine if you will, the headlines:

" 'Terry Embassy Attack on Convival Holiday Markers!' 'Vascular Fluids Flow in Street!' 'Invasion Under Cover of Diplomatic Immunity.' It would set Terran-Sardonic relations back to the Stone Age, early last week!"

"Yeah," Hy agreed gloatingly, "I'll get a release off right now." He turned to the Military Attache. "What'll I say, Fred? 'Enemy Forces Routed by Bureaucrats' sound about right?"

"Ahh," the colonel temporized. "Aside from the predictable outcry from the media, so vividly described by His Excellency, there would appear to be no flaw in the scheme from the military point of view."

"Colonel!" Shortfall almost choked on the word. "Am I to understand that you support the notion of firing on these high-spirited civilians?"

"I don't know from their spirits, Mr. Ambassador," Underknuckle replied gamely, "but they're out there yelling for a Terran diplomat, which I don't think they plan to hang no medal on him, and it looks like they decided to rush the Marines on the gate, so—well, you better start composing suitable letters of condolence to the next of kin—not that you'd get to mail 'em before they knock down the door here, and whack off our heads." He paused to unholster and check over his ceremonial sidearm. Holding it aimed carelessly in the direction of the door, he added: "I guess I can nail a couple of the blood-thirsty devils before they get me, or you, that is, Boss."

"No one, Chet, is going to 'get' anyone!" Shortfall spat, then jumped as yet another chunk of rubble impacted on the table before him, leaving a nasty gash in the urethane finish. "We are, after all, gentlemen," His Ex resumed firmly, "a diplomatic mission, not a commando; let us consider calmly—" he broke off with a yelp as a detonation rang the building like a cracked bell.

"Colonel!" he moaned. "Do you actually think they'd ah, 'whack off our heads,' is, I believe, the unfortunate expression you employed . . .?"

"Might stake us out and pour sweet-tar on us and let fire-weevils clean the meat off our bones," the colonel suggested. "I read up on this place in a Usually Deplorable Source," he added.

"That confounded Isolationist rag again, I suppose," Shortfall mourned. "See here, Chester," he continued. "I am not entertaining proposals for a theme for a blackout at the Benefit tonight! I am attempting dispassionately to assess the nature of any hazard with which we may be faced!"

"Sure, I know all that stuff, Yer Ex," the colonel reassured his chief. "But how am I spose to know what these infernal savages are gonna do next?"

"It is precisely your responsibility, Chet," Shortfall intoned heavily, "to keep your superiors, namely myself, informed well in advance as to the tactics the locals are most likely to employ!"

"We ain't got no crystal ball nor nothing, Mr. Ambassador," Colonel Underknuckle reminded his Principal Officer. "But whatever they pull, it'll be what they think will lose us the most face. They'll try to make us look like a bunch of monkeys!"

"While I see no point in casting unwarranted opprobium on innocent simians, Chester," Shortfall objected with a somewhat mournful 610-d (Looka Me, *I'm liberal!*) expression. "It is apparent that the unruly element among our hosts would indeed desire to discredit Terra, no doubt at the instigation of an irresponsible foreign power, in hope of influencing the devision of spheres of influence at the upcoming Summit over on Lumbaga."

"Everybody knows the Groaci got the fix in with the Sardonic Foreign Ministry," Chet riposted.

"Your sullen attitude, Chet, ill befits a field-grade officer dreaming of stars on his shoulder-tabs," Shortfall reminded his military advisor. "I suggest you turn your attention to the devising of a viable strategy to oppose precisely the Groaci strategy you cite."

"Sure," Nat Sitzfleisch of the Econ Section spoke up as One Who'd Been Awaiting an Opportunity to Weigh in on the Side of Enlightened Policy. "Sure, what we gotta do, we gotta get the fix in our own selfs."

"Nat," Shortfall said, almost kindly, "while it is self-apparent that the wisdom of Terran counsel should receive due consideration by the Sardonic Council—"

"Hold it!" Herb Lunchwell, Nat's second-in-command cut in. "That 'Terran counsel' and 'Sardonic Council' mixes me up. And right here in the Embassy ya got your Consular Officers, and your Counselor of Embassy, and now this local Council, and I don't see why the *Corps* don't come up with some new terminology, which it won't rely so heavily on homonyms!"

"The personal lives of our personnel, Herb, are no concern of the *Corps*," Shortfall rebuked the portly Second Secretary and Consul. "You will doubtless recall the landmark Kablitzki decision back in '86 which established that a policy of openness and official disinterest in such unfortunate matters would disarm in advance any supposed vulnerability to pressures to which deviant personnel might otherwise be subject. You were saying . . .?"

"We could call 'em 'Advisor of Embassy,' instead of 'Counselor of Embassy,' for openers," Herb proposed. "And how about changing 'Consul' to, say, 'Liaison'? I'm just noodling, mind you. And this here local Council; we could call it the Cabinet. Then maybe a fella'd know what he's talking about. And I didn't say nothing about no deviants."

"What *I'm* saying about," Shortfall said waspishly, "is the dire necessity for affirmative action on the part of this Mission, preferably *prior* to our demise at the hands of the unruly local element!"

"Too bad the unruly local element is the *de jure* government," Ted Whaffle, the Political Officer, put in glumly.

"And the *de facto* gubment, too," Hy Felix reminded him promptly. "So we can't hardly lodge no official protest with *them* babies."

"This Mission, Ted, does, as you suggest, face more than usual difficulties," Shortfall conceded. "I assume," he went on in a tone of Deep Synthetic Interest (12-w), "that you will now extend your remarks to include your proposed solution to the contretemps."

"As to that," spoke up young Marvin Lacklustre, the Assistant Consular Officer, "it appears, judging from the complaints lodged even prior to our arrival, with my office by the local Terran Entrepreneurs, Realtors, and Retailers Institute, that the local Ministry of Stuff expects to extract license fees, taxes, insurance, and protection, amounting to some hundred and fifty percent of gross transactions. It's highway robbery. They seem to imagine that TERRI has access to unlimited funds, of which they demand their exhorbitant cut. Shocking! A combination in restraint of trade of the most arrant stripe!"

"Pity Taft-Hartly's writ doesn't run here in Tip Space, Marvin," Shortfall murmured sympathetically. "I suggest you huddle with Herb Lunchwell to devise a viable strategy to counter this unrealistic policy."

"But, sir," Marvin protested. "I *did*! And still they're intransigent to a degree!"

"Sorry His Ex cut you off when you were going good, Marv," his immediate supervisor murmured consolingly as the lad resumed his seat.

"What *I* don't see," the irrepressible Hy Felix interjected, "is how TERRI got the local chapter which there ain't never been no Terries allowed in here."

"As you so cogently point out, Marvin, it's shocking," Shortfall intoned stonily, ignoring Felix's jibe. "Still, something must be done, and you're just the fellow within whose job description such action falls. Such are the burdens of the diplomat," he pursued his thesis with a resonate delivery suggesting that massed mediamen were recording each sonorous syllable, "selflessly saving mankind, and TERRI, too, on many a far-flung world!"

A spattering of spontaneous applause broke out, cut short, but not unkindly, at a gesture from the Great Man.

"Fellows," he almost whined, in an overly abrupt return to normal Staff Meeting tones, "if we could just find out what the devil it is these brigands want, we'd have made an important advance, BTCWYA*wise! So— thinking-caps, gentlemen! I want to see half a dozen constructive proposals on my desk by tea-time. Dismissed . . . yes, what is it, Magnan?" he concluded as the slender Budget-and-Fiscal man burst into the room, signalling for attention like a distressed schoolboy with an urgent Number Two.

"Why, Mr. Ambassador," Magnan responded in his thin voice, "why don't we just send someone out to ask them—since the Minister refuses to respond on the hot-line?"

"Never could pronounce that 'bitch-wa,' " Hy muttered.

"You surprise me, Ben," Shortfall told his underling

*Brightening The Corner Where You Are—a hallowed Corps principle

in the tone of One Whom Nothing can Surprise (717-d).
"Candidly, I had never given you high marks in the
'Suicidal Tendencies' column under 'Devotion to Duty'
on the ER's."

"Changed his tune," Hy remarked barely sub-audibly,
to Herb Sitzfleisch. "A minute ago they were 'high-
spirited merry-makers.' Now he's talking suicide."

Shortfall ignored the not quite sub-audible after all
remark with the elan of the seasoned diplomat. "Just
how, Ben," His Ex bored on, "do you propose both to
secure the relevant information and to relay it here to
me prior to your demise at the tentacles of these
Terricidal maniacs?"

"Whom? *I*, sir?" Magnan said, his voice tending to
crack on the personal pronoun.

"Whomever else, Ben?" Shortfall boomed, "when it
was you who volunteered. Yes," he went on gravely,
"yours is the honor, Ben, and you will find Terra not
ungrateful."

"In that case," Retief spoke up, coming up behind
Magnan, "I guess we'd better get going, Mr. Magnan."

"Yes, yes, that's all right," Shortfall snapped. "As
Ben's immediate subordinate, it's fitting that you should
go along to hold his coat. And by the way, I note that
both of you gentlemen are late, by a full—" he broke off
to consult an antique pocket-watch the size of a hockey
puck "—five minutes!"

4

Back outside, in the red-carpeted corridor, Magnan
mopped his forehead with a small, blackish tissue with
the embossed arms of the Fustian embassy, leaving
patches of purplish-dark dye on his face. He cast the
tissues from him as he noticed the stain on his fingers.
"Drat!" he commented. "I forgot Ambassador Whonk
likes to keep always at hand the aroma and pigmentation of
his native mud!"

"Just what did you have in mind, Mr. Magnan?" Retief asked his immediate supervisor.

"What *I* had in mind?" Magnan echoed in a tone of Deep Astonishment at an Unwarranted Assumption (246-z). " 'What did His Excellency Ambassador and Minister Plenipotentiary Theophilus Clyde Shortfall have in mind?' I assume you mean."

"A fine technical distinction," Retief pointed out. "But since it was indeed yourself, sir, who spoke up at the precise moment when His Ex was desperate for a patsy—or perhaps 'dedicated public servant' is the more dignified term—surely you had anticipated that anything you said would be seized upon to provide an Ambassadorial out."

"Doubtless," Magnan mused contritely, "I was imprudent. But it was good of you, Retief, to come along on what will doubtless be my final mission in the service of Terra."

"Just following orders," Retief pointed out. "So I can claim no credit. Meanwhile, we'd better work out some tactics, strategy being out of the question."

"I recall a somewhat irrational, but pertinent motto attributed to an admittedly obscure Venetian general of the Fifteenth Century," Magnan offered hesitantly: " 'When in doubt, attack!' "

"What happened to this general?" Retief asked. "I don't remember hearing of him."

"He died young," Magnan admitted.

"It appears the question is academic," Retief notified the skittish Budget and Fiscal Officer, as they turned to see a swarm of armed locals boiling up from the ceremonial main staircase, improvised weapons gripped in an improbable number of hard, purplish-gray fists, which they shook aloft in a manner universally recognizable as other then cordial. Above them, hand-made placards bobbed, crudely lettered in Standard: GET TERRY and SARDON FOR THE SARDONIC. As well as one hastily chalked card demanding: HAND OVER RETIEF!

"Great Heavens, Retief!" Magnan blurted. "The cheeky fellows intend to violate the Chancery itself! I'd best notify his Ex at once—" He broke off and ducked as a rusty iron spear wrenched from the fence outside came hurtling toward him, to crash noisily on the terrazo behind him. Retief caught the next one, reversed it, and swung it in a whistling arc which sent out one bold agitator reeling back among his associates, who paused in their heading advance to gather round him curiously.

"Not friendly clobber local citizen," one called in his squeaky voice. "Violate ancient Sardonic code of hospitality!"

"Be off with you, sir," Magnan returned briskly, "before I report you to the authorities!" He ducked a well-aimed spitoon.

"Rots o' ruck, Terry!" came the reply. "We *are* the authorities! Anyways, Chief Smudge is, which this Retief gave him a sore foof-organ where he can't be up here to arrest youse his ownself! Now hold still so I can get my placement right this time!" The spokesman pegged a medium-sized rock which Retief returned sharply, wielding his iron spear like a Louisville Slugger. The noisy mob split to allow the missile to pass through, to impact at last against the rump of a fleeing comrade, who yelled and accelerated his pace. At the top of the staircase, Retief grabbed Magnan and draped him over the ornate bannister which ran up the center of the broad steps, down which he slid, straight through the throng. Then Retief shouldered his spear and took a position astride the handrail, to slide quickly down to the lobby, where Magnan lay in a heap after his abrupt descent, surrounded by the throng, through which Retief had cut a swath in his arrival. Chief Smudge sulked near the ruined gate. Bill stood by, keeping an eye on him.

"Retief!" Magnan called feebly over the din from above. "I think I'm still alive!"

"See if you can move," Retief suggested, and gave him a hand up.

"I seem to be quite intact," Magnan reported. "By a miracle. It was quite unwarranted of you, Retief, to manhandle me in that undignified fashion!"

"Would you have preferred to be pillar-handled?" Retief inquired, indicating the yelling throng on the staircase, the bolder of which were beginning to descend cautiously toward the islotaed Terrans.

"Nice going, sir," Bill congratulated Retief on his ploy. "Left them pillars flatfooted."

"All right, you bums," Chief Smudge called to his troops. "This here one is that Retief I told you about, and you seen what he done to my foof-nodes, so put the arm on the miscreant without no more horsing around!" He backed away hastily as Bill made a sudden move in his direction, but continued his exhortations from beyond the iron grill, now propped up and hanging by one hinge.

"Don't let him get away! No, not *that* one, the big one!" He broke off and humped away as Bill reached through the bent latticework and grabbed at one of the alien's short arms. Then the mob reached the Marine and pinned him, by sheer weight of numbers, against the abused gate, which collapsed outward at last. Retief waded into the writhing mass of pillars.

"Retief!" Magnan squeaked from the periphery of the aroused crowd. "They're running amok! We have to *do* something!"

"I'll try to keep 'em busy, Mr. Magnan," Retief called between jabs at exposed yellow patches. "You'd better take the private lift!"

"What? Appropriate the Ambassador's *personal* conveyance?" Magnan yelped, but he stepped briskly into the waiting car, and the automatic doors slammed shut. Retief continued hauling the limber-bodied aliens back and tossing them aside, until he had cleared a path through to Bill, whom he assisted to his feet while the frustrated rioters boiled around the two, gnashing their fangs in fury. Chief Smudge reared up in time to receive a fist, full in his sense-organ cluster.

"Nice shot, Bill," Retief commented. "You think we can get through these fellows to the main drag?"

"Can we not," Bill replied, grinning through a smear of blood from his nose. "Lead on, General, sir!"

5

"What?" Ambassador Shortfall yelped, confronting Magnan, disheveled and gasping for breath as he tottered from the suddenly-opened door of the private lift. "Are *you* back here, Magnan?"

"No indeed, Mr. Ambassador," Magnan twittered daringly. "This is my astral projection; you see, sir, I was savaged by the mob, and—" he broke off, clutching at the arm of Major Tremblechin, who had hurried forward. "They've got Retief!" Magnan gasped. "We went down under a virtual avalanche of the ferocious creatures! When I last saw him, he was still battling, gamely but hopelessly, against literally overwhelming odds! We have to rescue him! Don't just dither, Fred!" he addressed the dithering Military Attaché. "*Do* something!"

"Magnan!" Shortfall barked. "I'm sure you're exaggerating! Tell Mr. Retief to report to me here in the Chancery at once!"

"But, sir," Magnan wailed. "You don't understand!"

"What, Ben Magnan, *I*, 'not understand'? You forget yourself, sir! You are addressing no mere mortal, but your very own Chief of Mission, a Career Ambassador! Now do as I say without further cavil!"

"But," Magnan objected Stubbornly (36-w). "I can't, sir! He's a captive of a mob led by the Deputy Chief of Police, one Smudge!"

"Don't try that feeble 36 on *me*, Ben!" Shortfall commanded. "As for Mr. Retief's choice of companions, that's not my concern at the moment. Go to the police, as you suggested, if you must, but get Retief!"

"That's just what the mob is yelling, sir," Magnan replied, retreating to the door, held open for him by Herb Lunchwell, who was wearing a Smug Look (14-b).

"Et tu, Fred?" Magnan gasped.

Behind him, Shortfall spoke up: "If even this roiling throng can grasp my instructions, Ben, surely *you* do as well!"

"But—but *they* want to tear him to pieces, Mr. Ambassador," Magnan temporized.

"As for myself," Shortfall commented quietly, "I have not yet decided on an appropriate course of action regarding a junior officer of this Mission who has egregiously ignored his Chief's instructions to disperse this nuisance. Especially as it was he who set off the throng in the first place. Get him in here, and I shall decide his fate, you may be sure."

"But, sir, he, that is, *we* tried! There are hundreds of those armed maniacs, all inspired by a fanatical hatred of Terries, inspired no doubt by Ambassador Flith's insidious propaganda program. But he was overwhelmed, Retief, I mean, not Ambassador Flith—"

"Enough of these baseless accusations against my very own colleague, the Groacian Chief of Mission!" Shortfall boomed, as well as one can boom in a feeble tenor.

"Gosh, sir," young Marvin Lacklustre spoke up hesitantly. "A comradely feeling for a fellow Ambassador is all very well, sir, but do you think it should outweigh your loyalty to your fellow Terries and subordinates?"

"Racism rears its ugly head," Shortfall intoned heavily. "Marvin, I'm surprised at you. I do hope you've not at any time given utterance to these illiberal sentiments in the hearing of others, perhaps less inclined than I to make allowance for youth and inexperience."

"You mean," Marvin came back promptly, "that it's OK for you to sacrifice one of your own officers just to keep the peace with your kiki-stone-fingering buddy, Flith!"

" 'Ambassador Flith' if you please, Marvin!" Shortfall corrected the lad. "Protocol, my boy, is not so lightly to be tossed aside, not in *my* presence!"

"Maybe the kid got a point at that, Mr. A.," Hy put in, sounding mournful.

"Enough, Mr. Felix!" Shortfall barked. "Get Mr. Retief up here to report at once, I say! There'll be no more discussion of the matter! He was already in trouble before daring to challenge my personal policies!"

"Nobody's discussing *that* matter," Hy muttered. "What we're discussing is, if it's cool to throw Retief to the dogs just so you can stay buddy-buddy with these local maniacs and that five-eyed little sneak, Flith."

"I warned Marvin about proper diplomatic usage, Hy," Shortfall stated bleakly, "as well as implied racism. Now *you* are so injudicious as to speak up to compound both indiscretions." He paused to jot a note on a leather-bound pad. "Perhaps, Hy," he went on, purringly, "you'd be happier after all, back at the city desk of the *Canny Poultrymen's Weekly,* or whatever sheet it was you formerly graced with your journalistic efforts."

"Too bad you got nothing to say about that," Hy retorted. "I get my instructions direct from the Agency; the Department's got nothing to say about it. I call 'em like I see 'em, Mr. Ambassadore!"

"Freedom of the press is not at issue here, Hy," Shortfall corrected the dour newsman. "And one calls them *as* one sees them, not 'like,' Hy," he added in a More Kindly Tone, (13-r) and jotted again. "I've spoken to you before, Hy," he went on, "about your usage 'Ambass*adore.*' As I jovially commented on a former occasion, I am not an avenue of ingress and egress. The word is Ambassador!"

"Yeah," Hy rejoined spiritedly. "But I seen a old historical filmclip showing about olden times and all,

and a big shot name of Ronnie Reagan said 'Ambassadore' just like me!"

"I recall the personage you mention, Hy," Shortfall
conceded. "He constantly outraged his foes by taking
actions which tended to serve his own nation's interests, rather than those of his avowed enemies, the
Blues, or Greens, or something. Hardly the diplomatic
way; poor choice as an exemplar, Hy."

"Reds," Felix supplied.

"I said about Blues or Greens or like that," Shortfall
reminded the stubborn Information Agency rep. "And
that's the same as if I said 'Reds,' right, Art?" He
turned to the Cultural Attache for confirmation. "But it
is the insubordination, verging on open revolt, of Mr.
Retief which is under discussion here!"

"Ha!" Hy Felix interjected. "Retief ain't even here!
How could—"

"You see?" Shortfall cut off the irreverent Agency
man. "After I distinctly ordered him to report to me at
once—and he's not even here!"

"So the guy's a couple minutes late fer Staff Meeting," Hy persisted. "That ain't hardly a hanging offense."

"I said nothing of hanging, *yet!*" Shortfall caviled.
"Still, when one considers that Retief's desertion was in
the face of an angry mob menacing this Mission, it
could well be regarded as a capital offense."

"Geeze," Hy sighed. "Next you'll be offering a reward, dead or alive."

"Preferably alive," Shortfall told the sarcastic fellow.
"As for the reward, I think one hundred guck would be
about right, eh, Nat?" He turned to his Econ Chief for
confirmation.

"Well, sir," Art spoke up sagely, if belatedly, "there
are perhaps those who would hold that while references
to the azure and vert tinctures are not the precise
equivalent of the gules, it is undoubtedly a fact that
Your Excellency was on the right track." This time it
was Hy who jotted.

"That 'ghouls,' Art," he called to the Culture man, "that's the same as 'red,' ain't it?"

"That is precisely my point, Hyman," Art replied, and busied himself stuffing a Yalcan clay pipe.

"You're *not* thinking of lighting that thing, I trust, Arthur," Shortfall said in the tone of one Reluctantly Mentioning the Unmentionable (3-z).

Art stuck the pipe back in the tobacco pouch and returned it to the bulging pocket of his Harris tweed hacking jacket.

"How do you like that?" he inquired *sotto voce* of an unheeding universe, "after I back him up and all, he won't even let a fellow have a little pick-up."

"Rick," Shortfall spoke abruptly to his Admin Officer, pretending not to have overheard Art's plaint, "better get some flyers run off, offering a reward for the return of Mr. Retief, alive and in one piece."

Rick Uptight nodded and jotted a note. "You *did* say 'dead or alive,' right, Chief?" he inquired disinterestedly.

"Naw, Ricky," Felix spoke up, "that was me: I was ribbing his Ex."

" 'Dead or Alive,' " Rick mumbled, jotting again.

"Then why din't you just say 'Red'?" Hy demanded out of context, of Art Proudflesh. "Always tryna ritz us common people, eh, Art?"

"A knowledge of heraldic blazoning terminology is a part of the education of any gentleman, Hyman," Art rejected the accusation.

"So now yer saying I ain't a genulman," Hy complained. "Ha! Next you'll be throwing me to the dogs—or pillars—like you done Jimmy Retief!"

CHAPTER TWO

Down in the lobby, Retief went first across the fallen gate. A nearly solid wall of intertwined locals reared up to oppose him, fangs bared, shredding hooks at the ready. He took a rusty kitchen-knife from the knobby grip of the nearest and poked it at the fellow's neck-region until it recoiled; then he seized the thus isolated creature just below the jaws and squeezed the pressure point until the fanged mandible opened to its widest gape. With the other hand, he scooped up a loop of the most conveniently placed local and wedged it into the yawning maw of the first, which reflexively closed, pinching the other's abdomen painfully, and eliciting a shrill screech. Thick umber ichor leaked from the wound thus inflicted, running down across the rumpled fur of its owner to drip reluctantly into the gutter below.

"Hey!" the bitten mobster yelled. "Whatsa idear, Leroy, you can't wait for chow?"

Retief released him and stepped back as he threshed and heaved frantically, until at last he threw off the grip of Leroy, who, jaws snapping, was at once engulfed in the suddenly writhing mass of rioters. The injured local continued to whip his elongated torso against the in-pressing mob until he had cleared a space of a few cubic yards in which he could inspect his hurtie in relative solitude. By then, a free-for-all was raging around him.

"Wonder what come over old Leroy?" the bitten one mourned. "Usely a nice, quiet feller. Where *is* the son of a gurge?" he added with sudden vehemence. "I'll teach him to go gnawing on his cell boss!" As he charged the writhing wall of his fellows, Bill reached him and delivered a hearty kick to the punctured area, setting off a new flurry of resentful body-threshing, accompanied by appropriate invective.

"This feller talks pretty rough," Bill said admiringly to Retief. "Must of ordered hisself one o' them black-market O & P tapes, guaranteed to outrage decency in a hunnert dialects and blaspheme all the gods from Azuz to Zuba." So saying he promptly assaulted the nearest bystander, only to be thrown promptly on his back. Retief grabbed him before he rolled off the edge of the narrow entry-ledge.

"Geeze," the husky lad commented, regaining his feet. "I guess you make it look easier 'n it is, General," he commented, rubbing a bruised shin, while waving away the ever-present gnats.

The focus of attention of the angry crowd was now shifting from their impromptu riot back to the two embattled Terrans. With the threatening locals snap-ping and jabbing him from every direction, Bill took up a position back-to-back with Retief, fending off teeth and daggers with lightning fast forearm blocks, dodging the more daring attempts at tail-blows, the accuracy of which was spoiled by the constant movement of both the aggressors' allies and their intended prey. Then Leroy reappeared, howling, closely pursued by the com-rade who had been bitten by him, and now quite appar-ently intending to return the favor. Leroy recoiled at sight of the embattled Terrans and instantly received a sharp nip near the tip of his elongated last somite, at which he lashed out in frustration, passing the bite along to a bystander, who retaliated in kind, setting off a chain reaction which again embroiled the entire crowd in a whipping, snapping free-for-all, ignoring the Terrans.

One group, ignoring the affray, was busy attaching handbills to every available surface. Magnan, retreating from the thick of the affray, got close enough to see that the documents being distributed were typical of those badly reproduced on the equipment in the Office of Information. It showed a blurry photo of Retief which Magnan recognized as having been surreptitiously snapped by Art Proudflesh during Staff Meeting. Above the picture was the legend, in bold block letters, 'RE-WARD FOR RETIEF Dead or Alive.'

"Why, the scoundrel!" Magnan blurted. "Or, rather, the incompetent ass! The very idea! All His Excellency intended was to assist a subordinate to safety. One would think he was a hunted criminal!" He turned away, muttering, jostled by the bill stickers.

Smudge, standing aloof beyond the fringe of the me-lee, yelled in vain for order. The noise-level decreased slightly: in the respite thus afforded, Bill blurted:

"We can't stay here, General; they'll remember us any second, specially with old Chief over there yelling 'Get Terry!' and blowing that whistle!" The Marine ducked a wild blow aimed by a local who employed half his length as a bludgeon, with his fanged head at the end, a blow which would have crushed the Terran's skull had it connected. Bill, shaken by the near miss, stepped back for a wide view of the crowd, saw rein-forcements crowding in along the avenue from the con-spicuously marked Police HQ, in the next block to the left.

"We got to get outa here, General!" Bill yelled over his shoulder; suiting action to words, the Marine rushed the heap of entangled battlers directly before him, made it across the two-by-four to the relative spaciousness of the boulevard, where he paused for only a moment before setting off at a sprint toward the somewhat less crowded area to the right.

"Hold it, Bill," Retief called, as a fresh contingent appeared ahead. "They've got us blocked both ways."

Bill skidded to a halt as yet another platoon of locals burst from a side street and swarmed over the boulevard directly in his path. He turned and dashed back to a cable-sized sideway and started out across it, holding his arms horizontally for balance, and shaking his head at the busy gnats, moving at a snail's pace while the locals rapidly closed the gap between their snapping jaws and the Terran's unprotected flesh. With a final lunge, he reached the beaver-dam-like structure at the end of the cable, secured hand-holds in the shedding surface and started up. His pursuers halted and began to pile up at the base of the fragile wall, which they were apparently reluctant to scale. As usual the persistent gnats seemed to avoid the locals, to swarm around the Terran faces.

Retief came up behind the press and began prying a confused rookie away from his grip on the cableway. The surprised fellow struggled to retain his grasp on the cable, but Retief inexorably broke one grip at a time until the frantic creature's full six-foot length was dangling by a single knobby fist.

"Tell you what, pal," the terrified cop proposed, his thin voice rendered even shriller by fear. "You give me a hand up and leave off stamping on my knuckles, and I'll leave you go this time, OK? I'm constable Bub," he added hopefully, as if giving his name sealed the compact.

"You've been watching too much classic telley, Bub," Retief counselled the fellow. "Real life isn't like that. But don't worry, you won't be lonely; I'll send some of your colleagues along very soon, to keep you company."

"That ain't the point," the cop complained. "It's the company I *will* have down there in them lightless depths and all that worries me."

"Tell me about it," Retief suggested. When the cop hesitated, Retief raised his foot into position to stamp on the overstrained fist which alone supported the obstinate constable.

"Wait!" the latter yelped. "It's like a state secret, as well as common tradition here on Sardon: the Underworld down there is inhabited by demons and aliens and goblins and outworlders, and ogres and foreigners and trolls and Terries: tear a fellow into small pieces and put ketchup on 'em and eat 'em rawr, is what they do. Don't let on I tole you, OK, pal? Now gimme that hand up."

Retief bent and grasped the wiry wrist attached to the hand at his feet and at once Bub whipped his nether end up and over in a bone-crushing blow which however, missed its mark, as Retief, unsurprised, stepped aside so that Bub's fourteenth somite impacted the cable with a force which nearly bisected him. In frantic reflex, Bub recoiled, releasing his hand-hold, to dangle, draped over the cable, doubled over with his head adjacent to his terminal pair of feet. He gazed mournfully up at Retief, who was now engaged in beating back another cop, this one less determined than Bub, relinquishing his grips in an effort to reverse himself so as to snap his yellow jaws at his assailant. Retief unceremoniously dumped him from the cable. He fell with a long drawn-out but abruptly terminated screech.

"Guess you won't want to give me another chance," Bub guessed correctly.

Retief went over the next half-dozen cops and reached the tattered wall with a final lunge which dislodged the most eager of Bill's pursuers, who had reared up half his length to snap chartreuse fangs six inches from the Marine's foot. Bill looked down, saw Retief behind him.

"Hi, General," he called over his shoulder, "glad to see you. I thought the mob had you cut off."

"They did," Retief conceded, "so I went around them."

"Musta jostled a few of 'em by accident," Bill commented. "Heard a few ceremonial terminal yells, like it says about in the Post Report."

"Could have," Retief acknowledged.

Below Retief, one of the mob-members was slamming his upper torso against the shaky, doorless structure to which both Terrans clung. Suddenly, there was a ripping sound and Bill shifted position abruptly, grabbing for a secure hold as he pitched forward, his head and torso disappearing inside the abruptly opened gap in the loose-woven fabric of the structure. Retief caught a glimpse of movement inside the rent just before Bill, with a yell, seemed to leap forward to disappear inside. Retief hauled himself up, looked inside, saw flickering hand-lights in the otherwise unrelieved pitch darkness.

"Hey, Mr. Retief!" Bill shouted. "They got me! And they ain't caterpillars! They're—" his voice cut off in mid-word. Retief heard threshing sounds, the *smack*! of a fist impacting on flesh, a brief scuffling, then silence, except for the howl of the frustrated mob outside, and a background of faint rustlings and creakings from the rickety building. He climbed in through the narrow aperture, found himself standing on a resilient and uneven floor which creaked underfoot. There did not seem to be any gnats here.

Retief froze, breathing silently. The yells of the frustrated cops outside were diminishing in volume as Smeer's commands gradually began to restore a degree of order. Inside the still, haystack-smelling space, nothing stirred. Retief called quietly to Bill, but received no reply. He lit a micro-flash and played its brilliant needle-beam around the room, on a shedding woven-grass partition, a high ceiling of decaying rattan and rushes. A black opening in a far corner suggested where Bill's captors had taken him. Looking in, Retief saw woven walls which had sagged until they nearly touched. He heard a faint yell, far ahead. He stepped in, proceeded quickly along the narrow passage, came to a dubious-looking down-ramp where the main corridor curved off to the right. He paused to listen, heard a faint murmur from the side. He went cautiously, using the light sparingly, and after a hard left turn, saw ahead a dim glow as of filtered daylight. Another ten feet brought him to a broad landing made of unexpectedly solid planks at the head of a long flight of equally firm steps. The light, such as it was, came from below. There was no sound from the stairwell. Retief descended, step-by-step; suddenly the light below brightened, and he heard the creak of a heavy door on unoiled hinges. Then a voice, unmistakably Bill's, yelled, "Whoopee!"

Shadows moved near the foot of the stairs, where, Retief now saw, a heavy timber blocked ingress. He went quickly but silently down to the barrier, squinting against the brightness. Someone loomed up in view just beyond the six-by-twelve blockade. It was Bill, his hair disheveled, a hand-blown flask in one fist.

"Mr. Retief!" the non-com boomed jovially. "I mean, General, sir. Come on in, if I can get this dang timber outa way. Run into some good fellers down here! Got some pretty good home-brew, one drag and I'm already pretty well juiced." He paused to take a grip on the unplaned timber and lift—to no avail. It remained firmly in place.

"Hold on, General, sir," he muttered. "I'll get Big Henry."

The space Retief could see beyond the turnstile was wide, low-ceilinged, illuminated by daylight filtering through chinks in the windowless wall opposite the stair. There were tables and chairs, and along one side, a crude counter, on which Retief saw a number of misshapen bottles similar to the one Bill had been waving. The place was crowded with crudely-garbed Terrans with the look of seasoned spacemen, all intent on their drinking and arguing.

"It seems we've found where the local Terry Colony hangs out," Retief told Bill, who nodded and set off determinedly to push through the heedless crowd.

"Too right, Matey," someone called cheerfully from near at hand. A bleary face in need of a shave appeared around the corner where the entry hall debouched into the room proper, followed by a small, skinny body clothed in rags with brass buttons.

"Call me Blinky, Mate," the newcomer suggested, and proffered one of the lumpy bottles, this one a deep green, with a crooked neck. Retief accepted, and took a taste, then braced himself and took a long pull.

"That's right, Mate," Blinky approved. "Man can't sip a good pale ale; don't taste right. Come on, meet the boys."

Retief tossed the barrier aside and followed his scrawny guide into the room. There were windows along one side, covered by slatted shutters. Behind the crude bar, a big, paunchy fellow with 'Spike' lettered on his pocket was polishing a ruby-red goblet clearly of Yalcan manufacture.

"Name yer pizen," he muttered around a well-gnawed cigar-stub.

"Bacchus black," Retief replied. Spike nodded and turned to extract a dusty green bottle from a shelf below the back bar. In the tarnished mirror against which bottles were stacked, Retief was surprised to see a reflection not of a sagging stick-and-grass architecture, but a gas-lit interior with red plush settees and a crowd of top-hatted dandies and bustled ladies in fantastic *chapeaux* sitting at tiny tables or standing crowded against yet another mirror across the broad room.

"Curious effect," Retief commented, and tasted his wine, which was rich and dry, of a deep jewel-red.

"What's yer loose-nation, stranger?" the mixologist inquired indifferently. Retief described the scene in the mirror.

"Oh, that's just old Will," the barman explained. "Got a lot of funny idears. He's what you call a pote."

Before Retief could respond, a deep, hoarse voice shouted across the room:

"What six varlets done messed with my set-up here on the door?" Retief turned to see a red-faced seven-footer dressed in the costume of a trideo pirate. "Taken me a halfa hour to wrassle that timber up there!" the newcomer continued. "Now I got to do it again! Hey, you!" he interrupted himself, thrusting through the crowd toward Bill, who stood, bottle in hand, awaiting whatever came next.

"I ain't seen *you*!" the giant accused. "You're new! Likely you know something about this!" He dropped the bottle and grabbed Bill by the front of his blue uniform-blouse and lifted the six-footer clear of the floor, whereupon Bill doubled a fist and delivered a hearty jab to the big fellow's jaw. He hardly noticed.

"Oh, frisky, eh?" the giant said.

"Hey," Bill interjected in a shaken voice as the big fellow drew back a ham-sized fist, "lemme down, Big Henry; you know me. Blinky gave us an introduction no more'n ten minutes ago."

"Yeah, I guess I seen you," Henry acknowledged regretfully; then his choleric eye fell on Retief. "But you I *ain't* seen, fer sure!" He dropped Bill, who staggered but retained his balance.

"Hey, Big Henry," he called to the giant's back, "that there's my pal, Mr. Retief. He's a OK guy. So. . . ." His voice trailed as Henry halted, confronting Retief, who, at six-three, was an inch shorter than the official greeter.

"What *you* want here, Sonny?" Henry demanded. "Don't you know no strangers ain't allowed in The Cloud-Cuckoo Club, excusin' they're friends o' mine?" His speech delivered, Big Henry reached as if to grab Retief's shirtfront, but Retief casually knocked the oak-like arm aside and chucked the bouncer gently under his unshaven chin.

"You did that real well," he commented. "Better let it go at that."

Quick as a snake, Henry grabbed Retief's wrist and was instantly thrown on his back.

"I don't like to be man-handled by strangers," Retief explained.

"Who's 'strange'?" Henry demanded indignantly. He climbed back to his full height and looked around belligerently at the awe-struck crowd. "Wheresa bum says this here feller—"

"Retief," his new-found lifelong pal supplied.

"Who says Retief, here, and me ain't old buddies? Which I'm prouda welcome him and his side-kick to the club."

No one volunteered, and Henry, flanked by Retief and Bill, retired to a table in a relatively quiet corner where a woven-grass screen intersected the bamboo wall, a spot embellished by a flowering green plant in a five-gallon putty-bucket. Henry leaned to sniff one of the showy white-with-yellow-streaks blossoms, then turned to the small, wiry waiter, clad in rusty black, with a small-checked vest, who had followed them.

"Three brews, Chauncey," Henry commanded. "My private stock," he added, then fixed his small, piggy eyes on Retief.

"You hear about some kinda official Johnnies done settled in, up Embassy row?" he demanded stonily, as the waiter returned with three dusty flagons and three heavy pewter mugs.

"The rumor is true," Retief told him.

"They gonna try and interfere with the Club, you think?" There was an anxious tone in Big Henry's voice now.

"They'll probably try to regulate the booze production," Retief suggested, "and maybe tax you boys a little."

"Taxes?" Henry spat the word like a doody-bug in his soup. "I like to see the slob collects any graft offen Big Henry Laboochy!"

"Taxes aren't actually graft, Henry," Retief corrected his host. "Just ordinary stealing."

"Ain't no mug gonna steal nothing off Big Henry

Laboochy neither!" Henry declared with vehemence. He took a long pull at the tankard.

Bill touched Retief's sleeve. "Mr. Retief," he said hesitantly. "What kinda place is this?" He looked around with a puzzled expression at the crowded room with its watery light. "Looks like a old 'movie,' I guess they useta call 'em, I seen once."

"What old movie?" Retief asked him.

"Name of the *Vikins*, or somethin like that," Bill replied uncertainly. "All about these guys useta row around in little boats with gargoyles or like that carved on the front end. Had little swords and iron hats with a cow's horns on 'em. Useta raid the churches and all. Then they went home and sat around and bragged and got juiced and started fights with each other. Don't sound too bad. But lookit them two bozos over there . . ." He nodded toward a table where two beefy, redfaced men with immense walrus mustaches had put down their glasses and were glaring at each other across the table. A frail-looking young woman with a pale face and large eyes sat between them, looking distressed. Bill looked at Henry.

"Well, how about it, Big?" he said challengingly, "you gonna let them two start a fistfight right here in the club? Girl might get hurt, them two heavies start in."

"Oh, Edgar," Henry called. One of the belligerent men responded by turning briefly to look inquiringly at the bouncer cum host.

"Yah?" he muttered. "Just a minute, if you don't mind, Hank, I got to teach this here feller a few things about Realism. Beat it, Minnie," he added, addressing the girl.

"Poor Edgar takes the epithet 'Intransigents' literally," the other fellow supplied, looking smugly at the back of Edgar's head. The girl, clad in a tight-fitting bodice and a voluminous skirt of unpressed pinkish cloth rose quickly and walked away.

"You guys finish it outside," Henry ordered. "And leave Minette outa it."

Henry returned his attention to his beer-mug, and the two art critics returned to their low-voiced quarrel.

"Mr. Retief," Bill said softly, sounding troubled. He pointed to the far side of the big room. "Look at them two fellas: getting ready to fight it out with their butcher-knives, and their buddies are egging them on."

Retief followed the young fellow's gaze, saw a pair of lean, mustached men in westkits and with ruffled shirt-fronts intent over a card-game.

"You're exaggerating, Bill," Retief told the lad. "They're playing cut-throat, but they're not cutting any actual throats."

Big Henry, who had been growling as he listened, rose suddenly and yelled, "Willy! Get it over here right now!"

The nearby crowd parted to allow a wraith-thin fellow whose face seemed all forehead to hurry up, clearly distressed.

"What wouldst, friend Henry?" he gasped. "Art displeased? Softly, pray. Thy wish is my command."

"OK, Will, take it easy," Henry soothed the nervous fellow. "Everything's jake, or will be soon's you lay off horsing around." Henry turned to Retief. "Old Willy likes to 'peer into the future,' like he says. Got a lot of funny ideas; his loose-nations are so clear they kinda spill over, know what I mean?"

"No," Bill put in, "*I* sure don't know what you mean. What's this here Willy's ideas got to do with a couple light-heavies starting a riot?"

Henry looked sadly at the young Marine. "You got a lot to learn about the Club, kid," he observed regretfully.

"I'm with Bill," Retief put in. "What's it all about, Big?"

"Well, it's kinda hard to explain to a feller ain't use to it," the big fellow told Retief. "But, what the hell, when I first come, I didn't catch on neither, for a while.

See, this here is a place where some kinda force lines or like that are in what ya call resonance with the alpha rhythm and all, get it? So it like reinforces the old imagery, OK?"

"That's an explanation?" Bill inquired in the tone of One who Still Doesn't Get It.

"Well, every guy's got a few ideas about where he'd like to go on shore leave," Henry pointed out patiently. "Some guys can see it in their head better'n others; it's what they call mind over matters and all. Will here likes to pick up on stuff that's coming up sometime later, and he brings it right into focus, so sometimes it almost drowns out I and the boys' loose-nations. See?"

"*I* don't get you," Bill complained. "Sounds like you're tryna tell us around here you imagine stuff and it's real."

"Sure," Big replied, nodding in reinforcement of his verbalization. "I already said about the loose-nations and all. So here we are."

At that moment there was a sudden stir near the entry, where the bandy-legged little fellow who had greeted Retief stood ready with a baseball-bat sized club to greet the next arrival. He swung and missed as a smallish, slightly-built man incongruously clad in a seersucker dicky-suit only slightly disheveled by contact with the mob at his heels, dashed through, shied at the near miss and uttered a yelp of protest.

"The very idea!" he cried. "A matron of *your* years clowning in such a disgraceful fashion!"

"What's a matron?" somebody called.

"Some kinda dance," another supplied. "He thinks Blinky's dancin!"

"Don't take it so hard, Mate," Blinky advised the newcomer. "What's goin on out there? Looks like we got a regular invasion here. How'd you boys get the 'pillars' all worked up, anyways?"

"Enough of your insolence, Madam!" the frail-looking new arrival snapped. He stood on tiptoes to scan the room over the heads of its occupants. Blinky moved in to block him off. "A spy, hey?" he charged, shoving the slightly larger, but unathletic stranger.

"It's OK," Henry advised his guests. "Blinky can handle it. Looked to me like one o' them topsiders. Wonder how he got past the patrol."

"That's Mr. Magnan, a professional associate of mine," Retief told the big fellow. "I'd better introduce him before Blinky does something a little too permanent."

"Suit yourself, pal," Henry conceded, and began to ply a well-worn toothpick on his large, square, yellow teeth.

As Magnan disappeared from his view in the gang of excited men, Retief rose. "Excuse me," he said. "Bill, order another round and I'll be right back."

"Retief!" Magnan yelled from the midst of the huddle of waving arms and raised voices. "There you are! I feared the worst! Get away, you hussy!" he snapped at a paunchy deck-ape type who was attempting to frisk him. "Take your grimy paws off my person instanter, or I shall be forced to resort to harsh measures!"

Blinky recoiled, blinking rapidly. "Zounds!" he exclaimed, whipping off his warped nautical cap. "Best belay that, me hearties," he advised his motley crew. "Most planet-lubbers know when to keep their jaw shut, but this here one seems to be made of sterner stuff!"

"Quite right, Madam," Magnan told the frustrated fellow. "You may now conduct me to your leader."

"Still too cheeky by arf," Blinky remarked, then, addressing Magnan: "You wouldn't be a shipmate of my chum Retief, I don't suppose?"

"Indeed I am!" Magnan averred. "Now stand aside."

"Sure, bub," Blinky agreed, backing away, shooing his minions from Magnan's path. "Any pal o' Retief and Big Henry is OK with me!"

"Big Henry, indeed!" Magnan snapped and forged

into the press directly toward Retief, who led him to the table.

"May I join you, gentlemen?" Magnan inquired rhetorically as he sank into an empty chair. He mopped at his forehead dramatically with an Ambassador-only issue hanky.

"Well!" he remarked to Retief by way of greeting, "I rather thought you could have come along sooner to assist me with that cutthroat crew, rather than continuing to linger here in low company, swilling whatever it is you're swilling."

"I was admiring your technique, Mr. Magnan," Retief explained blandly. "You handled matters quite well, I thought."

Magnan dug at his eyes with the heels of his hands. "Of course," he snapped, "I was at no moment at a loss for the correct mode of response to those hussies."

" 'Hussies,' " Big Henry echoed. "That's some kinda dames, ain't it? If you seen one, that's the second time the Number One House Rule's been broke this afternoon. Will don't really count, o' course, him bein' a pote and all, not like a regular humern bean. But now, this here swab—what's yer alias, bub?" His small porcine eyes suddenly bored into Magnan's.

"Uh, as to that," Magnan gobbled, "one wonders by what authority—I mean to say, while I have nothing to hide, of course, it happens that at the moment I am engaged on a most sensitive operation, and both honor and custom require that I decline to disclose that datum to one of your stripe, sir, in the absence of competent authorization, that is." He turned to Retief with an earnest expression.

"What sort of place is this?" he almost wailed. "Somehow," he confided, "it gives me the creeps. Everything seems so . . . so, well, I don't really know how to describe it, but my hair is attempting to stand on end. Let's go." He broke off to peer anxiously around. "A moment ago—" he began and fell silent.

"It's all right, sir," Retief reassured him. "Or, it's not exactly 'all right,' but it's not immediately disastrous."

"The disaster comes later, eh?" Magnan queried, still nervous. He looked distastefully at Henry.

"Where did the ladies go?" he wondered aloud. "And who is this . . . ah . . ."

"Henry," Retief put in, "may I present Mr. Magnan of the Econ Section. Mr. Magnan, Big Henry, also known as Sir Henry, and Lord Shivingston, as well as King Hank."

Magnan extended a shaky palm. "Honored, Your Majesty," he managed. "God Lord, Retief," he interrupted himself. "Why didn't you tell me? I'd have observed proper protocol."

"Didn't want to risk a fall when you backed into the Presence," Retief told the senior diplomat.

"In what way, Your royal Majesty, may I be of service?" Magnan inquired in his most unctious tone.

"Say, Retief," Henry addressed his guest, *sotto voce*, "you sure this here guy is a shipmate o' yours? Sounds like a spy to me. And you shunt of said about the boys electing me king and all."

"Hardly, Your Imperial Highness," Magnan objected, "and I do hope I have got your style right. A diplomatic member of an Embassy staff would hardly stoop to espionage!"

"Well, if Retief says you're OK, Bub, you're OK with me. Now, I was just tryna tell the boys here, about the Club. See, one o' the first Terries in here, a couple hunnert years back, was a big Swede, Captain Larson, and natcherly he had his own idears, all about the olden times, and he was one tough hombre, I guess, and he printed his old-time Swedes and all on the place so they still stick. Me and Willy together never got 'em all cleared out; but we got a good bunch here now; we all work together at a what you might say is a compromise set-up. Course, you fellers are welcome to add a few choice items o' your own, if you got the loose-nation

power to make it stick. Now, you, Bill, you was objecting to the knife fights and all—so what I say is, who
needs 'em? See? We aim to make a feller feel at home."

"We got a few house rules, like no nood dames—ner
no nood guys, neither. One time we hadda pair here,
name of Ralphie and Dood, had the whole place steamed
up, something you call a sharrom, whatever that is,
where some guys they call Rams hang out, and all.
Hadda throw 'em out. Ralphie and Dood, I mean, not
these Rams. But mostly we get along good. Jest don't
expect to be able to override me nor Willy: we got the
strongest loose-nations here, especially Willy, eh, Willy?"
Henry looked knowingly at the half-bald pote, who
nodded dreamily.

"Tis passing strange," he commented. "I dreamt of
days to come—and in the instant here was I, amid the
scenes I mused on. But for Hal's rude warriors, tis
true."

"Tole ya an I tole ya, Willy, them ain't *my* knaves,"
Henry objected. "Left over from old Cap Larson, like I
was telling Retief here. Wisht I could get ridda 'em.
Club'd be peaceful joint cept fer them rogues!"

"Easily done, friend Harry," Will said. "But concentrate your will, as I shall mine—and perhaps our guests
as well. We'll wish 'em to Hell, and no part of this our
club." He closed his eyes and frowned.

"Geeze!" Bill exclaimed. "Willya look at that! Old
Olaf and Helgi—least that's what they been callin each
other—jest got up and walked out, like they hadda go
or something. And the rest of 'em, too." He twisted in
his chair to scan the farthest corners of the cavernous
room.

"Well done, gentles!" Will exclaimed. "Better than
any putter-out at three to one had wagered, I trow!"

"Old Willy talks funny sometimes," Henry told Bill
behind his hand. "But he's larning."

"Methought twas your own rude dialect that 'casioned

fun," Willy observed mildly. "Still, so long as we can converse, what matters terminology, say I."

"Ere, ere," Blinky put in from a position just behind the windy pote. He raised his warped amber bottle and drank deep.

"Par me, Big, and fellers," he added. "I gotta get back on the gate. Gotta press a crew to get the timber back in place." He paused to eye Retief, half resentfully, half hopefully, "Lessen maybe Cap Retief here might wanta lend a hand."

"With pleasure," Retief acceeded, rising. "But may I inquire why it's necessary to set up a roadblock of such heroic dimensions?"

"You been lissening to Willy too much," Big Henry grunted. "But I get the drift: you wanta know how come we got to fortify the door."

"Precisely put, Your Majesty," Magnan supplied. "I think that is precisely what Mr. Retief was wondering, as I do myself."

"Well, you see, gents," Henry began hesitantly, "some slob named Goldberg or like that with a grudge against old Cap Larson they say, tried to bring in a horde of evil spirits and all, to drag old Wolf direct to the Bad Place, least that's what they usta say, the old boys was here when I come." He paused to empty his bottle and bellow for refills all around.

"Fact is," he continued, a trifle defiantly, "I seen 'em myself, once. Had a few too many, maybe a couple dozen brews and a jug o' rum, and had a notion to go outside for a looksee. And this here devil in the shape of a big old caterpillar or what ya call 'em rared up square in front o' me and said, 'Hold hard, Mate, notaries loud in the high street,' or like that." Henry uncapped a new bottle with a flip of his thumb and drank half of its contents in a gulp. "Fer meself," he went on thoughtfully, "I like a nice grog-shop where a feller can get some good brew and a nice plate o' eats and maybe get into a few friendly fights. No guys blowing that loud music and guitar-picking. And *no* dames—dames cause trouble," he explained. "Sure, I like a nice dame, but so does every other guy, 'cept Ralphie and Dood, o' course, and that's where the trouble comes in. Guys use knives over dames. . . ." As he spoke, Henry fingered a scar on the side of his neck. "Hadda bar one feller fer life," he added. "Say, talking about a nice plate of eats, what say we put on the feed bag, fellers?" He yelled and the black-clad waiter was back. He nodded at Big Henry's instructions, and was gone only a moment before returning with five heaped plastron plates balanced along one arm.

"I hope ya like a golosh, boys," Big said heartily. "My own recipe. Have it every day. Only one issue galosh to a batch, but it's got lots o' glimp eggs fer texture."

"Why I'm sure it's delightful, Your Highness—" Magnan burbled.

" 'Majesty,' " Henry corrected, "if ya wanta be technical. Retief mentioned I was king, remember?"

Bill sniffed his steaming plate and commented. "Seems like that galosh was a used one—GI, too."

Will averted his eyes. "Didst forget thy promise, good Henry?" he inquired. "'Twas agreed that I should prevail in the kitchen. In this my ideal pot-house, height *Ye Moulin Rouge*, I assure you the *chef de cuisine* is an artist."

"I dunno, Willy," Henry temporized. "That there Moolin Rooje grub might be a mite too fancy for the new—I mean my old pals here." He looked inquiringly at Retief.

"I'd be glad to try Willy's recommendation," the diplomat assured his host. "The restaurants in Paris in the 1870's have an excellant reputation."

"Didst say . . . 1870?" Will demanded breathlessly. "Three centuries beyond the veil of time, I trow. And how didst thou, good Retief, come to know this milieu, of mine own devising?"

Retief explained to the unworldly poet that he had imagined better than he knew, that he had visioned what was indeed to come to pass, and that even in Retief's time, a thousand years later than Will's, the restaurants of Paris had a reputation so high that it was even able to overwhelm the reputation of the Parisians' manners as those of super New Yorkers, and attract vast numbers of tourists from America and Japan and elsewhere.

"Thou dost pull my leg, I trow," Willy replied, grinning. "Savages, you'd have me believe, cross the ocean sea from the New World in order to dine in Paris. A most pleasant conceit, good Retief—and equal to mine own imaginings, forsooth!"

Magnan leaned close to Retief to ask, "That Will, whence—I mean where did he come from? He hardly fits in with the rest of these rude louts."

"Ask Henry," Retief suggested. Magnan did so.

"Oh, old Willy, well, he just was here one day," Henry reminisced. "Mighta been around a while fore I noticed him. Quiet feller; talks funny, like you, Mr. Magnan, only worse, no offense."

Magnan turned to Will, sitting slightly apart in the corner of the booth. "If you don't mind my asking—" he began but broke off as Henry came abruptly to his feet.

"Hold hard, mates!" the big fellow boomed, holding up a callussed hand. "I smell mischief afoot, as I draw breath!" He peered across the room toward the entry. "Aye," he commented, more calmly. "Tis the demon-worms, come again! But my brave lads will drive them off, as always. They've sharp teeth, these imps, but dull livers! Bother the rogues, we'll dine and be damned to them!" As he concluded his peroration, the waiter reappeared with two subordinates beside him, each bearing a silver tray laden with savory aromas.

"Beef Bourgignon," Magnan announced, "but of course, the *consomme au buerre blanc* first." He beamed approvingly as the Sevres china bowl of soup was placed before him. Henry had already dipped his spoon in his bowl and smacked his lips loudly.

"I've but little patience with slops in the ordinary way," he cried, "but this be no ordinary broth! Well done, Retief! I declare to all, you've effected an improvement on my own rude eats! And the beef good Chaucey bears tastes one half so good as it smells, tis a viand of rare delight!"

"Chow hounds," Bill commented, as he slurped his soup noisily. "They're all alike. Rather eat then run off the caterpillars."

"All in good time, Sergeant," Magnan reproved the lad. "Eat slowly, and savor your food. You'll not soon get its equal in the Embassy dining room."

"All that stuff seems like it's a long way off," Bill commented dreamily, as he took Magnan's advice and noticed the rich taste of the fine soup.

"But alas, it is not," Magnan said as he glanced toward the entry where men were crowding, obscuring the view. "I'll wager it's that scamp Smeer," he observed, "intent on seizing our persons in flagrant violation of diplomatic custom, the rules of hospitality, and common justice, to say nothing of Interplanetary Law." Magnan paused to tug at Retief's sleeve. "Hadn't we, that is, you, better—" he started, but Retief shook his head.

"Remember what you said about savoring the food?" he said as he tried his beef.

Magnan finished off his *mousse choclat*, leaned back and sighed. After a sip of his Chateau d'Yquem, he leaned toward Retief, cupped his hand beside his mouth and whispered:

"Am I actually to understand that whatever some of these fellows consider the ideal place to have a good time becomes manifested as though it were actual?"

"So it appears," Retief told him.

"That's impossible!" Magnan snapped.

"Certainly, Mr. Magnan," Retief agreed readily. "I didn't suggest that it's possible, only that it's happening."

"Well," Magnan ruminated, somewhat mollified, "that *was* a rather fine Chateau Lafitte-Rothschilde. An 89, or I miss my guess. So I suppose one may as well accommodate to appearances."

"I'm curious, Mr. Magnan," Retief said. "What did the place look like to you when you came in?"

"Why, it was a near-perfect duplicate of Ye Cozy Tea Shoppe back home in Salinas," Magnan replied, sounding surprised. "Charming place, really. One could pop in on a blustery winter afternoon and take a dish of Soochong and a really lovely crumpert, all in an atmosphere of the most refined propriety. But, alas, I was so happy to see the place, I made the error of impulsively embracing Madam Lachaise, the maiden lady proprietress, much to her and my own embarrassment, especially when she repulsed me like a termagent as if I'd been guilty of an improper advance!"

"And Blinky thought you were attacking him," Retief commented. "That's what precipitated the riot."

"Then, oddly enough," Magnan mused on, "the surroundings were different. Nothing actually changed, it seemed, but in some curious way, rather than the cozy tea-room on a chilly afternoon, it seemed to be some sort of dreadful, old-fashioned French bordello, but with bits and pieces of the sort of gin-mill one sees in unlikely pseudo-historicals about Pacific islands, where all sorts of unsavory riff-raff turn up and spend their time plotting to raid some forbidden temple or the like. All very confusing." He subsided, looking out past the potted geranium on the sill of the dusty window at the white sails of the pleasure-yachts on the breeze-riffled bay.

"Pleasant enough corner, here," Magnan observed. "And the food is superb. One wonders how the management is able to import the rare old vintages to this dismal backwater world so far off the trade-lanes. Odd I didn't notice a lake when we drove in."

"Will is responsible for the Gaslight Era Parisian milieu," Retief told his supervisor. "He's drowning out Big's mariners' roost, and between them they've pretty well suppressed Captain Larson's mead-hall. Your tea-room didn't stand a chance, I'm afraid. I settled for this corner table, and it seems to stand up pretty well. I suppose because it doesn't clash too much, and good food and service have a universal appeal."

"Fantastic!" Magnan blurted. "But—" he frowned at Retief, who was watching the heavily-draped wide double window across the room. Beyond its small panes, something moved. Then the glass and mullions burst inward with a prolonged *crash!*, and Smeer appeared, a cloud of gnats swarming in behind him. The cop coiled through the opening, apparently unheeding of the shards of broken glass over which he crawled, to take up a position with the first few feet of his sinuous body coiled on a table, from which four drinkers had fled, uttering yells:

"L-look out! It's the pillars comin again! Get Henry!"

"—outa my way, Leroy. *You* get Henry!"

"—thought we taught them worms a lesson!"

"Silence, lesser creatures!" Smeer commanded, and paused to await conformity with his order. As the hub-bub rose in volume, and a barrage of hurled objects came arching in toward him, he suddenly drew the remainder of his long form in through the shattered window and whipped it up and over and down with a force that splintered the adjacent table and sent two chairs and their occupants spinning. Glasses shattered, and an overturned bottle discharged its contents un-heeded on the floor, until someone darted in and grabbed it up, directing its flow to his mouth.

"Well," Henry commented. "Looks like I got a job o' work to do here, all over again. Them pillars don't learn too fast, seems like. Want to have some fun, Retief?

You, too, Bill. Mr. Magnan?" He looked dubiously at the latter who was still firmly seated, gripping the arms of his chair.

"One in my position can hardly associate himself with an affair of this kind," Magnan stated in a defensive tone.

"Oh, I get it," Henry replied, "OK if *I* and the boys do something, or you figger we're gonna just set here and let 'em take over the club?"

Magnan paused judiciously before framing his reply: "Inasmuch," he began portentiously, "as your 'club,' as you term it, is in fact located on a site wrested by force from its original owners, Enlightened Galactic Opinion can but look with approbation on the initiative of the latter to retain possession of their real estate—to fulfill their legitimate aspirations, that is to say."

"What was that part after 'however'?" Henry inquired doubtfully.

"Never mind, Big," Retief reassured him, "Mr. Magnan is just reciting some old traditional CDT spells that are intended to ward off disapproving glances from some source unspecified."

"Does it work?" Henry asked.

"Nope," Retief told him. "But it comforts Mr. Magnan to have the rituals to fall back on."

"These here 'disapproving glantses' and all," Henry posed his inquiry gingerly. "They anything like ten-inch Hellbores?"

"More potent by far, when intercepted by traditionalists like Mr. Magnan," Retief explained.

"Well," Henry ventured hesitantly, "seems old Cap Larson built this here clubhouse in a swamp on a pile o' dirt him and his boys dug up off'n the bottom, and the 'pillars' musta been thunk up by some slob of unknown origins like I told you about so, I guess we got a like obligation and all to run these here pillars off."

"Sheer yivshish," Magnan sniffed. "The very mud

dug up by this Larson person was the property of the autochtones!"

"Mud they can have," Henry muttered and advanced toward Smeer, who twisted his elongated form into a position of readiness, two hands gripping machetes deployed in front of his fang-studded visage. He seemed, however, to be looking past Henry.

"I say, Mr. Magnan," he called, "you're not figgering on pitting this here ruffian which there's a APB out on him, against a official of the law, I hope."

"Certainly not, Captain," Magnan replied, rising to shout after Retief and Bill, who were flanking Henry. "He's simply going to eject a trouble-maker, in pursuance of law and order."

"Oh," Smeer said, relaxing his defensive stance just as Retief and Bill simultaneously jumped in and grabbed the machetes, while Henry, dodging a snap of the yellow spike-studded jaws, took a casual arm lock on Smeer's person just below the head and wrenched the cop's face upside down, so that he could look him squarely in the eye.

"Seems like I seen you before, Bub," he told the astonished cop. "Looks like you'da had sense enough to stay outa where you ain't wanted."

"As for that breach of decorum," Smeer came back tartly, talking past Bill, "it is you yourself, Henry, and your cronies, who are at fault, as so great a man as S. Goldblatt conceded, long ago, at the time he so decisively transferred his operations elsewhere. And besides," he added, "youse are harboring a wanted fugitive, this here Retief, which they's a reward out on him."

"Naw, Chief, you got the wrong guy," Henry objected. "That Mr. Magnan buys that line o' crap, not big Henry Laboochy."

"So," the chief came back, "it is clearly Mr. Magnan to whom I should direct my conciliatory remarks." So saying, he gave a mighty flip of his forequarters, throwing Henry off, just as Magnan emerged from among jumbled tables into the clear.

"Good lord, Your Majesty," the Second Secretary and Consul gasped. "Did the brute . . .?"

Before Henry could frame a disgusted reply, Smeer arrived with a *crash*! that shook the floor, and at once threw a coil around the surprised Magnan and before the diplomat could so much as yelp, whisked him away through the shattered window. Henry made a fruitless lunge in the direction they had gone. "Hey!" he said without conviction. He turned to seek out Retief and saw him, approaching from a few feet away, Bill at his side.

"They done got pore old Mr. Magnan," Henry reported sadly, rubbing the elbow on which he had landed, as if to remind everyone that he, too, had suffered at the hands of the enemy. "Too bad. He was a nice feller, too. Used to call me 'my majesty' and all. Too bad, but— Hey, where you going, Retief?" he broke off to call as the latter bypassed him and continued toward the broken window. "Look out! That dang pillar's yonder! Where he's taken Mr. Magnan."

"Well, we can't just let him rob us of Mr. Magnan's scintillating company, can we, Big?" Retief said, as he climbed out through the ragged opening.

"Don't hardly know what that 'scent-lation' is," Henry objected. "But wait up, I guess I want a piece o' this." He hunched his shoulders and followed through the shard-rimmed sash, Bill close behind.

Henry looked down and saw spongy-looking black soil thickly grown with slender brownish reeds. He dropped down, found the footing treacherous. Retief had started down a path overhung with tall grasses. A few gnats hovered listlessly here, as if uncertain whom to harrass.

"Careful," Henry told Bill. "Don't bog down in this here muck." The ragged path beaten through the clustered vegetation led off in a wavering line toward the water's edge. No locals were in sight. A battered light-alloy rowboat lay in the mud, lapped by the oily water. Retief went to it, and from the shore caught sight of a large, clumsy-looking galley moving briskly away, propelled by multiple oars which moved in approximate unison.

"How we gonna catch 'em, General?" Bill asked as he came up.

"Got just the thing," Henry supplied, arriving beside the two. "Right the way round, hid out under the deck." He led the way along the barely visible path which followed a ledge of fairly firm ground along the periphery of the apparently derelict structure housing the club. Blinky trailed behind, muttering audibly.

"Don't like it, going outside the club, 'mongst all them pillars," he told his biographers. "No skin off *our* butts, they grab some outsider. Let it go, *I* say." Henry shushed the little man.

When they had arrived at their destination, a cavernous, black, echoic space under the building and behind the pilings supporting the club, Henry abruptly told Blinky to go back. He went, protesting.

"Ole Blink's kindy shy o' the pillars, since he spent a week with 'em," Henry explained, "time he went to check the weather and got hisself grabbed. Taken to some kinda headquarters-like and he was had up before a judge with a regular little peruke and five eyes peekin out from under it, so he says. Too bad. Useta be a good man, old Blink: come here 'fore I did. Come on." He stepped off into surprisingly shallow water and waded, ducking his head under the sagging joists, to a tarp-covered dory-sized boat moored to a piling. He stripped away the cover to reveal the sleek but work-scarred form of a regulation dispatch boat as long ago issued to the Terran Navy for ship-to-shore personal transport for Rear Admirals and Captains. A six-digit number was stenciled on the prow.

"That there trifib," Bill stated in a flat voice, "was

stole from the Navy, off the old *Imperator,* tell by the
serial code on her; *Imp* was lost on survey duty more'n
a hunnert years ago. Never found a trace of her until
now." He looked Henry in the eye.

"Where'd you get it?" he demanded in the tone of a
traffic cop almost politely requesting a citizen's DL.

"Right here when I come, boy," Henry told him, and
proceeded to climb aboard, then turned to lend a hand
to the Marine.

"Oh, boy," Bill said, almost gleefully. "Always wanted
to go joy-riding in the Captain's gig. She looks wore but
ship-shape."

"Durn right," Henry confirmed. "We taken good
care of her. Think you can back her outa here?"

Retief climbed aboard as Bill deftly maneuvered the
little craft out between the pilings, its almost silent
power unit setting up an eerie, hollow echo between
the riffled black waters and the underside of the club
floor, where only a few gnats darted aimlessly.

Retief studied the structure close overhead. "This
timber was cut with old-fashioned sonosaws," he commented. "So it must have been built by Terries—a long
time ago."

"Club's been here a while," Henry confirmed thoughtfully. "Some say hundreds o' years, standard."

Back out in the watery sunshine, Bill looked around
to orient himself, then steered alongside the unpainted
plank-sided structure, and out into open water, turning
the prow toward the fleeing boat, now a mile distant
and approaching a heavily-wooded point of land projecting into the water. Even here, he noted absently,
the gnats swarmed. He batted them away.

"Better step on it, before they land and skidaddle
into the woods," Henry suggested; Bill nodded and
opened the throttle; the hum of the power-pack deepened, and the prow of the boat rose as she leaped
forward, a crisp bow wave curling away from the sleek
hull.

The boat ahead passed the point, then curved in sharply and disappeared behind it.

"Wonder if the lift-unit still works," Bill muttered to himself.

"Better not try it, boy," Henry cautioned from the bow. "Oh-oh," he spoke up. "We got a stern chase on our hands, boys; there's a crick yonder; they'll get in it and try to lose us in the shallers."

"Look there!" Bill exclaimed, pointing toward the nearby shore-line. A man covered with black mud was staggering among mangrove-like roots, pausing to wave frantically.

"It's me!" Magnan's reedy voice came faintly across the water.

"Better pick him up, I reckon," Henry grunted as Bill curved in toward the shore, steering carefully between sandbanks just below the surface. Magnan waded out, paused to splash water over his face; his pinched features emerged starkly white against the black mud surrounding them. Bill reached, caught him by the arm and hauled him aboard amid the stench of sulphurous mud. Henry backed the skiff, twisting to look back over his shoulder to steer.

"Heavens!" Magnan gasped. "I'm indeed glad to see you! I feared the wrenches would do me in!" He paused to gulp air and slap ineffectually at the muck on his once-crisp late early afternoon informal dickey-suit.

"There are other Terran captives, you know," he commented tonelessly. "There's a sort of concentration camp back in the jungle. I caught a glimpse of it when I made my break, when they beached the boat. Terrans, in rags, herded like wild animals into that dreadful stockade, crowding around the locked gate, peering out mournfully. We must hurry back and inform His Excellency!"

"Maybe we ought to take take a closer look, first," Retief suggested, "so we'll know what we're reporting."

The boat was back in deep water now. Henry looked inquiringly at Retief.

"Let's go back a hundred yards," the latter said. "Stay inshore and we'll keep a sharp lookout. Bill, get in the prow, if you don't mind, and sing out as soon as you see the locals."

Bill nodded and went forward. At once he raised a hand.

"Hold hard, Henry," he said. "Easy. They're on the beach; seem to be getting ready to hike inland; unloading the boat."

Henry halted their forward progress. Small ripples lapped at the hull with a gently slapping sound, over which could be heard the gabble of the pillar's wheezy voices, echoing across the flat water.

The Terrans arrived unnoticed at the edge of the small stream fifty feet from where the kidnappers had grounded their boat.

"I had managed to free my ankles," Magnan told Retief. "And I awaited the proper moment; while they were engaged in pushing the boat up on the mud, I slipped over the side and was off!"

"Nice work, sir," Retief congratulated his associate. The boat from which Magnan had escaped was a heavy, flat-bottomed affair with an untrimmed tree-trunk serving as mast and a much-patched sail drooping, unsheeted, from the yard. The oars, apparently chopped to shape with an axe, were heaped in a disorderly pile.

Rounding the prow of the beached galley, they saw a lone guard stretched out, partially coiled, in the shade of the close-growing jungle.

"Hadn't we, that is, you best, er, deal with this fellow before going furthur?" Magnan suggested in a gingerly way, as one Mentioning the Unmentionable, Just This Once (1206-a).

Retief shook his head, "Our best bet is to go around him quietly."

They moved up, treading silently on the soft ground, past the prow of the galley and into the shadow of the wattle-and-daub stockade. As they paused at the corner of the ten-foot-high barrier, they heard a faint sound, like the hiss of escaping steam.

"Hark!" Magnan said softly. "Did you hear that faint sound, like the hiss of escaping steam?"

"It ain't no steam that's escaping, pal," a hoarse voice whispered through a chink in the rude wall. "It's me: Looie Segundo." The voice continued: "Youse fellers can help. Jest get ready to decoy that dumb piker sleeping it off over there, and I'm over the top in nothing flat."

"Wait!" Magnan whispered urgently. "If you arouse the sentry, we shall be caught here in the open, exposed to his gaze."

"It ain't his gays you gotta worry about, chum," Segundo cautioned. "It's them fangs o' his. Can chew a feller's leg off in two shakes of a cat's whisker—jest ast Gimpy, here, he can tell ya. Lucky they don't like Terry meat: he spit out the leg and let it go at that."

"I find nothing implicit in that datum tending to refute my thesis that caution is in order," Magnan replied tartly.

At that moment, the pillar guard raised its head and opened its mouth, like a small drag-line bucket, to expose the very appertenances under discussion. If it noticed the intruders, it showed no sign, but merely rearranged its sinuous body in a new configuration indistinguishable from the original one.

"Quick!" Looie hissed. "Gimpy here's gonna give me a leg up—that's a little joke, see? He only got the one leg and I said he's giving me a leg, see. The point is—"

"Enough, Mr. Segundo," Magnan cut in. "The jape is an ingenious one, and we fully appreciate its subtlty. Now you'd best hurry. At any moment it's going to occur to that alert guard that its duties do not include passive supervisions of an escape attempt."

"They don't care," Segundo replied off-handedly. "Why *should* they? It's *us* fellers livin off the fat o' the land.

It's just I got this little ole gal back on Oort station, got two er three nippers, reckon I orta get back to see 'em if I can."

"Naturally, Mr. Segundo," Magnan hastened to assure the confinee. "Just let's get on with it; I fear we'll be apprehended ere we can effect your release!"

"Hang loose, old buddy," Looie urged. "I jest remembered I got to say goodbye to Dottie and Frou-frou and old Hungry Annie and all, and my ole buddy Hump, too. Gimme a minute. Be right back."

"Well!" Magnan sniffed. "He doesn't seem very appreciative of one's efforts on his behalf." He went close to the shedding wall to peek through one of the many chinks in the ragged barrier.

"Their captors seem remarkably lackadaisical about restraining them," he commented, picking at a loose slat which fell away to open a six-inch wide gap. "Why," he went on wonderingly, "one could easily tear away that whole plank. . . ."

"Better not," Retief cautioned. "Since the boys inside haven't already done so, there's probably a reason."

"What possible reason could prompt a free-born Terry spaceman to languish voluntarily in durance vile?" Magnan addressed his appeal to the circumambient air.

Retief glanced through the newly-made opening, saw grass and shade-trees and a bank of imported flowering bumbum vine, all colored like a hand-tinted postcard. A whiff of a delicate floral perfume wafted through. One of the ubiquitous reward posters had been plastered on a tree-trunk.

"A curious sort of concentration camp," Magnan commented, looking over Retief's shoulder. "Just look at that burbling brook, and the wildflowers as countless as the stars that shine and twinkle in the Milky Way!"

"Wordsworth?" Retief inquired. "Or Shelley?"

"They're tossing their heads in sprightly dance, too," Magnan added.

"Who, the prisoners?" Bill inquired.

"No, don't be silly: the daffodills!"

"All this and Dottie, too," Retief said. "Maybe Looie has a point."

"Damn right!" Looie's voice spoke up close at hand. Magnan looked up to see a beardless face, with blackened eyes and ochre bruises peering down at him from the top of the wall for a moment before the wall bulged outward under his weight and collapsed. Segundo, who was a short, muscular fellow neatly dressed in a loud sportshirt and overlong Bermuda shorts, got to his feet, muttering. "Damn wall, made me look like a fool! Hi, ole buddies," he addressed the diplomats. "Be right back." With that, he stepped back across the ruins of the fallen fence and disappeared into a grove of purple-fruit trees.

"Well, I never!" Magnan informed Galactic Public Opinion. "The scamp didn't so much as acknowledge our efforts on his behalf!"

"We didn't actually make any, sir," Retief reminded him. The sound of the collapse had at last attracted the attention of the lone sentinel, who came undulating across the mud toward the two diplomats.

"Say, you fellows are out of your bailiwick, eh?" it called cheerfully. "Old Smeer won't like that too good."

"Chief Smeer isn't obliged to like it," Magnan retorted tartly. "As fully accredited diplomatic members of the Terran Embassy staff, bearing the Exequatur of your own government, we enjoy the prerogative of visiting this installation to ensure that all is being conducted in accordance with solemn interplanetary accord."

"Naw, nothing like that, pal," the pillar objected. "What we're worried about, we find a creature don't thrive too good outside of its natural enviarment and all."

"I assure you, my good fellow," Magnan stated loftily, "that we Terrans can thrive in virtually any environment, simply provided we have access to fresh air, clean water, and a modicum of nourishing victuals."

"Well, yeah, I guess that's right," the guard agreed dubiously. "But what I read, you fellows are just like you was Sardonic: you need a few extras, too, to really live it to the hilt; onny we can't figure out just what extras you need. Nookie, maybe, or slamph-balm. Now, you take old Looie, always tryna bust out: all he got to do is sign out at the main gate, and we got transport laid on to take him anyplace he wants, except outa his right envirament, o' course."

"Possibly it is precisely therein that the key to your problem lies," Magnan theorized. "The point being, my ma—good fellow—that is—that Looie wants to do whatever Looie wants to do, not choose from predetermined alternatives of another's devising."

"That don't make no sense," the pillar returned shortly. "Prang-nuts is prang-nuts, right?" he pursued the point. "Whether you find 'em inna woods, or they're dispensed by a autofeeder."

"It's not the same," Magnan insisted stubbornly. "Mr. Segundo—and the other illegal retainees as well, are free born citizens of the Terran Autonomy, not subject to arbitrary confinement by your local constabulary, or anyone else."

"So who's confining 'em?" the pillar persisted. "I tole ya the gate's open."

"Really?" Magnan demanded in a tone of Utter Scepticism (3-W). "In that case, why do they not depart at once?"

"What I was saying," the guard returned doggedly. "What ye'r doing, buddy, ye're jumping to conclusions and all, wrong ones, too." With that, he coiled up in a loose heap and blanked off his multi-faceted compound eyes from behind, an effect like having a blind pulled down in one's face.

"Well, we'll just ask," Magnan stated, and turned to pick his way across the fallen section of wall.

"I better do a recce o' this here wall," Bill volunteered, and set off at a trot.

CHAPTER THREE

"There's no one in sight," Magnan announced superfluously. "Odd," he commented. "The infernal gnats seem to be absent. I wonder why everyone's hiding. Probably frightened by the sound of the collapsing wall."

"Nope," Looie contradicted. "Nothing like that. They jest got better things to do than rubberneck at what's going on over here." He followed Magnan, shooting a sharp glance at Retief as he passed. "Hey," he commented. "I seen yer pitcher. What's yer racket, pal?"

"Precisely what *is* going on here, Mr. Segundo?" Magnan demanded as he halted abruptly. "Nothing which will redound to the benefit of Terran-Sardonic relations, I fear. And I had the impression," he added severely, "that I saw a naked young person dart into the underbrush over there."

"Prolly old Nudine," Looie hazarded. "Likes to shake up the new boys which they don't know the ropes yet."

"Mr. Retief and I," Magnan announced grandly, "are definitely not 'new boys.' And on second thought, I was

95

probably mistaken: just a flash of white, most likely a white bathing costume."

"Nudie didn't wear no costume when she bathes off, nor no other time, neither," Looie dismissed the idea. "Come on, I'll innerdooce youse."

"I hardly think . . ." Magnan began hesitantly. "That is, to burst in unannounced on a young lady who is about her *toilette*. . . ."

"Now, the terlet's over the other side," Looie reassured the nervous diplomat.

"I didn't mean. . . ." Magnan started.

"Let it pass, Mr. Magnan," Retief suggested. "Whatever the local customs are, it's not up to us to try to reform them."

"Yes, that's all very well, when we're speaking of the abominable habits various unenlightened peoples have with regard to nasal-orifice-picking, or infant exposure, but that was a bare derriere I saw flitting through the begonias."

"Maybe we'd *better* have a closer look," Retief agreed. He parted the flowering shrub and was looking into a wide-set pair of cornflower blue eyes. It was a young Terran female, wearing a golden sun-tan and a shy smile.

"Hi," she said, stepping back out of Retief's path. "You're new here." Her voice was mild and melodious. Magnan, close behind Retief, uttered a shocked gasp. "Heavens!" he exclaimed. "We seem to have blundered into a nudist camp! Our pardons, Miss!"

"Forget it," the girl dismissed the matter. "You come over here to the pond to bathe off, or what?" By this time she was knee-deep in a pellucid pool, casually rubbing a bar of soap up and down her curvaceous hip. "Through in a sec," she said over her shoulder. "Come on in; plenty of room."

"Retief!" Magnan muttered in a catatonic voice to the bigger man. "We'd best be off at once! What if His

Excellency should learn we'd been ogling some forest dryad at her ablutions?"

"We're not ogling, sir," Retief corrected his supervisor gently. "Just admiring the scenery."

The girl gave him a smile. "You're nice," she told him. "What's the matter with your father there?"

"I am not—" Magnan started. "That is, *he's* not—"

"Hand me that towel, will you, Pop?" the young lady requested. As she waded out to stand before Magnan, unselfconscious as September Morn, he groped the towel from the convenient bush, and handed it over, trying to look over, or possibly through the naked woman. She patted her face dry, then draped the towel carelessly over her shoulder.

"What's the matter, Pop?" she inquired solicitously. "You have a bad experience with some hard-hearted dame once, or what?"

"It's just . . ." Magnan choked and tottered away, muttering, inconspicuously tearing a reward poster from a tree as he passed. Retief helped her up the slight slope. She thanked him prettily and asked:

"How about some lunch? I'm in the mood for a chicken sandwich, or maybe a blurb-beast salad. And a nice cold pale ale." She extended an arm into the shrubbery and did something. At once a brisk voice spoke from the foliage: "Yes?" it said, and paused.

"Two Number Ones over the pond," she said to the bush.

"Coming up, Nudine," came the reply.

"My name's not really Nudine," she told Retief and settled herself comfortably on the cool, lush grass. "That's just a dopey nickname old Buzzy came up with. I'm really Jacinthe."

"Nice name," Retief commented. He sat down with his back to a sycamore-like tree. "Just call me Retief."

"What's your last name?" she asked.

"That's it," Retief told her. "First name's Jame, or Jim as it's usually pronounced."

"Hey," Nudine exclaimed, her eyes on Retief. "You're the feller on the new signs." He nodded.

"Well, Jimmy, what brings *you* here to Danazu?" she queried.

"I thought it was Xanadu," Retief commented.

"Oh, just lost, huh?" she decided; then a small, inconspicuous fellow dressed all in black emerged from the underbrush pushing a laden tea-cart. He put the tray, bearing frosty mugs of ale and a stack of fat sandwiches, on the grass between them and ducked out of sight.

"Thanks, Buzzy," Nudine/Jacinthe said belatedly. "He used to be a Heller before old Worm got him," she confided in Retief. "Worm straightened him out good and give him something useful to do." She dropped the subject and took a pull at her ale. Retief picked up a sandwich. Before he could take a bite, there was a thrashing in the underbrush. Nudine looked up, surprised.

"What—?" she started, as Magnan stumbled into view.

"Oh, there you are!" he yelped, as one solving a mystery. "I just stepped out to look around, and found I was lost; then I heard voices."

"I know," Retief told him. "Sit down, try one of these."

"Oh, I do love club sandwiches!" Magnan gushed, and sank down, breathing hard; he shied as he noticed Nudine's inadequate towel, but accepted a sandwich and took a hearty bite. "I was starving!" he said as he chewed. "Where . . . ?"

"Jacinthe," Retief said formally, "this is Mr. Magnan, First Secretary of the Terran Embassy to Sardon."

"Where's that at?" the girl inquired. "Hi," she added. "You look hot, Mister. Why don't you take off that old coat?"

"Thank you," Magnan replied coldly, still standing aloof. "I shall retain *all* my garments."

"You gonna bathe off with yer clothes on?" she persisted.

"I have no intention, Madame," Magnan told her, "of 'bathing off,' as you so curiously phrase it."

"What did Mister say?" Jacinthe appealed to Retief.

"He disapproves of your informal attire," Retief explained.

"Don't misunderstand me, my dear," Magnan interpolated. "I'm no bluenose. I understand that under primitive conditions, one necessarily relaxes the more restrictive social taboos."

Nudine frowned prettily at Retief in puzzlement. "Why don't Mister talk like folks?" she asked.

"Mr. Magnan bears a great burden," Retief explained between bites. "He is charged with maintaining the Image."

"I don't see no image," Nudine objected.

"Yes," Retief agreed. "That's precisely the problem."

"I guess you fellers are both kinda weird," Jacinthe commented. "Gorblorian chocolate pie OK fer desert?"

"Ideal," Retief conceded.

"How about you, Pop?" she queried Magnan, who, though still averting his eyes, seemed a trifle calmer now. He nodded absently, and looked about as if noticing the idyllic setting for the first time, and drew a deep breath.

"That's it, Pop, loosen up," his hostess encouraged. She spoke again to the bush:

"Three blurb flops on a biscuit," she commanded. Then, to Retief: "A bottle o' the good stuff with that?" she offered. Retief nodded.

"OK, Buzzy," Nudine amplified the order. "Nice cold Chateau d'Yquem with them flops."

"You call Gorblorian chocolate pie 'blurb flops'?" Magnan inquired distastefully.

"What it looks like, Pop," the girl affirmed.

Magnan leaned back on one elbow and fanned himself with one hand. "One can't help think of Manet's *Dejeuner sur L'herbe*," he commented contentedly.

"Rather set Paris on her ear back in eighteen-seventy-something Old Style."

"Except that Jacinthe has a considerably better figure," Retief corrected.

"To be sure," Magnan agreed, at last looking her over openly. "It's not so bad, actually, if one simply thinks of it as an artless work of art, so to speak."

"Thanks a *lot*, Pop," Jacinthe put in coldly. "That musta been some bitch!"

"Your language, my dear!" Magnan gasped.

"Let's leave my language lay, Pop," she suggested just as the pie and wine arrived. Buzzy showed Retief the label, then uncorked the flask and offered the cork to Jacinthe to be sniffed, then poured the deep amber nectar into paper-thin glasses.

"Buzzy don't do the whole number with letting the hostess sample it first," Nudine explained. "Waste o' time. Our stuff is always good. After all, figgerin how we get it, I guess it oughta be."

"And just how *do* you get a chateau-bottled wine here in this remote backwater?" Magnan asked.

"Same way as we get the rest o' the stuff," Jacinthe told him. "Old Worm," she added.

"Oh," Magnan said, as if enlightened. "But," he went on briskly, selecting one of the three many-layered wedges of gooey brown dessert. "Um, smells heavenly," he interrupted himself. "But we didn't come here to spend the time in idle conversation. Par me," he concluded, swallowing. "Frightfully rude of me to talk with my mou' full. I was trying to say we came as liberators, my dear, but so far all we've done is accept your hospitality."

"Anything wrong with my hospertality, Pop?" Jacinthe challenged. "Have another slug of good ole Wykwim."

"That's 'Eekem,'" Magnan corrected as she filled his glass.

"What I said," the girl replied. "Good stuff; goes good with vaniller ice cream."

"As I was about to point out," Magnan put in, sounding pained, "our mission here is that of emancipators, not gourmets. So perhaps we'd best just finish up our blurb-flops, and be off about our business."

"I got no business," Jacinthe corrected gently. "Anything I got somebody needs, I give 'em some. Like the pie," she added.

"And what was that about worms?" Magnan queried belatedly.

"Well, you know. And its 'the Worm,' not 'worms.' "

"But indeed I do *not* know," Magnan corrected sharply. "If I knew, I should hardly waste breath in requesting clarification."

"Yer doin it again, Mister," Nudine pointed out. "All I said was about old Worm gives us the stuff."

Magnan stared at her with a bewildered expression. "Some local god?" he managed.

"Nothin like that," Nudine dismissed the suggestion.

The halcyon mood was abruptly shattered by a yell as of mortal agony, or insane rage, or both, followed at once by the crash of something—or someone—bursting through the rhododendrons.

"Awright, let's shape up here," Looie growled, for it was indeed he.

"Good Lord," Magnan moaned. "At first glance it looked like Mr. Segundo; and it is indeed he."

"You mean it's 'him,' I guess," Nudine corrected. "Hi, Looie," she continued. "What's biting your ass this time?"

"Same as before," Segundo snarled. "Tole ya I can't stand seeing anybody having a good time. That's what you call 'morals.' So you better beat it before I get mad. Arrghhh!"

Magnan rose defensively; Segundo knocked him aside and advanced on the girl. As he reached for her towel, Retief knocked him down, then hauled him half-upright by one arm and pitched him back in the direction from which he had come.

"You can re-escape now," Retief told him, ignoring the surly fellow's roars.

"Changed my mind," Looie said in a normal tone. "You done spoiled it fer me, you and that Mister Magnan. No offense to you, Nudie."

"Plenty of offense to me, Lou," she returned spirit-edly. "When you come busting in on me and my friends, Jim and Pop here, I get offended. Now, since Jimmy says you can go, I guess maybe you better, less you want to go fer a dip with yer pockets full o' rocks." She picked up one of the latter and pegged it at the now-whimpering Looie and turned away, recovering her towel with a quick grab as it almost fell. This time she draped it over the other shoulder.

"You know you ain't allowed in this part, Lou," she reminded the crestfallen intruder. "Thought you was planning a big escape."

"No fun," Lou grunted. "Damn pillars never done nothing to stop me."

More trampling feet heralded the arrival of another large man who blundered to a stop before Nudine and after a quick glance, bowed from the waist. "Par me all to hell, honey, if I busted in on yer ablutions and all," he said formally. "Seen smoke yonder," he added, point-ing vaguely.

"Why, it's Mister Big," Magnan remarked brightly. "And where, pray, is young Bill?"

"Oh, he's horsing around with some comedians thought they knew something about martial arts. Be here in a minute, I reckon. Hi, Retief." Big Henry looked around. "Right purty spot," he commented. "Oh, you been having blurb-turds on a flapjack," he exclaimed as he noted the leftovers of the meal. "Some nice-looking wine, too. Got any more?"

Retief introduced Henry to Jacinthe, who promptly ordered lunch for him, and for the not-yet-arrived Bill as well. Retief had escorted the grumbling Looie off along the path, passing Bill on the way in.

"Good riddance to *that* feller," Big commented to Magnan. "Name's Dirty Eddie; come in the Club once, and tried to start trouble. I hadda run him off."

"Precisely," Magnan agreed. "Except he told *us* his name was Mr. Segundo. The ruffian burst in upon us here, and would have created a scene had I not spoken sharply to him. Do sit down, sergeant," he added as Bill arrived.

"Usually takes more'n talk to get rid o' old Eddie," Big observed, nodding to Retief as he returned.

"Well, Retief *did* fell the scamp," Magnan conceded. "But I had already let him know he was unwelcome."

"*That* don't bother Eddie none," Big pointed out. "Wonder what's burning yonder?" Nudine looked worriedly where he pointed to a smudge of smoke above the trees.

"Say, Mr. Retief," Bill spoke up, "what kinda place is this? Over the other side, the gate was wide open. We come in, and hadda sock our way through a gang o' crudbums didn't wanna excape. We told 'em, 'OK you're free; we come to liberate yousel' And they trieda jump us. Big hadda lay some slobs out cold, and I gave a couple of 'em some lessons in counter-punching. All talking at once, sounded like *we* was the enemy. Funny kinda place. And now here's you and Mr. Magnan having brunch on the grass just like that old painting I seen once, only the lady here ain't fat. What's there, yonder?" He switched subjects abruptly, pointing toward the cluster of golden domes visible above the foliage downstream.

"What we were just wondering, my boy," Magnan supplied.

"Them's—" Big started.

"Don't ast," Nudine advised.

"Don't matter to me," Bill dismissed the topic. "But who are these here Terries think they're so tough?"

"I think you just happened to run into the local over-privileged element," Retief told the lad. "Having used up or smashed everything they could find, and refusing to do anything useful, and at the same time making trouble for everyone they met, they're naturally dissatisfied with the social order, but instead of leaving quietly they prefer to stay on and bitch about injustice. It's a lot like every other place, as well as I can judge from what Looie told me."

"Oh, I heard plenty about that Looie," Bill replied. "One o' them boys jumped us said somebody name Looie, or maybe the one they call Eddie, trieda set hisself up as boss and got hisself beat up some and he taken off."

"Not very far," Magnan sniffed. "He was here, introducing a discordant note into our idyll, but a moment since."

Bill sat down and started in on the sandwiches. After a brief conference with Big, Nudine had ordered more, plus a hearty stew for the leader of the Cloud-Cuckoo Club, which he devoured single-mindedly, along with an oversized mug of the poteen.

"Plenty good eats, Miss Jacinthe," he acknowledged. "Booze ain't bad, too." He belched comfortably in confirmation of his remark. "Near as good as the Club."

"Now, Sergeant," Magnan addressed the young Marine seriously. "You say the men we saw crowding against the fence declined to be emancipated?"

"Naw, nothin' like that," Bill protested. "They just didn't wanna excape."

"Old Bimbo and his bunch," Nudine put in. "Them boys is pretty dumb, but not *that* dumb. Outside, who'd they have to give a bad time to? Not to say nothing about eats and nookie and all."

"You *are* coarse, Miss," Magnan reprimanded. "And mind your towel; it's slipping again."

"Here, I'll help you," Bill volunteered, stepping forward, to be blocked off by Magnan, who nearly fell down, attempting to avert his eyes. Meanwhile, Big had finished off the sandwiches and pie, and was downing the fine dessert wine from the neck. Magnan noticed and uttered a squawk of protest.

"Sounds like you orter join up with the boys over the other side, Pop," Jacinthe commented. "If the big feller's got a little thirst on him, let him drink: 'swhat it's made for."

"To be sipped, yes," Magnan corrected. "Not gulped like beer."

"Well, OK, if it worries ya, Mr. Magnan," Big conceded gracefully. "But whatta ya think we oughta do about Eddie and the rest o' them trouble-makers?" He waved absently at the persistent gnats.

"Do?" Magnan echoed as if amazed (7-v). "I fail to see that it is our responsibility to *do* anything, so long as they congregate at the exit and limit their activities to hooting at newcomers." As they wrangled, Retief rose and inspected the immense tree spreading above them.

"How's about *this*, dumbum?" a coarse voice demanded as at the same instant, half a dozen large, ungroomed men leapt from the branches overhead; one felled Magnan, another rebounded from a hearty haymaker delivered by Bill, and a third ruffian seized Nudine.

"Help!" Magnan cried, picking himself up and looking around wildly. "Where's Retief?" he demanded. Big was busy picking up the new arrivals one by one and tossing them out of sight behind the blossoming azaleas. When one kicked him in the solar plexus, he carried him to the pond and threw him well out from shore, where he floundered and uttered choking cries.

"Looks like the sucker can't swim," Big commented indifferently, at the same time taking a firm grip on the nape of the neck of the rawboned fellow who was fully occupied with retaining his grasp on Jacinthe. Big kicked

him hard, once, and cast him toward his drowning
associate.

"Better rescue old Bimbo fore he drownds," he suggested to the latter, as he handed Nudine's towel to her
with a courtly bow. "Sorry about that, Miss Nudine,"
he said. "Skunks ain't got no manners at all."

Magnan was on his feet, backed against a thick-boled
tree by a hulking gorilloid in a faded Three-Planet Line
uniform.

"You'll rue the day, fellow!" Magnan predicted as he
ducked under a swipe of his tormentor's oak-root like
arm.

"Sure, Junior," the ex-Merchant spac'n agreed, showing square, widely-spaced, black-spotted teeth in a grimace which caused Magnan to yelp and try again, only
to rebound from the arm which had moved surprisingly
quickly for a member so formidably muscled. Big, noting Magnan's distress, took the ape-man from behind in
a strangle-hold. The space'n twisted his head to give
the big fellow a puzzled look.

"I don't think I had the pleasure, pal," he grunted,
and reaching around, thrust out a callussed hand. "Tiny
Tim's the handle," he said. "I didn't catch yers."

"Me, too," Big grunted. "Small Henry's what you can
call me, Tiny." He released his grip. "Sorry about
that."

"By the way," Small went on, addressing Magnan,
who was now peeking around Tiny. "Whereat's old
Retief? He don't wanna miss all the fun." Suddenly
Tiny uttered an *oof!*, leapt forward, off-balance, nearly
knocking Small Henry down. Retief dropped down from
a low bough from which he had delivered the kick
which had interrupted Tiny's concentration on Magnan,
and greeted the latter. "When I heard them sneaking
up through the trees," he told the older man, "I thought
it would be a good idea to go up to meet them. I was
delayed by the need to immobilize a couple of fellows I
ran into."

"At least you arrived before this Pithecantropus Erectus actually did his worst," Magnan acknowledged breathlessly. "Now, see here, fellow," he addressed Tiny, who had regained his balance and was dusting his hands and looking ominously at Retief.

"You orta look where yer goin, feller," the gangleader advised the diplomat. "You could get in trouble swinging down outa a tree without looking first."

"Oh, I looked," Retief corrected him. "I didn't see anything much."

"I guess I'm big enough to see," Tiny protested. "Six-eight in my sock feet and not a ounts o' fat on me!"

"I saw *you*," Retief amplified. "I just didn't see anything *important*."

"Well," Tiny grunted. "I guess I can overlook it this here time, you bein new and all—"

"But I think I've spotted an ounce of fat after all," Retief interrupted. He took a step toward the subhuman giant and slammed a hard right to his gut. Tiny yelled and folded forward, as if bowing from the waist. Retief straightened him up with an uppercut that snapped the flat skull back and glazed the small dark-brown eyes. Magnan bustled forward and gave the gasping man-mountain a sharp poke with his forefinger. Tiny fell backward like a felled Sequoia.

"Nice going, Mr. Magnan!" Small cried, while the remaining aggressors muttered and eased around Magnan and out of sight into the shrubbery.

"Retief helped," Magnan said modestly. "But I must revise my former opinion. This Bunch must be dealt with. Spoiled the sandwiches, too," he added mournfully, surveying the remains of the *al fresco* repast, now trampled in the grass. Through a gap broken in the bank of flowering arbutus, he caught a glimpse of something white. "Why," he exclaimed, "I see a glimpse of something white! I wonder . . ." Without completing his period, he stepped past the ruins of the shrubs broken off by the hastily retreating gang, emerged into a patch of smooth-cut lawn, sun-lit amid the towering trees. At its center in a puddle lay the broken fragments of what had been a small, exquisite marble fountain, from which water was still oozing.

"The vandals!" Magnan yelped and went forward to attempt to restore the snow-white sculpture to an upright position. "It's no use," he moaned, realizing that both pedestal and basin were broken in two. "How *could* they?" he lamented. "This is a genuine Frumpert, from his early classic revival period, or I miss my guess!" He sank down on a white-painted bench beside the tiled walk which bisected the once jewel-like clearing.

Retief came up behind him, along the path of patterned, green, white and gold tiles, and paused to examine a small bright-metal ring set in a glossy green ceramic rectangle. He stooped, inserted a finger and lifted. The tile hinged upward, exposing a cavity, dimly lit by a glare patch. "This is strange, Ben," he commented.

"Oh, dear, Jim," Jacinthe's voice spoke close behind causing Magnan to jump back. "You really mustn't, you know," the girl chided. "Only the Emergency Crew are allowed to touch the Connection."

"For heaven's sake, girl," Magnan snapped, "don't creep up on me like that! 'Not allowed,' eh? Then perhaps you can tell me who it is who's 'allowed' to smash fountains and tread on my sandwich!" He stepped up beside Retief to gaze into the hollow exposed by the lifting of the lid and at the intricate apparatus inside. "Why," he exclaimed, "that looks like—and these tiles, Jim: they're definitely the type made from lava on Io; how in the worlds would they have gotten here?" He turned back to Nudine.

"I've asked you, Miss; who vandalized this charming spot? Even those confounded midges don't seem as persistent here!"

"That was Tiny and his bunch, call 'em the Spoilsports," she returned spiritedly. "They don't pay no mind to the rules. Crew'll get to 'em by and by, I reckon."

"Sit down, Miss," Magnan invited sternly. "Now I think it's time you explained matters here: Retief and I, and Big and Bill as well, came here at risk of life and limb to liberate the Terrans reported under restraint here. We find a sort of public park with the gate guarded by ruffians who will allow no one *in*, rather than out. We find anarchy and immodesty if not immorality; waste, disorder, civil disturbance and vandalism; and now you presume to order me to ignore a most interesting find, in the name of some unspecified 'Rules,' administered, presumably, by the equally mysterious 'emergency crew.' Who make up this 'crew,' and where may I examine the rules?" He ducked to avoid a cloud of dancing gnats. "But for these pesky mites," he griped, "this would be an idyllic spot."

"I can tell you the rules, Pop, if you act real nice," the girl informed him. "The Crew, well they're busy right now—"

" 'Busy,' you say—" Magnan cut in savagely. "While Bimbo roams free and Tiny destroys our lunch! If the latter fails to qualify as an emergency, though expeditiously dealt with by my people and myself—I fail to imagine what does!"

"Sure it does," Nudine agreed. "Qualify, I mean," she amplified. "Well, problem is, we got Bimbo wrecking the Temple up north end, and asetting fires in the Grove. Gotta stop the slob before he upsets old Worm any more'n what he already done."

"Then why, may I ask, are we sitting here jawing?" Magnan demanded. "And you're nattering of worms again, while disaster stalks us all, undeterred." He rose and started past Small, who had just poked his head into the clearing.

"Hold hard, Mister Magnan," the big fellow said, catching his arm. Magnan attempted to shake the grip loose.

"Let me go, Big," he snapped. "Didn't you hear?"

"Sure did," Small replied calmly. "We seen more smoke and Bill went off to have a look-see; I stuck around to look for you and Nudie. We gotta keep calm and wait here."

"But—but—I found—!" Magnan blurted, and turned to point. "There's a state-of-the-art nexus-box installed just there! It's surely significant, if one only knew the significance! We must investigate!" He started back toward the concealed apparatus.

"Seems like I heard about them there neck-us boxes," Small commented. "Something about Relativity and all, ain't they? Or like that," he amended, in the interest of the precision demanded by the high-tech subject.

Retief said, "I'd better check on that smoke," and left the clearing. Jacinthe rose to bar Magnan's way, her towel over her left shoulder now.

"I tole you, Pop, against the rules!" she stated with surprising firmness. "Small, you better reason with Pop; don't want him messing up now."

"By what authority, Miss Jacinthe," Magnan demanded, "do you presume to order me about, in full knowledge of my diplomatic status here on Sardon?"

The girl shrugged her shapely shoulders, almost losing her towel, which she slapped back in place with a sharp rebuke; "Stay put, dammit, don't want to go getting Pop all upset. I'm the enforcer," she added.

"And just how, pray, do you propose to go about *forcing* me to ignore so provocative a find?" Magnan demanded tartly, and made a move toward the nexus box. Nudine made a lightning-fast move and flipped Magnan backwards across the bench, then peered anxiously after him, at the same time retrieving her towel.

"You OK, Pop?" she queried.

"I would be, if you'd stop fooling with that damned towel," Magnan came back spiritedly. "As an ecdasiast, you have no peer, that I'll grant. Now help me up, and no more of this impudence!"

Jacinthe lent a hand to pull Magnan back to an up-right position.

" 'Enforcer,' indeed!" he muttered, as he got to his feet. "Has no one suggested to you, my dear, that it's most inappropriate for a fragile young lady to presume to represent the forces of, ah, force?"

"Last one did, hadda have extensive dental work did," Nudine replied confidently. She turned to Small. "Better keep a eye on Pop," she ordered. "Don't want him getting into no more trouble." She blew on her knuckles and gave the towel a final tug as she turned to leave the clearing.

"I better go along and see what Jim's doing," she added over her bare shoulder. "Shouldn't be no smoke over there, near the Place; you boys coming, or what? And you, Pop, stay clear o' that Connection, OK?"

"I shall of course accompany you," Magnan muttered. "But I warn you; my colleague is unlikely to be so compliant as I, regarding your improvised 'rules.' "

"Smoke was over thataway," Small said, pointing. He was interrupted by the abrupt reappearance of Bill, soot-smudged and breathing hard. "Got big trouble!" he gasped out.

"Hold hard, boy," Small ordered. "What kinda big trouble? Retief OK, or what?"

"It's got him surrounded," Bill explained. "He's holed up in a kinda cave we found. He kept it busy while I snuck past."

"May I inquire," Magnan put in cooly, "precisely to what the pronoun 'it' has reference in that context?"

"Prolly old Worm," Nudine supplied. "I guess I shoulda tole him more about that, but seem like we was having such a nice time . . ."

"That is hardly encouraging information, Miss Ja-cinthe," Magnan commented faintly.

"The rest is worser'n that," the girl supplied. "You want to be encouraged, or you want the facts?"

"Facts, to be sure, my dear," Magnan replied in a

tone of Mild Reprimand (14-b). "Just what else can you tell us about this Worm?"

"Couple hunnert feet long, maybe," Nudine told him. "Not that nobody never up and measured it. Moves too fast for that anyways." She batted absently at the hovering gnats.

"My dear," Magnan put in gently, "we must avoid the double, and in this case, triple negative. In effect, you negate what you intend to express, by the redundant multiplication of negative particles."

"Oh," Jacinthe said without emphasis. "Anyways, you get the idear: Worm's big, can get inside yer head, too. Not like wibbly-nits in a log, but it *talks* in yer head. Says some pretty wild stuff, too. If it's got Retief surrounded, means it's noticed him. Best bet's to not get noticed."

"Speaks in one's head, eh?" Magnan mused to himself.

"Seen the fire," Bill put in. "Bunch o' them crudbums from over the gate, putting the torch to a nice little shed, looked like a bank. Purty spot; shade trees, you know, and flowers. They was stealing a lot of stuff from inside, pots and little statues and like that."

"Looting and burning the Temple," Small grunted. "Heard tell about the place. Ain't right them rogues should wreck it." He nodded in agreement with himself.

"Mr. Retief went around back," Bill continued, "tole me to stay put, clobber any of 'em got close. Then a minute later they come yelling and hollering, shoving each other outa the way, couldn't get outa there fast enough. I figgered the coast was clear, so I went around where Mr. Retief went, and seen this here critter, like a snake big as a tube-car and covered with like feathers. I seen the cave and snuck into it; the snake never seen me. Minute later Mr. Retief come in and tole me to take off and tell Miss Jacinthe here what I seen. The old snake whipped around fast and went outa sight, and here I am. We gotta do something. Mr. Retief's pinned down in that hole in the ground. He tole me to go, otherwise I'd of stuck with him."

"Of course you would have, sergeant," Magnan soothed the lad. "You did precisely the right thing." He turned to Nudine. "Is this Worm a carnivore?" he inquired. "And what do you mean about it talking in one's head? Mere folklore, I'd have assumed, but for certain curious phenomena."

"Ain't no folklore," Nudine retorted sharply. "Old Worm stays in a cave yonder, nice and cool down there, till some dang fool like Dirty Eddie comes along and gives him a hard time, like tryna burn down the neat little shed somebody built over the mouth of his cave and all. Come on: Jimmy ain't got a chance less'n we do something!" She ended sharply and strode off.

"And what, pray, can one, ah, 'do'?" Magnan demanded anxiously as he fell in behind the indignant girl. Bill and Small came along, muttering.

". . . need us a howitzer," Bill's voice rose above the crash of thrust-aside shrubbery.

". . . tis but ill to tarry near the lair of the fabled beast," Small contributed. Nudine ignored them and moved on boldly. After a quarter-mile of progress through forest seemingly as ancient as the hills it clothed, enfolding an occasional plot of sunny greensward, an excited man clad in unwashed rags burst into view. He halted momentarily and gave Nudine a careful scrutiny, which she ignored; then he rushed up to Magnan.

"You're a big shot," he stated breathlessly. "I can tell 'cause you got socks on, and that there's one o' them ties, ain't it?"

Magnan shook loose the fellow's clutch and hurried on.

"Need help here, you honor," the derelict yelled after him. "You gonna jest ignore a feller tryna tell ya about our Big Trouble?"

Magnan halted and turned a stern look on the unkempt stranger. "We have quite sufficient Big Trouble of our own, sirrah," he rebuked the importunate man. "Go along, now!"

"Wait a minute, Pop," Jacinthe suggested. "Looks like old Raunch here has got something to tell us. Maybe important. You seen old Worm, Raunch?" she concluded, addressing the newcomer.

"*Seen* it?" Raunch echoed in a tone of Stunned Incredulity (an awkward 271-g, Magnan noted).

"Never attempt subtleties, my man," he advised, "the technique of which is quite beyond the non-diplomatic mind. You should have tried for a 14-a (Mild Surprise at an Opponent's Lack of Preparation). Now, what's this all about?"

"Gee, sir," Raunch stammered, "I never meant to tempt no suttle T's nor nothin. Jest wanneda say old Wormy got some fellers cornered up his cave, which they ain't got a hope. So long." With this, Raunch abruptly withdrew.

"Here, fellow!" Magnan yelped. "I have not yet dismissed you! I require more details of this matter!"

"You, Raunch!" Nudine yelled. "You get yer butt back here pronto: I wanna talk to yew, boy!"

Raunch reappeared, looking sheepish. "I was gonna take a look, see if they was sneaking up on us," he mumbled.

"Who?" Nudine demanded.

"Us!" Raunch reiterated indignantly.

" 'Us' what?" Nudine persisted.

"Us getting snuck up on, nacherly," Raunch responded, as One Whose Sensibilities Have Been Wounded (2-w).

"There you go again," Magnan mourned. "Were I not a sophisticated interpreter of nuances, I'd have taken that for a 71, (How Can You Pick On a Sick Man) about a -g."

"I don't believe yer sick at all," Raunch announced flatly. "Don't nobody get sick here in Zanny-du."

"I didn't say I was sick, you simpleton!" Magnan snarled. "Oh, dear, what's the use?"

"Right, Pop," Nudine seconded. "Guys like old Raunch here don't care *how* sick a feller is."

"I am not, and I emphasize NOT, sick!" Magnan yelled. "Whence did that foolish notion arise?"

"You said so, Mr. Magnan," Small supplied diffidently. "I heard ya my ownself. You was asting how old Raunch here culd pick on a sick man, and it was you he was picking on, so—" He let it go at that.

"I see I've been too long among civilized bureaucrats who have enough couth to conceal their ignorance," Magnan moaned. "I simply can't cope with morons."

"Yew ain't calling me no moe-roan, are ya, Pop?" Jacinthe guessed. "Musta just meant Small, and o' course Raunchy."

"I had enough," Small barked. "I'll see you at the club sometime, Nudie." With that he turned, brushed past Raunch and disappeared into the deep forest.

"How far is it?" Magnan asked the girl. "Is this woods endless?"

"Naw, onney about twice five miles," she reassured him. "That's including all the gardens which they're bright with sinuous rills and all—and plenty o' spots o' sunny greenery, too. But we better get going. Retief's gonna freeze solid in them ice caves, even if old Worm don't get him."

"Perhaps I'd best hurry along," Magnan suggested, and plunged ahead along the faint trail.

2

After leaving the party by the pond, Retief had followed a well-marked trail toward the cluster of golden domes from near which the smoke was rising in a diaphanous white cloud. Drawing close to the blaze, he heard hoarse voices yelling tunelessly:

"Oh, the King of Grote was a hell of a note,
And his horns was tipped with brass,

      And one grew out of his upper lip, and
      The other grew out of his ump-te-ump . . ."

Retief motioned Bill left and himself circled to the right to come up behind the tiny, classically designed structure from which the smoke originated, pouring out between the pristine white columns.

One of the incendiaries came out to the fringe of the woods surrounding the temple to relieve himself. Retief waited until he had completed the chore, then stepped in front of him as he headed back to rejoin the fun. The man, squat, scruffy and red-headed, lowered his head and charged with a bellow of rage. Retief stepped aside, and as the redhead tried to change direction, he took him almost gently by the collar of his greasy pea-jacket and swung him around.

The man gave Retief an astonished look as he tried without success to free himself.

"I ain't ever *seen* you!" he yelled.

"Quiet, Red," Retief ordered. "It'll just be you and me for now."

"You nuts, or what?" Red demanded, but in a more moderate tone. "Old Worm's like to slip up on us any time. What we done," he went on, sounding as proud as a five-year-old reporting how he has just used the fingernail scissors on his baby sister's face, "we waited till old Worm come out, then we poured in a couple drums o' high octane we found and lit her off and she's burning what I mean *hot!* Old Worm's ice'll all melt and he won't have no place to go. Have to listen to reason, then."

"Just what would you call reasonable, in this context?" Retief asked. Red gave him a puzzled look and dug at his scalp with a blunt, black-crescented fingernail.

"He's the one got all the stuff, ain't he?" he whined. "Jest want it to hand it over. No use it setting on all the stuff. *It* cain't use it!"

Just then, Magnan arrived, breathless and disheveled. "I *heard* that!" he declared indignantly.

"You're losing me, Red," Retief told the unhappy fellow. "What 'stuff' are you talking about?"

Before Red could frame a reply, Bill came into view. Retief rose and signalled. Bill came over, frowning.

"Where's Jacinthe?" Magnan and Retief asked together.

Bill jerked his head. "She'll be along, I guess," he told them off-handedly. "She knows how to take care of herself. What's going on?" Bill demanded. "Seen two o' these crum-bums coming outta the church or whatever, with a case o' Scotch."

"Twelve-year-old plus," Red said dreamily. "Smooth as a angel's wing."

"That ain't right," Bill told the red-head. "Storing yer booze in a church."

"Ain't no church," Red protested. "Jest a kinda shed over the entrance to the cave."

"How do you know?" Retief asked.

"I guess we seen it go in there to get the stuff it hands out, ain't we?" Red demanded.

"This Worm gives you things?" Magnan wanted reassurance.

"Sure; extra stuff *it* cain't use—like duds and eats only fit fer humerns," Red confirmed.

"It bestows largesse on you, but you want it all, is that it?" Magnan persisted.

"Guess we got a right to it," Red deduced, sullenly now. "Don't know what that there large S is," he added.

"Never mind, Ben," Retief suggested. "The rationalizations of those who want everything free are beyond logic."

"What else you got in there?" Bill demanded.

"*I* ain't got nothing in there," Red contradicted sharply. "Old Worm got it all. That's why we come over to roust it."

"Sounds nutty," Bill told the now-cocky captive. "I seen that dragon; a hunnert foot long if it's a inch, big as a beer truck, and got these like colored scales all over. It never seen me, or I wouldn't be standing here gabbing when we oughta be hiking for the tall timber, hey, Mr. Retief?"

"Not yet, Bill," Retief countered. "The Worm, as the locals call it, seems to be perfectly peaceable, as long as nobody comes along and starts a fire in its lair."

"These slobs done that, eh?" Bill said thoughtfully. "What for? Just meanness?"

" 'Meanness,' the kid says," Red jeered. "We figger that critter got no use for *our* supplies, so it was up to us to liberate 'em! Nobody else had the guts to try, but *we* did!"

"What supplies he talking about, Mr. Retief?" Bill wanted to know.

Red answered eagerly: "I'll tell you what supplies, punk! The eats and booze and duds and sneakers and all! *That*'s what supplies! How long'd we last in this here Central Park withouten no supplies, hah?"

"You appear sufficiently well-nourished," Magnan pointed out.

"That ain't the pernt!" Red protested. "It's jest, well, with all that stuff stored yonder, we could set up a like retail operation and clean up a pile. Wouldn't be no competition. Too bad yer too late to get cut in fer a slice o' the action; corporation's closed."

"No one of civilized sensibilities would for a moment consider participation in such a scheme!" Magnan snorted indignantly. "Grand larceny, monopoly, and doubtless price-gouging into the bargain!"

"Yeah, it's a real professional operation," Red agreed dreamily. "Got to hand it to old Eddie, planned it all out—but first we got to fox this here Worm. Tell ya what," he continued in a confidential tone, "way old Eddie figgers it, old Worm's got a back entrance to his cave. We go around there and hit him from behind."

"Are you mad?" Magnan demanded.

"Naw, I'm a good-natured kind of slob," Red pointed

out modestly. "Even if the big feller here *did* clobber me some, I don't hold no grudge."

Bill blocked him as he attempted to slide casually off the path into the underbrush. "Mr. Magnan don't mean that kinda mad," he told Red. "He means 'nuts'–mad. And I say ya must be, tryna louse up a nice deal like you got here."

"Hey, look," Red protested in an attempt at a reasonable tone. "What we gotta do, we gotta get around back and sneak up behind, afore old Worm takes a notion to come back in head-first. Then we'd have them jaws and all to deal with, see? Come on." He darted past Bill, who looked to Retief for advice, but Magnan spoke first.

"Don't just stand there," he commanded sharply. "Follow him!" He trailed after Bill as the Marine fell in on Red's heels. "Coming, Retief?" Magnan addressed the latter.

"I might as well," Retief agreed. He paused to listen. "The boys are still busy," he commented. "It seems they haven't missed Red."

"They've set fire to that lovely little Doric temple," Magnan complained. "Sheer vandalism! And in this idyllic setting, too."

"Something strange going on up ahead," Retief told Magnan. "Over this way." He angled off to the right, between the mossy boles of giant trees. A faint murmuring was audible, coming from somewhere ahead.

"Why, it's a faint murmuring sound," Magnan announced, "coming from somewhere ahead." He mimed Puzzlement over the Treachery of Physical Law (3-V). "Whatever can it be?"

There were sounds as of a brief struggle from the slightly divergent direction in which Bill had followed Red, concluding with a *smack*! like a ball bat striking a gourd. "Don't try that one again!" Bill's voice said sternly, followed by inelegant expostulation from Red.

"I'm onney tryna show ya a short-cut, ain't I?" he whined.

"Hadn't we better . . . ?" Magnan proposed uncertainly, his attention again on the murmuring sound, now more like a roar.

"I think not," Retief vetoed the idea. "Just a little further now."

"It's louder," Magnan said. "It sounds like Pookapoo Falls, that I saw as a boy, back in New Peoria. There was this yacht, wrecked on the rocks just above the Falls; and a little farther upstream, a derelict barge. Fascinating stories! And once a man named Fred Heisenwhacker gained immortality, at least in the New Peoria area, by going over the cataract in a barrel. Fred was never the same after that: used to stop and pound his ear at odd intervals, whatever he might happen to be doing. Oh, here we are!" He concluded his reminiscences abruptly as they emerged on a rocky slope adjacent to a foaming torrent issuing, wreathed in a mist, from a cleft in the rock-face. At the same moment, Red, followed closely by Bill, appeared on the opposite side of the turbulent stream.

"Hey!" Red yelled. "How'd—? Never mind! What we got, we got a foul-up on our hands here! We can't go in, 'cause somebody done flooded the whole place! We got to keep a sharp lookout and get the good stuff when it washes out! Old Eddie ain't gonna like this!"

"If old Eddie sets a petrol fire in an ice-cave," Retief pointed out, "it's to be expected that ice will melt, and inevitably the resultant water will flow downhill."

"Me and old Ed never thought o' that," Red confessed. "But we'll salvage what we can, and maybe Eddie won't take it out on me, which I was just follering orders, up till you fellers come along." He gave Bill a resentful look.

"Fascinating!" Magnan burbled, pointing to the exposed strata in the rock-face. "Look there, Retief! A layer of fossil ice, doubtless the remnant of an ice cap laid down during an era of glaciation, then covered with insulating sediments and preserved here in the shade of the ridge! What's that you said about an ice-cave? Have you noticed? Those confounded midges aren't so thick here."

"Red tells me the Worm, which he says looks like an overgrown 'pillar—lives in one," Retief explained. "Eddie and his crew baited it out and then poured highly inflammable fuel in, and ignited it. So the melt-water is running out the back door. But I don't see any of the goodies Red expected to loot."

"I don't hardly unnerstan," Red grieved. "Place gotta be full o' good stuff, but none of it ain't washing out! Must be another way out," he concluded.

As they watched, the torrent diminished to a modest flow, on which bits of trash, paper, leaves, and charred wood fragments floated gently past.

"Huh! Musta burnt up all the stuff!" Red mourned. "Shunt never of let Eddie take over from Bimbo. Bim had the right idea: sneak in quick and grab a load while old Worm was out." He reeled back as a horde of gnats swarmed from the cave.

GO AWAY, the Voice demanded abruptly.

"No, *you* go away!" Red yelled, looking astonished.

The flow from the hole had dwindled to a trickle, wreathed in pale smoke; the midges had dissipated as quickly as they had appeared.

Red stared into the orifice, now dry; he kicked idly at a stone, then halted in his tracks, his mouth open.

IT IS BETTER THAT YOU WITHDRAW NOW, the Voice spoke gently, but disturbingly as always. Magnan looked about wildly but said nothing.

Red yelped and blurted: "I'm getting in outa this!" and lunged for the shelter of the cavern.

"Better wait until the fumes clear, Red," Retief advised the terrified fellow, taking a restraining grip on his arm. "That was Number Three you burned in there," he reminded him. "The gas is carbon monoxide. Bad for the health." Retief released him. Red clapped his hands over his ears and backed off, babbling:

"—go away! Tole you, go away! Say, Mister, let's get outa here!" He came lurching down the slope and made a grab for Retief, not as one who attacks, but as one seeking refuge. Retief caught him by the arm, and spoke gently:

"It's all right. The voice won't hurt you!"

Red jerked at Retief's restraint. "Guess I know what'll hurt me," he protested. "Anyways, I don't wanna be left out when the loot's divided up," he explained, shaking his head as if to free it of fumes.

"There isn't any loot, remember?" Retief reminded the frightened fellow, who was whimpering and tugging at Retief's grip.

"Take it easy, Red," Retief said soothingly. "We're going. Nobody's after you, except us, and we've already made friends with you, remember?"

The redhead was still shaking his head as if to dislodge foreign matter and the corners of his mouth went down like an infant about to bellow. He continued to mutter, as if disputing with himself.

"But I don't *wanna* go topside," he wailed, at the same time starting up the steep slope. Retief pulled him back.

Magnan spoke up abruptly: "It won't do, it simply won't do!" He broke off and stared about him, an expression of deep puzzlement on his narrow features. "Curious, Jim," he said. "These gnats don't seem to bite. One wonders—"

"Say, Mr. Retief," Bill said, ignoring Magnan's remarks. "Didn't that little gal say something about voices inside yer head?" He shook that member vigorously. "I got 'em," he added. "Says to 'just come in the front way like a good chap' is what it's saying. What should I do?"

"Ignore it for the moment," Retief replied, as Magnan simultaneously yelped, "Get it out, get it out! No! I'm not going, so there!" Then he fell to his knees and looked up at Retief in desperation. Behind him, Red was on the ground, openly weeping, knuckling his eyes, but doggedly trying to creep uphill. "Feller's gotta do it," he explained, aggrievedly. "Heard stories about fellers went nuts," he added. "Why we come up here, get ridda the damn thing. Never bleeved them stories, but looks like—all right, I'm coming, ain't I? Or I would be if this here dumbjohn'd leave go my leg!"

Magnan had scrambled up beside Retief. "Hurry!" he urged. "We have to do as it says! Otherwise. . . ."

"Mr. Retief," Bill blurted. "Don't *you* hear it, too? Looks like Mr. Magnan and this slime-ball can hear it same as me."

"I didn't hear anything to scare a Marine," Retief told the excited lad. "Now be calm, Bill, and tell me exactly what's happening."

Magnan clutched at his arm. "It's telling us to come around and enter by the front," he gobbled. "We're to deal with some ruffians, too, and above all, save the eaters! Then . . . then . . . I'm not sure," he broke off uncertainly, and forged past Retief and scrambled up the slope. "Hurry," he called over his shoulder. Then: "Don't you understand the urgency?" he scolded.

"Nope," Retief said. "I suggest you sneak up on Eddie and his friends a little more cautiously, sir—"

"Who in the world are Eddie and his friends?" Magnan yelped as he halted and slid back downslope.

"My pals, up there," Red contributed. "Prolly in a bad mood counta no pickings after all, plus that monster got 'em treed on a rock spire. Sounded mad last time I seen 'em. Better not get caught sticking the old nostrils in, Mister, prolly get 'em stuffed fulla lint."

"Retief!" Magnan barked, stepping over Red to confront his subordinate. "Am I to understand these Eddie people have intimidated you?"

"Never met 'em," Retief replied. "Excepting Eddie, of course. But at four or five to one, you're taking on too much to chew, single-handed."

" 'Single-handed'!" Magnan spat. "You intend to let

Bill and me, and—this Red person, too, if you'll release him—confront the enemy alone?"

"There's no need for a confrontation just yet," Retief corrected. "There's a cave here that needs investigating."

Magnan stared at the dark, smoke-leaking orifice in dismay. "*It* might be in there—" he started, and broke off. "Yes, Mother, I'm coming," he added in a conversational tone, and again began the ascent of the steep escarpment. "Coming, sergeant?" he called. Bill grunted and followed. Retief released Red's ankle, and the scruffy fellow hesitated, looking puzzled for only a moment before trailing along, muttering, "I'm doin my best, ain't I?"

Retief was scanning the crest of the slope above, noting the overhanging cornice, when the Voice spoke quite clearly, impinging not on his ears but thrusting in among his thoughts.

. . . THERE'S A GOOD FELLOW! I WAS BEGINNING TO THINK YOU'D NEVER LOWER THAT IMPRESSIVE SHIELD OF YOURS! NOW, IF YOU'LL JUST COME ALONG WITH THE OTHERS, I WANT TO EXPLAIN CERTAIN MATTERS TO YOU, BEFORE DISASTER OVERTAKES US ALL, EVEN THE INOFFENSIVE EATERS! QUICKLY, NOW!

Retief went to the black opening amid the crumbling strata, from which a brisk draft was issuing. He sniffed, detected no poison, and entered the dank, chill chamber. As he did, Bill uttered a hoarse yell from above, and came sliding down an icy chute to arrive in a cascade of rubble.

"Mr. Retief!" the lad yelled. "Whatever you do, don't go up there—that's where *they*'re at! Look out—" he broke off, and dashed out of the cave. Retief heard a sound from ahead, and turned quickly to see a carpet of wriggling foot-long creatures with large glowing eyes advancing toward him in an undulating wave; then a silent impact behind his eyes, and blackness closed in.

3

Cutting across the lightless void, a crystalline pattern appeared, like a glowing meander of infinite intricacy, which quickly resolved into silent speech:

. . . DEAR LITTLE EATERS, the words took form in Retief's head like his own thoughts. BUT CLIMB ABOVE THEM AND THEY'LL FORGET YOU. AT THIS STAGE OF DEVEL-OPMENT THEY HAVE LITTLE OR NO INTELLECT.

Light returned. Retief looked ahead. As the worm-like creatures, each with gaping jaws formidably armed with oversized teeth were about to reach him, Retief stepped up on a low ice-ledge, then climbed higher as the living blanket of eaters rolled past, thrusting on until they reached the sunlit entry, at which point they recoiled, surging back across their siblings, returning whence they came as relentlessly as they had come, and Retief stepped down.

THANK YOU, the pattern said clearly. I DO APPRECIATE YOUR CONSIDERATION. NOW, THAT RED FELLOW, NOT AN ALLY OF YOURS, I SEE— HE'D HAVE TRIED TO TRAMPLE THEM AND BEEN STRIPPED OF HIS SOFT PARTS IN A MOMENT. BAD FOR THE EATERS, YOU SEE, A BLOOD MEAL AT THIS STAGE; AND THEY GROW UP TO BE INSATIABLE CARNIVORES. BUT NOW, PLEASE COME ALONG AWAY FROM THAT APERTURE BY WHICH YOU ENTERED. WHY DON'T YOUR COMPANIONS JOIN US?

"They seem to think that there's something danger-ous in here," Retief explained. "Maybe it's the eaters Red had in mind."

BUT HOW SILLY, the pattern shifted to communicate mild mirth. AS IF I'D LET THEM—NEVER MIND. YOUR FRIENDS ARE EASY OF ACCESS, UNLIKE YOURSELF, BUT LACKING IN SUBTLETY. AS FOR THE CHARMING EATERS, IT IS OF COURSE QUITE NATURAL THAT THEY SHOULD EAT, EH?

"No doubt," Retief agreed, "but somehow I got the impression they would have eaten *me*. I'd be against that."

WHY, OF COURSE YOU WOULD. BUT NEVER MIND; 'TO UN-DERSTAND ALL IS TO FORGIVE ALL.'

"That's gracious of you," Retief commented. "What do they eat when there are no Terries sticking their noses in here?"

OH, NO SUCH TIME HAS YET COME, NOT SINCE DEAR CAPTAIN GOLDBLATT FIRST OFFERED HIMSELF, THEREBY AVERTING—BUT NEVER MIND. ALL THAT WAS LONG AGO; ONE'S RECOLLECTIONS GROW DIM. The pattern communicated nostalgia. STILL, I REMEMBER HIS CRIES OF JOY AS HE MADE HIS NOBLE SACRIFICE OF HIS OWN PETTY EXISTENCE IN FAVOR OF THE YOUNG, WITH THEIR LIVES STILL AHEAD . . .

"Altruistic, indeed," Retief commented. "Unfortunately, all the history books have to say is that Captain Goldblatt was lost in space."

BUT I FOUND HIM, AND GUIDED HIM IN TO A SAFE LANDING HERE, the pattern affirmed. I EVEN HELPED HIM FILE HIS DISCOVERY REPORT.

"That was the last that was heard of him," Retief pointed out. He had found that it was unnecessary to voice his remarks: they were communicated unerringly as soon as they formed in his mind.

"Red and his bunch had an idea there was a lot of salable merchandise stored here in the cave," Retief remarked, looking around at the bare rock walls and the porous layer of rotten ice from which water trickled.

OH, YES, THE TROUBLESOME FELLOWS I WAS OBLIGED TO CHASE, BUT NOW, the reply came as clearly as if printed out.

"The fire didn't bother you?" Retief inquired.

GRACIOUS NO, the pattern reassured him. ACTUALLY, I RATHER ENJOYED THE BATH, AND OF COURSE I INGESTED THE ENERGIES: I ABHOR WASTE.

"You consider a hundred-and-fifty octane fire just a bath?" Retief asked.

TOO LONG EXPOSURE *COULD* DAMAGE ONE'S ZANG-TEMPLATE, was the reply, BUT A BRIEF IMMERSION CLEARS AWAY THE ERGNITS.

"Oh, the erg-nits," Retief repeated, unenlightened.

"Now that you know what Eddie and the others tried, what will you do with them?"

'DO'? the pattern echoed in turn. THEY'RE QUITE AT LIBERTY TO WORK OUT THEIR OWN SHABBY DESTINIES. I SHALL OF COURSE PROVIDE SOME SMALL GUIDANCE, NO MORE. IN THE MOMENT OF EMERGENCY, I WAS CONCERNED ONLY TO PREVENT THEIR INTERFERENCE HERE. TOO LARGE A MEAL WOULD GIVE MY LITTLE EATERS INDIGESTION.

"What about the supply of goodies?" Retief persisted. "If there really are any, where do you keep them?"

THEY REMAIN LATENT UNTIL EVOKED BY THE YEARNING OF A DEPRIVED PSYCHE, the pattern stated in a matter-of-fact way. WHAT A PITY THIS EDDIE AND HIS FRIENDS HAVE NEVER PAUSED TO CONCEPTUALIZE JUST WHAT IT IS THEY GENUINELY DESIRE.

Just then Red burst in through the triangular entry, stared about blindly, and blundered away into the darkness, whimpering.

"What do their desires have to do with anything?" Retief wanted to know, ignoring the interruption.

BUT, YOU SEE, for the first time the silent Voice seemed uncertain, THE HABIT OF DISPLACEMENT IS SO DEEPLY IN-GRAINED, ITS VICTIMS ARE UNABLE DIRECTLY TO PERCEIVE THEIR OWN DEEPEST YEARNINGS. This as if clarifying the obvious.

"Eddie and his friends deeply yearn to give every-body a hard time," Retief pointed out. "And they also like the idea of accumulating cash, especially if in the process, they gain power over people."

THOSE TRIVIALITIES ARE OF COURSE, THE SURFACE MOTI-VATIONS, the thought spelled itself out a bit severely. BUT ONE MUST PROBE DEEPER TO FIND THE TRUE GENERA-TIVE LEVEL.

"Oh," Retief commented. "By the way, Jacinthe said you were responsible for Jitty's reformation. Anything in it?"

HARDLY A RE-FORMATION, the pattern corrected. I ONLY EXPOSED AND REVEALED THE TRUE FORM.

"Why?" Retief asked.

BECAUSE IT IS MY NATURE SO TO DO, the pattern spelled out patiently.

"What about the Chateau d'Yquem and blurb-flops?" Retief persisted.

A MATTER OF A MINOR REORGANIZATION OF AVAILABLE MOLECULES, the pattern stated dismissingly.

"That's quite a trick," Retief commented. "Can you rearrange the molecules to produce whatever you like?"

FOR WHATEVER A YEARNING PSYCHE PROVIDES A TEMPLATE. The pattern seemed to come into clear focus. CURIOUSLY, IN YOUR OWN CASE, THERE APPEARS TO BE NO TRULY BASIC CRAVING FOR THE MATERIAL, OTHER THAN PASSING THOUGHTS OF CHATEAU BRIAND WITH BEARNAISE SAUCE, AND THE LIKE, WITH THE APPROPRIATE APPURTENCES, OF COURSE. At once Retief caught a whiff of a delightful aroma. He turned at a *clink*!ing sound and saw Red, clad in a crisp tuxedoall, laying a place at a small, linen-covered table which had been placed on the Isphahan covering a smooth patch of cave floor, adjacent to a wrought-iron standing lamp which shed a mellow light on the Haviland service, the Waterford crystal and the Jensen silver.

"Better make that two," Retief suggested. "I'm sure Mr. Magnan would like to join me; I expect him soon."

"To be sure, sir," Red said, and quickly laid a second place, just as the muted tones of a Chopin *Nocturne* started up from somewhere in the shadows. There was the scrape of a shoe at the narrow entry and Magnan came in, peering doubtfully at the pool of light in the enveloping gloom.

"Retief?" his reedy voice said doubtfully, "wherever *are* you? Are you all right?" He advanced to the table, where Red ceremoniously drew out a chair for him, which he accepted.

"Good lord," he muttered. "Good thinking, Jim. I'm famished! After that brisk trek, I've quite recovered my appetite in spite of having overindulged in the blurb-flops." He gazed at the meticulously set table.

"However did you manage this?" Magnan blurted. "Ah, sublime," he added as he took the first succulent bite. "Hung to the hour and broiled to the second."

"I didn't exactly manage it," Retief told him. "I was chatting with Voice, here, and the subject came up, and here it is."

"This is a strange sort of world," Magnan said thoughtfully, "but not entirely displeasing. Thank you, Red," he added as the latter filled his paper-thin stemmed glass with an aromatic red Burgundy.

" 'Voice'?" Magnan exclaimed in belated response to Retief's reference. "You mean Worm? Where? I didn't see any horrid slimy worms, thank Heaven!"

"That was him you were talking to outside," Retief explained. "He's telepathic. Nice fellow."

"What's come over Red?" Magnan demanded in a stage whisper. "He darted in here suddenly, and a moment later he's serving table as graciously as a graduate of Snively's on Europa. Quite astonishing!"

"It just come to me, sir," Red said diffidently. "I were wasting me time mucking about there, and I seen I was needed here. So here I am. A bit of the crispy, sir?" he offered, waiting, carving knife poised over the prime ribs steaming gently on the salver. Magnan nodded vigorously.

"One feels a bit of a glutton," he confessed. "But when again shall I know the opportunity?"

"Whenever you like, sir," Red supplied.

"This is all very well," Magnan said, in a return to his brisk manner. "But we can hardly be said to be implementing Ambassador Shortfall's instructions to clarify the situation, Terry-Sardon relationswise. Unless, of course," he went on, "the estimable Mr. Red can tell us a few things. Do take a chair, Red," he urged the black-clad servitor. Red shook his head, a stiff expression on his coarse features.

"Twould hardly be proper, sir," he rebuked Magnan. "One has, after all, one's code."

"Excuse me, excuse me," Magnan gobbled. "No breach of etiquette was intended. You can explain quite as well standing, I suppose."

"Never had much of a childhood, sir," Red grunted. "Folks killed, I reckon. First I remember is dodging about the loading quays at Marsport; used to pick up bits and pieces that spilled, see. Then went on to opening a bale now and again, helped it to spill, you see? Sold the swag for what I could get. Fences in Marsport has hearts o' duralloy. Went to space at about ten. Doc looked at my teeth, said I was nine or ten. I chose ten. Bigger, you know. Never got along good with my mates; too soft, they said, too goody-goody, never would join in to raid the captain's pantry and all. Went on fer years that way. Then one time we set down here. Poor job of landing; broke her back. I taken to the woods; found some likely lads and used to raid the native village over the other side. Caught us right one time, and me and Eddie got clear and been hiding out ever since. Then a little while ago, it come to me I wasn't having no fun; tired o' being on the dodge, see? I figured what could a feller do? The Voice, you see, started talking to me then; said come into the cave and all of a sudden them fellers grab me, never hit me, jest give a shave and a wash and give me these new duds; Voice tole me what to do. Old Voice was right there all the time, saying about pulling out the chair and a serve from the left and all. Funny, I kinda like it. Got a job to do and know how to do it. Feels good."

"You consider that an explanation?" Magnan demanded.

"You ast me," Red pointed out sullenly. "You said tell you a few things. So I done."

"I had in mind some disclosures regarding this entire foolish business. This so-called Worm, for example."

"Watcher speck me to tell ya?" Red demanded aggrievedly. "Old Worm ain't 'so-called.' It's right here, talking to me right now . . ." his voice faded off and his face assumed a far-away expression.

"Do close your mouth," Magnan advised sharply. Red's slack jaw closed. Magnan looked at Retief in puzzlement. "What's this about the Worm talking?" he demanded.

I SHALL TELL YOU ALL ABOUT IT IN DUE COURSE, BEN, the Voice told him calmly. RED IS UNDER A BIT OF A STRAIN JUST NOW.

"It's back!" Magnan yelped and nearly spilled his demitasse. "It went away for a while, but now it's back! It says it's going to explain, I think," he concluded doubtfully. "But, Retief—" this with abrupt urgency. "Why are we sitting here stuffing ourselves when that monster could return at any moment, with consequences too horrid to contemplate!" He paused to look about nervously, then remarked, "I seem to have developed a voracious appetite quite suddenly. At this rate I'll soon outweigh Herb Lunchwell, but, never mind, the dinner is delicious, so why not enjoy it, eh? It quite diverts my mind from our eminent demise." He returned his attention to his blurb-steak.

HARDLY, MY DEAR FELLOW, the Voice cut in urbanely. WHY DO YOU ASSUME THE WORST? WOULDN'T IT BE PLEASANTER TO CONCEIVE OF ME AS A BENIGN BEING?

"You!" Magnan blurted. "You mean *you're* the Worm?" he stared wildly at Retief. "The Worm is telepathic! It says it's a benign being!"

"And so it is," Retief replied, nodding. "I'd say this little lunch indicates that quite convincingly."

"The Mad Tea Party," Magnan muttered. "It's traditional, after all, to give the condemned a hearty last meal."

IT'S ESSENTIAL THAT WE TALK, the pattern stated. Magnan jumped, looking at Retief in interrogation. He nodded.

"So I'm not just going dotty," Magnan reassured

himself, "if you can hear it, too. But what in the Nine Worlds will we talk about? The stockade, those horrid bullies, Eddie, the one they call Bimbo, and all their friends, I suppose . . . the temple? The fire? The blurb-flops, the Club . . .? I'm at a loss as to where to begin!"

SHALL WE START WITH THE IMMEDIATE? the silent Voice suggested. AT THIS MOMENT, THE ORGANISMS KNOWN AS EDDIE AND BIMBO ARE APPROACHING FROM THAT DIREC-TION. Somehow the listeners knew the direction the Voice meant.

Magnan's head turned numbly to stare into the depths of the cave. "Of course," he muttered. "They're looking for loot, just as Red was. What are you going to do?"

PROBE THEM FOR THEIR FUNDAMENTAL NEEDS, OF COURSE, AS I EXPLAINED; the Voice communicated a sharpness of tone. AHA, it went on, OUR BIMBO HAS A DEEP NEED FOR SECURITY. PERHAPS AN ENCOUNTER, NON-FATAL, OF COURSE, WITH THE LOVABLE EATERS WILL SERVE TO BRING THAT NEED TO THE FOREFRONT OF HIS AWARENESS . . .

A yell came echoing from the darkness. A moment later, a seven-foot grizzly of a man arrived at a lope, his path illuminated by the brilliant beam of a vacuum helmet's light. He skidded to a stop when he saw Red.

"Quick, Red!" he blurted. "They're coming! I seen 'em. A zillion big worms with teeth. I just barely got past 'em by taking a detour down a side passage—been lost in there fer three days! C'mon, let's get outa here."

"Hold it, Bim," Red objected. "Three days ago you was over the gate, tryna tell Eddie how to take over the action! I seen you outside a half a hour ago my ownself!"

"We got to get away," Bimbo stated, ignoring Red's objections. "Bunch of pillars out there, too, trydda grab me. Some big shot name of Smeer wanted to know was I some guy you call Retief; I told him I never heard o' the bum!"

"This here," Red told his former boss, "is Mr. Retief,

which he's havin lunch right now and don't wanna be disturbed. Why not sit down, and I'll bring you a nice plate o' eats. Must be hungry after them three days in the cave you was saying about."

"I don't like no cops to hassle me on account of some other slob got 'em riled up," Bimbo announced. "So after I work over this here Retief, I'll turn him over the cops my ownself, after I soften him up a little first." He glared ominously at the two diplomats still at the table, then advanced on Magnan.

"OK, you," he started, but Red blocked him off. "No, you don't wanna do that," he told his boss. "Anyways, it's the big feller's Retief, like I tole ya—" He stumbled back as Bimbo stiff-handed him in the ribs.

"Don't much matter, I guess," Bimbo announced. "I'm not gonna overlook any of 'em. You boys better eat up," he concluded. "You got about a half a sec before I start cracking heads."

"Well, Retief," Magnan chirped nervously, "are you simply going to sit there and allow your chief to be browbeaten in this fashion?"

"It's been my observation, Mr. Magnan," Retief replied, "that when a fellow means business, he gets to it. He doesn't waste time beating his chest, or his brow, either. You can relax. This Bimbo doesn't want any trouble."

Listening, slack-jawed, Bimbo started to say something, but instead advanced and hooked his fingers under the edge of the table. At once, Retief put both hands flat on the damask cloth. Bimbo lunged upward, failed to lift the table, looked astonished, bent his knees and strained to no avail; his face grew pink and his breathing slowed and deepened.

"Mr. Magnan," Retief said easily. "If you'll check this poor dumbell's right hip, you'll find a 2 mm. I don't think he should be allowed to play with dangerous toys."

Magnan bobbed his head, emptied his wine glass at a

gulp and rose, looking up at Bimbo's rapidly purpling face, set in a ferocious scowl.

"Goodness," he murmured, averting his eyes, "one is reminded of a mask of the Aztec god of war."

Bimbo snarled and strained again, then heaved a deep sigh and slacked off. "Never knowed it was bolted down," he muttered. With a quick dart, Magnan slipped behind him and deftly lifted the holstered needler. Bimbo failed to notice the swift maneuver; he turned to Retief and snarled, "Wise one, eh? Tryna make a monkey outa me."

"That's not necessary," Retief countered. "All you need to do, Bimbo, is grow yourself a tail."

"No use tryna talk me out of it—" Bimbo began: then his brutal face belatedly registered astonishment which quickly changed to rage. He bellowed and took a step toward Retief, who caught the big fellow's oncoming fist and twisted it. Bimbo uttered a soprano yelp and sank to his knees.

"You wouldn't wanna kinda leave go my arm, I guess," he mumbled. "You know," he went on in an attempt at a sprightly tone, "I been thinking a lot about retirement lately, you know, when the thrill ain't there no more, it's time to quit and leave a younger fella take over."

"Boss!" Red blurted. "Does this mean—?"

"Kindly don't call me 'Boss,' Albert," the retiring kingpin requested. "Just 'Clarence' will do. No need for empty titles among old comrades, eh?" He turned his tormented gaze upward to Retief.

"Could I have it back now, sir, please?" he entreated. "Purty please wid sugar on." He uttered a sigh as Retief released his grip and resumed his seat.

"Be a nice fellow, Bimbo," Retief offered, "and I'll order you some ice-cream."

"Maple-walnut?" Bimbo queried hopefully.

"With whipped cream," Retief assured him.

COMING UP, the pattern responded as from a distance. NICELY DONE, it added. IT WOULD HAVE BEEN A PITY TO

ACTUALLY TEAR HIS ARM OFF AFTER I HAD SOFTENED HIM UP.

"I thought he folded rather too easily," Retief remarked.

"Easily?" Magnan echoed. "Why, he held out for a full five seconds. I once saw a Garoobian hivemaster collapse, whimpering, after less than a second of your persuasive fist-twister. Bimbo was quite a man."

"Still is," Retief amended. "Just getting some sense, is all."

"Sure, Mr. Retief," Bimbo gobbled. "I got some now; wanna make amends, is what I wanna do. Need to apologize to old Busky, which I hammered him up purty good once, and old Hunk, too, nice feller, Hunk, you'll like him. I see now I shoulda listen to him. Guess I ain't made too many friends. . . ." He broke off as Red placed a pressed-glass dish of tan ice-cream before him. He threw away the cookie, and dipped in with the long-handled silver spoon.

"Boy!" he said gluttonously, "maple-walnut, jest like you useta get at old man Jenkin's over on Colvin. Never had a double-dip before, though." He fell silent and devoted himself to swallowing.

"I always like chawklit best," Red offered.

"*Do* sit down and have some," Magnan cried. "No, no, I insist. I'll just nip back and fetch it." He darted away into the dim recesses of the ice-cave.

To his surprise, the cavern widened, opening out to an echoic space like the grand concourse at Granyauck Consolidated, which he saw with surprise was a broad, grassy plain under a blue sky with fleecy clouds. At the same time, the trickle of water flowing down the center of the cave floor beside the table broadened until it was an impressive stream, flowing now between grassy, tree-shaded banks, all in an eclipse-like twilight. He saw a light on the lawn off to one side and hurried over, to find a tiny white-painted booth, bright-lit, and occupied by a heavy-set woman wearing a faded ball gown, with bedraggled ostrich plumes in her unkempt reddish hair. She bobbed her head as Magnan came up, and at once dipped three dark-brown scoops into a blue bowl, and handed it over with a smile.

"I always use a blue bowl fer the chocklit," she commented. Magnan grabbed the dish and paused in confusion, while reflecting that the smile made her almost attractive.

"Is there a charge?" he inquired uncertainly.

"Naw, don't kid me, buddy," she returned, then looked at him more closely. "Ain't seen you before, handsome," she said.

"Mind your tone, my girl," he chided. "I can't abide cheekiness. Did you call me 'handsome'?"

She partly averted her face. "I always did like a snappy dresser," she replied diffidently. "Sorry if I was outa line."

"Not at all, not at all, my dear," Magnan reassured her. She patted back her hair, said "Excuse me," turned abruptly and disappeared through a tiny door in the back of the booth. Magnan stood gaping, then put the cold bowl on the narrow counter and leaned forward to examine the interior of the phone-booth-sized structure. He saw bare walls and a worn floor, directly lit by a glare panel in the low ceiling. There was no visible evidence of a stasis-box for cold storage.

"Curious," Magnan remarked for the record, and walked around behind the tiny booth. Its back was a plain white rectangle, with no discernible door. Magnan looked wildly about.

"Then where, in Heaven's name did she go?" he wailed.

"Right here, sir," a sprightly feminine voice spoke up behind him. He spun and found himself facing a sturdy, but slender, pretty girl whose auburn hair, in an elaborate coiffure interwoven with pink and red feathers, glinted in the crepescular light. "Didn't mean to startle you, sir," she said when Magnan leapt back with a yelp.

"N-not at all," Magnan babbled, "but where did your mother go?"

"Ma's been gone for years," the young lady replied, looking puzzled. "Glad you come along," she added. "I was getting pretty tired. Not to complain," she explained quickly. "I picked the job—course I was pretty young, but I got what I wanted: all the ice cream I wanted for as long as I wanted it. And you know what? I guess I don't want it anymore. Rather have home-made soup. So I guess it's time to move on. OK if I go with you?"

"Are you sure you want to?" Magnan queried anxiously. "After all, I'm not going much of anywhere." He paused to search the horizon. "Which way is the river?" he asked.

"You *are* new," the girl told him. "I thought everybody knew old River Alph goes in a circle; anyway you go, you'll hit the river."

"Not *my* river," Magnan objected. "It dwindles down to a trickle and disappears among the rocks. It's only melt-water from the ice-caves, you know."

She shook her head. "No, I didn't know," she said vaguely. "Don't know much of anything, I guess. But I *do* know I'm glad you come along. Been waiting a mortal long time."

"Waiting for what, my dear?" Magnan asked.

"You, you good-looking devil," she replied and took his arm possessively. Magnan looked around as if searching for a route of escape, waving aimlessly at a small swarm of gnats.

"Ah, from which direction did I approach?" he inquired nervously.

The girl pointed. "Yonder," she said. "Let's go." He allowed her to urge him in the direction in which she had pointed.

"Wait," Magnan objected. "Before we go—tell me, where did you come from—and where did the old bag go?"

"Me and the old bag are the same," the girl said teasingly, and danced out ahead of him to pirouette gracefully. "All in what yer looking for," she added, as if in explanation.

"I *still* don't understand!" Magnan carped.

"Why fight it?" the girl challenged. "You like me better this way, don't you?"

"Vastly," Magnan agreed compliantly. "But—"

"But me no buts, my fool," she said and kissed him on the mouth. He staggered back, then caught himself. "What the devil am I doing?" he inquired of the circumambient air. "Thinking of what the ambassador would say, at a moment like this." He took her in his arms and returned the kiss with interest.

"I told you you were sweet," she murmured, gently disengaging herself.

Magnan asked no more questions as to her identity, but instead broached the subject of the door through which the old bag had exited the booth.

"Wait a minute!" he interrupted himself. "I'll bet—" He broke off and went back around to the front of the booth, stooped, and began to examine the corrugated skirting, half-concealed in the lush grass. Suddenly he uttered a *yip*! and jumped up.

"It's a nexus repeater box," he declared. "I found the data-plate. No wonder—but why? Out here in the middle of nowhere . . .?"

"Don't know what ya mean, handsome," the girl said. "Old stand been right here all along. What do you mean, 'the middle of nowhere'?"

"Never mind," Magnan waved the question away. "By the way, Miss, I'm Mr. Magnan, of the Terran Embassy. May I enquire your name?"

"Sure, go ahead, Mister," she answered.

"Well?" he snapped.

"Go ahead and ask me. I'll be glad to tell ya."

"What . . . is . . . your . . . name . . . please?" Magnan demanded icily.

"Gaby. Short for Gabrielle," she told him.

"Lovely name, Gaby," Magnan said. "You may call me 'Ben,' rather than 'handsome.' "

"I like 'Handsome' better," she replied saucily.

"Very well. But not in the presence of others," Magnan specified sternly.

"What others?" she asked looking around the broad, deserted parkland.

"Well, there's Red . . ." Magnan specified. "And young Bill, and possibly Jacinthe and Small and that Tiny person, and most of all, Retief—and a gross fellow called Looie, or possibly Dirty Eddie—and others as well."

"Suits me, handsome. I never heard of any of 'em. Where do they stay?"

"That, Miss," Magnan said lugubriously, "is a deep, dark secret. Everything about this curious place is a mystery. That reminds me: I forgot Red's ice cream. Probably melted by now, anyway." He turned and went toward the booth, sitting empty on the lawn, its lights gleaming cheerfully in the deepening twilight. His eye fell on the blue bowl on the counter where he had left it a quarter-hour before.

"Why, the ice-cream hasn't melted!" he exclaimed.

"Did you want it to, Ben?" Gaby asked.

"No, of course not! Silly question—but—"

"You sounded disappointed," she said. "Might as well eat it now our ownselfs; won't last forever." She used the slim silver spoon to scoop up a morsel and offered it. Magnan opened his mouth to receive it.

"Marvelous!" he cried. "Makes the blurb-flops seem like tapioca!"

They finished off the dessert, standing by the cheery booth, she in her red-glitter ball-gown, he in his somewhat wilted late mid-afternoon hemi-semi-demi formal coverall. Somewhere a bird twittered.

"Why, a bird twittered!" Magnan exclaimed. "Or

something did. I don't suppose there are any birds here on Sardon."

"Zanny-du," Gaby corrected absently.

"Well, we can't stand here—have to get back," Magnan declared when the bowl was empty. He turned and set off abruptly. Gaby fell in at his side. After a quarter of an hour's leisurely stroll across the close-cropped, tree-dotted meadow, they saw ahead the line of trees which marked the river's course. "Odd!" Magnan cried. "It seemed closer before."

CHAPTER FOUR

In the chilly cave, Retief and Bill were discussing the curious silent Voice, which they had not heard now for a few moments.

"Maybe it's gone," Bill offered. "Guess Mr. Magnan's not coming back. Let's get outa here, Mr. Retief. This place gives me the willies, and Small and Nudine'll be wondering where we got to."

I AM HARDLY GONE, the pattern stated clearly. I SUGGEST YOU REMAIN HERE FOR A TIME. THERE ARE A NUMBER OF INCORRIGIBLES LOOSE OUTSIDE.

"What about Red?" Bill asked dubiously. "Should we run him off?"

"He hasn't had his ice-cream yet," Retief pointed out. "Mr. Magnan seems to be taking his time."

YOUR ASSOCIATE HAS MADE A NEW FRIEND, the Voice informed them. HE'LL BE ALONG PRESENTLY.

"Prolly another old maid," Bill muttered. "No offense, Mr. Retief—"

"Oh, not so old," Magnan's voice spoke up cheerfully as he emerged from the darkness, leading Gaby by the hand.

141

"Geeze!" Bill said reverently.

"Geeze, indeed!" Retief seconded the notion, as he offered the slim beauty a chair, into which she sank gratefully.

"I'm sorry about the ice cream, Red," Magnan told the glowering fellow. "We ate it."

"Don't matter," Red grunted. "I'll get my own." He rose and started toward the rear of the cave.

I WOULDN'T, the Voice spoke clearly. THE DRAGON, YOU KNOW.

"Old Worm?" Red and Bill said together. "He's a pussycat."

"But—!" Magnan started. Bill nodded. "Yeah, the Voice *is* the Worm. I don't get it."

THANK YOU, INDEED, was the reply. BUT NOT ALL MY MANIFESTATIONS ARE SO BENIGN.

"Pay no attention, Retief," Magnan whispered. "That's nonsense. Actually there's a rather pleasant valley just beyond the first turn."

BE NOT DELUDED, came the stern warning. VENTURE THERE AT YOUR PERIL—

"Yeah, lissen good, fella," Red burst out. "Old Bim started to check that out back there wunst, and he come out shook plenty. And I been partway through there, too, one time. Nothin but ice—and if old Voice says there's a dragon, I'll believe him!"

"Well," Bill put in jauntily, "I guess a little peril would liven things up. I'll take a look." With that he was off, disappearing after a few steps in the deep, clammy darkness.

"Retief!" Magnan exclaimed as he watched the young fellow out of sight. "Why didn't you stop him?"

"Bill's an adult," Retief pointed out. "He'll be all right. You said so yourself."

"But the Voice said—well, you know very well what it said."

While they were still discussing the matter, Bill sauntered back into view, whistling softly.

"What happened?" Magnan demanded. "Was it blocked?"

"Changed yer mind, hey, soldier-boy?" Bimbo sneered.

"What do you mean?" Bill exclaimed, sounding surprised. "I just had the best three days of my life in there. I come out here to report, and I'm going right back. So long."

He turned and would have returned whence he came, had Retief not caught his arm.

"Just a minute, Bill," he urged. "Tell us more. You said 'three days.' "

"About; maybe four. Funny place. Never got dark, underground there, but we slept twice. Figure about seventy-two hours. I'm ready to rack out now, only the boys are waiting for me."

"What boys?" Retief insisted.

"Chip and Bill and Buck and Horny—you know; my old boot platoon. Even Lieutenant Frong; the whole outfit."

"Isn't that rather a coincidence?" Magnan wondered.

"Sure," Bill agreed. "So what? Swell bunch of guys."

I WOULD URGE YOU TO MOVE ON, TERRIES, the pattern formed, MUCH AS I HAVE ENJOYED YOUR VISIT AND YOUR CURIOUS CONCEPTIONS OF THE DESIRABLE.

"Yes, oh, we were just going," Magnan supplied, bustling toward the glare of the narrow entryway.

"Go ahead," Red urged. "Old Eddie's got a surprise fer you."

Magnan checked in mid-stride. "I dislike surprises intensely," he stated. "As for this Eddie person, I am assured he's been treed on a rock-spine by the fearsome Worm itself."

"Don't count on him staying up there," Red dismissed the objection contemptuously. "Old Worm's not so bad. You seen that yerself."

MAKE NO ILL-CONSIDERED ASSUMPTIONS, the Voice urged.

Magnan turned back. "Oh, by the way," he addressed the invisible presence. "Retief told me about the, ah, 'eaters.' Where did they go? I saw nothing of them in the cavern yonder."

DOUBTLESS THE DEARS ARE IN AN ESTIVATING PHASE PRIOR TO METAMORPHOSIS, was the reply.

"Oh, yes, of course," Magnan mumbled. "Will they be coming this way again?"

NOT FOR SOME TIME, the Voice told him. BUT ENOUGH OF THESE TRIFLES, it added. YOU HAVE LITTLE TIME REMAINING BEFORE—the Voice broke off, as, at the same moment, a hoarse voice yelled from the entry.

"Ahoy! there, mates! Gladda see ya! We got us a problem here!"

"Hey, Red!" another voice yelled. "Hulk wants you! Better getcher ass out here where he can chew on it!"

Small crawled in through the opening and paused to backhand a whiskery fellow who was attempting to follow.

"They got the gal," Small remarked.

"You mean Jacinthe?" Magnan yelped.

"That's Nudine," Small corrected. "Gal with the towel. She clawed some, I'll tell ya. But they was jest too many of 'em."

"I hardly see what you expect *me* to do," Magnan objected. "Brawling with ruffians is not the strong suit of a diplomat, after all!"

"Thought maybe Retief and Bill'd like to have a little fun with them suckers," Small explained, and whirled suddenly as Dirty Eddie's face appeared at the opening.

"I'll take care o' this, Hulk," he called over his shoulder, and started in. Small seized his head and gave it a hearty hundred-eighty-degree rotation before thrusting the noisy fellow back outside. "C'mon," he remarked and went after him. Bill hurried over as if to follow, but paused and cast an inquiring glance at Retief.

"Better wait," Retief advised. "I think this is more than just another rumble. We've got at least three separate gangs on the prowl simultaneously. How about it, Red?" He turned to the now docile thug. "What's up?" he asked him.

"Why ast me?" Red yelped. "Better ast old Bimbo—all his idear, anyways. Besides, ain't nothing up!"

There was another stir at the narrow entry, and Nudine scrambled through, draped in a plaid shirt six sizes too big. She jerked it into approximate alignment and commented. "Slobs! Tryna interfere with me in the performance o' my duties and all!"

Magnan had dashed to her and was ushering her to his vacated chair, at the same time trying to interpose his thin body between the near-nude girl and Gaby's innocent gaze. Nudine sank down gratefully and Red at once served her a generous slice of tender beef. Small hovered over her solicitously.

She looked around at the cave, chewing. "Howdy, Gabe," she greeted her table-mate. "You boys got a nice layout here," she went on. "I always did like them potted palms and fancy wrought-iron railings and like that. But old Worm's liable to come back any time."

"It's already here," Magnan informed the girl. "Haven't you heard it speaking in your mind?"

"Aw, poor old Pop," Jacinthe said sympathetically, and put down her fork to pat his hand. "Just you take it easy, and purty soon you'll be all right."

Magnan withdrew his hand stiffly. "That remark, I take it," he stated coldly, "indicates that you have in fact not been aware of the Voice."

"Not inside o' my head, Pop," she returned spiritedly, and looked around at the others for their reactions. "How long he been hearing these here like voices?" she asked Retief.

"We've all been hearing it," he told her. "Seems it's the Worm, communicating telepathically."

"Looky, Mr. Retief," she said seriously. "Don't you go cracking. I got to talk to you. There's mischief afoot here, you mark my words. Never seen so many drop-outs and congenital psychopathic inferiors and slime-balls on the move all at once. They're cooking up something, I got a feeling! We hafta break it up now, afore they present us with one o' them *fate I come please!*"

"I seem to recall, Miss," Magnan put in coldly, "that it was you yourself who first told me of the Worm's telepathic abilities."

"Well, yeah, sure, that's something we always tell the new guys, and about how you better not never come over here near the gold domes and all—just kind of kidding, you know? Don't mean I'm spose to believe it my ownself."

"Oddly, the story is quite correct," Magnan told her. "Though I must decry your irresponsibility in attempting to delude me. You also mentioned an Emergency Crew, I believe you called them. Was that—?"

"Ain't seen the Crew lately," Jacinthe told him. "Should of been on the job, rounding up these here Spoilsports."

"And one other thing," Magnan persisted. "What about your being the, ah, Enforcer, here?"

"Got elected, fair and square," Jacinthe replied, unabashed.

"And what, pray, are the duties of your office?" Magnan demanded.

"Say," Red interrupted. "I guess I better tell youse, me bein stuck in here with youse: Boys are gonna block the entry, here, so we better—" He broke off as a handful of gravel clattered on the rock floor, followed by a baseball-sized stone, which Bill deftly caught and threw back, eliciting a yell from outside. Retief stepped past the lad as a boulder as big as a watermelon was thrust through the opening. He caught it, lifted it overhead, and hurled it back. More yells ensued, followed by a moment of stillness.

"—Get a pit mortar in there!" a hoarse voice was audible.

"Heavens, Retief!" Magnan cried. "We'd best withdraw at once. After all, you can't go on all day returning their serves!" He turned to Gaby, who was still seated at the table, finishing her repast.

"Come, my dear," he urged. "At any moment these ruffians will be upon us."

"No hurry," she replied calmly. "That's just the Spoilsports, trying to discover a new thrill."

"I'm sure the old thrill of braining innocent bystanders will serve as well," Magnan snapped. "Come!" He caught her hand and tugged her to her feet.

"Hold on, there, Mister," Red blurted. "We need every man to keep that hole open!" He suited action to words by grabbing up a rock and tossing it past Retief, only to see the ragged triangle of wan daylight further diminished by a new rock shoved into place from outside.

"I wonder," Magnan said nervously to Bill, "what's become of the Voice—ah, the Worm, as the locals call it. One would expect it to assist in this moment of peril."

—SORRY, BEN, the Voice said, faint and faraway, AT THE MOMENT I'M BESET BY A HORDE OF STRANGE EATERS— ROGUES, IT APPEARS, IN COMPANY WITH A GROUP OF TERRANS LIKE YOURSELF.

"What?" Magnan yelped. "Terries in league with locals?"

"Smeer," Retief announced from the portal. "And Counselor Overbore, and a couple of others. That's Colonel Underknuckle, in the disguise, I think. I'm going out to see what they're up to." With that, Retief climbed out through the now tight crevice. Too late, Magnan leapt to attempt to restrain him.

"He'll be killed!" he whimpered. "Those ruffians will assault him without mercy!"

"I reckon Mr. Retief can take care of hisself," Bill commented in a matter-of-fact tone. Small went to the opening, dodged an incoming, and peered out.

"All's well," he announced. "Retief's talking to some fat guy, and I don't see nothing of Tiny, nor Dirty Eddie, nor Bimbo's bunch neither. No pillars in sight."

"Hold it," Red interrupted. "Look yonder—back of that line of brush—" He broke off as Retief abruptly took the plump man's arm and urged him toward the hedge-like growth to which Bill had referred. A whiskery fellow in archaic clothing stood nearby.

"That's Chief Smeer hiding backa there," Bill explicated. "And looks like Retief's going to ennerdooce him to Sid Overbore."

"I hardly think it appropriate," Magnan said glacially, "for a Marine guard of non-commissioned rank to refer to a Counselor of Embassy by his first name, and a nickname at that!"

"This'll be good," Bill predicted. "Old Sid badmouths the pillars worser'n anybody. Now he's gonna hafta shake hands with one."

"I venture to predict," Magnan sniffed, "that Counselor Overbore will conduct himself with the panache of the career diplomat, however such contact may repugn him personally."

"Hiya, Sid," Smeer's wheezy voice could be heard greeting the reluctant Terran Deputy Chief of Mission familiarly. "The next arms shipment about ready?"

Overbore drew himself up stiffly. "Chief Smeer," he began. "I can't imagine—"

"Yeah, that's one o' yer problem areas, Sid," Smeer dismissed the objection. "How about it? Them rocket launchers coming in on schedule or what? I don't know how long I can keep my boys in hand—especially with this *agent provacateur* Retief stirring up the natives and all." As his large, faceted eye fell on Retief, he uttered a yelp. "Hey! that's him! I know the rascal good, seen his pitchers, and seen *him* the time he like massacreed me and my boys in the performance of our duty and all! Get him!"

As Overbore turned, startled, to follow Smeer's excited gesture, he was thrust aside by two pillars who had erupted from the shrubbery at the chief's outburst.

"Where's he at?" one demanded. The other knocked

Colonel Underknuckle to the ground, dislodging his false whiskers and tricorn hat. The colonel clapped a hand over his eyes as if to render himself invisible. "I told you!" he yelled to Overbore. "It was a mistake for us to venture out here into the wilderness, unaccompanied! But no, you wouldn't listen! Said you had the confounded locals under your thumb!"

"That will be quite enough, Fred!" Sid cut off the excited colonel coldly. "I'm sure the chief will be only too glad to assist you to your feet—" He broke off to peer sharply at Retief.

"You're that undisciplined fellow Retief!" he accused. "What are *you* doing here, meddling in high-level GUTS-security matters? Well, I'm waiting! Eh, what's that?" He paused to cup his ear as if listening for distant birdcalls.

"I'm to 'be silent and return whence'?" He frowned at Retief, then shook his head impatiently. "Couldn't be," he concluded. "Voices in my head—and such impertinence from a mere Second Secretary from the Econ Section—are equally impossible!" He turned his back to Retief and assisted Fred Underknuckle to his feet.

"Don't bother with that silly hat," he advised the colonel. "Can't think from whom you imagine you should attempt to disguise your identity, in any case. But your cover is blown now, so throw away those whiskers at once!"

"Don't want any nosy press personnel leaping to conclusions," Underknuckle grumped. "As if the Terran Military Attache would be associated with illegal schemes to overthrow the local authorities and—"

SILENCE FOOLISH ONE! the ubiquitous Voice commanded. YOU'D BEST CLEAR OUT, NOW! YOUR VENAL SCHEMES WILL AVAIL YOU NAUGHT, I AM NOT DISTURBED BY YOUR PATHETIC ROCKETS AND BULLETS.

"I never said about no bullets," Fred protested. "And they're far from 'pathetic,' I assure you! At the last trials—" He stopped in mid-bleat and looked around wildly.

"You, there," he addressed Retief, who was busy shoving one of the Sardonic bodyguard's elbows into the jaws of the other, who was reflexively gnawing the intruding apendage, while both yelled in protest.

"Stop fooling with those chaps!" the confused Colonel ordered. "At a serious moment such as this, when the fates of worlds, to say nothing of my career—and Sid Overbore's, too, for that matter, are hanging in the balance—to indulge in horseplay is inexcusable! And how dare you order me to 'shut up and clear out' in that insidious manner?"

"I didn't, Colonel," Retief replied cooly, "but it wouldn't be a bad idea." He turned and spoke quietly to the two pillars and dismissed them with a hearty shove apiece. They retired to the shelter of their chief, who slithered forward to confront Retief.

"Hey, you can't alien-handle my valiant troops that way! You seen him, Sid! You gonna let this criminal brutalize we deserving locals like that?"

"One moment, Chief," Overbore objected. "While Mr. Retief was, perhaps, a bit precipitate in his rejection of your minions' implied threat, he is still an accredited diplomatic member of the staff of the Terran AE and MP, hardly a mere criminal!"

"Oh, yeah?" Smeer countered cheekily, and unrolled a rather soiled copy of the poster bearing the smeary photo of Retief and the legend 'Reward for information, etc. s/His Terran Excellency.'

"You misunderstand," Overbore improvised, "His Ex was merely concerned for the safety of one of his subordinates who had unaccountably disappeared!"

"I see what I see," Smeer dismissed the alibi. "I'm hunting this here enemy of society, and so's yer boss; he must be a desperate bad hombre. So I'm taking him in!"

Listening at the cave mouth, Small poked Magnan

with his elbow. "Well, we gonna resacue old Retief, or what?" he grunted, and started past. "C'mon."

Magnan caught at the burly fellow's coattail. "Wait! I'm sure Retief can deal with the situation. Just lie low and watch!"

Small muttered but subsided. Outside, on the trampled patch of emerald grass, Smeer was reaching for Retief's arm. Suddenly, Retief jabbed quickly, and the caterpillar-like officer of Constabulary whipped up and over to slam the ground like ten feet of infuriated, scaled and fanged rug-beater hitting a carpet. Leaves flew, and both Sid Overbore and Colonel Underknuckle uttered sharp cries and dashed off into the underbrush, whence they were promptly retrieved by Smeer's two retainers, who had at last succeeded in ending their reflexive gnawing at each other's impenetrable hides.

Smeer rose slowly and painfully. "Dirty pool, Retief," he complained. "Who told you about the Achilles heel of us noble Zanny-duers? The sensitive zata-patch is our most guarded state secret; in fact it's our only state secret, whatever that is."

"A fellow named Big, or Small Henry told me," Retief informed the chief.

"I heard o' that Terry," Smeer declared. "Runs some kind o' off-limits dope den or something, spose to be in some unknown part of the valley, never could find the place."

"Your boys raided it just a couple of hours ago," Retief corrected.

"Dang!" Smeer spat. "That's that pushy Lieutenant Blot, tryna make Captain! Tole him it's better to keep the criminal element all pinned down in one spot, steada spooking 'em so they run in ever direction."

"You were right," Retief said. "Things will never be the same again. And you can forget your deal with Sid."

"See here, young man," Overbore burst out as he bustled forward to confront Retief. "I'll brook no insolence from trouble-makers of your stripe!"

"Suits me, Mr. Overbore," Retief replied quietly. "But it's only fair to let this poor sucker know the plan is blown."

" 'Blown,' you say? After months—nay, years of the most delicate finessing by seasoned diplomats, you propose to butt in and destroy the basis of the Sardon-Terra accord?"

"No, sir, I don't propose," Retief corrected. "It's already done."

"Look here, Mr. Retief," Overbore said in a more placating tone. "I'll be candid with you. Chief Smeer and his gang are, of course, merely a mob of thugs. But better an alliance with them than no alliance at all on this hell-world of anarchy! And in addition—those stories of some horrid great monster terrorizing the hinterlands—I'm persuaded they're true!"

HOW YOU DO RUN ON, SID, the silent Voice commented. WHERE DID YOU GET SUCH A SILLY IDEA?

"I've told you not to speak impertinently to me, sir!" Overbore barked at Retief. " 'Silly idea,' indeed! I have that direct from George, the janitor, our very best Usually Reliable Source!

IMPRESSIVE, the Voice said. I MUST SPEAK TO GEORGE. IT SEEMS THAT WHEN WE LAST TALKED, HE WAS EITHER MORE OR LESS DRUNK THAN I ESTIMATED.

"You'll do no such thing!" Overbore yelled, whirling to look behind him. "I absolutely forbid it!"

CALM DOWN, the pattern shaped the command clearly. DON'T BECOME AGITATED WITH RETIEF; HE HASN'T SAID A WORD.

"Well, I guess I know what I heard!" Sid snapped. "Still, as you suggest," he went on with an effort at suavity, "it ill-graces a senior diplomat to blow his cool in the presence of a subordinate. Forget that outburst, Retief. I'm not myself. Alone, here in this monster-infested wilderness, betrayed by ally and opponent alike—"

"*I'm* here, Sid," Fred Underknuckle spoke up. "You're not *quite* alone, even if you don't count Retief."

"You see the problem, Retief," Overbore appealed. "How Fred ever made field-grade, I shall never comprehend. And those false whiskers! Egad! I've fallen among maniacs!"

"You don't hafta knock my get-up, Sid, which it prolly fooled Retief here for a good five seconds," Underknuckle protested. "At least if they got any spy-eyes focused on us, they got no proof Mrs. Underknuckle's boy Fred was anywhere around when the trafficking with the enemy was going on."

"I shall personally testify at your court-martial," Overbore told the Colonel. " 'Traffic with the enemy,' indeed! Chief Smeer here is hardly the enemy, but a firm friend of Terra, Terrans in general, and the Terry Embassy in particular, especially the Counselor and his confidant the Military Attache!"

"A minute ago you was railroading me," Fred grumped. "Now I'm yer confidant all of a sudden. Better decide which way to swing before that Worm you been talking about comes charging outa the bushes, breathing fire and all."

"Where?" Overbore yipped, turning to look behind him with such vigor that he almost fell. He grabbed Retief's arm.

"Get me out of here in one piece, fella, and I'll see you're rehabilitated!" he hissed. "Look! There's a cave over there, looks like. Let's try that."

"After you, sir," Retief replied; Sid scrambled for the dubious shelter of the narrow aperture.

"Uhh! Looks like rotten ice," the Counselor remarked, but plunged through without hesitation.

WELCOME TO MY HUMBLE ABODE, Retief overheard.

"What do you mean your 'abode,' Ben Magnan?" Sid yelled. "And who's this pack of undesirables? You've fallen among bad companions, Magnan!" he added, almost not yelling.

WOULD YOU CARE FOR A REST, A BATH, OR A SNACK? the Voice inquired concernedly. YOU SEEM QUITE FRAZZLED, SID.

"Everybody's doing it!" Overbore yelled. "Suddenly it's 'Sid this,' and 'Sid that!' What's become of protocol, to say nothing of common etiquette?"

DO YOU DISLIKE YOUR GIVEN NAME, SIDNEY? the pattern wondered. I SEE THAT ACTUALLY YOU'RE FOND OF IT, HONORING AS IT DOES YOUR WORTHY GREAT-UNCLE. WHY THEN THE OBJECTION TO ITS USE?

"Magnan, I must say I resent your unwonted familiarity!" Overbore snapped. "Uncle Sid was always a great favorite of mine, ten million guck or no!"

"But sir," Magnan babbled. "That wasn't *me* being cheeky!"

"I say it *was* cheeky, in the extreme!" Overbore dismissed the objection. "And whence did you learn that trick of talking without moving your lips?"

"Sir, I haven't said a word!" Magnan wailed. "Except just now!"

"You slipped that time, Ben," Overbore interrupted cooly. "I saw your lips move."

"Of course my lips moved!" Magnan confirmed. "They always do when I speak."

IT WAS NOT BEN MAGNAN, BUT I WHO MADE REFERENCE TO YOUR HOPES OF INHERITANCE, SIDNEY, the Voice interpolated.

"Who's this mug, anyways?" Small demanded belatedly, "calling a lady, and me, too, 'undesirables'?"

"Stay out of this, you!" Sid turned to dismiss the query. Small responded by knocking the formerly dignified Deputy Chief of Mission against the wall, sending the luncheon table flying. Gaby rose with a yelp and Magnan went to her side protectively.

"Mr. Henry," he addressed the big man, "I must protest your untoward violence. You not only assaulted my very own Counselor of Embassy, you very nearly upset Miss Gabrielle!"

"Big deal," Jacinthe commented, attempting without success to do up the buttons of her borrowed shirt.

"You, sergeant!" Overbore yelled from his supine position. "It's your duty to protect me from this ruffian!"

"Maybe, Mr. Overbore," Bill conceded, "but you shunta called us all a bunch of undesirables, maybe. Now, Nudine here: Nudine, meet Mr. Overbore. She's head Enforcer in these parts, Sid, and a real nice gal to boot."

"Why, thank you, Billy," she cooed, and looked up at him searchingly. "You know this bum?" she inquired, eyeing the fallen diplomat contemptuously.

"He's a big shot in the Embassy," Bill hastened to explain. "Usually he's a cool article, but I guess he's a little shook right now." He extended a hand to assist the Great Man to his feet. "This here's Big Henry, manager o' the Cloud Cuckoo," he pointed out formally. "Big, meet Counselor Overbore. Over there," he went on, pointing, "that's Red, he's a prizner of war, but kinda reformed."

I SUGGEST, the Voice cut in silently, THAT YOU TAKE AFFIRMATIVE ACTION AT ONCE. OBSERVE THE ACTIVITY AT THE ENTRYWAY.

Bill and Magnan turned as one to see the last sliver of daylight abruptly cut off.

"Hey!" Bill yelled and charged past them to hurl himself in vain against the barrier.

"Must be a big one they done shoved in there, boys," Small announced, after pushing without effect. "Come on, Bill, and you too, Red. You better lend a hand, too, Mr. Magnan. If'n we can't budge this mother, what we are, we're buried alive!" He set himself and heaved again.

As Magnan and the Marine crowded in to help push, Red sauntered over casually. "I got no worries," he told them. "Them's my buddies yonder. They ain't going to bury their pal Reddy alive."

"One can't make a souffle without breaking eggs, Red," Magnan reminded the insouciant fellow. "They can hardly bury us alive without inflicting the same fate on you, pal or no."

"Well, I dunno," Red hedged. He went to the former opening, and yelled: "It's me, Eddie! Lemme outa here!" Then he fell to, gained a foothold and added his force to the effort, but uselessly. The rock held firm. Then Retief stepped up and pushed it aside.

Behind them, shoe-leather scrapped on rock, and Magnan turned in time to see Overbore disappear down into the darkness at the back of the cave.

Jacinthe was the first to react. "Hey, Mister!" she shouted after him even as he was engulfed in the darkness.

THAT WAS PERHAPS UNWISE, the thought formed in the mind of each one present.

"Yes, but—" Magnan offered and looked questioningly at Retief. "Hadn't we better . . .?"

"Right, sir," Retief confirmed promptly.

"What's happening, Mr. Worm?" Magnan demanded aloud. "Is he—?"

YOUR TERRAN MINDS ARE VERY COMPLEX, was the only reply.

"Very possibly," Magnan conceded, "but what has that to do with Counselor Overbore getting lost in that underground labyrinth?"

ONCE AGAIN YOU SURPRISE ME, the pattern told him. DID YOU ENCOUNTER A MAZE WHEN YOU VENTURED THERE?

"No, of course not," Magnan conceded readily. "Actually, it was a lovely, park-like valley, quite odd, actually, considering it was underground. But how could it have been? I saw a blue sky with fleecy white clouds, and afternoon sunlight. Somehow, I must have wandered out onto the surface. Curious, I'm not given to such lapses. . . ."

YET YOU FOUND IT PLEASANT ENOUGH, DID YOU NOT? the Voice insisted.

"Most pleasant!" Magnan agreed. "Especially when I so unexpectedly met Gaby." He turned to peer about in the gloom. "Gaby, dear, where've you gotten to?" he queried uncertainly.

At that moment, Sid Overbore's voice, at its most authoritive, rang sharply from the darkness. "Are you fellows—and ladies," he added with awkward gallantry, "still here? We're wasting time!" He emerged into view, breathing hard.

"Ye gods!" he declaimed. "Three days in a retirement home for worn-out bureaucrats! The dinner-table conversation, Ben, was less than scintillating, I can assure you—and, you know, I had always had a vague sort of idea that's where I'd find peace at last, some day. Now I realize that worked-out diplomats don't retire, they're junked. Horrid. Do have Red bring me a dish of tea; I'm quite undone." He stumbled, and Red instantly took his arm and eased him into a Chippendale chair.

"A retirement home, sir?" Magnan queried uncertainly.

"Where'd you get that idea?" Overbore snapped.

"Why—it's what you said," Magnan blurted. "I heard you quite plainly—so did—"

"Then why the devil are you asking me if that's what I said, Magnan?" Sid demanded scornfully. "We've no time to waste. I overheard a couple of old fellows from Sector discussing certain long-range strategic plans for this infernal worm-infested world. We must act at once if we're to save our skins!"

"Long-range strategic plans, sir?" Magnan quavered, and then caught himself. "Of course, long-range strategy is *so* important. What scheme has Sector devised to ensure the integrity of this rather strange, but actually quite charming planet?" he babbled on. "I've a theory, sir, about some of the apparently fantastic phenomenon we're witnessing here—it's all perfectly rational, once one has somewhat revised one's conception of 'rational.' " He fell silent and waited expectantly.

" 'Actually quite charming,' eh?" Overbore snarled. "Dammit, now you've got me doing it. So you want to preserve the so-called integrity of this dismal cold, wet, cave, is that it? Have I misconstrued you, Magnan?"

"No, sir, I mean 'yessir,'" Magnan blurted. "You haven't misconstrued me, I mean. Why, Retief and I have uncovered a large-scale conspiracy on the part of certain disaffected individuals, to destroy the Worm himself! We interrupted them in the very act of fire-bombing his lair, here."

"Is that why the place reeks of number three?" Sid snorted. "Enough to destroy one's palate." He broke off to confer with Red over the wine list.

"How perceptive, sir!" Magnan cried. "They poured the fuel in and ignited it. However, the occupant was outside, and suffered no harm, you'll be glad to know. Hardly even melted the ice—it's only a rather thin layer on the limestone, you know. Oddly, only a trickle of water from the melt flowed out the crevice yonder, which is how we found it—the fissure I mean—but most of it flowed into the cave, and gave rise to the broad river that flows through the caverns."

"River? Caverns? You've snapped your cap at last, Ben, as the lads used to say when I was a boy—quite a vivid metaphor, that; one envisions—well, never mind what one envisions, Ben! Stick to the subject! I've told you disaster is upon us!" He waved to Red to clear away the dishes, and unrolled a war map on the linen cloth. "This," he stated, stabbing a finger at the sketchy chart, "is our present location, or so Fred Underknuckle assures me. You see that all these pink arrows I've drawn in converge on this very site."

"Whatever can it mean?" Magnan dithered. "We were aware, of course, that groups led by Bimbo, and Tiny, and a few others were all headed this way, some of them having already arrived, and of course we've just seen both Chief Smeer's troops and you yourself, sir, not that—"

"Of course not, Ben!" Sid barked. "The colonel and I are here simply to look into this matter!"

"Somehow I had the impression you had planned the rendezvous with Smeer," Magnan put in stubbornly.

"To be sure," Sid purred. "The chief is cooperating in the apprehension of the evil-doers."

"Certainly!" Magnan agreed. "That's plain as day, sir! I do hope you didn't think I entertained any idea of treachery?"

"Of course not, Ben," Overbore dismissed the thought. "But now we really must get cracking."

Magnan nodded emphatically and took two brisk strides before pausing to ask:

"Crack *what*, sir? I haven't the foggiest."

"*Au contraire*, Ben," Sid corrected. "The foggiest is precisely what you *do* have."

"Say, Mr. Magnan," Bill put in, "I needa ast you something. You know I said what a great time I had back in the cave, there—kinda spooky, seeing all the guys, even Smokey and Buck, which they was both kilt at Leadpipe. And *you* went in sir, and met Miss Gaby, in kind a big park-like; so I got the idea that every feller finds whatever he wanted back there—some kind of a jazreel trip, I guess—all but old Sid, here. He says he spent his time in some dump full of wore-out diplomats. Some place! I wonder . . .?"

I CONFESS, the Voice spoke up with silent firmness. I PERMITTED SURFACE MOTIVATIONS TO INTERVENE; THE ENORMITY OF WHAT I FOUND IN MR. OVERBORE'S LATENT LEVEL WAS SUCH THAT I GUIDED HIM INSTEAD TO THE ACHIEVEMENT OF A GOAL HE HAD LONG CLAIMED AS HIS HIGHEST ASPIRATION, RATHER THAN PERMITTING HIM TO ACTUALIZE THE FULL ELABORATION OF HIS DEEP LATENCY YEARNINGS.

"I suppose that means something," Magnan commented. "But I confess I can't think what."

"Musta been some pretty dirty schemes old Sid was hatching," Bill commented, "to get old Worm so shook."

"I protest this entire proceeding!" Overbore blurted. "You, Ben Magnan, whom I personally never recommended for summary termination! Such gratitude! Now you accuse me of some vague crime, only contemplated, you concede, and poison the minds of everyone present against me." He sobbed abruptly. "I just want folks to like me," he stammered. "Wanted to be a big enough man they'd all admire me. Never did any of that stuff you were talking about. I guess nobody ever did really like me. Not even Mother, always carping at me because I got tired of her bossing me when I was over forty and a Foreign Service Officer of Class Three! I'm a failure, never even got one gang of thugs calling themselves a *de facto* government to accept a no-strings treaty and a billion guck grant! And that retirement home: found every blockhead and petty tyrant I ever met in thirty years of dedicated service! All of 'em higher ranking than me, too! I was lucky I got out alive!"

I OFFER MY SINCERE APOLOGIES, the pattern said in what seemed a humble tone. I YIELDED TO THE TEMPTATION TO ALLOW YOU TO ACTUALIZE YOUR OWN DECLARED AMBITION.

"You goofed, whoever you are!" Overbore barked, turning to peer into shadowy corners. "Where the devil are you? And *who* are you? I can hear you, but I can't exactly seem to see you!" He turned to Magnan. "What's going on, here, Benny?" he entreated. "Sorry about accusing you just now, but I can hardly be blamed for thinking. . . ."

"Sure not, sir," Magnan chirped. "And about that next ER: I do hope to see some more charitable marks in the Big Picture column."

"I suppose I could bump you from 'Unbelievable' to 'Hopeless,'" Sid conceded. "But right now, let's see you get me out of this mess you've lured me into."

"'Lured,' sir?" Magnan faltered. "I, sir? How in Heaven's name am I responsible for your forging into the hinterlands?"

"Followed you, Ben," Sid said shortly. "Hadn't had a

report from you since you departed Staff Meeting so precipitately."

"But, sir, I was *commanded* to go at once, by the Ambassador himself! Right after Art went to see about running off that infamous WANTED poster. Surely you remember? And I've hardly had a moment to catch my breath, to say nothing of preparing Progress Reports in triplicate!"

" 'Progress,' Ben?" Overbore queried icily. "A Retrogression Report would be more apropos."

"I tried, sir!" Magnan cried. "I'm still trying, sir!"

"They don't hand out any Better Bureaucrat prizes for nugatory efforts, Ben, more's the pity," the Counselor reminded his subordinate. "But I was talking about your apparent inclination to interpret my zeal on your behalf as some sort of discreditable act," he resumed redundantly. "What about that, Ben? Do I scent latent insubordination here, or what?"

"Sir, I didn't breathe a word," Magnan gasped. "Your secrets are safe with me—"

"Magnan, I have no secrets!" Overbore snapped. "And if I did, do you suppose that I'd have allowed an underling of your gabby proclivities to learn of them?" He turned his back on the hapless Magnan.

"The Voice told us," Magnan whimpered.

"Never mind, Mr. Magnan," Bill spoke up. "I seen him out there chumming with that pillar, too! I'll testify at yer trial!"

"Aren't you rushing the pace of affairs a trifle, Sergeant?" Magnan dismissed the offer. "The Counselor and I were nattering of glowing ER's looming on my personal career horizon, not preferment of formal charges!"

"Guess I got the wrong idea, Mr. Magnan," Bill explained. "Sometimes when you diplomatic fellers talk, it's hard to say if you're for or against."

"That, Sergeant," Magnan said loftily, "is precisely the essence of enlightened diplomacy."

"Where the devil's Fred?" Overbore barked abruptly. "Fred!" he called. "Where've you gotten to?"

"Oh, don't you remember, sir?" Magnan offered. "You abandoned him to his fate, outside there, with Chief Smeer and those rascals of his."

Overbore whipped out a pad and jotted swiftly. " 'Abandoned,' eh, Ben?" he purred. "I see you've decided to risk all on your feckless campaign to discredit me. Pity—and you with such bright career prospects, until this!"

"Bill saw you, too," Magnan yelped.

"Leave me out o' this one, Mr. Magnan," Bill interpolated. "I got a few career objectives, too."

"Worm, if you *are* Worm," Retief interrupted the exchange, "let's go back to where you were confessing. I picked up a sort of subliminal hint that there's more to tell."

YOU ACCUSE ME OF LYING TO YOU? came the shocked response. AFTER ALL, I NEVER CLAIMED—

"You never denied, it, either," Magnan pointed out.

FEE FIE, FO, FUM, a silent Voice boomed in the crania of all present. I NOTICE ACTIVITY IN THE TABOO PRECINCTS!

"Heavens," Magnan gasped, covering his ears with his palms. "That doesn't sound like Worm! Who's there?" he quavered. "*Do* accept my, that is, our deep personal regrets if we've trespassed. Worm! Where are you now that we need you?"

I'M JUST HERE, the familiar mild Voice replied at once. I, AH, FEAR THERE ARE ONE OR TWO DETAILS THAT I NEGLECTED TO MENTION. AS TO DRAKEN, THE ENTITY WHO SPOKE JUST NOW OF TABOO PRECINCTS, SHE'S NOT THE BEST-TEMPERED LADY ON SARDON, ALAS. AND SHE'S SOMEHOW GAINED THE IMPRESSION THAT YOU, OR WE CONSTITUTE A THREAT TO HER PLANS. NONSENSE OF COURSE, BUT—

YOU CALL WHAT I SAY 'NONSENSE'? the Big Voice boomed again.

"N-not *me*, Madam!" Magnan hastened to clarify. "Why, that's not nonsense at all!"

YOU MEAN, PETTY CREATURE, THAT YOU DO IN FACT CONSTITUTE A THREAT TO MY WORLDVIEW?

"Good lord, no!" Magnan yelped. "Quite the contrary! It's just that as I understand it, the cave is full of eaters which would eat me alive, if they could!"

NOT ALIVE, BEN, the cave-filling silence corrected curtly. AS FOR YOU, JUNIOR . . .

GEE, FELLAS, a weaker pattern formed hesitantly, in the wake of the Big Voice's thunderous declaration, I ONLY TRIED, I MEAN, YOUR INTENTIONS WERE SO INNOCENT, SORT OF, I ONLY WANTED TO HAVE A LITTLE FUN, IS ALL. I'M PRETTY TIRED OF BEING BOSSED AROUND BY A——

JUNIOR, the Big Voice rang out silently, THIS TIME YOU'VE GONE TOO FAR. THE AFFAIR GOLDBLATT WAS NOT, IT APPEARS, SUFFICIENT WARNING OF THE DANGERS OF FECKLESS MEDDLING WITH MINDS MORE HIGHLY DEVELOPED THAT THOSE OF THE FRESHMAN LARVAE.

As the Voice paused in its furious rebuke, Retief touched Magnan's shoulder.

"Time to go, sir," he suggested.

"Doubtless!" Magnan concurred. "But in which direction? If we remove the blockage and venture outside, Chief Smeer and his bullies are waiting. And if we retreat into the cave, we're likely to end up in Sid Overbore's retirement farm!"

"Hey!" Bill put in, "I don't mind seeing the old platoon one more time. Let's go!" He suited action to words and disappeared into the darkness where a row of the luminous flecks still glowed an eerie yellow-green.

"The Worm, or rather, ah, Junior warned us," Small contributed. "What do *you* say, Nudie?"

"Don't ast me, Small," she countered, "try asting Miss fancy Gabrielle, she come from there."

"Gaby?" Magnan croaked, as he looked about him wildly, scanning the shadowy recesses, now lit only by a few vagrant rays penetrating the chinks among the boulders blocking the entry. "Gaby, dear, where've you gotten to?"

"Prolly went back inside," Red offered. "Kinda nice in there, except for them guys grabbed me. Pool tables, nice bar, not too much light, neat little broad selling cigars—almost like old Dinny's Billiards back in my home slum. I'm going back in." He turned and strode off into the darkness.

"He's insane," Magnan said dully. "It's a beautiful park-like meadow, acres of lawn, lovely old trees, and a lone hotdog and ice cream stand. And Gaby!" He too, hurried to the back of the cave—and hesitated.

"What's back there, anyways?" Small queried. "Don't no two of you fellers say the same thing. I guess I got to see for myself." He strode out purposefully into the back of the cave and was gone.

"I reckon I better stick with old Small," Nudine remarked. She yanked down on her shirttails, and departed.

YOU HESITATE, RETIEF, the small Voice noted. DO YOU FEAR, BOLD ONE, TO EXPERIENCE YOUR DEEPEST DESIRES?

"Maybe so," Retief replied. "I don't know what my deepest desires really are. I suppose I'm hung up on some ideal of peace and order."

UMMM . . . the pattern communicated a sense of thinking it over. I SUPPOSE YOU'RE RIGHT, it conceded hesitantly; PERHAPS, it went on judiciously, NOT UNMIXED WITH HONOR AND GLORY. TO SAY NOTHING OF LOYALTY AND JUSTICE.

HAVE DONE, JUNIOR! the Voice cut in. I SHALL DEAL WITH THIS MATTER.

"I have nothing against any of those qualities," Retief agreed. "If you can find them."

"Speaking of loyalty and justice," Magnan spoke up from the shadows. "Gaby's gone back in there—to heavens knows what hellish situation of another's creation."

"I doubt it, sir," Retief reassured him. "She was all right before you came along."

"Still, it's hardly a life for a vital young girl at the peak of her beauty," Magnan protested. "Standing there in the hotdog stand, all alone! It's ghastly! I must go to her at once!" This time he turned and plunged ahead. The sound of his footsteps on the wet cave floor ceased abruptly.

Disregarding Overbore's protests, Retief went to the blocked entry opening. Through an interstice he saw Fred Underknuckle sitting disconsolately on a rounded boulder. Neither Smeer's troops nor the Terran roughnecks were in evidence. Retief thrust the boulders aside and climbed out. The colonel looked up, startled at the sound.

"Great Heavens!" he blurted. "You're that fellow Whatsisname! What have you done with poor Sid?"

"I was about to ask you, Colonel, what you've done with the Chief of Police and Tiny and Bimbo and the other boys."

"Why, I dismissed them some moments ago," Underknuckle said, as one stating the obvious.

"That was clever of you, colonel," Retief commented.

YOU REALLY MUSTN'T REMAIN IN THE OPEN, Junior's voice spoke up, sounding somehow furtive. TAKE COVER BEFORE HERSELF COMES BACK, AND—the thought remained incomplete.

"Whatever for?" Fred yelped and jumped to his feet to stare about wildly. "What are you talking about, Retief?"

" 'Whatsisname,' colonel," Retief reminded the officer.

"What's who's name?" the agitated officer demanded wildly. "First you utter a cryptic warning, then you speak of mysterious strangers!"

"I didn't utter a warning, sir," Retief told the plump colonel.

"I distinctly heard you!" Fred countered. " 'Whatsisname,' you said!"

"Yes, since you called me 'whatsisname,' then 'Retief,' I thought you'd prefer to be consistent," Retief explained.

"Why do you speak in riddles, Retief?" Underknuckle demanded. "Now you accuse me of inconsistency! I insist you explain why I shouldn't remain in the open! And just who is 'Herself', may I inquire?"

"Sure, go ahead," Retief agreed.

"Go where?" Underknuckle demanded. "I've had quite enough of your obfuscation, sir! I demand an immediate explanation! Where would you have me go, eh?"

"I meant 'go ahead and inquire,' " Retief explained.

"You imagine that I require your approval before I can investigate the matter?" Underknuckle demanded. "I'll remind you, sir, that as a full bird, and a military attache to this Mission, I rank with and after a First Secretary—and you're only a Third!"

STOP IT! Junior cut in. WHY DO YOU SPEAK NONSENSE, EVEN AS YOUR DOOM APPROACHES?

"You presume too far!" Underknuckle declared vehemently. "I'm getting all this on tape," he went on, tapping his lapel, the gold wire insignia on which served as antenna to a sophisticated recorder, as Retief well knew.

"I'll play back your insubordinate remarks," Fred announced. "You'll hear with your own ears what you said but a moment ago! Then you won't dare to deny it!" He fingered one of the buttons on the tunic he wore beneath his disguise.

"—And you're only a Third!" his own voice declaimed in a triumphant tone. After a two-second silence, he barked: ". . . You presume too far!"

The colonel looked puzzled, ran the tape forward and back at the high scanning rate: "—then you won't dare to deny it!"

"Just what is it I'm denying, Colonel?" Retief asked quietly.

"Why, what you said!" Fred barked. "You heard it all played back but now! That insolent reference to my cogent remarks as 'nonsense.' " He ran the tape past again at 1:1 speed.

"B-but, I *heard* you!" he wailed at last. "Somehow it got wiped! How did you do that, sir?" he demanded.

"Show me the trick and I'll take it into account in my report to the Ambassador, with a copy to Sector."

"I didn't do anything, Colonel," Retief told the frantic attache patiently. "To the tape," he amplified. "The recorder didn't pick up Junior's remark, because it was in the telepathic range, which your Mark XII can't handle."

"I know what I heard!" Fred wailed. "I'm *not* losing my marbles, do you understand! I suppose driving me daffy is part of your plan, but I won't have it! An Underknuckle is not so easily disposed of!"

DO HURRY! the silent Voice urged. TAKE COVER AT ONCE! LOOK IN THE FAR CORNER OF THE DEN, RETIEF, AND YOU'LL FIND MY LITTLE RETREAT, AN EMERGENCY PLACE OF REFUGE OF WHICH SHE KNOWS NOTHING! AND PREPARING IT WITHOUT ONCE LETTING IT SLIP WAS NO EASY TASK, I ASSURE YOU!

"Now you're talking to yourself," Underknuckle muttered. "Poor chap; gone right off his onion," he commented in a milder tone. "Talking aloud to yourself; even addressing yourself by name. Your hardships have dented your gourd, sir! I realize now that I was insufficiently restrained in my remarks just now. I assure you that had I known of your unfortunate condition, I'd have spoken more gently. By the way," he switched subjects with breathtaking verbal agility, "just why did you decoy me here in the first place?"

GO NOW! Junior commanded. Retief motioned Underknuckle ahead and they returned to the heaped rocks at the cave entry.

Underknuckle stared into the shadowed crevice; his expression suggesting Incredulity (21-b) mingled with Righteous Wrath Restrained by a Will of Iron (422-m). Retief went past him into the cave and crossed to the darkest corner of the vestibule and scanned the ice-covered rock.

There was a deep vertical fissure where the uptilted strata had separated. A breath of warm smoke-and-booze-scented air wafted from it. From deep within, he heard voices as from a great distance. The opening, he estimated, was barely wide enough to squeeze through— or get stuck in.

"What are you doing in there, Retief?" Colonel Underknuckle's voice rasped from outside the cave.

"Just looking things over, Colonel," Retief told him. "Come on in."

"You're sure it's not dangerous?" Underknuckle inquired.

THE FELLOW'S AN ARRANT COWARD, Junior commented.

"I am not, just cautious is all!" Fred corrected.

Retief put an arm into the fissure; the stone was icy cold, and dry.

Behind him, the colonel was chatting with Counselor Overbore.

"Good job you finally decided to rejoin me, rather than skulking out there with those rude persons," Overbore remarked.

"I? Skulking?" The colonel began a protest, but subsided, his meaty features registering discouragement at Egregious Intransigence of Trusted Colleagues (1209-D).

"Fred!" Overbore barked. "This is no time for recrimination. It's time to twenty-three skidoo!"

"What am I supposed to be looking for, Junior?" Retief asked aloud.

"Why ask me?" Underknuckle yelped in a tone of Astonished Indignation, or Indignant Astonishment, (409-A or -B). He backed away from Overbore. "And who do you think you're calling 'Junior'?

"I want you to realize, Retief," he said loudly, "that I always stuck up for you when the others were blaming you. Surely you'd not repay such loyalty with brutality!" He continued to search the shadows for the object of his remarks.

I PERCEIVE THAT THE ORGANISM KNOWN AS WINDY IS THE VICTIM OF UNUSUALLY DEEP-SEATED CONFLICTS, Junior contributed.

"How dare you, Retief!" Fred yelled. "Why, no one has called me 'Windy' since I was a private last class! How did you ever hear of the eke-name?"

"Never did," Retief replied from his shadowy niche. "That's Junior you heard, sir. Or rather, didn't hear. He communicates directly, mind-to-mind."

"Do you imagine," the colonel cut in, "that any such flimsy story will avert the Righteous Wrath of an insulted Underknuckle? And, just where is this 'Junior'? I see no one present but ourselves. Not even Magnan!"

"He's hiding," Retief informed the excited Counselor.

"Uh, so he's hiding!" Overbore mimicked with Heavy Sarcasm (112-N). He stared about him, now miming Honest Confusion (73-b). "I fail to see where even a junior could conceal himself in this bare cavern—unless he's fled away down the passage at the back and is even now joining old Miss Murkle and a gaggle of retired Econ Officers at breakfast! And the sobriquet was never justified; I've always been a chap of few words!"

HOW THEY DO RUN ON, the Voice commented. IT APPEARS 'WINDY' IS INDEED AN APPROPRIATE EPITHET FOR BOTH OF THEM. POOR FELLOWS! ONE FEELS AN URGE TO HELP . . . the pattern faded.

NO MORE MEDDLING, JUNIOR! the Big Voice's pattern imposed itself over the small Voice's relatively feeble one. I UNDERSTAND THE TEMPTATION TO SOOTHE THESE TROUBLED PSYCHES BY RESOLVING THEIR CENTRAL CONFLICTS. BUT AFTER SIXTY-ODD YEARS IN THESE UNFORTUNATE MOULDS, TO FREE THEM NOW WOULD PROBABLY DESTROY THEM. HAVE DONE, I SAY. I SHALL DEAL WITH THESE MATTERS PERSONALLY.

"How do you do that?" Underknuckle yelped. "You speak—and loudly—without a movement of the lips or throat! That's clever, Retief, I'll grant you that—but the Corps Diplomatique is hardly the proper venue for such tricks! A carnival midway would be a fitter outlet for your skill!"

Sid, who had been hovering nearby, tugged at Underknuckle's sleeve and led the now somewhat deflated colonel off to one side. "We've got to work together, Fred," Sid told the panicky colonel. "We came out here to lay the trouble-maker Retief by the heels—"

"I thought we were here to demand the release of hostages, Sid," Fred objected mildly.

"You've seen the posters yourself, Fred!" Sid reminded him. " 'Reward for Retief' they say! 'Dead or alive.' Bringing him in will be a coup that will doubtless net you your first star!"

"Sure, but . . ." Fred faltered. "There's been some kind of foul-up. His Ex was just kidding about the 'dead or alive' part. Art Droneflesh took him seriously! Bad show, Sid. After all he *is* a Terry diplomat, same as us; maybe we oughta consider siding him, just until he can round up and dispose of those dacoit types that interfered with us just now."

"Perish the thought, Fred!" Sid dismissed the proposal. "Those posters don't say 'Reward for Retief' for nothing, after all! Chief Smeer will deal with the banditti!"

"Sure, Sid, but after all, Art wrote the copy in error, like I said," Underknuckle persisted. "My idea is, first we get his help to get clear, then we run him in. How's it sound, Sid?"

TREACHEROUS IN THE EXTREME, Junior put in.

"Now *you're* doing it!" Fred and Sid cried together, then launched into a confused exchange in which the expressions 'trickster,' and 'how dare you!' recurred frequently. Then they paused for breath and looked around the cave as if seeing it for the first time.

"He's gone!" Fred exclaimed, just as Sid said, "Where did he go?" and turned a demanding look on Fred.

"I'm sure *I* wouldn't know," the latter said reprovingly.

"You seek to imply that I *would*?" Sid countered. "That, Colonel, is unwarranted, inappropriate, insubordinate, and unendurable!"

"Also 'imaginary,' " Fred pointed out. "I never came

out and said you were actually responsible for letting the miscreant slip through our fingers."

"Maybe it's just as well," the Counselor suggested. "He *is* rather a physical type, and I had never planned to seize him without the assistance of Chief Smeer and his loyal cops."

"A fat lot of good *they* turned out to be!" Fred complained. "They quailed at the first glimpse of that thug they called Tiny."

"Well, after all," Overbore alibied, "Smeer *was* only up on a vagrancy charge when I found him in the lockup. He aspired to better things—which is why he leapt at my offer of a chieftainship. Otherwise he'd have sneered at my offer like all the other confounded locals."

"Sure, I know all that stuff, Sid," Underknuckle said impatiently. Then he inquired in an oily tone, "Doesn't it strike you, Counselor, that it was just the teensiest bit devious of you to seek in the first instance to discredit an officer of the Terran Mission, albeit a junior one, in order to create a context in which raising, in effect, a private army of local malcontents would seem not unremarkable, all in pursuit of your own personal objectives—"

"*And* your star, remember!" Sid cut in. "Look, Freddy, we've almost got it made: all we need to do is order this mere Third Secretary, this obscure Vice-Consul, to surrender himself, and we'll take him back to the capital in figurative chains, and the prize is ours!"

"Suppose he don't want to?" Fred countered.

I THINK YOU TWO HAVE POLLUTED THE AIR OF THE SACRED CAVE LONG ENOUGH, Junior announced. Sid and Fred leapt as if prodded by hot pins and stared wildly about.

"Disembodied voices!" Overbore breathed.

"Spooks!" Fred corrected.

"Possibly the disembodied voices of spooks, as you suggest," Overbore conceded. "In any event, the suggestion inherent in the insulting remark is not without

merit. Let's get out of here," he added in translation of
his own convoluted syntax.

"And leave Retief here, to the mercy of the spooks?"
Fred objected. "Good idea," he went on. "Then we
won't hafta try to arrest him. Let's go!" the two senior
diplomats dashed for the narrow exit. After a brief
struggle they burst through and found Chief Smeer
awaiting them.

"Gladda see you boys," the chief greeted them. "Some
o' my cops hadda go back to town on urgent business—"

"What urgent business, may one inquire?" Overbore
demanded.

"Sure," Smeer asserted. "Go ahead and ast me. Keeping alive," he added. "Can't blame 'em fer that."

"And what of the ruffians you were ordered to place
under arrest?" Overbore persisted.

"Oh, you mean that rogue Terry, Retief," Smeer deduced. "Well, he went inna cave with you, Fred. I
figger you got him bottled up good."

2

Inside the cave, Retief, having squeezed halfway into
the crevice, heard a woman's scream, then saw movement farther ahead along the narrow niche.

"Retief!" Magnan's voice called. His face appeared,
pale and strained, only a few feet ahead. "I'm stuck!" he
groaned. "Can't go any farther and can't go back. Thank
heaven you're here! I can hardly breathe. Extricate me
at once!" His arms groped toward Retief's extended
hand. "I . . . can't . . ." He whimpered. "What a dreadful way to die! Trapped in the bowels of an alien world
inhabited by ravening monsters and sarcastic voices! Do
hurry! Gaby needs me! They've got her!"

"How'd you get in there?" Retief asked. "And why?"
His effort to reach Magnan's hand fell short by a few
inches.

"I thought they'd taken her this way," Magnan explained. "Here among these tumbled rocks where the

river emerges from the mountainside, I saw a dim light coming from this cleft. So I tried to come through—and here I am. Make haste, Retief! There's no telling what atrocities those terrible creatures will inflict on the poor child!"

"What terrible creatures are those?" Retief wanted to know.

"I think they're what Junior called eaters," Magnan whimpered. "You don't suppose they're—"

"Not a chance, sir," Retief assured his immediate supervisor. "They eat nothing but glow-worms, Voice told me. And by now they're estivating."

"But—I thought—never mind," Magnan stammered. "Good lord! She was never in danger at all, and my effort was all for naught!"

"Not quite, handsome," Gaby's voice spoke up, near at hand. "It's a wonderful thing for a girl to know her lover would put his life on the line for her. Hurry up, please! Let's get out of here!"

"Gaby!" Magnan called awkwardly. "Are you all right?"

"For now," she replied. "But you better get a move on! They're getting close."

"Who, the eaters?" Magnan yelped. "They're harmless, my love!"

"Naw, some ugly mugs I never seen before, make old Dirty Eddie look like Sir Galahad!"

"Exhale, Mr. Magnan," Retief suggested, as he did the same. "And try to relax; I'm going to try something." With that, he wriggled back out of the crevice, not without difficulty, over Magnan's spirited, though muffled protests.

"I gained perhaps an inch when I breathed out!" he called excitedly. "But that's no reason to abandon me now!"

"I notice that the bottom of this fissure is ice-free," Retief told the older man. "It's not water-tight, it seems. But if I pack it with cloth . . ." He paused to rip an inch-wide strip from the ruffles adorning the cuff of his

early mid-morning semi-formal shirt dress, middle three
grades, for the use of, and pressed it down into the
narrowing lower edge of the crack in the cold rock; then
he scooped a palmful of water from one of the many
puddles on the floor, and dribbled it on the fabric
caulking. At first, it soaked out of sight in an instant;
then the wet cloth glazed over and became reflective,
as a film of water built up on it, between the converging walls of stone. In the bitter cold, the thin film
crystalized almost at once, and in so doing expanded
minutely. There was a resounding *CRACK*!, and the
fissure widened by perhaps one sixty-fourth of an inch,
Retief estimated. He dumped in more frigid water and
called encouragingly to Magnan. "Give it about five
minutes, and I think you'll feel the difference."

"I do!" Magnan blurted. "I'm sure I felt a relaxation
of the pressure! I'm going to try. . . ."

"You'd better go back," Retief suggested. "I don't
think there's room to squeeze through."

"Very well," Magnan agreed doubtfully. "But how
am I to do so? I can't find any purchase."

"Relax, Mr. Magnan," Retief suggested. "I'll go around
and pull you back out."

"Do you think you can find the right crevice in which
to look for me?" Magnan groaned. "That was an incredi-
ble jumble of boulders. I was a fool to have tried . . ."

"It was for Gaby, remember?" Retief encouraged his
trapped friend. "Relax and breathe," he added. "I won't
waste any time. Ta." He backed out, noted Counselor
Overbore and the colonel still wrangling near the exit,
and without disturbing their concentration on their de-
bate, went along the wall to the opening of the deeper
cave, took two steps and encountered a solid wall of
stone. He explored for a few yards to the right, found it
to be a seamless continuation of the side wall, curving
in to form a cul de sac.

"How about it, Worm?" he said aloud.

CONFOUND YOU, JUNIOR! The Big pattern communicated fury. NOW YOU'VE CREATED A CLASS ONE PARADOX WITH YOUR CARELESS MEDDLING! STAND FAST, ALIEN BEING, it added more calmly. I SHALL SEE WHAT'S TO BE DONE.

"You there, Retief!" Underknuckle's wheezy voice spoke up abruptly behind him. "Who, or whom, I suppose, are you talking to? Or to whom are you talking?"

"Never mind that, Fred," Overbore's sarcastic voice cut in. "I'm not grading on syntax today. But as for you, Retief, what's your excuse?"

"For existing, you mean, Mr. Overbore?" Retief inquired innocently.

"For participating in this plot against the peace and dignity of the CDT!" was the irate reply. "And what was all that about paradoxes—? You said you'd see what was to be done. You! A mere FSO-7: and with a career minister present! It is precisely *I* who shall determine the correct course of action!"

"Swell, Sid," Fred commented eagerly. "OK," he went on, "I'm as ready as I'll ever be. Let's do it, before the monster comes back."

"Do *what?*" Overbore demanded. "What monster? This is no time, Fred, for precipitate action!"

"You're asking me, 'Do what'?" Fred demanded. "You just said you had a plan all ready to go, so let's do it! And you know darn well what monster: the one all the locals were saying about, and Tiny, too, not to say nothing about Chief Smeer, your own protege!"

"Smeer was a tool to be used and cast aside," Overbore explained to the colonel. "Now, as for you, Retief, it was you who volunteered to 'see what's to be done,' your very words."

"Not quite, Mr. Overbore," Retief contradicted the Counselor politely. "That was Voice. He's the big cheese around here."

"You deny making the declaration which both Colonel Underknuckle and myself clearly heard?" Sid turned to the Attache. "Right, Fred?" he purred.

"Sure, Sid, uh, Counselor Overbore, I mean. No disrespect intended. Just palship, you know, Sid?"

"The informality will be overlooked on this occasion, Fred," Sid conceded in a tone of Gracious Condescension (104-B).

"You don't need to go pulling no 104 on *me*, Sid," Fred carped. "They used to call you 'Windy,' eh? I *coulda* called you that."

"But you didn't, Fred, and you won't," Overbore reminded the colonel coldly. "For very good reasons well known to us both; you're in this far too deeply to attempt to weasel out now; if I fall, you fall first. Now buck up, man, and take that effective action to extricate us from this awkward contretemps, just as you boasted!"

"Whom, I, Sid?" Underknuckle asked as if Amazed at an Unreasonable Attack From an Unexpected Quarter (1127-M).

"One should never essay subtleties beyond one's capability, Fred," Sid told him coldly. "Your attempted 1127—yes, I recognize your intention—was pitiful at best, and by a less experienced professional than myself would have been interpreted as a 707, about a Q, I'd say."

"Anyways," Fred counterattacked gamely, "it was *you* that said about the paradox! A Class Two, you said, as if you were an old hand at classifying paradoxes, or paradoces, if you care about correct Latin inflection."

"Which I emphatically do not!" Overbore riposted vigorously. "Your attempt to attribute to me your own immoderate remarks is one which I shall not fail to include in my post-op debriefing Report!"

"If you ever get to fake up your lousy PODR," Fred challenged. "First, we gotta get outa here alive, right? And I never said a word about paradoces!"

Sid turned to Retief, who was leaning against the wall with his arms folded.

"What about it, Mr. Retief?" Sid barked. "Are you or are you not a witness to the colonel's remarks?"

"I'm afraid you're both mistaken," Retief told the dumbfounded senior officials. "Neither of you said that, and neither did I. That was something known as Worm."

"The dread monster of the Taboo Cave!" Underknuckle groaned at the same moment that the Counselor sneered.

"Oh, back to that nonsense, eh? Tell me, sir, just where *is* this mysterious Worm? I challenge you to show him to me!"

YOU'LL REGRET THAT PIECE OF INSOLENCE! the silent Voice boomed. GET BACK AGAINST THE WALLS THERE, ALL OF YOU, LEST I SQUASH YOU BY INADVERTANCE!

CHAPTER FIVE

"How did Retief do that?" Sid whimpered as he flattened himself against the cold, wet rock surface at his back.

"H-how do I know?" Underknuckle objected from his position flanking the almost completely obstructed exit-crevice.

TAKE IT EASY, GENTS, Junior's lesser voice seemed to creep stealthily into their excited awarenesses. OLD VOICE WON'T HURT YOU UNLESS YOU GET HER A LITTLE RILED, AND THEN IT'D JUST BE AN ACCIDENT. STAND FAST AND LET HER GET IT OFF HER CHEST—

I HEARD THAT, JUNIOR, the Big Voice cut short the lesser one. NOW, AS FOR YOU, TERRIES AS I BELIEVE YOU CALL YOURSELVES, WHAT IN TOPHET ARE YOU DOING HERE IN THE FIRST PLACE?

"Well," Fred spoke first. "Sid here, Counselor of Embassy Sidney Z. Overbore III, FSO-1, I mean he came to me yesterday afternoon with this plan, see? He said where the Terry Mission was getting no place in pacifying the locals, because they were already too peaceful—didn't have a regular war going to speak of, just the constant dacoit activity. Plus the renegades, of course, were hazing the illegal Terries. Said if we could organize the action where the media could have something to get their teeth into, then we could step in and pacify the whole works, and take our places in the annals of diplomacy as the Great Pacifiers! So, naturally I leapt or leaped at the chance to bring the joys of halcyon peace to the poor overworked locals, and all. Terries, too. Members of TERRI were always reporting a colleague's disappearance, or worse. So I hadda clear duty to do something affirmative, like they say."

'ANNALS OF DIPLOMACY,' INDEED, Junior cut in sharply. 'ANNALS OF VILLIANY' IS CLOSER TO THE MARK!

FOR ONCE YOU'RE RIGHT, JUNIOR, the Big Voice thundered. BUT THIS IS A MATTER FOR ME TO HANDLE. WATCH CLOSELY AND OBSERVE MY TECHNIQUE, WHICH, YOU WILL NOTE, DOES NOT RELY ON BRUTE FORCE AND SUPERFICIAL MANIPULATION.

AS YOU DESIRE, BIG SHOT, Junior agreed tamely. BUT I WAS HOPING TO SEE THE FAT ONE FACE-TO-FACE WITH HIS SECRET YEARNINGS . . . !

THIS IS NOT AN OCCASION FOR PERSONAL GRATIFICATION, JUNIOR, the Big Voice rebuked sharply. INDEED, THAT IS THE FIRST LESSION TO BE LEARNED. NOW OBSERVE!

"I'm going mad," Fred Underknuckle said quietly in the thunderous silence which followed the Worm's pronouncement. "I just heard old General Faintlady chewing me out, just like in the old days at the Academy. Ah, those were the great days! We had some solid values then, like promotion and pay! Now it's all politics—like *this* dumb caper. Stir up a war so we can settle it, the man says, and make some underling the patsy. I better go make a clean breast of the whole thing to His Ex before it's too late."

"You'll do nothing of the sort, Fred," Overbore barked. "Don't let a mere ventriloquist unman you, man. Remember the Fighting Underknuckles from whom you claim descent!"

" 'Claim,' hell, Sid Overbore!" the colonel snapped. "I have a fully authenticated genealogy showing Field Marshall Lord Underknuckle was my paternal four-greats!"

"I recall the career of His Lordship," Overbore replied. "Died manfully at Bellybutton, as I recall. Well, I have no intention of dying manfully, or any other way, just now. Instead, we shall proceed in a deliberate, calculated fashion to draw total success and vindication from the shambles of shameful defeat—a defeat which would have been due solely to your lack of soldierly qualities, my dear Colonel!"

While the two senior Embassy officers were wrangling, Retief had examined the wall which blocked his way. The feeble available light revealed an uneven line of juncture along the left side. He took from his pocket a steel tool, useful for opening recalcitrant doors, and inserted it in the hairline crack. Something inside said *'click!'* and a sliding panel moved aside to open a vertical aperture.

HEY, THAT'S NOT CRICKET! Junior objected. Both Overbore and Underknuckle at once responded by objecting to the other's supposed accusation of foul play. Retief ignored the hubbub, and taking a two-handed grip, he forced the thin, tough slab aside, and stepped through into a somewhat larger cavern, with no sign of the heaped rubble where Magnan was trapped. Without delay, he started down the almost lightless passage. Behind him, Colonel Underknuckle uttered a yelp: "He's escaping! Do something!" Overbore's reply was inaudible. Retief went on, studying the water-worn walls as he went.

YOU'VE TAKEN ME UNAWARE, Junior complained. I HAD EXPECTED YOU TO FOLLOW MAGNAN INTO MY HIDEAWAY—OR TO BECOME JAMMED IN THE PASSAGE IN THE ATTEMPT! YOU'VE SPOILED A MOST ARTISTIC PLOT!

ONCE AGAIN, the Big Voice rang silently, YOUR

INEXPERIENCE HAS LED YOU INTO FOLLY. YOU MAY AMUSE YOURSELF WITH THE SHALLOW BEINGS IN THE OUTER CAVE.

WAIT! Junior pled, I HAD A REALLY NEAT PLAN GOING, AND I CAN STILL BRING IT OFF, IF YOU'D JUST LEAVE ME ALONE A FEW MINUTES.

A side passage debouched to the left. Wan daylight shone from it.

SEIZE THE INTRUDER AS SOON AS HE VENTURES HERE, Junior ordered, somehow furtively.

Retief flattened himself against the cave wall as two men in tight black clothing appeared from the dimness.

" 'Grab the intruder when he pokes his nose in,' the Boss says," one of them sneered. "So how do we grab some sucker when nobody ain't poked his nose in, eh, Manny?"

"Shut up, Boony," the other replied curtly. "He gotta be clost." He moved uncertainly past Retief. "Cain't see nothing in the dark," he muttered.

"Wrong, Manny," Retief said, imitating the penetrating, though silent voice of Junior. " 'Nothing' is precisely what you *can* see in the dark."

"OK, OK, I get it," Manny replied irritably.

"Who you talking to, Man?" Boony wanted to know. "I didn't say nothing."

" 'Nothing' is precisely what you *did* say, wise guy," Manny retorted. "I guess you ain't no smarter'n me, huh?"

"Don't start nothing, wise guy," the slightly larger Boony advised.

"I'll pass that one," Manny said. "Din't you hear old Boss, too?"

"Boss ain't said nothing 'cept clobber some bum," Boony objected. He had paused directly before Retief; his unshaven jaw was a barely visible target in the gloom.

"Hold that pose, Boony," Retief said, and as Boony reflexively jumped, he pole-axed him with a straight right. Manny scuttled over to peer down at the limp form of his partner.

"What's got inta ya, Boony?" he demanded. "This here is serious business. Lay off the clowning!" He poked Boony's limp form with one booted toe. "Come on, Boonsy, get up, OK? We got a job to do." When there was no response, he squatted and began to shake the slack shoulder. From this point of vantage, he discerned a pair of feet planted immobile just beyond Boony's outflung arm. Manny rose quickly. "Oh-oh," he commented. "I was just going," he added in a conciliatory tone, and grabbed Boony's arm as if to lift him with a fireman's carry. "It's just my pal here, which he's having one of his spells," he babbled. "Soon's I get him back to the nutch. . . ."

"Never mind that, Manny," Retief told the panicky fellow. "I'm not going to hurt you—yet. I need some information. Do you feel like supplying it?"

"Sure, chief, you bet. Information? Heck, I'm a gold mine. I got information I ain't even used yet. Wanna know where old Boss keeps the booze?"

"Not yet," Retief told him. "Start with what you're doing here."

"Well, like we was saying, we come over to clobber some clown which he was like intruding in the Boss's private turf and all."

"Why?" Retief pressed the man.

"Cause them was our orders," Manny stated defensively.

"Who gave the orders?" Retief insisted.

"Well, Boss did who do ya think?" Manny replied as one Stating the Obvious (702-C).

"Where'd you learn that 702?" was Retief's next question.

"You mean the dopey look?" Manny inquired. "Picked that up from a old wino said he was a diplomat—but he couldn'ta been."

"Why not?"

"Never had no striped pants," Manny supplied bluntly. "Name of Ebbtide. Never had no pants at all. Said he was 'set upon' whatever that is, by brigands, whatever them are."

"Very well," Retief said soothingly. "Who are you, Manny, and how did you get here?"

"I'm Manny, like you said," Manny said in a puzzled tone. "And I walked over from Vegas. What's so funny about that?"

"Vegas," Retief told him, "is a town on Terra, some forty-five hundred lights from here."

"Naw, you got the wrong dope, pal," Manny cut in impatiently. "Vegas is just around the bend there, five minutes maybe, if you walk slow."

"What does this Boss of yours look like?" Retief asked next.

"Never seen the guy," Manny replied promptly. "Kinda weird sort of fella: sneaks up and whispers stuff in your ear, and ducks out before you can turn around. Guess he's kinda shy about anybody identifying him."

"Why do you take orders from him?" Retief demanded.

"I heard what happens to guys that don't cooperate," Manny admitted glumly. "Like Roy; nice quiet guy, too. Boss tole him to go collect stores from the hopper, and he was on a hot roll and he says to Boss, 'Fetch 'em yer own-self,' and he never rolled nothing but deuces all night. Fell over his own foot going out. Roy was a guy with a like curse on him from then on. Like me and Boony will prolly be when we don't bring you in."

"Perish the thought," Retief reassured Manny. "As soon as Boony awakens, I'll be glad to accompany you back to Vegas."

"Yeah?" Manny said wonderingly. "Put her there, pal!" He extended a callussed hand, and when Retief took it, he instantly attempted a hip throw which somehow went awry, so that it was Manny who hit the wet stone floor face-first.

"Par me, pal," he said through bruised lips as he climbed to his feet. "Just what they call reflex," he explained lamely. "Guess I din't do it right."

"Your technique *could* stand a bit of polishing," Retief told him. He glanced at Boony, who was now sitting up, groaning. "If you'll help Boony up, we can be off," he told Manny.

"You mean—you don't hold no grudge?" Manny queried. "You're still game to go in wit' us, and ack like we taken you and all?"

"Why not?" Retief replied easily, and watched as Manny dragged Boony to his feet, whispering urgently to his dazed partner.

Then he came up to Retief and jabbed him roughly with a well-chewed forefinger. "I tole Boon you was a right guy," he stated. "Let's move the dogs," he ordered.

Retief caught the thick wrist and squeezed. "Keep your pinkies to yourself, Manny," he advised the lout. At that point Boony staggered over and commented.

"You two boys holding hands or what?"

"What we're doing, Boon," Manny answered him, "we're holding our lip—like you oughta be doing."

Before Boony could voice the resentment which was revealed in his snarling expression, Retief turned slightly to block him away from the object of his annoyance.

"No time for personal gratification just now," he told the frustrated chap. "You were taking me to the boss, remember?"

"Well, not egzackly *to* the boss," Manny hastened to clarify, as he tugged at the restraint; and Boony set off ahead, along the passage from which the two enforcers had first emerged. "Just where Boss said, is all," Manny completed his explication. "You gotta leggo my arm, pal, which I can't hardly walk backwards too good, OK?"

Retief released the wrist, which Manny hugged to his chest like a mother bear recovering a straying cub, and massaged it gently.

"It's prolly broke," he lamented. "Look at this here bump—it usta be way over here." He demonstrated the fancied displacement with the twin to the finger with which he had incurred the discomfort.

"I was careful, Manny," Retief reassured him. "By tomorrow it will be as good as new—just keep it close to home in the meantime."

"You bet I will, pal," Manny said. "I guess Manuel Lipschitz is a guy which he's a fast learner."

Bright lights glared ahead. The passage made an abrupt right-hand turning and as the trio rounded it, the sounds of a nervously excited crowd abruptly blared.

Boony paused at the entrance to a brilliantly lit casino; the formally attired throng, intent on their wagers, ignored the new arrivals. Here in the light Retief saw that both his escorts were neatly dressed in old-fashioned tuxedos. His own travel-worn, torn and stained early late-morning informal coverall was in stark contrast.

"See?" Manny told Retief. "I tole you it was onny a few minutes walk and all."

YOU NEEDN'T BE EMBARRASSED, Junior spoke up unexpectedly. IF YOU'LL TURN TO THE ALCOVE ON YOUR RIGHT, YOU'LL FIND A MORE SUITABLE COSTUME.

Manny and Boony turned as one to shush Retief.

"Hold it down," Manny hissed. "We figger to make a like inobtrusive entry and all."

"The costume I'm wearing," Retief replied to Junior subvocally, "is just right for what I have in mind."

I DO HOPE YOU INTEND NO VIOLENCE, Junior communicated. I ABHOR MAYHEM, YOU KNOW.

"Whatta ya mean, 'violence'?" Manny demanded, backing away. "I thought we had a nice modus vivendi worked out here. Me, I'm a non-violent guy, and even old Boon here don't never do no violence unless he really gotta. Right, Boon?"

"Sharrup," Boony replied curtly. "I gotta think!"

"Geeze!" Manny turned to Retief miming awe. "He got-ta think, pal! Just think o' that!"

"That does it, dum-dum," Boony snarled and rammed a short left into Manny's ribs. "I taken all yer crap I'm gonna take, see?" He fended off Manny, who had folded against him. Abruptly Manny lashed out, catching Boony a smart clip to the side of his lumpy head. Boony muttered a muffled yell and staggered backward through the archway, jostling a plump woman in a tight scarlet gown and clashing blue hair. As she recovered her balance, muttering, a powerfully-built man with smooth gray hair stepped forward truculently, but the overweight woman caught his arm and led him away, scolding as she went.

"Nice joint, see, pal?" Manny remarked. "Class, see? No hassle even if old Boon had a few too many and goes knocking down the fat old dames. Come on, I guess the cover is broke anyways. I'll innerdooce youse around." He advanced into the deep-carpeted room, grabbing Boony by the elbow as he went past, and steering the dazed fellow alongside. Retief lit up a hyacinth dopestick and followed. His attention was caught by a long board like an outsized billiard table, marked in an intricate pattern in red, yellow and white lines, with a black disc at the center.

"Try your luck, chum?" a tall croupier type said ingratiatingly.

"Where's the zoop tower?" Retief countered.

"Oh, you'll find that over the other side, outside my turf," the croupier replied with a yawn.

"Nix, pal," Manny objected, "you don't wanna mess with no zoop tower nor with no blim-blam rig neither. Them boys play for keeps."

"That's fine," Retief reassured him. "When *I* win, *I* keep."

"Yeah, but nobody don't never win over Slick," Manny stated with finality. "He ain't no dummy."

"I assume you mean he *is* no dummy," Retief replied. "Nonetheless, I'd like to observe his technique."

"Technique got nothing to do with it," Manny pointed out. "See, I never said 'ain't' that time."

"You're a quick study, Manny," Retief conceded. "Have you ever tried studying?"

"You mean like looking at books and like that?" Manny's hoarse voice expressed Amazement at a Totally Inappropriate Suggestion, a close approximation of the official 2731-a, or even a 'b,' Retief estimated.

"You seem to have a natural flair for diplomatic subtleties," Retief complimented Manny, who very nearly dug in a toe and blushed, but stopped short of saying 'corn shuckins.'

"Yes, books, and tapes, and maps and diagrams," Retief confirmed. "You might find it interesting to discover something about the universe you live in, and how it all came to be."

"Don't need to, I awready know all that stuff," Manny dismissed the idea.

"Then tell me, in a few well-chosen words," Retief proposed, as they paused beside a relatively quiet porp table, where a leather-vested Hoom gaulieter seemed to be in the process of breaking the bank.

"Well," Manny replied, "you see, a long time ago, Zanny-Du here was just a ordinary little backwater world. Point eight-seven T, it was, whatever that means. Then this here life-form done arose and all, and it had a like yen to get plenty of eats and plenty of rest, onney there was too many meat-eating fellows bigger'n it around alla time, so it seems like it come up with this here tricky nervous system and all, where it could mess wit the other critters' brains, what they had of 'em, to make 'em *think* they was getting a full meal, while the victim eased off inna underbrush and got clear. Old carnivores went away happy, and pretty soon they all died o' starvation, see?"

"Fascinating," Retief encouraged the suddenly talkative fellow. "Where did you learn all this?"

I TOLD HIM, Junior's crisp Voice supplied. I SIMPLY

HAD TO TALK TO SOMEONE. YOU SEE, MR. RETIEF, I'M NOT
LIKE THESE THUGS; I'M THOUGHTFUL, INDEED PHILOSOPHI-
CALLY INCLINED. I CONFESS THAT TRAIT, WHILE A SOURCE
OF PRIDE, HAS CAUSED ME A GREAT DEAL OF DIFFICULTY IN
MY LIFETIME, AND I'M ACTUALLY STILL QUITE A YOUNG
FELLOW.

JUNIOR, the Big Voice boomed out. I'VE WARNED YOU
FOR THE LAST TIME! NOW I'M FORCED TO TAKE ACTION!

Retief noticed a flurry of activity across the room.
People were retreating from the path of a short, stout
man, who had dashed out through the door marked
Private, slamming it behind him.

Manny and Boony hurried to the scene of the excitement, and conferred with other dinner-jacketed thugs.
Then one went to the slammed door and wrenched it
open. At the instant *slam*! of a hardshot, Boony staggered back and fell across a crap table. Two of the
others at once grappled with Manny, who had started
toward the fallen man. Manny yelled, "Boony! How
bad are you?"

OH, DEAR, Junior's voice, sounding nervous, lamented.
I REALLY DID HOPE THERE WOULDN'T BE NEED FOR VIO-
LENCE. POOR BOONY: I WONDER IF. . . .

The man lying across the table flopped an arm as if
groping for support, then sat up. He shook his head like
a dog drying itself after a swim, then slid down off the
table to his feet, one hand pressed to his chest. The
other men recoiled, looking horrified.

"I never figgered old Sol would do it," the risen man
stated, still fingering his wound. "I thought we was
pals, him and me. We been together a long time. Great
guy, old Sol, in spite of what he done." Boony took a
step toward the door, but halted at the same moment
that Junior's voice cut sharply across Retief's awareness:

NOBODY BUT NOBODY COMES IN HERE, UNDERSTAND? THAT
MEANS YOU, BOONY, AND MOXIE AND AL, TOO. MANNY, YOU
GO GET RETIEF: HE'S THE ONE WITH THE SHOULDERS ACROSS

THE ROOM THERE. IT'S OLD WORM'S FAULT, CALLING ME
'JUNIOR,' THE UPSTART! GOT ME MAD. . . .

Manny pushed his way through the crowd, which
had stood silent and unmoving since the first stir by the
Private door. Retief waited for him calmly.

"Geeze, Mr. Retief!" Manny offered as he came up
hesitantly. "Guess Boss wants to see you. You going to
come nice, or have I gotta blow the whistle?"

"Whistles are bad for my nerves, Manny," Retief told
him affably. "Let's go."

The other henchmen of the mysterious Boss waited
silently as Manny came up, elbowed his way through
them, and halted by the door. His hand went out and
hesitated, not touching the knob.

Retief went past him and flung the door open. At the
other side of the spacious room, a plump, nearly bald
man sat behind a chromalloy desk clearly salvaged from
a ship of the line. He grunted and waved Manny back,
picked up a fat cigar from an ashtray chipped from a
five-pound carbon crystal, drew on it thoughtfully while
examining Retief from head to toe.

YOU DON'T LOOK LIKE A MUSCLER-IN, Junior's voice
rapped out shockingly loud.

"Don't kid me, Captain," Retief dismissed the remark. "You know exactly who I am and why I'm here,
and the sooner we get on with it the better."

"You like my layout?" the Boss inquired in a mellow
voice quite at variance with his rough-and-tough appearance.

"I thought it was *Manny's* idea of Heaven," Retief
replied.

The Boss nodded. "Right, Mister; old Manny was
responsible for the basic layout, but I added the refine-
ments." He pressed a hidden button and with a soft
humming, a fully equipped den-style bar deployed from
the adjacent wall, complete with ice-bucket, booze and
water dispensers and bowls of tasty snacks. "Have a
drink, Retief," the Boss urged. "Lay off the rye, that's

Manny's; it ain't up to my standard. The gin is tops. And how come you called me 'Captain' when you come in?"

" 'Captain Goldblatt' would have been more precise," Retief said, and took the chair which had rolled into position before the desk. "Quite an enterprise you've undertaken here," Retief went on. "And it almost worked."

"Whattaya mean, 'almost'?" the Boss demanded, a worried look abruptly on his fleshy features. "My name's 'O'Reilly,' " he added. "Big Red O'Reilly, six-oh, two-twenny stripped, and still plenty tough."

"Shanghaing a few Terry spacers was all right," Retief told him. "Nobody much noticed that for a while. But when you started meddling with the Terran Embassy you went a little too far."

"What, that bunch of stuffed shirts?" the Boss jeered. "I got them dopes where I want 'em: right here." He opened and closed his right hand. "Take that phoney Sid Overbore: thinks he's little Jesus, or maybe little Moses I should say. All I hadda do was take him on a little mindtrip, and he caved in like a hull full of shipworms!"

"Naughty," Retief reproved. "Do you have a blackboard?"

"Why—" Boss started, then pressed another button. At once a panel slid back to reveal a dull green chalkboard.

"Now," Retief directed, "you're going to write 'I will not play with the head of the Counselor of Embassy of Terra,' fifty times."

"I dunno know how you spell that 'Counselor,' " Boss objected, "and there ain't room to do fifty. Maybe twenty-five." He rose and picked up the chalk and started in briskly. After he had managed to spell 'Counselor' three different ways, Retief called him off. "Start telling me things, Captain," he ordered the shaky Boss.

"How do **you** plan to make me?" the Boss demanded

truculently. "This is *my* turf, Mister! I been here a while, and I don't need any gang of bureaucrats coming along, telling me what to do! What's your beef, anyway? You've had it pretty nice, mostly, I'd say."

"JUST DO AS YOU'RE TOLD," Retief cut off the objection, miming the Voice.

Boss looked shaken; he stepped back, keeping his eyes on Retief. "All right," he almost yelled. "I see I made a few miscalculations; just take it easy and we can work something out!"

"ALL YOU NEED TO WORK OUT," Retief contradicted, "IS WHERE TO START. I'D SUGGEST THE BEGINNING."

"Like I said," Boss temporized, "that's been a while. I dunno how long; I don't keep in touch with Outside. But I guess a few years. Started losing my hair, till I put an end to all that."

"YOU'RE MAKING ME IMPATIENT, JUNIOR," Retief told the shaken man.

SURE, BUT THIS HIT ME PRETTY SUDDEN, the familiar silent Voice objected. I GOT TO HAVE TIME TO ADJUST TO ALTERED CIRCUMSTANCES. WHADD AYA MEAN, 'JUNIOR'? I'M STILL NUMBER ONE. GIMME A BREAK!

"THE SAME KIND OF BREAK YOU GAVE MR. MAGNAN?" Retief demanded.

HEY, BEN'S OK. JUST GOT HIM LOCKED IN A HOLDING CELL, IS ALL: TO KEEP HIM OUTA MY HAIR. BOY, WAS HE FULL OF PLANS! I TRIEDA TELL HIM BUT HE WOULDN'T LISTEN! ANYWAY, I WAS JUST GOING TO LET HIM OUT!

"Pass that for now," Retief said aloud. "I'll see about the formal charges later. Just get him in here, clean, well-fed, healthy, and right now."

AS I SAID, THAT WAS PRECISELY MY INTENTION, came the silent reply. CAN'T BLAME ME: HE COULD HAVE SPOILED EVERYTHING.

Boss went to an inconspicuous door marked Supplies and opened it. In the semi-darkness, Retief saw Magnan, standing on an upended shoe-rack, his head and shoulders out of sight as he struggled to climb higher through an open hinged panel in the ceiling of the cramped space.

"Retief!" Magnan's muffled voice cried into the space above. "Only a little more! I can see light! Just catch my hand and give me a little boost!"

"Relax, sir," Retief said behind him; Magnan started, lost his footing and fell to the floor with complicated *thump*ling. He struggled to his feet at once, peering out into what must have seemed to him the brilliant glow of the well-lit office.

"Don't come up *behind* me like that!" he wailed. "I was almost through, now I've got to start it all again!"

"Never mind, Mr. Magnan," Retief soothed. He gave his distraught senior a hand out. Magnan saw Boss and shied.

"Retief!" he yelped. "Look out! Behind you!"

"That's the fellow they call Boss," Retief replied unperturbed. "Actually he's Line Captain Sol Z. Goldblatt, presumed lost in space but actually quite well, as you see."

"B-but that was over a century ago!" Magnan objected, sidling so as to keep Retief between himself and the object of his glassy stare. "Anyway, there's a monster loose with green and yellow scales, and the *biggest* fangs I ever saw! Look out! It's about to leap at you! I barely escaped into the closet, before . . .!" He leapt for the door to the storeroom, but Retief intercepted him.

"Be calm, Ben," he advised the struggling First Secretary: then, to Boss, again miming the Big Voice:

"STOP FOOLING, JUNIOR!"

"Help, Big Voice!" Magnan screeched. "Make it go away!"

Retief restrained the panicky senior diplomat and turned to Boss. "No more tricks, Captain," he instructed the stocky man, who nodded eagerly.

"I don't get it," Boss complained. "I got the feeling there for a minute that *you* were Worm. But that can't be, because I happen to know you Embassy Johnnies only been here on Zanny a week, and old Worm has been here longer'n me! So how about it, feller? What goes on?"

"You were just telling me, remember," Retief countered. "Go back to where you were losing your hair."

"Oh; well, after I got things kind of shaped up here—cleaned out Boony's alley and all; I figured, why shave? So I done away with my whiskers, and itching—never did like to itch much—and fat, too." He patted his firm belly. "I got like padding, but I ain't fat."

"Good thinking," Retief congratulated him. "But maybe you'd better go a little farther back."

"Uh, to Before—I see what you mean," Boss acceeded readily. "Well, I was conning my command—old Tiglath-Pileser III, in to a cold turkey approach on this here uncharted planet—which I registered her with GPS, called her Goldblatt's Other World, seeing's I already registered the first Goldblatt's—but in the log I named her Zanny-du, after a book or something I heard about—that was after I survived the clobber-in—I can't call it a landing—and found the ice-caves." Boss paused to catch his breath.

"Damn Worm was responsible," he said in a less enthusiastic tone "—contacted me a Luna out, made me see a Class One installation where there was nothing but jungle and gnats; even gave me bogus contact numbers from Approach Control. Some wise guy, that Worm. Well, it took me a couple days in the automed to get it together, and another couple to cut my way outa Command Deck—I'll tell youse, them bulkheads was folded up like a deck chair—anyways, I looked around, and found out I'd discovered me a .999 Terry world. Not a bad place at all, except fer them damn gnats. Ain't as bad lately. I was kind of lonely, at first. My crew got clear in the lifeboats and took me a year to find most of the boys. A few are still MIA. So, I found this nice little joint with a neon sign and all and I went in, and—"

"One moment," Magnan interrupted curtly. "You mean to tell us that, while wandering through an uninhabited jungle on an unknown world far off the spaceways, you came upon a commercial establishment, there among the hang-a-man trees?"

"Sure," Boss confirmed promptly. "I guess I seen what I seen."

Magnan turned to Retief. "Are we to listen solemnly to this ruffian's outrageous lies?"

"Remember the Cloud Cuckoo Club," Retief cautioned his colleague. "And Nudine, and the rather good service back in the ice-cave. We've seen stranger things than a neon sign."

"To be sure," Magnan conceded distastefully. "And in any case what's this nonsense about Captain Goldblatt? It's well-known the captain died heroically over a century ago, as I said. What I want to know is what's he done with Gaby?"

"Don't know no Gabby," Boss grunted. "Had a Lippy around here a while back, but old Worm got him or something," he added indifferently.

Magnan caught Retief's arm. "Make him tell, Jim! I know he's kidnapped her, just as he did me! Poor child, alone and frightened half to death stuffed in some closet or worse."

"Why, Benny," Gaby's melodious voice spoke up from the outer door. "You really *do* care!" She came quickly across to Magnan, took his hand and patted it. "I'm all right," she reassured her patron. "Old Boss here tried to give me a hard time, but I know him too well for that! Last time I got him pissed off, he stuck me in that hot dog stand out in the park—but that worked out all right, too, Benny: you came along and here I am!"

Magnan gazed wonderingly at her. She was dressed now in a gown of metallic wine-red and had a fresh gardenia in her hair. He squeezed her hand. "Now that

I know you're all right, I can deal with this scoundrel," he told her, and turned to face Boss.

"You may as well get on with your fantasy," he ordered. "Just what did you find when you went inside this neon-lit commercial enterprise you'd have us believe in?"

"I don't care if youse believe in it or not," Boss muttered. "This here feller ast me to tell it, so I was doing like he said, that's all—only there's something funny going on here: I hadda idea old Worm poked his snout in . . ." He looked at Retief with sudden crafty suspicion. "But that was *you*, fooling around with my dome, right?"

"DON'T BOTHER YOUR PRETTY HEAD," Retief commanded.

Boss jumped. "There!" he yelped. "You done it again! Old Worm won't like it when he finds out you been impersonating him!"

Magnan looked at Retief in puzzlement. "What's he talking about, Jim?" he demanded. "How in the world would a Terran diplomat imitate this fabulous Worm?" He hugged Gaby as he spoke. She responded with a radiant smile, then freed herself and said, "I got to get back on the tables, Benny. See you." She kissed his forehead and was gone. Magnan's "Gaby! Wait!" came too late.

2

"IT'S NOT HARD," the words which Magnan recognized as Retief's formed silently in his awareness. "IT'S JUST A FORM OF FURFLING, WHICH YOU RECALL DEAR OLD D'ONG TAUGHT US. HOLDING IT TO A TIGHT PERSON-TO-PERSON BEAM IS THE ONLY DIFFICULT PART."

"Oh," Magnan nodded wisely. "Furfling, eh? I'd almost forgotten those silly tricks. But at the moment, hadn't we better be getting on with it?" He looked expectantly at Boss.

"Well, OK," the latter responded, "so inside, this place turned out to be a billiards room, which I'm pretty good with a stick, so pretty soon I'm the new owner. This fella had it before, name of Vince, trieda hustle me, the schmuck. I never missed a shot." Boss paused reminiscently.

"Well, after I found out how good I was, I thought about it and seen there was a little sort of trick to it: hadda make a pitcher in my head, like, of that ball dropping, and then sort of *push*. So I got this idea: why not try it on somethin' else besides the spheres, eh? So I was remembering about this holoplay I seen once, where the Boss had this really class office back o' the club, with these red carpets and chrome-plated steps and all, so I went inna back room—and there it was! Am I dumbfounded! I check the built-in-bar, and it's stocked with the best: genuine Cordon Bleu and Old Smoky bourbon, and Bridgit Terry's potheen, and Blue-beard's rum, and Marlowe rye, and Scotch that was made by the Tuatha de Danaan and a hunnert years in the keg, and a cooler fulla real aged Pepsi—the works! I and my boys had it made! Then one day when I'm onna phone to the Coast, this strange voice cuts in and yells at me to lay off the seventh order stuff, which I'm stretching the space/time/Vug continuum pretty thin, it says. Well, I got to admit I was a pretty cocky guy, with my three Bentleys in the garage out back, and seventy-two suits in the closet, all cut by a angel and all; used to giving the orders, not taking 'em, so I up and says back to old Worm—cause that's who it was, see—which I hadn't heard from him in a long time—rascal growed since then—anyways, I says, 'you stick to your turf and leave me handle my own business!' " Boss shook his head and looked at the toes of his well-shined shoes. "So all of a sudden two mugs which I never seen 'em before come busting in here and try to get heavy with me. ME! The Boss, and they're tryna tell me to lay off—started talking all that hot jazz about—what'd they call it . . ? 'Bolixing up the seventh order harmonics' or like that! I tole 'em I don't play no harmonica, nor no

Jew's harp neither—and the onney order I caller in was for a medium pepperoni pizza, hold the anchovies! Them bums was nuts!"

"Yes, yes," Magnan prompted. " 'Seventh order harmonics'—it's all beginning to make sense. Pray continue."

"Well, I taken and thrown 'em out, and just then old Worm—anyways a little later I found out it was Worm—done that trick again of getting at me from inside: HAVE A CARE, it says. YOU'VE CAUSED ME A TRIPLE NODE-ACHE EVER SINCE YOU POPPED UP ON MY PSYCHONIC INTERFACE! It always talks funny like that. But I tipped wise and started watching close how it done it, and I seen right off it was doing like when I *push*, onny it give it a little *twist*-like, and I tried it my ownself, back at Worm, and I says, *You stick to your turf, Junior, and I'll stick to mine, OK?* Now I ast you," Boss peered anxiously at Magnan, "that's fair enough, right? But old Worm still tries to gimme a hard time and all of a sudden it gives a little extra *twist-twist*, and my red Wiltons are gone and I'm standing on bare concrete! The nerve o' the bum! So natcherly, I use the same trick and put it back, and then it fades out to a dirty pink, and I make it deep purple and then all of a sudden old Worm folds his hand; I'll never forget it:

I PERCEIVE THAT I DISSIPATE MY ULTRA-ORDINAL ENERGIES, he says, AT AN EXCESSIVE RATE. YOUR CURIOUS MIND, THOUGH UNTRAINED—"hah!" Boss interrupted himself—"And me with a Trade High School diploma!" IS POSSESSED OF QUITE EXTRA-ORDINARY LATENCIES. I SHALL ACCORDINGLY IGNORE YOU FOR NOW, AND DEAL WITH THE PROBLEM LATER. MEANTIME, I SHALL TEMPORARILY CONCEDE TO YOU THE VOLUME OF SPACE/TIME/VUG YOU NOW CONTAMINATE, THEREIN TO ACT IN THE CAPACITY OF MY LIEUTENANT. I ASSIGN TO YOU AN APPROPRIATE DESIGNATION: JUNIOR. HAVE A CARE, JUNIOR, it tells me, and since then I had no more problems—until the Embassy big shot comes along and start sticking his nose in, which he's likely to get it stuffed fulla lint yet!" Boss swept his visitors with a defiant stare and fell silent.

"Do you imagine, sir," Magnan demanded sternly, "that you can easily intimidate duly accredited officers of a Terran diplomatic mission?"

"Old Worm don't mess around," Boss commented. "It'll flame ya where ya stand without scorching the carpet, which it don't like no wise guys tryna hassle its very own lootenant already!"

"Well, I didn't mean, I mean, I only meant—" Magnan explained.

"Mr. Magnan is too polite to say it," Retief interjected. "But as for myself, I flunked Hypocrisy at the Institute. You used to be one hell of an astrogator, Captain, but you're a damn poor liar."

Boss arranged what he thought was a dumbfounded expression on his round face, an effort which caused his bushy eyebrows nearly to merge with his hairline. He pointed a stubby forefinger at his chest. "You calling me a liar, or what?" he growled.

"You got that one right," Retief confirmed. "You picked up a few tricks, all right," he went on, "but not by studying the Worm's sub-vocalisms; the fact is, you're holding a hostage—the real Junior. Worm's talented offspring, no doubt. That's why Worm hasn't redistributed your component atoms as a fine dust on the cave floor."

"Retief!" Magnan objected. "What possible grounds could you have for that remarkable accusation? Here in the center of Mr. Boss's stronghold, we're dependent on his good will, don't you realize that? Why antagonize him?"

"I guess it's because I kind of liked Junior," Retief told his immediate supervisor. "I think the captain here took advantage of his good will and inexperience to sucker him. That about right, Captain?"

THAT IS PRECISELY COR—the unmistakable tones of the Big Voice boomed out, abruptly cut off.

"See?" Boss crowed. "Even old Worm ain't saying nothing against me! Now I guess I had about enough o' you two wise guys!" He started defiantly past Retief, who put out a foot and deftly jerked it back. Boss hit the red carpet face-first and looked up with an expression like a spoiled infant gauging the most effective microsecond to utter a wail.

"It can't," Retief told the fallen Boss patiently, "while you have Junior. Let's get back to your story."

"Me? I got no Junior!" Boss started as he climbed to his feet. "Let's see you prove anything!"

"That neon sign you found in the woods," Magnan said, "it didn't by any chance read 'Cloud Cuckoo Club,' did it?"

"Naw," Boss made a brushing-away gesture, "nothin like that." He paused as if listening intently. "Well, maybe," he amended, then, "OK, OK, I get it!" He put his hands over his ears and looked resentfully at Retief. "Anyways, I went in, and after I gave this sharpie a few lessons in cuemanship—"

"Cuemanship, or prestidigitation?" Retief asked, as if idly.

"You tryna say I cheated the sucker?" Boss demanded hotly, and mimed Wrath Held in Restraint (732), a weak -c, Magnan estimated.

"Look here, Mr. Boss," Magnan spoke up in the reasonable tone of a lynch mob victim suggesting that his captors quit kidding around now, and join him in a drink. "You must remember that my colleague and I are after all, men of words, not deeds, and I'm sure Mr. Retief meant no disrespect."

"Save that for yer memoirs. Jest in case you live to write 'em," Boss suggested curtly. "I clipped that Vince pretty fair and square, almost—anyways, it was all going to waste—them fellers never knowed what they had—I seen it and I taken it without hardly no blood-shed! After, the Worm come and faked-up the town around the club. And I ain't giving it up—not after nigh two hunnert year! I guess the Statute o' Limitations done run out some time ago. So just you boys beat it back to yer boss and tell him Goldblatt's Other World is shipshape and bristle-fashion, and don't need no outsiders coming along to start messing things up!" As Boss concluded his outburst, his jaw dropped, his eyes widened, and he slapped his own jaw with a sharp report.

Magnan drew a deep breath to begin his assurances that all would be as Boss decreed, but Retief caught his arm.

"Don't fold our hand yet, sir," he urged, then paused as a sensation like a hot needle in his brain jabbed once and was gone. "Did you feel that?" he asked Magnan. "A sort of probe, not quite in the audible range."

Magnan jerked his arm away from contact. "Do let me be!" he yelped. "It's not you, Retief! It's something else—it's poking me in the head!" He put both hands over his ears and screwed his eyes shut. "It's not quite . . ." he muttered between clenched teeth. "No! Stop that!" he yelled. Behind him, Boss had sunk to his knees and was shaking his head as if dazed.

"I'll *do* it!" he roared. "I tole ya I'd do it, and I'm gonna do it!" His eye fell on Magnan and he leaped at the slender diplomat and seized him in a bear hug, eliciting a sharp yelp and a kick in the shin from Magnan. As the two struggled, Retief became aware of a second curious hot-wire sensation behind his eyes. Vision blurred; the floor turned soft under his feet. Waves of hot and cold struck him like palpable blows. Now skyrockets were spewing fire in his mind.

I'M SORRY TO CAUSE YOU DISCOMFORT, the giant carved-from-granite words loomed in the foreground. THE TIGHT BEAM WAS MY ONLY HOPE; I PRAYED YOUR MIND COULD ACCOMMODATE IT. SO FAR, SO GOOD. YOUR COMPANIONS ARE MOMENTARILY NON COMPOS MENTIS, BUT THEY'LL SOON BE ALL RIGHT, EXCEPT PERHAPS FOR SOME RESIDUAL LOSS OF THE REAL/ UNREAL DISCRIMINATORY FACILTY. NOW TO MATTERS OF IMPORT:

With an effort, Retief focused his attention on the

giant stone words: Voice, it appeared, was concentrating its phenomenal mind-to-mind faculty on a 'private-line' linkage. He gathered his forces, and, using his own imitation of the alien being's 'voice,' interjected:

"TONE DOWN THE GAIN. YOU'RE KNOCKING MY CONSCIOUSNESS OFF-LINE."

SORRY, came the prompt reply, now at a comfortable level. FRANKLY, I NEED YOUR HELP. THIS BOSS PERSON HAS DISRUPTED MY PARADIGM. I HAVE TRIED TO ACCOMMODATE HIS INTERFERENCE INTO MY OWN HALCYON GESTALT, BUT THE INCOMPATIBILITY RUNS TOO DEEP. I SENSE IN YOU A KINDRED SPIRIT—A LINK, I HOPE, BETWEEN MY WORLD-VIEW AND THAT OF YOUR UNFORTUNATE BUT UNDOUBTEDLY POTENT KIND. WILL YOU JOIN ME, EXPERIMENTALLY, JUST FOR A MOMENT?

"You'll have to show me how," Retief said aloud.

DON'T MUMBLE, PLEASE, was the prompt response. BUT YOU ARE WILLING TO MAKE THE ATTEMPT, I GATHER. NOW JUST LOWER THAT BARRIER THERE. . . . an impalpable pointer indicated a ghostly structure deep in Retief's subconscious. He made an effort of will and felt the wall dissolve. At once, Worm's Voice came in more intimately, now in a small concise elite typeface rather than megalithic form.

THE ONLY WAY TO REJECT THIS INTRUSION INTO MY PRIMARY POSTULATE IS TO FIND COMMON GROUND BETWEEN HIM AND YOURSELF, NONE EXISTING LINKING ME WITH HIS DEEPEST FANTASIES, WHICH ARE OF VIOLENCE AND VAINGLORY, CONCEPTS WILDLY ALIEN TO MY OWN PEACEFUL ASPIRATIONS, the Voice expatiated. HMM, I'LL HAVE TO RUMMAGE A BIT . . .

Retief was aware of a disturbing sensation somewhere behind his memory; bright flashes winked and faded, then steadied. He looked down, saw the sturdy legs of a ten-year old, his feet in polished boots with jeweled spurs. His hand went to his side, found the hilt of the chrome-plated saber that hung there. He drew it, snapped down the chin-strap of his helmet, and started along the tiled street in the deep twilight. High facades in a classic style lined the avenue, and at the end a great edifice towered. Retief felt his heart beat faster. He was seeing the ruined city of Northroyal—as it once was.

No one moved in the silent street, but light glowed in a window here and there, and the portico of one radiant edifice blazed with lights. It was the Hall of the Fallen in Battle, Retief realized, from pictures he had seen of the ruins, yet here it was, pristine.

NOT QUITE, a Voice spoke up suddenly and bewilderingly. Retief's thoughts roiled; he felt vaguely that he should recognize the silent voice, but the thought was elusive; it slipped away and he caught half-glimpsed impressions of cold, deep darkness, a table laden with exotic food, a red carpet and a man—almost but not quite familiar. As he watched, a whole side of the portico ahead went dark. He heard faint sounds, followed by a sharp *smack!* and another element of the glowing design disappeared. He hurried toward the sounds. A man appeared—no, he realized, a boy, slightly older than himself, a stocky lad with a truculent swagger. The boy advanced to the lighted archway above the grand stairs, then paused and raised his hand. The arch went black. The boy laughed raucously and executed a clumsy parody of the *Grande Pavane*, the ancient stately dance of Northroyal.

Retief ran forward, heard himself shout in the uncertain tenor of a pre-teener: "Stop that, you!"

The capering boy halted and looked around, a surprised expression on his blunt features. "Who're you, dummy?" he called derisively, and concluded his insulting parody by bowing from the waist. Retief climbed up the wide steps to him, and the vandal fixed his eyes on the drawn sword and mimed astonishment. "Would you cut down an unarmed man?" he yelped in pretended terror. Instead of replying, Retief sheathed the weapon and the other lad at once produced an eighteen-inch truncheon from his ragged sleeve. He made a tentative pass at Retief, who grabbed the club, jerked it from the other's hand

and threw it clattering down the white marble steps.
The older boy backed off, then turned and ran off
between the looming, half-lit columns. Retief went
around to the right side, where the running boy reappeared a moment later; he skidded to a halt as he saw
Retief.

"What do *you* care about this old dump?" the boy
demanded, circling warily in an attempt to maneuver
Retief into a position with his back to the steep drop-off
at the end of the column row. "I know you," he stated
defiantly. "You're one o' them kids from the Old School.
Whatta *you* know?" As Retief said nothing, the boy's
derisive tone became more confident.

"I heard youse boys are all sissies," he sneered.
"Well, I'm Mean Soup, and I do as I like." He fumbled
at his belt and produced the energy weapon with which
he had shot out the lights. Retief kicked it from his
hand, and Soup jumped to recover it, but Retief tripped
him down the steps. At the boy's yell, two other teen-
agers appeared; they were slightly older than Soup, and
dressed, like him, in tattered cast-offs. Retief put his
back to the wall, watching both of them as they fanned
out, one left, one to the right. But immediately, two
more ragamuffins emerged from the shadows of the
columns, then more, until Retief was ringed in by a
dozen unkempt louts, each of them carrying an object
Retief recognized as an antique unit battle honor pried
from the walls of the temple. The tallest of them swag-
gered forward and stepped ten feet from Retief and
assumed a *dai-ako-nichi* stance.

"We're the Trashers, jerk," he announced. "I'm Dude,
the War Chief. You looking for trouble?" He advanced
a step, then leapt, aiming a kick at Retief's head. Retief
knocked the extended leg aside, stepped in, and kicked
Dude's other foot from beneath him. The nearly adult
Trasher's head struck the marble paving-slab with a
bonk! and enough force to scramble his eyes out of
focus. He made pawing motions, then relaxed and lay

supine. No one else moved. Soup had crept back up
the steps. He got to his feet and yelled at the others:

"Are you bums Trashers, or choir-boys?"

"Put everything back," Retief ordered. Soup turned
on him with a yell, nearly fell down the steps again, and
said:

"Just who are you, creep, all dressed up like Mama's
little soldier-boy? Get that fancy suit," he called over
his shoulder. "Let's see how that gold braid and them
fancy buttons look on *us!*" He edged closer, as if casually, and Retief knocked him back down the steps. This
time the boy got up and loped away up the empty
street.

"Well, how about it, Trashers?" one gang-member
spoke in the lengthening silence. "Are we going to
watch how this kid cleans up on Trashers one at a time,
or do we teach him some respect, or what?" No one
moved or replied. Retief pointed at a husky lout of
about eighteen, who was holding an enameled Badge of
Merit engraved with the name of a famous Brigade.

"You first," Retief ordered. "Put it back." The boy
dropped the heavy casting with a brazen *clang!* which
echoed among the columns. At Retief's level look, he
stooped and recovered the centuries-old relic.

"Durn thing's heavy," he complained. "I din't want it
anyways." He turned and went back inside the Hall.
The others muttered and closed ranks. Retief looked at
another boy, this one with the three-hundred-year-old
rhodium-plated helmet of a Battle Officer of grade five
perched incongruously on his unkempt mane of bushy
hair.

"You, too," Retief ordered. The boy backed a step as
if to blend into the crowd.

"Whatsa matter with you?" he demanded. "What's
wrong with having some fun? Who are you, anyway?"

"He's some big shot's kid," another volunteered. "Look
at the fancy outfit. He's dressed up like the Prince
Imperial."

"Got him a toy sword, too," commented another, a well-grown boy with a few straggly whiskers. He brought out from behind him a sheathed cavalry saber dating back to the days of Rhoxus I. He drew the blade and threw the sheath aside.

"I rated Master Swordsman in my YMNA class," he stated, and advanced a step. "You want to try me, kid?" Without awaiting a response he crouched slightly and executed a *dorchoi* leap which put him within three feet of Retief, his extended saber having passed between Retief's arm and chest. His grin disappeared when he realized he had come to rest with the needle-point of Retief's saber prodding his throat.

"Put it back," Retief said quietly.

"I was *going* to," the boy muttered as he leaned back, away from the sword-point. The whole gang followed him back in between the columns.

YOU SEE NOW HOW FECKLESS THESE HEROICS WERE, AND ARE, the disembodied voice put in gently. NOW TO MORE IMPORTANT MATTERS. As the voice ceased, the darkling sky dimmed into instant deep twilight, then full darkness. For a moment the glow from the remaining lights above the classic architrave illuminated the steps; then it, too, winked out, leaving Retief in darkness. Something stirred close by.

"Retief, where *are* you?" Magnan's worried voice spoke up near at hand. Retief blinked, concentrated on gathering his awareness, saw dim light on a red carpet and polished woodwork. Magnan stood dithering before him in the gloom, and across the room Boss was crouched against the wall, whimpering:

". . . like I was scared of," he babbled. "I done went nuts! Can't stand bein' crazy!" He got to his feet and looked around as if seeing the luxurious office for the first time. "Who are youse guys!" he demanded as his eye fell on Retief and Magnan.

"N-nobody, Mr. Boss," Magnan hastened to assure him. "That is, I'm just B and O officer, and this is, ah,

Retief; he handles the semi-annual requisition and that sort of thing. We were just going." He tugged at Retief's sleeve and edged toward the door.

"Nobody, huh?" the Boss echoed. "That does it! Now I'm having a conversation with guys which there ain't nobody here." He clutched his head with both plump, be-ringed hands and sank into a chair.

"Just a minute, sir," Retief demurred. "Before we go, hadn't we better find out where we've been?"

"*Been?*" Magnan cried, as if Astonished at an Unwarranted Leap in Logic, third class (1291-3-a). "Why, we've been right here in this dismal cave, where else?"

"A cave with red Aga-Khagan carpets?" Retief queried. "And why were you locked in the closet?"

"Why, as to that," Magnan temporized, "I was simply wedged in among the rocks there. . . ." His voice trailed off as he glanced toward the still open door of the tiny chamber in which he and been confined. "Oh, dear, Jim," he muttered. "We'd best hurry back to the Embassy and lie down; I'm having one of my dizzy spells."

"I've never heard that you had dizzy spells, Ben," Retief commented.

"This is the first one," Magnan snapped. "You know, like 'the first annaul golf tourney' and so on; candidly, Jim, I've felt rather off my feed ever since we first saw that Cuckoo Club. It's as though the whole planet is out of alignment with the entropic vector; especially Vugwise."

"And so it is, Ben," Retief agreed. "Something to do with the problyon flux, according to Boss."

"Then perhaps I'm *not* going dotty," Magnan groaned. "And I still haven't actually rescued poor Gaby from this den of vice."

Retief strolled across to Boss, who was still holding his head and moaning softly.

"Where's the lady?" Retief asked quietly.

Boss looked up, miming indignation. "What dame's that?" he yelped. "I keep no dames in my office! Got a couple out on the floor to hustle the marks, but I don't hardly never see 'em."

"I'm interested in one named Gaby," Retief told him. "She was here just a moment ago."

"Oh, her," Boss groaned. "Tryda make friends with her once—a long time ago—and she like rebuffed my kindly overtures and I hadda exile the broad. Run her off and tole her not to never come around no more. Don't know how she got in here. Whatta *you* know about old Gaby, anyways?"

"She left here only a moment ago," Magnan supplied, having come up beside Retief. "Before that, she was helping me extricate myself, then I heard her scream—and now where is she?"

"Must be a different Gaby," Boss said indifferently. "Onney dame around here today is a dice-girl they call 'the Glutton.' She come in to get a new supply of dominoes, tole her I was busy and she left in one o' them huffs—into the john, there." He indicated a discreet door adjacent to the storage closet. "Must still be in there; I locked it, and it got no winder nor no back door. Take a look."

"But," Magnan objected, "one can hardly invade the 'Ladies'; do summon a female employee."

"I tole you, no dames is allowed in my office!" Boss growled.

"Except La Goulue (that's 'glutton' in French)," Magnan snapped back.

"I never ast for no Frog lessons," Boss grumped. "OK, I guess you ain't going to let up until I check." He strode to the door, and pushed the latch button savagely; the door swung inward and Gaby stepped into the room. She saw Magnan immediately and rushed across to hurl herself at him. Magnan patted her on the back, and over her shapely shoulder eyed Retief wildly.

"Really, my child," he rebuked the now-tearful girl, "such a display in public is likely to give rise to rumors as to our relationship!" He managed to disengage himself, and holding her at arm's length, looked uncertainly at her.

"What relationship?" she demanded. "You don't like me . . ." The words dissolved into a wail.

"See here, my girl," Magnan started sternly.

"Wrong play, Mr. Magnan," Retief put in. "This is where you kiss her. Go ahead, I won't look."

"It's not a matter of looking," Magnan objected, then, addressing the tearful woman: "Where have you been, dear? This boss person said he locked you in the Ladies!"

"I wasn't in no ladies," Gaby dismissed the idea. "What I was, I was lost in the Gray Place—and it's *his* doing!" She stabbed an accusatory finger in Boss's direction. "He's a bad 'un," she concluded. "What you going to do with him, Benny?"

"Why, just now I'm going to use him to get us out of this den of iniquity," Magnan stated, in the tone of an adman presenting a promotional campaign to a demanding client.

"Before we go," Retief put in, "we need to find the real Junior."

"I suggest you forget that silly idea, Retief," Magnan said loftily. He offered an arm to Gaby, who took it tenderly in both hands. "Oh, Ben, you're so masterful," she breathed.

"If you insist," Magnan acknowledged, then to Retief: "Just how do you plan to negotiate our escape route through this bewildering maze of now-you-see-it-now-you-don'ts?"

YOU FIND IT ALL QUITE SIMPLE, ONCE YOU HAVE REDE-FINED YOUR PRIME POSTULATES, the Big Voice boomed out.

"I suppose that has to do with the Vuggish aspects of the contretemps," Magnan commented dubiously.

WHAT ELSE? was the curt reply. Magnan looked pleadingly at Retief, trying to avoid Gaby's appealing look.

"That wasn't me," Retief assured his supervisor.

"T-then . . ." Magnan stammered. "Then, *it's* listening! It can help us!"

UNFORTUNATELY, Big Voice replied, SO LONG AS THE TRICKY CAPTAIN HOLDS IN THRALL MY SOLE GENETIC LEGATEE, I CAN DO NOTHING.

"But that's impossible!" Magnan objected. "Voice is virtually omnipotent! How could this mere tramp skipper exercise any restraint over him?"

MY JUNIOR IS BUT YOUNG. AS FOR HIS 'OMNIPOTENCE,' HE IS AT BEST A JOURNEYMAN TRICKSTER; AND THIS GOLDBLATT ENTITY IS CAPABLE OF A GUILE BEYOND THE EXPECTATIONS EVEN OF A SOPHISTICATED BEING. FREE JUNIOR TO RECEIVE HIS LEGACY AND YOU WILL FIND ME NOT UNGRATEFUL. FAIL, AND I SHALL BE FORCED TO UNLEASH DESTRUCTIVE FORCES OF THE EITHTH ORDER TO ACCOMPLISH THE CHORE MYSELF. THIS GALAXY WOULD FIND THAT REGRETTABLE. ACT PROMPTLY, BEFORE JUNIOR'S LATENCIES ARE FOREVER CURTAILED. THIS IS THE CRITICAL STAGE OF HIS EVOLUTION, AND TO START ANEW NOW WITH ANOTHER EATER LESS BOUNTIFULLY ENDOWED WOULD LIKELY CONSTITUTE AN ENTERPRISE EXTENDING BEYOND MY SCOPE, VUGWISE.

"Retief," Magnan whimpered, tugging at his subordinate's sleeve. "What are we to do? Clearly, we need to do it at once, but one might as well call on us to levitate as to take effective action anent this contretemps. Did it say 'Eighth order'? Gracious, I'm beside myself. Although one *could* whaffle, I suppose. But to what end?"

"Is everybody around here going nuts, or what?" Gaby demanded, giving Magnan's arm a proprietary yank. "A minute ago you were ready to conquer the world for me; now you're crying the blues!"

"Really, my dear, you must excuse me," Magnan babbled. "I'm quite at sea, with all these disembodied voices, and Retief's burlesque of them, and that closet I seem to have thought was a pile of rocks, and you, and—and . . ." He trailed off.

"And *me*?" Gaby echoed, looking discouraged. "What have *I* got to do with you losing your grip?"

"Why, when I first saw you—" Magnan attempted, but gave it up.

"Never mind sorting it out now, Mr. Magnan," Retief suggested. "We can do that when we've cleared things up a little better."

"But, Retief!" Magnan objected. "Perhaps you aren't aware of it, but our very own Counselor of Embassy, in connivance with Fred Underknuckle, the sneak, are involved, with Chief Smeer, in a diabolical plot to implicate the Mission in actual warmongering, to say nothing of eliminating you and me—and quite possibly Gaby and Nudine and Small as well—because we Know Too Much!"

"I already had a run-in with that Underknuckle character," Boss spoke up aggrievedly. "He come in here with some kind of self-appointed local flatfoot, tryna raid the joint, he says, but I know a muscler-in when I hafta deck him with his own bodyguard!"

"Yes, yes, Mr. Boss," Magnan dismissed the remark, "but you mustn't judge *all* diplomats by a single backslider! Most of us are dedicated public servants of the highest character! It is your clear duty to assist us in restoring a modicum of order to this chaotic situation. You may begin by divulging the wherabouts of the real Junior—and while you're about it, you may as well describe precisely how you managed to establish supremacy over an apprentice superbeing, and be brisk about it!"

"Well," Boss started, more calmly, "what I seen, when this here Junior first stuck his oar in—I seen right away he didn't have it all together, like old Worm; he was pretty clumsy with his psychojuntures and all—and I bet the kid never hadda handle a incipient vortex on the Vug level in his whole life! So that makes it easy for me to slip him a fast one—con him into dipping down below the alpha and get hisself all bolixed up in that mess down there—so I take over the kid's prime directive before he knows what hit him, and from there on, he was my property—hadda follow my lead or lose his grip and spin out along the Vug coordinate—and you know what that means?"

"I do?" Magnan replied dazedly. "It sounds most underhanded, Mr. Boss."

"Oh, you can call me 'Captain,' " Goldblatt suggested. "That Boss stuff is OK for the rubes and flatlanders, but you and me got to like conduct our negotiation on a little higher plane and all."

"What negotiation was that, Captain?" Magnan wondered aloud.

THAT WAS A MOST ILLUMINATING DISCLOSURE, CAPTAIN, the Big Voice spoke up. IT GIVES ME PRECISELY THE ANGLE OF IMPINGEMENT I REQUIRE TO EXTRICATE JUNIOR FROM INVOLUNTARY SERVITUDE. I AM INDEED GRATEFUL TO YOU, BENMAGNAN, FOR TEASING THE FACTS OUT INTO THE OPEN BY YOUR CLEVER SIMULATION OF IDIOCY. NEATLY DONE!

"Well!" Magnan said huffily, but Retief caught his eye. "I suggest you pass on that one, sir," he said. "After all, it *was* intended as a compliment."

Magnan seemed to be about to pursue the point, but instead he winced, and blurted. "Easy! Easy! Look here, Big Voice, or Worm or whatever you call yourself—that's an actionable invasion of privacy—one more like that and you could get *me* disoriented along the Vug axis!" He turned to Retief. "I've been considering our situation; consider: we perceive the time axis as a substrate, in constant uniform motion; space is the static substrate against which we ourselves have some limited power of locomotion. Now, the Vug axis is itself, like time, in motion, and confers independent motion upon matter—ergo: *if* I should find myself divorced from the natural one: one relationship therewith, I'd likely find myself flying off along either the spatial or the temporal axis, or perhaps both! Since you seem to enjoy a certain influence with Worm, *do* tell it to stop meddling with my tertiary postulate!"

I WILL RESPECT YOUR WISHES IN THIS MATTER, BENMAG-

NAN, came the prompt response. BUT OF COURSE I HAVE NO
INTENTION OF ALLOWING THE DESTINY OF THE SOLE CUSTO-
DIAN OF MY GENETIC HERITAGE TO BE ABORTED BY THE CAP-
TAINSOLGOLDBLATT ENTITY. WILL YOU, JIMRETIEF, JOIN ONCE
MORE WITH ME IN AN EFFORT TO PRY LOOSE THE AFORE-
SAID ENTITY'S ILLICIT GRIP UPON POOR JUNIOR'S PSYCHE?

"Sure," Retief replied. "But this time let's stay away
from the daydreams."

AS YOU WISH; STILL THE CHARADE DID UNCOVER, PERIPH-
ERALLY, ONE OR TWO OF YOUR CONCEPTUAL FOUNDATIONS.

This time, the tiled avenue was thronged with people, a crowd gathering, for what seemed to be some
public event. Over the babble of excited voices, the
blare of the ancient long trumpets echoed; then the
crowd parted to reveal a pair of mountainous beasts
brilliantly caprisoned, whose long, recurved tusks were
tipped with deep red core-jewels as big as tennis balls.
In a noudah atop one of the tandem dire-beasts, there
sat a man, broad and deep of shoulder and chest, clad
in the Imperial green. As he raised a hand in friendly
hail to the population, a bolt of white fire lanced out
from a narrow black-fronted building to his right, to
detonate in a blinding flash which left the dire-beast a
tottering ruin of torn flesh and gouting gore, while the
castle and its occupants had disappeared completely.
The cry that went up from the horrified crowd was like
the death-scream of a monster hill-devil. The other
dire-beast tottered and collapsed, blood-splashed but
apparently unhurt. Retief, quite involuntarily, leapt forward, pushed through the press of people, some struggling toward the scene of carnage, some wildly fleeing.
Even as he heard himself scream the word, 'father!', a
big man in the silver and green of the Guard caught his
arm and pulled him aside.

"Nothing you can do, Jimmy," he said as he lifted
the boy. "But there is that which I must do."

"No!" the boy Retief yelled and sought to grab the

big man's hand. "I command you, Captain Count William!"

The big man smiled uncertainly. "As you desire, Milord."

"My name's 'Jame'!" he shouted. "Let's go!"

LET IT GO, RETIEF ENTITY, a gigantic, disembodied voice boomed from the sky. LINK EASILY WITH ME AND WE WILL PREVAIL! NOW LET US EXTEND AWARENESS. AND PERHAPS. . . .

Instead of complying, the boy turned and ran into the shadowed interior of the temple. He stopped in the lee of a column of soap-smooth stone. On the glistening white marble block lay a small gold coin. Retief picked it up absently and stood listening. There was only silence. He started on, and at once the great, strange, silent voice boomed out, somehow more distant now. THERE YOU ARE! HOLD STILL! WHY DO YOU SEEK TO ELUDE ME? COME, JOIN WITH ME AND TOGETHER WE SHALL SOON DISCOVER WHAT WE SEEK. COME, NOW, JUST GENTLY, NO NEED FOR IMPULSIVE ACTIONS. DO COOPERATE.

Retief probed the darkness and encountered a maze of intangible barriers, like a series of nets guiding him in *that* direction. He turned and faced the opposite way.

A dim light sprang up, all around the periphery of the long rectangular platform surrounded by the columns. Cool air flowed across his face, bearing the scent of night-blooming flowers and perfumed smoke. Retief took a tentative step toward the shrine-like structure at the center of the uncluttered floor. It was a small rectangle of cut stone, and before it a fire smouldered on a brazier.

WHERE ARE YOU, NOW? The Voice demanded. I HAD YOU PLOTTED TO THE DEMINIT AND NOW AGAIN YOU SLIP AWAY. THIS IS NOT TO BE TOLERATED IN AN ALLY! SHOW YOURSELF LOYAL TO OUR COVENANT! HEED ME AND FOLLOW MY GUIDANCE WITHOUT FAIL! YOUR INTRANSIGENCE COULD TRIGGER A DISASTER! BE PRUDENT. THE FORCES INVOLVED

ARE BEYOND CALCULATION. NOW! the Voice commanded.
GO FORWARD TO THE STONE OF HROLFR, AND—

"What's inside there?" Retief asked the circumambient gloom, indicating the shrine.

EH? THAT IS NOT YOUR CONCERN! the Voice reprimanded
sharply. FOLLOW MY INSTRUCTIONS, NO MORE, NO LESS.
THE FORCES WE SEEK TO MANIPULATE WILL BE IN ALIGN-
MENT—AND A MIS-TOUCH COULD COLLAPSE THE PARADIGM—

At that point, Retief closed his mind to the insistent
Voice. At once he was aware of Boss's garish office and
Magnan's nervous presence. "Very well," he addressed
Voice patiently. "So far, you've communicated to
me, very poignantly, that something of value is threatened. Very well, I'm willing to help save it; so no more
charades."

AS YOU WILL, the Voice agreed grumpily. DIRECTLY TO
THE NEXUS, THEN.

As the silent Voice trailed off, Retief felt himself
catapulted into a whirling chaos of flashing lights, er-
ratic pressures and cacophonous sound. At the center of
the maelstrom, a vivid blue-white glare was the sole
constant within his perception. He moved toward it
against impalpable pressures. Magnan clung to his arm
with both hands. Retief saw it come into focus as a
glowing crystal as big as a baseball, multi-faceted, glittering. As Magnan whimpered behind him, Retief
gripped the doorknob, turned it, and stepped into a
small, drably furnished room where a young child, perhaps eight years old, thin, dirty-faced and clad in rags,
crouched in a corner. Magnan crowded in behind Retief.
A big, swarthy man in need of a shave sat with crossed
arms as big as pork hocks on a sagging wooden box
labelled PRODUCE OF BEGONIA. At sight of Retief,
the boy exclaimed and started to his feet, then at a snarl
from the swarthy man, fell back silently.

"Got a sick kid here," the man grunted in a surprisingly mellow baritone. "Can't do nothing with the little
devil; seems like he's went kinda off in the head. Tried

everything; hit him, starved him, chained him fer awhile—but no, he's got these big ideas. They call me George the Stick." He rose, hitched up his belt and waited.

Magnan swallowed audibly. "Ah, I am Mr. Magnan of the Embassy," he croaked. He indicated his companion. "This is Retief, my, ah, assistant. Please pardon the intrusion; it was noisy out there."

"Cheese!" George burst out, his eye roving past Retief and Magnan as if in expectation of a crowd at their heels. "There's what you call a Class One Discordancy going on out there and the guy waltzes through and says it was noisy! You must be quite a man! I don't know your angle, chum, but I'm on your side, you bet!"

"Relax, Vince," Retief suggested. "We're not here to choose up sides. Just answer a few questions, if you don't mind."

"And if I *do* mind," Vince came back in a defeated tone, "I guess you ast 'em anyways, right? How'd you know I'm Vince Scumelli?"

"Just a lucky guess," Retief told him. "Captain Goldblatt mentioned you."

Vince tapped his temple with a blunt forefinger. "That nut-case send you?" he barked. "What *more*'s he want?" Then he slumped on his broccoli box.

"Just a minute," Magnan put in sharply. "First this fellow said his name was George; now it's Vince." He glanced sharply at Retief. "How can we trust a man who's unsure of his own name?"

"I ain't unsure o' my name," the swarthy man contradicted in a surly tone. "Name's Vince Scumelli, just like yer partner said. What *I* said was they call me George the Stick, which I'm pretty good with a cue, see? Least I was until this Goldblatt come along. Come in one night, looking like that Robin's son, Caruso. Said his vessel done clobbered in, and big-hearted me, I let the bum in and he asts fer a game, so next thing I know, he's the new owner, and I'm shoved inna back room. That was maybe a couple weeks ago, and I been locked in here ever since, then yesterday the door opens and they shove this kid in here. Natcherly, I ast him what gives, but he ain't talking." Vince paused to grab at an imaginary fly in front of his face. "I'm ready to talk deal," he concluded gloomily. "Onney just lemme outa here."

"He's insane," Magnan commented without emphasis. "It's been well over two centuries since the Captain's disappearance."

"We were talking to him ten minutes ago," Retief reminded him.

Magnan shook his head impatiently. "I suppose there's no sense seeking logic in this irrational paradigm," he instructed himself firmly.

LOGIC IS FIRMLY GROUNDED ON THE VUG AXIS, the Voice put in. IT IS QUITE INDEPENDENT OF THE SPACE AND TIME DIMENSIONS. ONCE THE VUGGISH ORIENTATION OF THE PARADIGM HAS BEEN ALTERED—AND I WARNED HIM!—NO LOGIC CAN BE EXPECTED.

"I awready said I'll deal," Vince reminded his guests' back. "You don't need to go doing no ventriloquist tricks."

At that point the door opened and Captain Goldblatt/Boss staggered into the room. He slapped his forehead and recoiled at the sight of Retief. "You, again!" he lamented. "Whattaya want outa me?"

"The truth," Magnan responded promptly. "At first you said you'd been here for two centuries—a palpable absurdity; then you said two weeks. That, Mr. Boss, is quite inconsistent, as I'm sure you'll agree."

"Two hunnert year, two weeks, whassa difference?" Boss challenged. "You try sitting in a cell a while, you'll find out there ain't no time-posts to tell you how far you come. Ain't even got a watch."

"Why is this boy here?" Magnan demanded relentlessly.

"Vince already tole you, they shove the kid onto me

one day to make me miserabler'n what I already am. Kid's nuts; acts like he thinks I'm his valet or like that. How about it, kid?" He turned to the lad, who had gone to the vacated box and was sitting, looking calmly at Boss.

"You feel better now?" Boss suggested.

"Better than what, Mister Boss?" the kid asked. "I resent being confined," he added. "And it's your doing. I want—well," his voice faltered, "I don't exactly know what I want, but it sure isn't this—being locked in here with this surly lout."

Boss lunged toward the boy and somehow found his ankle hooked by the child's foot. The boy jumped back as Boss crashed on the crate, flattening the flimsy slats back.

"Kid's got no respeck, j'ear what the punk said? Talks like a book, 'surly lout,' he calls me! Me!" The swarthy man sat breathing hard and glaring resentfully at the boy.

"Who are you, lad?" Magnan asked in a kindly tone, with just a hint of Sternness Available As Needed (981-c).

"Don't waste no 981 on that lousy kid," Boss advised. "He wun't bat a eyelash if a full Ambluster unleashed a 989, Now You're Really Going to Get It, on him. Even a Z-plus. Hard as tube linings." Magnan ignored the comment and continued to look at the boy with benign expectancy. The lad returned a defiant look then stared into a corner.

"Really, my boy," Magnan said a trifle testily, "it's no good standing mute. We want only to help you, you know."

"All I need is for these guys to go away and stop bugging me," the boy muttered. "I was doing OK until they came along."

" 'They'?" Magnan queried. "I see only one guard."

"There's more of 'em," the boy told him. "Outside."

"There's nothing outside," Magnan objected, "except a, ah, class one discordancy, brought about, no doubt, by meddling by half-informed individuals."

"They're ahead of me," the boy grumbled. "Nobody informs *me* of anything, ever since—" His voice trailed off and for the first time he looked like a lost child.

"Still," Magnan pointed out, "we're here now—and the situation must be dealt with, not merely deplored. Now, Retief and I represent the Embassy of Terra— and the first order of business is for you to tell us all you know that would assist us in grasping, and thus mastering the situation. All right?"

"Whattaya talking to the kid for?" Boss demanded. "This here is man's work."

"He's lying to you," the boy told Magnan. "Said he was here first. He's lying."

Boss lunged again, but shied as Retief stepped into his path.

"Go sit down, Captain," Retief told the frustrated fellow, who went to a broken chair beside the door, pushed aside an empty carton, and perched tentatively.

"Now, tell us your name, boy," Magnan urged the child. "How old are you?" He waited, beaming. "Come, come, boy," Magnan said sharply. "I am a First Secretary of Embassy of Terra," he stated importantly. "How dare you offer me mute insolence?"

"Easy, Ben," Retief interjected. "From his point of view you're just a nosy stranger." He went over to the boy, and asked: "Would you like to get out of here?"

"That I would, sir," the child replied promptly.

"So would we," Retief told him. "Maybe you could give us some information that would help."

"You'll take me with you?" the lad responded eagerly. Retief nodded.

"Of course we'll take you," Magnan said impatiently. "But where? There's nothing outside that door but chaos. How are we to regain stable ground?"

"Got to rotate under it," the boy said, as if it were obvious. "See, old Capgoldblatt tricked me: Pried me loose from my primary postulate, and the whole Shrödinger function collapsed, anyways that's what Humphrey says. Well, it's pretty obvious we'll have to bypass all that and sneak out along a paradigmatic error of closure."

"Why, wherever did you learn such big words?" Magnan queried dazedly. " 'A paradigmatic error of closure,' you said. Why, the very concept is disconsonate with the fundamental postulates of modern physics. And who, pray, is this Humphrey?"

"Then you better find some new postulates," the boy dismissed the objection curtly. "And Humphrey is my friend. Don't look like much, but he helps me a lot, talking to me, and all."

"Talks to you?" Magnan echoed. "Just how does he do that, when you're confined here alone?"

"I don't care if you believe me or not," the lad stated defiantly. "How do I know how he does it?"

"Oh, dear," Magnan dithered. "I fear we've gotten off on the wrong foot. . . ."

The boy made a production of angling his sneaker-clad feet and eyeing them suspiciously.

"*My* feet are OK," he declared with finality. "Must be yours are mixed up." He craned in an exaggerated fashion to peer at Magnan's once-elegant but now scuffed melon slicers.

"Look OK, too," he decided. "So I still say it's your postulates. I think you got yer coordinates knocked slanchways coming through the Vortex. Better recalibrate."

"That's easier said than done," Magnan replied testily. "In the absence of reliable parameters."

PERHAPS I CAN HELP, the small voice spoke up abruptly.

"Good lord!" Magnan yelped, covering his ears. "After all these hours of silence, I thought you'd gone. Have you no duties requiring your attention?"

Meanwhile, the boy had backed away, then went past Magnan to take a stand beside Retief. "Look out for the Big Scary Voice," he yelped. "I don't want—"

WHAT YOU WANT, ALIEN EATER, IS OF LITTLE CONSE-
QUENCE, the Voice boomed out with such force as to
send Magnan to his knees, clutching his head as if to
prevent it from exploding.

Retief put a hand on the boy's unkempt head. "What's
your name, fella?" he asked.

"Sobby," the boy blurted. "I wasn't spose to tell
anybody. But I guess it's OK because that's only a
nickname."

"Who gave it to you?" Retief prodded.

"Old Marshall," the boy said promptly. "Use to call
him Barky, and one day he heard me. Said to you,
lad, I'm Field Marshall Prince Barcarol. And as for
yourself, by the same principle of nomenclature, the
rest of the lads will henceforth call you 'Sobby,' rather
that 'Sobhain,' or 'Milord.' "

"So your real name is 'Sobhain,' " Retief confirmed.
"That's a noble name, Milord. On his home world, a
few centuries ago, he was a national hero, 'the Prince of
the Green,' was his sobriquet. Your parents made a
good choice. Who were they?"

"They're the Anointed of Rohax," the boy stated flatly.

"So I had begun to suspect, Milord," Retief informed
the lad. "Can you tell us how you came to be here?"

"That man laid hands on me and dragged me in
here," Sobby said, giving Boss a look colder than the
core of Icebox Nine.

"That look was as cold as the core of Icebox Nine,"
Magnan contributed. "Colder. Why did he drag you in
here? Earlier, you said you were here before him."

"That was before," Sobby explained. "He locked me
in here, alone, and later on someone threw him in,
too."

"To be sure," Magnan mumbled. "But that's not
what Retief meant—"

"Retief?" the boy exclaimed, staring up at the tall
man with an astonished expression. "I knew Barky would

send someone—but, no, I suppose he didn't . . ." His voice trailed off uncertainly.

"He probably did," Retief said. "But you're correct: it wasn't me. I didn't know. But I'd like to help you, if you'll tell me what happened."

"Well, Battle Commander," the boy responded readily, "Captain Lord William came in one night and woke me up, told me about the—invasion I guess it was, not a revolution like that upstart Knout told everybody. Captain Willy got me out and aboard a fleet boat, and we made it to Vanguard without an intercept, and he made a deal with a Tip trader, Captain Goldblatt, to take me to the place Willy had made ready for me. He left me aboard and went out on an errand and never came back; so I did as he'd said and we shipped out. Three days out, the First Officer led a mutiny, and then they got to fighting over who was in charge, and let the maintenance go and burned the main coil, and got lost and made an emergency landing in the last world Goldblatt had in the navigator. They set up camp and nobody was watching me, and I escaped and wandered around in the park until I found the house, and then old Runt, from the ship, came along one day and hit me over the head, and I woke up here. Vince was the First Officer that killed Captain Goldblatt, and—"

"Hold hard, you little rat!" Boss yelled. "Don't you start lying about *me!* Matter of fact, I ain't even dead yet!"

"Be calm, Captain," Retief advised. The boy stood his ground calmly, but fell silent.

"That's why you're afraid of me," the lad told Boss.

"Go ahead, Milord," Magnan urged the boy. "You were just saying that some person named Runt assaulted you—"

"He must have waited for me," the boy explained. "I decided to go back out and try to find a loyal crewman, but as I stepped through the door, he struck me down, the cowardly swine."

"Calmly, lad," Magnan admonished. "That's all over and done: now we must apply our thoughts to the problem of escape."

"Why not just open the door and walk out?" Sobby suggested. "Now you're here, Boss won't be able to stop us."

As Boss started up with a reflexive snarl, Magnan waved him back. "Your only hope for clemency, sir," he advised the unshaven fellow, "is to lend us your assistance now. I assure that good behavior at the juncture will weigh heavily in your favor at the inquiry which will inevitably follow this farcical affair."

"Yeah?" Boss rejoined scornfully. "I don't see no junction. And what about the Vortex old Worm got set up out there?" He went to the door and opened it wide to reveal whirling snowflakes visible against the blackness.

"Close it, close it!" Magnan yelped. "We'll freeze in that icy wind!" He turned up the brocaded collar of his early mid-morning semi-demi half-cloak, official occasions, for use during, then turned a despairing look on Retief.

"Whatever are we to do?" he implored. "I confess I've quite lost my grasp of the tactical situation. After all that confusion in the closet-cum-rockpile, and then that dreadful chaotic state of affairs out there! All I can grasp is that this poor lad appears to be some sort of kidnapped princeling, and it's surely our duty to assist in his repatriation."

IT WAS PRECISELY TO THAT END THAT I LED YOU HERE, the almost forgotten Big Voice put in. I HAVE SUFFERED QUITE ENOUGH DISTURBANCE TO THE NATURAL ORDER OF THINGS. TAKE THE APPROPRIATE ACTION AT ONCE, AND RID ME OF THIS NUISANCE!

"Have a care, Big Voice, or whoever you are," Magnan responded testily. "It is hardly appropriate that a mere disembodied voice—and a silent one at that—should presume to issue commands to Terran diplomats. You

might try asking nicely," he added, in a more conciliatory tone.

"You heard Big Scary Voice too!" Sobby blurted. "So
it's not me going off my head, like old Runt said!"

"Anyway," Magnan added sulkily, still addressing the
Voice: "I already said we should help to rescue this
poor child. We're committed to do so!"

"I'm getting out of here," Boss stated. Hearing no
contradiction he enlarged on his thesis: "I can't take no
more!" He broke for the door, and they let him go.

"It's as well," Magnan commented. "He'd only have
been a nuisance in any event. Besides, I doubt he'll get
far in that cataclysm raging outside."

Retief went to the closet whence he had extricated
Magnan, opened the door and carefully examined the
interior. He turned and motioned to the boy. "Come
over here, Milord," he suggested; the lad complied.
Retief pointed to a space between stacked boxes and
hanging garments. "See if you can squeeze through
there," he said. "It was a bit too tight for Mr. Magnan,
but you should be able to make it." He lifted the lad
and boosted him up to the dark crevice, into which the
boy squeezed easily.

"What do you see, Sobhain?" Retief asked.

"It's home!" the boy called, his voice somewhat muffled but clear. "It's the field, and I see the Shallow Sea!
Boost me just a little higher, Commander, and I can
catch that branch and climb out of this hole. I don't
understand, but I like it! I thought I'd never see home
again, and all the time it was next door!"

"Not quite, Milord," Retief corrected.

Magnan crowded up behind him. "I smell fresh air
and spring flowers," he cried. "What's happening, Retief?
Have you found an escape route?"

Before he could reply, the boy cried out. "Oh, no!
It's a Rath raiding party, the scoundrels! As bold as can
be, riding in echelon across the Plain! Where are the
Guardians? Quickly, Battle Commander, we must give

warning!" As he spoke, the lad scrambled up and through and was gone.

"What's happening?" Magnan yelped. "What did he mean, about a raiding party? Where is he?"

"He got through, Mr. Magnan," Retief told his excited colleague. "I can't see anything through the opening except a dim light."

"Poor child," Magnan mourned. "And poor us as well, I fear. What are we to do, Retief? We seem to be sinking deeper and deeper into alien paradigm within alien paradigm! How are we ever to find our way out?"

"Let's start with the door," Retief said, and went to it. Boss was there before him, his back to the door.

"No, you don't, Mister. I know what's out there, and you ain't letting it in here!"

Retief gently pushed him aside.

"Just go sit on your chair and think enobling thoughts," he suggested, and flung the door wide open on a blast of discordant sound and garish light. Magnan, at his side, hunched his shoulders and averted his eyes from the chaotic spectacle. Retief took his arm and urged him through, and in an instant they were caught up in a hot, buffeting wind which nearly knocked Magnan from his feet. Retief hauled him upright.

"Try to ignore the distractions," he suggested. "Close your eyes and imagine we're walking across a level floor to the door across the room."

"B-but—" Magnan protested, "Boss's office should be here, not this kaliedophonic nightmare! We'd better go back!"

"We can't," Retief told him. "We can only go ahead. There's nothing behind us, not even chaos."

Magnan twisted to catch a glimpse, closed his eyes and shuddered. "It's the Vug dimension; I knew that meddling with that would only end in disaster! Lost in the Vug dimension! It's too grotesque to conceive! And for what? I came back to look for poor Gaby—and you came after me—we meant no harm. It isn't fair!"

FAIR! the Big Voice came faintly, muffled by the roar of reality in collapse. THAT CONCEPT IS A CURIOUS CONCEIT INVENTED BY YOUR OWN DEVIANT SPECIES. THE UNIVERSE KNOWS NOTHING OF JUSTICE! YOU DID WELL IN EXPELLING THE TROUBLESOME EATER FROM THIS PARADIGM. NOW TO CLEANSE THE NODE OF THE OTHER, LESSER, YET STILL DISTURBING NUISANCES. PROCEED AS YOU WERE. I NOTE AN ATTENTION OF THE ENTROPIC DENSITY ALONG *THAT* VECTOR. As the Voice fell silent, a glowing pink line traced itself across the tossing surface of pre-matter that lay at their feet. It dimmed and disappeared in the writhing, light-shot mist. Retief followed it, Magnan trailing, muttering half aloud.

". . . none of this can be so much as mentioned *en paspant* in my report. After who can say how many days of unauthorized absence from our posts of duty, we can do no more than say we were detained by circumstances beyond our control—that's if we ever do get back to sanity."

YOU CONSIDER AN AMBASSADORIAL STAFF MEETING TO BE 'SANITY'? the now-muffled Voice inquired. I SUGGEST YOU ABANDON THESE FRAGILE CONCEPTS, BENMAGNAN, AND CONCENTRATE YOUR FACULTIES ON THE IMMEDIATE PSEUDO-REALITY CONFRONTING YOU.

"Really!" Magnan huffed. "Your intrusiveness is exceeded only by your impracticality! How can one deal realistically with the unreal?"

REALITY, the Voice intoned, MAY BE DEFINED AS 'THAT WHICH APPEARS TO BE REALITY.' ABORT THIS STERILE CONCEPT AND PROCEED BOLDLY!

Retief took a step and disappeared from Magnan's view. "Retief!" Magnan yelped. "You *can't* go off and leave me here like this!"

"It's all right, Ben," Retief's voice replied calmly, as if emanating from directly ahead.

CHAPTER SIX

Looking about him, Retief saw nothing but a dense blackness; then a strip of greenish light appeared, which widened a moment later into a view of a sunny hillside, broken by a heap of blackish boulders apparently deposited by a melting glacier. Suddenly a great black horse came into view, walking calmly, with a small boy perched in the elaborate saddle.

"Hail, Sir Knight," Retief called cheerfully. "Didst thou unhorse the outlaw Farbelow?"

"Not I, Commander," Sobhain replied. "I saw the scoundrel scuttling from the thicket yonder, and captured his mount. At sight of him, his mob of rascals fled hither." He came up to Retief, just as Magnan, looking bewildered, emerged from behind the stone-pile, looking about fearfully. He halted at the sight of the horse, apparently not noticing the diminutive rider, and ducked back behind the boulder.

At that point, Boss hurried past Magnan and disappeared with a long-drawn wail like a man falling from a height.

"There!" Magnan bleated. "You see? Poor Mr. Boss 'proceeded boldly' and just look what happened to him!"

AND WHAT, PRECISELY, HAPPENED TO HIM? the Voice demanded relentlessly.

"Well, I don't rightly know," Magnan replied reluctantly, "but it surely wasn't anything pleasant."

IF YOU ARE HERE IN SEARCH OF PLEASURE, BENMAGNAN, the Voice countered, YOU HAVE PERHAPS ERRED IN VENTURING ABROAD TODAY.

"I'm here in the discharge of my duties as First Secretary of Embassy of Terra; specifically as Deputy Counselor of Embassy For Trivial Affairs!" Magnan rejoined testily.

THEN LET US HEAR NO MORE OF 'PLEASURES,' the Voice closed the subject.

"Stand fast, sir," Retief called to his immediate supervisor. "I'm going to try something."

"Try what?" Magnan yelped. "I demand to know what you propose. After all, my life is at stake! As well as your own, of course," he added.

"Reasonable, Mr. Magnan," Retief said, "but there's no time. Prince Sobhain is out there alone."

"Merely more illusion!" Magnan dismissed the idea. "In any case, I'm sure a case could be made that we've done all we could. Hardly our affair if the lad chooses to interfere in matters outside his legitimate interest-cluster!"

"Still," Retief countered. "It can hardly be our duty to stand idly by while he intercepts a gang of Rath cut-throats."

"Idly?" Magnan queried as if Amazed by an Egregious Non Sequitur, (1214-m). "We're lost in chaos, struggling to regain a stable paradigm, and you call that 'idle'?"

"Precisely," Retief confirmed. "Have you noticed the pattern of the events—or apparent events—of the past few hours?"

"Of course!" Magnan confirmed emphatically. "The pattern consists of our plunging ever deeper into matters not properly of concern to the Embassy of Terra. And I say it's high time that we take action to extricate ourselves from the deepening maelström!"

"Close, Ben," Retief commented. "But it's more structured than that."

ENOUGH! the Big Voice, now only Middle-sized, interjected. THESE SPECULATIONS REGARDING MATTERS LYING WELL BEYOND YOUR ABILITIES TO CONCEPTUALIZE, ARE FECKLESS!

"I guess they're feckful enough to require further investigation!" Magnan stated sharply. "After all, there's only one reality!"

THIS 'REALITY' TO WHICH YOU SO FREQUENTLY ALLUDE, the Voice began in a tone of disparagement, CAN YOU DEFINE IT MORE COGENTLY THAN IN TERMS OF APPEARANCES?

"Certainly!" Magnan promptly assured the bodiless entity. "It's ah, well, perhaps I can't actually define it, but you know as well as I—"

TELL ME, BENMAGNAN, IS THE PAST REAL? IN THE SAME SENSE AS THAT ITCH YOU ARE NOW EXPERIENCING BEHIND YOUR LEFT PINNA, FOR EXAMPLE.

"Yes, indeed," Magnan replied.

AND THE FUTURE? the Voice pressed him relentlessly. IS IT, TOO, AN EXAMPLE OF YOUR 'REALITY'?

"Precisely," Magnan stated, unperturbed.

AND NOW, THE PRESENT? IS IT THE SAME?

"Well, no, they're not all the same, of course," Magnan hedged. "The present is what we preceive as immediate experience. The past is that which we experience in retrospect. The future is that which is experienced in anticipation."

THEN THE MODE OF YOUR PERCEPTION IMPOSES CONSTRAINTS UPON EXTERNAL TIME, SPACE, AND VUG? The Voice's tone was unmistakably sarcastic.

"You're twisting my words," Magnan rasped. "Anyway, that's the well-established Anthropic Principle."

I AM ATTEMPTING, the Voice contradicted, TO GRASP YOUR CURIOUS CONCEPTION OF THAT WHICH IS AND WILL

CONTINUE TO BE, QUITE INDEPENDENTLY OF YOUR OPIN-
IONS. ONE CAN HARDLY EXPECT THE WRIT OF THE ANTHROPIC
PRINCIPLE TO RUN HERE.

"As to that," Magnan bluffed. "We shall see!" He
turned to Retief, and inquired earnestly: "What do *you*
think, Jim?"

"Voice is ahead on points," Retief told him. "You
better try for a knockout."

"Here's one for you, Mister Smarty," Magnan addressed the circumambient space/time/vug: "Conceive
of space/time/Vug as an endless strip of paper; stretching off *that* way is the past, and the other way is the
future. Now, with a sharp shears, we cut the strip right
across; to the left is the past, to the right, the future.
The cut is the present. The paper hasn't moved, any
more than the space dimension; the two halves are in
contact, the cut is of zero width, and is merely a position relative to past and future. Not one atom of paper
is in the cut; every one lies on one side or the other of
the cut. That position represents the present, which
endures for no finite period. Ergo the present is not a
substantive phenomenon."

NOR IS THE UNREALIZED FUTURE—NOR THE DISCARDED
PAST. IN SHORT, THERE IS NO REALITY. IS THAT YOUR THESIS?

"Only that there's no real difference," Magnan
amended. "If I'm traveling in a ground-car on a highway
and I see a signpost ahead, very well. I continue to
approach it, and for one infinitely short instant I am
beside it; then it is behind me. And all the while, the
signpost is unchanged."

YET WE CAN CHANGE THE FUTURE BY OUR ACTIONS NOW,
the Voice reminded him.

"And that is precisely what I intend to do!" Magnan
stated triumphantly. "What do you say, Retief?" he
went on; "what should we do *now* to improve the future
which rushes at us so relentlessly?" Receiving no reply,
he spun on the uncertain footing, peering into the
light-shot darkness. "Retief, where *are* you?" he wailed.

"Oh, dear, abandoned, alone in chaos with a disembodied voice which offers nothing but sophistries and yivshish! What am I to do?"

"Stand fast, Ben," Retief's voice spoke near at hand. Magnan jumped, staring even more frantically into the confusion of whirling, colored wisps and glittering streamers all around him. At least, he consoled himself, there were no pesky gnats here.

"One hardly has a frame of reference by which to establish one's position," the bewildered diplomat carped. "And where *are* you? It's bad enough talking with the Voice, without having one's own colleague abruptly disappear!"

"You're merely perceiving me, or not perceiving me, in an inappropriate mode, sir," Retief pointed out. "Concentrate on perceiving me as immediate experience, as you describe it."

"Well . . . I'll try," Magnan offered uncertainly. He made an effort to envision Retief, clad in impervious armor, seated on a mountainous white horse, lance in hand; somehow his effort slipped its focus, and he felt a sudden weight across his narrow shoulders, and sniffed a powerful aroma of horse-sweat. Looking down, he discovered the source of the aroma directly beneath him. He raised his surprisingly heavy hand to his forehead, with a slight squeak, and heard a metallic *clatter!* as his ingeniously jointed gauntlet touched the raised visor of his helmet, the weight of which, though mostly carried by his shoulders, was swiftly giving him a headache.

"No, confound it!" he barked. "*I* didn't want to be somebody's knight-in-armor!" In expressing his resentment at this unexpected turn of events, Magnan unintentionally kicked his feet, thereby putting spurs to his mount, which responded by leaping into a full charge. Magnan's visor *clang!*ed down, reducing his view to what could be seen through three narrow hand-filed slits in the steel. He was gripping a wad of leather reins in his left hand, while his right gripped the shaft of a long but light-weight spear with a flaring hand-guard, quite inadequate, Magnan noted in panic; and the shank of the lance was firmly clamped against his side by his upper arm.

"Help!" he yelled, his voice having an echoic quality inside the heavy casque.

What he saw through the visor was far from encouraging: swirling fog, wisps of vapor, layer on layer, growing more opaque with each bound of his mighty steed.

"I'll be killed!" he yelped.

THAT IS HARDLY A WISE POSITION TO ADOPT WHILE IMMERSED IN A MALLEABLE EXTRA-SPATIAL, NON-TEMPORAL, INFRAVUGGISH ANOMALY, the Voice commented casually.

" 'Adopt' my aunt Prissy!" Magnan yelled furiously. "I happen to be caught in an avalanche of misfortune, swept along like a drop in a tidal wave, and you natter of 'adopting a position' as if I had deliberately chosen this grotesque form of self-destruction! Why don't you do something helpful, instead of giving redundant advice!"

VERY WELL, came the silent reply. I SHALL DO WHAT I CAN TO RATIONALIZE YOUR SEEMINGLY IRRATIONAL SITUATION.

At that moment, the fog seemed to thin ahead, then Magnan burst through a final wispy veil of mist into a sunlit glade, a smooth-clipped lawn surrounded by the giant oak trees of an apparently impenetrable forest. A faded 'Reward for Retief' poster was tacked to one of the biggest oaks. Then, from the black shadows before him, a black shape stirred. A gigantic black horse emerged from the darkness, on his back an equally gigantic man in glittering black armor, bearing on his sable shield a griffon or in sinister chief, a bend gules, and in dexter base a human skull proper.

"The Black Knight of Farbelow!" Magnan realized at once, not knowing how he knew. Even as he thought frantically, "I've got to get out of here immediately," he settled himself in the saddle, set his feet firmly in the stirrups, gripped his lance, adjusting its angle to just below the horizontal, and put spurs to his mount. The black knight seemed to pivot lazily to face him squarely, then appeared to grow larger with astonishing rapidity as he charged to meet Magnan's attack. How big, sharp and close his lance-point seemed! Before Magnan had time for further thought, the shock came, the lance vibrated under his arm and shattered, but Lord Farbelow, looming gigantic, was tottering in his saddle, the stump of his lance tossed aside. Magnan was only dimly aware of a great pain in his ribs as he fought to retain his seat; then the black charger was past. There was a great *crash!*, and Magnan wheeled his sturdy Lippenzaner and looked back to see Farbelow lying on his back, while the black horse cantered away. The fallen knight raised himself to his elbows, lifted his visor to reveal the face of Counselor of Embassy Sidney Overbore, his eyes unfocused, and a trickle of blood dribbling from his nose.

"Gosh, Sir," Magnan babbled. "I didn't mean—"

"I crie thee mercie, Sir Knight," the fallen warrior blurted dazedly. "Spare me, and I shall make my devoir as thy vassal before all men on Lordsday next!"

"Gee," Magnan persisted, heedlessly. "I only; I mean, I wasn't . . ."

The man on the ground tossed his dented shield from him. "Bother this bootless quest for chivalric honors," he grunted, then caught Magnan's eyes. "And what boots it for *thy* honor, sirrah, to slay a helpless man?"

Magnan abruptly realized that he had drawn his unconscionably heavy sword from its jeweled sheath. At the third try, he returned the great slab of edged steel to its place. "Gee, sir, I hope you didn't think—" he started, then changed his mind.

"Arise, Sir Knight," he commanded, "and let me not again have report of your terrorizing your subordinates!"

"Sure, sir," Farbelow/Overbore hastened to agree, as he clambered heavily to his feet, his gleaming black grenouilliers stained with brown earth and green grass, at which he brushed noisily with a steel-encased hand.

"Throw down your baldric," Magnan ordered. "Place your helm beside it. Retrieve your horse and begone!"

The black knight hastened to comply, at the same time edging toward the nearest clump of bushes. Magnan heaved a great sigh and relaxed slightly.

"Tis well yon varlet brast his spear," he muttered to his attendant angel. "Else I'd have gone down over my horsetail instead of he. Whew! That was dreadful! And *now* what do I do?"

As if in reply, a feminine voice called 'Help!' from the shadowy woods. Magnan scrambled down from the big, smelly white horse and hurried over to assist Gaby through the last barrier of brush and out onto the smooth-mowed lawn, where shafts of sunlight striking through the forest canopy made patches of vivid green against black shadow.

"Oh, Benny," the girl breathed. "How brave! How noble! I saw it all. T'was soothing to my wounded pride to see the great bully brought low by my paladin!" His reply was muffled by her enthusiastic kiss. He struggled free, protesting.

"Really, my child, this is most unseemly! What in the world happened to you? What did that great ugly brute do . . .?"

"Fear not, my brave one," she quickly reassured him. "My virtue is just as good as it was before. The bum didn't even take off his armor!"

"Come," Magnan urged, taking one hand, "let's find a way out of this gloomy woods."

"No sweat, Ben," she replied. "We're only a few rods from Transfer Point Sixteen."

"B-but . . ." Magnan stammered. "Where have you been? What happened to you? You went to the back of the cave, and—and after that, in Boss's office . . ."

"And you came to my rescue, Benny," she supplied.

"That was cute. I was just admiring the scenery, until old Blackie came along. He had big idears, the jerk."

Magnan looked about nervously, saw only the big black Percheron grazing at the edge of the wood. "Where is he?" he inquired vaguely. "If he should come back—"

"I know, Benny. You'd have it to do all over again; but he ain't coming back, honey," Gaby reassured him, while running a finger along his profile. "I seen you brast a spear on his lunch. He'll be back in there, heaving, till dark." She cast a glance at the sun, just above the treetops. "And that won't be long; maybe a hour. We better get clear o' the woods 'fore dark. C'mon." She took his gauntleted hand and tugged it. He went along dazedly.

"I suppose," he said, as if judiciously (27-b), "that we may as well. Waiting won't help."

"Don't go wasting that 27 on me, Ben," Gaby chided gently. "Just be candid, spontaneous-like. Be yourself. If waiting around here for Blackie makes you nervous, hell, it would anybody."

"Me? Nervous?" Magnan inquired with a ghastly parody of a chuckle. He strode ahead, tugging the girl along.

"Hey!" she protested. "The transfer point's yonder!" She pointed off the way Sir Farbelow had staggered. Magnan allowed her to turn him. They pushed into the thick underbrush.

"Damn this armor!" Magnan blurted. "It's heavy hot. Wait a minute." He halted and began to fumble with the fastenings of his cuirass.

"Not that way, silly," Gaby said, brushing his hands aside. "You got to do the gorget first." She demonstrated. "A body'd think you never had on a suite of proof before. . . ." she mused.

"Well," Magnan started, "actually, that is, how silly, my dear. Now just get these confounded greaves loose if you will, and we'll be off."

"Why, Benny!" Gaby cried. "Embroidered long-johns! That's real sporty!"

Magnan at once turned away in response to an obscure impulse toward modesty, then, remembering the ludicrous trap-door seat, kept turning, executing a clumsy pirouette.

"Aw, Benny," Gaby exclaimed. "Yer full o' surprises! I never knowed you could dance and all!" As she spoke the sound of a five-man combo sprang up from an invisible source, playing *I Won't Dance.*

" 'Can't make me,' " he murmured in consonance with the music. " 'Never gonna dance, only gonna love . . .' "

Gaby seized his arm and snuggled up to it. "Ben," she sighed, "yer so romantic and all. . . ."

"Nonsense, my girl," Magnan replied severely, disengaging his arm. "Now, we've no time for dalliance; we must get back and tell the others!"

"What others?" Gaby asked, releasing her grip reluctantly. "Tell 'em what?"

"Why, as to that," Magnan temporized. "The Ambassador, for one. Heavens! He has no idea of the dangers lurking here in the boondocks! But, come to think of it, *he's* likely involved!"

"This here ain't the boondocks, Benny," Gaby objected. "Them's yonder." She pointed vaguely. "What's that got to do with anything, anyways?"

"Though the Counselor's errand in the bush was, undeniably, venal and treacherous in the extreme," Magnan orated, "nonetheless, it is one's duty to warn him of hidden danger."

"What dangers was them, Benny?" Gaby cooed. "Old Blackie was the only danger in these parts, and you trimmed him down to size. If he didn't dirty his underwear, he's got a bad case o' constipation!"

Magnan recoiled. "Gabrielle, how gross!" he objected. "Surely you're aware that there are matters to which a lady doesn't allude!"

"I don't know how to allude," she pointed out. "Anyways, I ain't no lady. I'm what you call a *grisette*, that's 'little gray' in Standard, means a chippy, you know, I ain't never claimed different, Ben; I thought you knew it and liked me anyways!"

"I *do*, I do," Magnan hastened to reassure her, as her tears started. "*Do* don't cry," he urged, confusedly.

"Cry if I wanta," she sobbed. "Aw, heck! It ain't nothing like Eddie said!"

"Eh?" Magnan came back sharply. "Would that be Dirty Eddie, otherwise known as Looie Segundo?"

"Sure! 'Dirty' is right!" she snarled, turning on Magnan. "I shoulda known—you and yer white horse—just more o' his tricks!"

"I assure you, Gaby," Magnan stated firmly, "that I am not a part of anyone's tricks. I am Benjamin O. Magnan, late of Caney, Kansas, and a Foreign Service Officer of Class One in the Terran Foreign Service, a Consul General of Career in the Terran Consular Service, and a Career Minister in the Terran Diplomatic Service, now assigned as Deputy Counselor and Budget and Fiscal Office to the Terran Mission to Goldblatt's Other world, or Sardon as it's officially listed."

"See? Three people at once," Gaby retorted. "Come off it, Benny—or whatever your name really is—show yourself—if there *is* any self—or are you just something Eddie thought up to tease me? Even if you're nothing at all, you musta had a good laugh at the way I come on to you—" She paused to resume sobbing.

"Good lord," Magnan remarked. "What in the world can I do to convince you that I'm a real, live human, from Terra itself?"

"See?" Gaby challenged hotly. "You can't just be humern, you got to come on like a pure-breed from Terra—if there really is any such place and it ain't just a myth!"

"I assure you, my child," Magnan tried again, "I give you my solemn assurance that I am not only a true

Terran, but an official representative of Terra in her contacts with other worlds!"

"You keep taking in even more and more territory," Gaby charged sadly. "I wanna believe in you, Benny, but how can I?" She looked up beguilingly at him with large violet eyes from which tears had washed the paint. He grabbed her and kissed her. She sighed and snuggled up to his arm, which she clutched possessively. "OK, Benny," she murmured. "I'll take what I can get, even if you ain't real."

"B-but," he started, then wisdom belatedly prevailed and he fell silent.

"C'mon," she urged, "let's get outa this loose nation." He followed uncertainly as she tugged him toward an azalea in full flower. She led him around behind it to a patch of velvety grass, and just as Magnan was readying a shocked protest, Retief came around the bush and said:

"We don't have much time. The Vug flux is approaching critical density for a phase-change."

"Hello, Jim," Magnan greeted his colleague. "I won't bore you by asking where you've been—or where *I've* been, but please indulge me by saying something comprehensible." He paused to fan himself with his hand. "I must say I'm quite undone by all this. Do you happen to know the way back to the cave?"

"Steady, Ben," Retief counseled. "This is a little heavy, I know, but we're *in* the cave. It's just a matter of focusing your awareness on the correct level of vibrational phenomena."

"You did it again!" Magnan charged. "I specifically asked you to say something comprehensible!" He looked around wildly. "Where's Gaby?" he demanded. "Indeed, where are *you*?"

"Look behind you," Retief suggested. Magnan spun and saw, a few feet away, a small-white-painted booth—one which he had seen before. He dashed to it, rounded the side and saw Gaby behind the counter of the ice-cream stand, just as he had first seen her: middle-aged, work-worn, coarse-featured. She looked at him in astonishment.

"Hold on, dearie," she said quickly and turned her back. "I got to fix my face."

"Gaby! It *is* you!" Magnan blurted, "but—but what's happened?"

"It's what *hasn't* happened," the woman corrected, and turned to face him. To his astonishment, the work- and time-worn look was gone.

"Gaby!" Magnan blurted. She recoiled. "You was going to take me out of all this!" she reproved sadly. "We was to of wed, respectable, and settle down!"

"Gabrielle, my dear," Magnan said in a shaken tone, "you appear to have somehow gained an erroneous impression. I am hardly ready to retire to a life-of-wedded-bliss-in-a-rose-covered-cottage, or any other form of domicile!"

"Why not?" Gaby demanded. "I guess I ain't enough of a lady fer ya," she tried vainly to hold her delicate features in an expression of contemptuous fury, but to her own obvious annoyance, a tear dribbled down from one large violet eye to the top of her turned-up nose.

Magnan was quick to produce a monogrammed hanky to wipe it away. "Really, my child, I didn't mean—" he stammered. Then she was hugging his arm in her usual possessive manner.

"Tell me one thing, Benny," she cooed. "How'ed you know about the rose-covered cottage? Took a deal o' horse-manure to grow them flars in this here lousy soil, too."

Magnan leaned back to stare at her. "Y-you mean . . .?"

She tugged at his arm. "Right over here," she said over her shoulder.

2

Retief was standing beside Magnan in the whirling, multi-colored, but gnat free fog listening to the Voice

saying WE CAN APPARENTLY CHANGE THE OSTENSIBLE FU-
TURE BY OUR LATENT ACTIONS. Magnan, beside him, said
something and abruptly Retief found himself immersed
in a dense billow of smog.

"Stand fast, Ben," Retief called. Magnan replied, and
they chatted for a few moments; then the Voice spoke
up again:

I SUGGEST YOU REMATCH PARADIGMS, QUICKLY, it said,
in a tone of urgency. IT WOULD BE UNWISE TO CONTINUE
IN THIS UNSYMMETRICAL MODE.

"Oh, we're getting close to something, eh?" Retief
replied, and focused his attention on detecting the direction from which the Voice emanated.

HERE NOW, NO MEDDLING OF THAT SORT! the silent
presense reprimanded sharply.

"Retief!" Magnan's voice was a wail, receding in the
distance.

"Right here, sir," Retief called. He took a step toward the reedy voice, and the surface underfoot seemed
to dissolve into a heaving layer of golf-ball-sized peb-
bles, into which he sank to the waist.

"Wrong scale." He directed the thought toward the
sense of the Voice. "You can't drown me in golf balls."

THOSE ARE HYDROGEN ATOMS! the silent Voice corrected
sharply.

The consistency of the entrapping mass changed, became gravel-like. Retief disengaged his feet from the
loose material, climbed a low slope to emerge in sunlight. When he looked back, the wisps of luminous fog
were drifting away, dispersing, to reveal a shadowy
hollow. Far below, there was a flicker of movement, as
a large slug-like creature scuttled for concealment. Retief
picked a shallow gulley as the most navigable route,
went across the grass and descended into the shadows
where the thing had disappeared. Barely visible under a
slaty overhang was a black opening. Once again, the
persistent gnats swarmed about him.

DON'T YOU DARE! came the sharp warning. Retief

sensed that its source was close—dead ahead, inside the tunnel. He picked up an apple-sized rock and threw it into the recess, eliciting a meaty *whap!* and a low grunt, followed by scuffling sounds. He selected a larger missile and pegged it after the first. This time, the unhandsome triangular head of Chief Smeer emerged, marred by a greenish contusion below one yellow eye.

"That done it!" the cop barked. "Yer unner arrest!" He hauled his ungainly length out into the open, awkwardly attempting to assume a look of dignity while at the same time brushing mud and debris from his cop-blue harness with two large, multi-fingered hands.

Retief expanded his telepathic sensitivity in the way he had mastered by conversations with the Voice, and at once picked up sub-vocalization:

. . . *let this outlaw give me the slip now. Old Fussbritches wouldn't like that. And I guess I got a score or two to settle my ownself* . . .

As the slug-like cop leaped at him, twisting onto its back as Retief stepped aside, he looked down at the long, armor-plated underside of the creature, located the ochre patch just aft of the third pair of short, scuttling legs, and delivered a jack-hammer kick to the leathery hide. In instant reflex, the long torso whipped itself into a tight ball, the projecting legs no longer able to reach the rocky ground. Smeer's bug-like face looked at Retief with what he interpreted as a despairing expression.

"Dirty pool, Retief," Smeer said mournfully. "I bet you looked up Sardonic physiology in a book or like that."

"On the trip out," Retief conceded, "I did happen to glance through an article on exobiology."

"Oh, you come here *planning* to attack us kindly locals," Smeer commented as if granting an interview to a Groaci sob-sister.

"I learned a number of other interesting things, too," Retief told him.

"That's ridiculous," Smeer dismissed the idea. "I've protected all sensitive data under four levels of obfuscation—which reminds me: how is it you're not still spinning your wheels in that lovely null-entropic pseudo-environment I evoked just for you?"

"You work on that," Retief suggested. "In the meantime, I *might* consider not knocking your IQ back down to the pre-goldblatt level, if you just drop the whole scam right here."

"What? And disappoint poor Sid?"

"Sid will survive to hang," Retief assured the unhappy creature. At the same time, he extended his awareness in a fine-focused tendril with which he lightly brushed the surface of the alien consciousness, noting the weak suture lines.

"Really!" Smeer objected, simultaneously beginning to waggle his antennae in an uncontrollable reflexive search for the source of his discomfort. "Drat it!" he carped, at last stilling the primitive snoof organs, except for a residual twitching.

"I haven't done *that* since I was a *very* small eater," he commented, as if confiding in a sympathetic interviewer. Then he fixed a baleful eye on Retief. "Alas, you force me to unleash my big guns, unhappy meddler!" he intoned, the impressiveness of his pronouncement somewhat marred by his awkward curled position, peering out from under his own appetite. "Just wait'll I get uncurled here, fellow, and I'll show you a few tricks you ain't seen yet!" he concluded.

"That might be a while," Retief told him. "I took the time to fuse your primary motor ganglion in that position.

HAVE A CARE, RASH TERRAN! the Voice warned, somewhat muffled. WOULD YOU ATTEMPT TO DEFY THE SSP?

"Oh, I already did that," Retief replied cooly. "You gave yourself away, back in the entropic vacuole."

TO BE SURE, Voice conceded. YOU DUPED ME: BUT EVEN THAT APPARENT KINK IN THE HARMONIOUS UNFOLDING OF DESTINY CAN, WITH A TRIFLING ADJUSTMENT TO ONE'S

WORLDVIEW, BE SUBSUMED WITHIN THE SSP. ONE OF THE
CHIEF VIRTUES, REALLY, OF THE CONCEPT.

"I'm talking SAP," Retief informed the gabby alien
with finality. "As principle which required Mr. Magnan's
gestalt and mine re-converge now!"

"Oh, dear," Magnan's voice groaned from near at
hand. Retief turned to see his colleague hurrying past,
his back to Retief.

"Hold on, Ben," Retief called after him. Magnan hesitated, half-turned, stammering: "B-but Gaby is just—oh,
it's *you*, Retief: Gracious, I hardly know where to begin. Where have you been?"

"Right here, sir," Retief reassured the agitated First
Secretary. "It's just a matter of viewpoint."

"Viewpoint?" Magnan yelled. "While I was being set
upon by metallic monsters—"

"Just one, Benny," Gaby murmured coming up behind him. He leapt as if jabbed by a sharp stick.

"Gaby!" he choked. "Don't *ever* creep up on me like
that!"

"I never crept," she objected. "Oh, hi, Jimmy." She
wisely dropped the subject. "What's next?"

"I was hoping," Magnan blurted before Retief could
speak, "that *you* could tell *me*—or us, that is, child.
You said something about Transfer Point Sixteen, I
believe: you seem to know your way around this maze.
So, shall we be off?"

"What about the rose-covered cottage and all?" Gaby
protested. "You ain't changed yer mind?"

"Mind?" Magnan echoed. "I feel as if I've lost it."

"Not quite, Ben," Retief corrected. "In fact, it's your
mind that's complicating matters at the moment."

"Who, me?" Magnan wailed. "I categorically deny
that! Jim," he appealed to his colleague. "Why in the
world would I—?"

"It's quite involuntary, of course," Retief pointed
out. "And unconscious. It's an automatic response to
being suddenly immersed in the SSP."

"What's that?" Magnan demanded. "A supersonic some-thing-or-other? Kindly explain yourself, Retief!"

THE RETIEFBEING REFERS TO THE STRONG SARDONIC PRINCIPLE, the Voice put in sharply.

"You see," Retief explained, "when Captain Goldblatt took the young worm under his wing, so to speak, and by patient training, taught it to communicate, he thereby unleashed its latent intellect, with the natural result that the Strong Sardonic Principle came into play, evoking the curious universe into which we've wandered, because we naively accepted its basic postulates, while our own Universe, generated by the Strong Authropic Principle, became attenuated to the status of an unrealized potential. We have to stop fighting the problem and solve it instead."

"Indeed? And just how does one go about that, may I inquire?" Magnan yelped. "It reminds one of the old limerick:

'A Phi Beta Kappa named Carradine
Once stepped outside of his paradigm
And since he came back, he hangs round the track
and he says, "pal, can you spare a dime?" ' "

"Apt indeed, sir," Retief congratulated his immediate supervisor. "But now, let's get busy."

"Damn," Gaby wailed, "I'm scared! The ground is getting all bumpy, and this here fog—"

"Ignore that, my dear," Magnan counseled. "Your surroundings are purely illusory."

"I guess this here gravel I got in my shoe ain't no dern loose nation!" she riposted spiritedly. "Already got blisters, chasing around in the hot sun, and—"

"Of course your blisters are real enough," Magnan conceded soothingly. "But then we must recall that all reality is illusion."

"I can't recall nothing I ever heard of, and something silly as that anyways—" She broke off and recoiled as if suddenly noticing Chief Smeer for the first time.

"Hey!" That there's one of them pillars!" she told her biographers. "Quick, Benny! let's go!" She seized his arm and hauled him, protesting, into the shelter of the boulders. "We got to *do* something!" she hissed. "Them critters is mean as a snake!"

"Don't be absurd," Magnan chided unemphatically. "Chief Smeer represents the forces of Law and Order here on Sardon." He favored the local cop with a Congratulatory Smile, Second Class, Inferiors, for the Encouragement of.

"Don't go showing *me* no second class SSCIE, Terry!" Smeer rebuked him sharply. "I rate a first-class Grimace, Ritual, Relations, for the Cementing of!"

"Benny!" Gaby put in. "You gonna let that there pillar smart off at you?"

"I really must protest your use of the pejorative epithet, Gabrielle," Magnan rebuked the indignant girl. "As for his 'smarting off,' I'm sure Chief Smeer meant only to suggest adherence to established protocol, in which, of course, he was quite correct. Do excuse me, Chief: I was a bit carried away for the moment, I fear."

"Talking about carried away," Smeer riposted cheekily, "I and my boys are gonna take this here wanted crinimal away right now, which they's a reward out on the sucker. Stand aside, there, Ben."

"I can hardly stand idly by, Chief," Magnan stated firmly, "while you violate the diplomatic immunity of a diplomatic member of the staff of the Embassy of Terra."

"Yer own boss throwed the sucker to the throng," Smeer reminded him sharply, and abruptly uncoiled. The sinuous alien used two of the arms grouped at his upper end to rub his thorax gently. Magnan's eye was caught by the glint of polished black metal briefly exposed below his cuff. Impulsively, he reached out quickly and grabbed the armored wrist.

"It's him!" he yelped. "Retief, the Black Knight of Farbelow was really Chief Smeer here! Somehow, he assumed the form of a high Terran official—"

"Nope," Smeer corrected. "*You* done that, Ben. I taken that mental image o' yours, and used it to mould the latent energies and all."

"He's a tricky one, aren't you, worm?" Retief challenged.

"Yer on a bum lay, jailbird," Smeer retorted. "If you think *I'm* the one that's been lousing up the paradigm. That's old Worm—"

ENOUGH, the Voice cut in sharply. Smeer fell silent in mid-expostulation.

"Retief," Magnan appealed. "*What* is going on here? I confess I'm quite at sea."

"I suggest you avoid vivid analogies for the present, sir," Retief replied, waving away the shadowy vista of white-capped surf which for a moment had almost blocked off the jungle view. "The space/time/Vug continuum appears to be in a highly malleable state just now/here/vorg, because the SAP and SSP are in head-to-head confrontation, thereby attenuating what we may as well think of as the fabric of space/time/Vug, so the latent energies tend to assume any form offered as a template by a strong visualization."

"I see, sort of," Magnan replied vaguely. "And in that case, let's just visualize ourselves safely back where we belong!" He closed his eyes as if in concentration.

"Hey! Don't go—" Smeer started, but subsided when Retief thrust him aside. "I suggest you proceed carefully, sir," he told Magnan. "Let's give the matter some thought at this point, rather than acting impulsively."

"Just think . . ." Magnan mused aloud. "If only we hadn't been in such a hurry to get to Staff Meeting on time, we'd never have become embroiled in this madness. So it's all the fault of Ambassador Shortfall, really, for being such a martinet!"

"If that thought soothes you, Ben," Retief said, "I'm sure it's all right to go ahead and have it."

"Darn right!" Magnan confirmed. "And things were going so well: after my stunning *coup* in making contact with TERRI in the person of Big, my career was assured! I was dreaming of promotion: just savor the sound of it: 'Career Ambassador Benjamin O. Magnan.' Sensuous, eh?"

"Virtually pornographic, sir," Retief confirmed.

" 'Of all sad words of tongue or pen, the saddest are these: 'it might have been,' " Magnan quoted gloomily.

"Hey, that ain't the way it goes!" Smeer corrected at once. "I seen it in a Terry tape once: 'The saddest words on sea or shore

Are 'once it was and is no more.' Whatever that means."

"That's a corruption of the original." Magnan dismissed the idea.

"Oh, yeah?" Smeer retorted. "Well, I guess the SSP is as valid as the SAP on any day!"

"That is a question for the philosophers," Magnan adjudicated. "Or possibly the Cosmologists. In fact," he went on, "if I ever everge from this contretemps, I have decided, on the basis of the SAP, to do so with a large fortune, in gold. Oddly perhaps, gemstones don't move me, but the solid bulk of gold coin—that's fat city. This is no mere greedy impulse, you understand, Retief; I shall employ an adequate portion of my wealth to endow a Chair of Experimental Cosomology at Omaha State, my old alma mater.

"You might object," he mused aloud, "that no such discipline as Experimental Cosmology exists—but it *should*, if every Tom, Dick and Meyer is going to go around begetting his own Universe. No wonder there's no harmony in human affairs. The thing must be reduced to a strict scientific basis!"

"How do you figger to haul all this jack out of here?" Smeer inquired sardonically. "Kinda heavy to back-pack."

"So long as I am evoking the mineral from primordial energies," Magnan replied loftily, "I may as well evoke it neatly stacked in the vaults at the Corn Exchange County Bank, over on Choctaw."

"Good idea," Retief approved.

"Still," Magnan rambled on, "all this is still highly theoretical: the Philosophical Discourse Dogma of course assumes the existence of other powerful intellects, equally capable with Man of evoking realities. But nobody expected them to be like *this!*"

YOU CONSIDER SUCH INTELLECTS TO BE HYPOTHETICAL? the Voice thundered, having regained its former volume and timbre. SURELY YOU DO NOT ATTEMPT TO DENY THE COPERNICAN PRINCIPLE, OF WHICH THE PRINCIPLE OF MEDIOCRITY IS BUT A SPECIAL CASE.

"Well, not exactly," Magnan temporized, "but after all, it's far simpler to suppose that I'm merely hallucinating. That's Occam's Razor, you know: the simplest thesis is the best one."

SIRWILLIAMFOCCAM KNEW NOTHING OF COLLAPSIN SCHRÖDINGER FUNCTIONS, the Voice reminded him curtly.

"That's not the point," Magnan whined.

WHAT, THEN, *IS* THE POINT? the relentless Voice demanded.

"Well," Magnan started gamely, "the point is, Retief and I were dispatched on a perfectly routine errand, and were set upon by a mob led by Chief Smudge, and took refuge in an unlikely establishment known as the Cloud Cuckoo Club, where Will Shakespeare was a regular; then a mob of local dacoits burst in, and I was raped away to a jungle fastness."

WHAT IS A 'JUNGLE FASTNESS'? the Voice wanted to know.

"Well, it's just what the term suggests," Magnan explained. "A thieves' den in the jungle. Or anyway, that's what it looks like. They were about to clap me into a concentration camp when my colleague Mr. Retief chanced along, and things grew rapidly worse!"

YOU CONSIDER THAT AN EXPLANATION? the Voice boomed silently.

"How can I explain when I don't understand myself?" Magnan demanded, not illogically.

ONE SHOULD NEVER UNDERTAKE TO EXPLAIN THAT OF

WHICH ONE HAS NO COMPREHENSION, the Voice chided sternly. PRAY ALLOW ME TO ENLIGHTEN YOU . . .

"Can you?" Magnan yelped. "*Will* you? Please do! I fear I'll lose my sanity soon—"

"Easy, Ben," Retief counseled. "I think we've stumbled into a node here, a point where the two paradigms overlap, like two overlapping circles, only in four or five dimensions. All we have to do is get outside of it, and the SAP will be in charge again. Meanwhile, what we think of as reality is malleable, and we're forming it with our minds. Captain Goldblatt was the first human here, so he impressed a basic pattern on the whole scene: we've only been modifying the details."

Magnan groaned. "The captain must have been a strange character," he commented.

"What makes you think so, Fancy-pants?" A resonant voice demanded from directly behind Magnan. He leapt, startled, and hit the ground running, but halted after a few paces and stood dithering.

"It's no use, I suppose," he declared, looking around hopefully as if for someone to contradict him. All he saw, besides Retief and the suddenly subdued Smeer, was a middle-aged but still burly red-head in a handsomely tailored but well-worn yachting outfit. "Like Boss but younger and broader!" Magnan burst out.

"Naw," the stranger dismissed the remark and thrust out a work-hardened hand.

"Sol's the handle," he said in a confident tone. "Sorry if I snuck up on you, Mister—"

"Magnan," the frail diplomat blurted, grasping the proffered member. "Hi, Sol," he added. "Actually we've met—or will meet, or—anyway Retief and I were just going, ha, ha, so if you'll excuse us. . . ."

"Going where, Mister Mumble?" Sol challenged, not releasing his firm grip on Magnan's hand. "Reckon you boys better stay put until I can get things straightened out here some."

"What things were those, Mr. Sol?" Magnan wondered aloud.

Sol waved a burly arm in an all-encompassing gesture. "I reckon you noticed a few little 'nomalies,' " he suggested vaguely. His eyes strayed to Smeer, now flattened against the major boulder as if attempting to squeeze under it. "Like that there grateful critter," Sol amplified. "Got too big fer its britches which it ain't even got any."

"Have a care, Cap," Smeer snarled. "You seem to forget the Accommodation."

"You boys came up with that one," he dismissed the complaint. "I never agreed to no Accommodation. The old SAP can steamroller yer lousy SSP any day o' the week. Now, I'm telling ya: you lay off messing around, or I'll lay the whole thing on Herself."

"Don't be a fool!" Smeer cautioned sharply. "If you should disturb her meditations with such trivia, she might well eliminate the entire nuisance from her Event Horizon. That includes you and your ill-considered arrangements, as well as my (innocent) self! We can work this out so that the interests of all parties are protected. Shall we begin by restoring the present time/space/Vug locus to its primordial pre-realization mode?"

"Now *he's* doing it," Magnan groaned. "Can't anyone talk sense?"

SENSE IS OF THE ESSENCE OF MY UTTERANCES, the Voice reproved. I CALL TO YOUR ATTENTION SNUT'S THIRD LAW OF MOTION—

"Not so fast," Magnan cut him off. "The H theorem has never been rigorously confirmed, so that leaves Snut's Law in abeyance."

WOULD YOU HAVE RECOURSE TO THE PERFECT (SO-CALLED) COSMOLOGICAL PRINCIPLE? the Voice taunted.

"Hardly," Magnan dismissed the suggestion. "Still, it *was* established by Crmblynski's work that the cosmic background radiation emanates from a pattern of widely distributed nodal points, one of which, of course, is located congruently with Goldblatt's Other World, rather than from the entire Universe; and since the Copernican Principle still holds sway . . ."

NEXT, YOU'LL BE INVOKING THE CRYPTIC CONCEPT, the Voice predicted.

"I would hardly dignify such an absurdity by discussing it," Magnan announced to the Galactic Press. ("Go ahead and quote me on that, fellows, and that's M-A-G-N-A-N, Benjamin O.").

UNWITTINGLY, the Voice informed him, YOU ALLY YOURSELF WITH THE PROPONENTS OF THE SAP, AND THE SSP AS WELL, FOR THAT MATTER, WHOM YOU AVOW TO CONDEMN.

"Yivshish!" Magnan charged. "Pure Yivshish! I wash my allegorical hands of the entire matter!"

"Not quite yet, I suggest, Ben," Retief contributed. "We still have some unfinished business here." At that moment, as if on cue, the sound of a horse's frantic hooves sounded from beyond the boulder. Magnan flattened himself against the giant stone and eased around to catch a glimpse of the source of the sound.

"Heavenly days!" he gasped, turning a stricken glance back at Retief. "It's a gang of horrid ruffians!"

"Staff meeting?" Retief suggested.

"Jape if you must," Magnan snapped, "but these fellows appear to mean business!"

"What are they doing?" Retief asked.

"Apparently, they're literally beating the figurative brush," Magnan supplied. "Do you suppose they're looking for *me?* Or for us, rather, of course."

"Why would they do that?" Retief inquired.

"Well, we are, after all, interlopers on their presumed turf," Magnan pointed out.

"Hardly," Retief countered. "We're the guests of Chief Smeer here; right, Chief?"

"Don't try to get *me* mixed up in *yer* private problems," the local grunted. "I got plenty o' my own. Them Rath guys got nothing to do with *me*."

"You're far too modest, Captain," Retief told the surly fellow.

" 'Captain?' " Magnan and Smeer echoed as one. "Why, the rascal is a mere local Chief of Constabulary," Magnan elaborated his objection.

"Here—" Sol blurted and fell silent.

"—lost yer reaction mass, Mister," Smeer was muttering.

"Actually," Retief told Magnan, "I suppose there's not much left of the original Goldblatt persona after two hundred years of submergence in a paradigm incompatible with his existence."

"I'm losing you again, Jim," Magnan complained. "As I understand it, Captain Goldblatt made planetfall on this unexplored world, inhabited by the caterpillar-like people we know as the Sardons: in his extremity, marooned here, and wounded after an uncontrolled landing, he was helped by a local animal of which he made a pet. The creature, and indeed all its kind, were at the threshold of a mentational breakthrough into higher-order intellectual levels; under the captain's tutelage, his pet achieved that breakthrough and his latent intellect was manifested; accordingly, it altered space/time/Vug, it, or should I say he-or-she evoked a Universe, as required by the SAP. Previously, other highly intelligent races had not evoked observable universes, because it is characteristic of the peculiarly human way of thinking so to organize the exocosm, and of course that first Sardonic genius, whom I suppose we may as well call the Great Worm, having had his intellect shaped by a Terran, acquired that same capacity, and its evocation was accordingly compatible with the Captain's. Do you agree?"

Retief nodded and Magnan went on: "Then, it appears, a second Terran vessel, wandering far from the space-lanes, arrived here, and abruptly Worm was presented with several dozen new paradigms which, originating virtually in superimposition with its own, and the compatible one of the captain, tended to overwhelm its own halcyon conceptualization. It of course resorted to appeal to the captain to join it in rejecting the intrusions. He agreed. . . ." Magnan's voice trailed off. "That's about as far as I've puzzled it out," he admitted. "And none of it actually helps us to deal with the situation. Where are we now, *actually*, Jim?" Magnan whimpered. "And why is this place so unlike the city, and that idyllic park we found inside the fence, as well?"

"Because we blundered," Retief told him. "We somehow penetrated the paradigmatic surface-tension and got out of one paradigm, but not into the adjacent one, but only into the zone where they partially merge. At least that's my analysis." He turned to Smeer. "What do you say, Captain?"

"Look here," Sol began, but the police chief spoke louder:

"Why," Smeer demanded coldly, "do you persist in addressing me in that manner? You may call me 'Chief.' "

"The fact, as I analyze it," Retief said, "is that as the Goldblatt paradigm began to conflict at various points with his erstwhile pet's world-view, under pressure of the new arrivals, the locals—you, chief, in your new, over-educated state, began to feel resentful of your formerly well-beloved mentor, and undertook to oppose his paradigm. This led, after some time, to a direct ego-to-ego confrontation. The pressure thus generated on the Cosmic All by two powerful entities of *almost* identical character, led to a merging of paradigms, a hitherto totally non-existant situation, since no two Terrans of equal potency had ever so opposed each other, and all previous alien Strong Principles were too mismatched to the SAP to mesh in that fashion. In the process, the Goldblatt persona was submerged in that of Worm, though not completely; he was, and is, still able to follow exocosmic affairs through the Worm mind, and to express himself as the false Junior. He also selected a prime specimen from the local population to act as his vehicle; he controls Smeer here, and sees through his eyes. So to some extent, the Chief here can be thought of as representing Captain Goldblatt himself."

"B-but—" Magnan objected. Sol, meanwhile, had moved a few feet and stood with his back to the others.

"There's something in what you say," Smeer conceded glumly. "But I insist the presence of this pesky Terran inside my cranial cartilage doesn't make me *him!*"

"Ignore us," Retief suggested. "Just relax your alertness, and let the Goldblatt aspect of your compound mind come to the fore."

"That's it," Smeer's vocal organs gasped. "With that damn pillar asleep, now maybe we can get someplace. Sure, I'm Sol Goldblatt; got into some strange places in my time, but this one beats 'em all. I been listening: you're dead right about that pillar coming along to help me out there at the beginning, when I was alone and lost and starving. Took me right along to as nice a tavern as ever had a roaring fireplace and fresh bagels and lox, and plenty o' rare steaks and cold draft. Good stuff, too. Reminded me a lot of the home-brew lager an old uncle of mine used to lay down every year. Then the sumbuck—the worm, not Unc Izzy—started trying to change things: kept stocking the reefer with some kinda lightning-bugs, and putting hoob-juice in the kegs—stuff like that. At first I didn't know what was going wrong, but after a while I figgered it out: he was trying to make the Club over to suit him. So I called him on it, and he tried to pull a fast one on me—locked me up in the ladies' room—no ladies here then, so it was OK—but I outfoxed him and tricked him into Bottomless Cave, but I blundered: I let him sweet-talk me into the cave to see it, and he faked up a replica of my old neighborhood, and I went for it, went charging into my old house like a kid, expecting to see my Ma and all—got confused, lost my head—and he *had* me. Sorry about old Smeer here giving you a hard time, but I couldn't help it. I was still in the Cave, o' course, and he and the army of pillars he'd conned into being his slaves bustled me through a tunnel and into the Park— said it was twice five miles o' farmland; had a wall around. Left me in the woods, crippled, as if my mind was wrapped up in cobwebs. I try to break out, but it's too tough. I'm locked in some kinda room, maybe underground; no windows. After a while, I noticed you fellers' mind-fields and started trying to contact you on the same level of abstraction as I had to talk to Worm on, and it worked, after a while. It was Retief here had a strong enough persona to punch through old Wiggly's shielding. Then, as you know, Herself butted in and started to mess things up. I couldn't get through until just now, when Wiggly konked out all of a sudden and now I. . . ." Smeer's body went limp and his voice ceased.

"Just who," Magnan put in urgently, "is this Herself to which you refer?"

"Beats me," Sol admitted. "But I do know she's the one behind the trouble here. Me and Wiggly would of got along good, only she kept butting in."

Retief probed gently, found the flaccid, immaterial membrane that was Smeer's endocosm-exocosm interface. He explored its surface, found the complex extrusion formed by the encapsulated ego-gestalt of the captain; he shaped his probe and punctured the confining membrane.

"—and now all of a sudden," the unconscious Smeer boomed out. "Hold on, I think I'm free. . . ." As Smeer spoke, Sol turned back toward Retief.

"Careful, Captain," Retief cautioned. "The membrane has kept you isolated from entropy. That's what's kept you alive all these years. Easy, now. You need to feel your way back into your own neurons."

"It's . . . strange," Smeer's strained voice said. "Like if a fella was to try to put on starched longjohns. It hurts my hair, but I can almost—" the voice broke off and Smeer uttered a groan and his jaw fell slack, as did the mind-form under Retief's touch.

"Good lord," Magnan muttered. "I'm not sure I understand what's happening here. In fact, I'm quite certain I don't."

"Over that way," Gaby suggested; she had retreated a few feet when confronted by the worm-like Smeer; now she advanced uncertainly. "Only shack around here's yonder," she offered, pointing. "Sod dug-out," she explained.

"Gaby—not our rose-covered cottage!" Magnan blurted.

"Sure not," Gaby reassured him. "Other side o' the hill. More like hole in the ground." She forged ahead.

Retief was maintaining contact with the intricately convoluted, but rapidly dwindling shape which represented the captive mind of Captain Goldblatt. Still holding close rapport, he felt out across the adjacent substrate which was the redoubtable mind-field of the super Sardon known as Chief Smeer, who, or which retaliated with a desperate lunge of mind-force which Retief struck down.

"Be reasonable, Chief," he urged, probing an attenuated area on the impalpable surface, which winced at his touch.

"Let go," Retief urged the shaken entity. "We can probably work out an accommodation that will give your paradigm ample room for expression, but if you kill a Galactic hero, it will be war to the knife."

CHAPTER SEVEN

Gaby had strolled ahead to pick a bouquet of wildflowers from the masses growing inside the faint trail. Suddenly she looked up, halted, and uttered a faint yelp! She shot Magnan an appealing look and turned back toward him. As she did, a burly arm reached out from the concealment of the brush and caught her slender wrist, jerking her off-balance. As she fell, her captor thrust through the foliage to leer down at her, a seven-foot heavyweight with the look of a pirate. He was showing irregular teeth in a broad grin.

"Hiya, Gabe," he growled, as he glanced toward Retief and Magnan. "Who's the marks?"

Before either Gaby or Magnan could reply, the piratical fellow stooped to grab Gaby's ankle and drag her toward him. She yelled and reached appealingly toward Magnan. He helped her up and embraced her while the pirate glowered. Then, at a sound from beyond the boulder which blocked the view of the trail, yet another unshaven oaf appeared. He paused to ogle Gaby, then, leering, stepped into her path, tripping her.

"Here, sir!" Magnan objected gamely, stepping forward. "What—"

"Here they are, Boss!" the lout yelled over his shoulder, ignoring Magnan except to elbow him aside. Retief caught the senior diplomat and steadied him on his feet, then felled the intruder with a sweep of his arm, and helped the young woman to rise. She spat at her fallen captor.

"Wait'll I get you alone, you piggy! Sneaking up on me like that, and dragging me like a trash-bag!"

Piggy got to his feet heavily, rubbing the side of his head. "Geeze," he commented mildly, looking resentfully at Retief, "I ain't even *seen* you."

"Seize him at once!" Smeer yelled, flapping his well-worn copy of the reward notice. "That's none other than the notorious Retief! There's a price on his head! Grab him before he gets away!"

"No hurry," Retief countered. "I'm not going anywhere. Neither are you," he added, blocking off Piggy as he attempted to slide around the boulder. "Relax," Retief advised him. "We're going to have a nice little talk. Who's your boss, and what's he up to? What's the idea grabbing the young lady?"

" 'Lady,' hah?" the crestfallen fellow snorted. Magnan leapt forward to confront him.

"Mind your tone, my man!" he commanded. "Now, apologize!"

"Aw gee, I'm sorry, Gabe," Piggy growled, peering past Magnan at the girl. "I never meant nothing, just yakking, you know."

"Skip it, Pig," Gaby dismissed the plaint and took Magnan's arm in a possessive clutch. "C'mon, Honey," she urged. "Let's blow. We got a late date, remember?"

Magnan tried awkwardly to disengage without appearing to do so. "Now, just be patient, dear," he urged Soothingly (702-w). Thus repulsed, she stumbled and fell, yet again.

"I tole you before, don't go using no 702 on me," she

reminded him, looking up resentfully. "Uh, it wasn't a 702 last time, OK," she amended. "But you know what I mean. Just be natural—like me!" She attempted to rise, struggling with her skirts, then relaxed and fell back, lay in his path, looking up at him and blocking his way.

"Here, my girl!" Magnan rebuked her sharply. "It's hardly appropriate for one in your position to be seen in such an undignified position—or to propose to serve as a role-model to a Foreign Service Officer of Class Two of Terra! After all, I'm number five man in the Embassy!" He hovered uncertainly over her. "Here, get up!" he hissed. "You're making a spectacle of yourself."

"And what *is* my position, Benny?" she cooed, holding the gaze of her large violet eyes fixed on Magnan's small brown ones. "Now don't go making no obscene quips, neither," she cautioned. "After all, I'm not prone to argue."

Piggy snickered. "That's some broad you taken up with there, Mister Big Shot," he commented. Magnan stooped, picked up a jagged rock as big as his fist and slammed it against the side of Piggy's head with a hearty *whack*! Piggy recoiled and uttered a wail of pain.

"Any more of your cheek, and you'll receive more of the same," Magnan told the astonished fellow. "Now, keep a civil tongue in your head, and explain yourself."

"Esplain *myself*?" Piggy echoed. "What am I supposed to be, some kinda metaphysician? On a material plane," he added more mildly, noting the gleam in Magnan's eyes, "you might say I'm a example of Homo Sapiens, the product of maybe twenny million years o' primate evolution, as shaped by some pretty tough experiences over a span o' maybe thirty-one hard years, which nobody ain't never really give me no love. See? I'm a like innocent victim o' heredity and avirament." As if incensed by this sudden realization, Piggy snarled and reached for Magnan who retreated to the top of the adjacent boulder.

"Or," Piggy resumed, "you could say I'm the inevitable end-product arising from proto-biochemical processes spontaneously initiated in the primordial *urschleim*, just like everybody else, even you, I guess."

"Explain what you're doing here—prior to your capture, that is," Magnan specified, testily, sliding down from his perch.

"Well," Piggy responded, "I and the boys are scouting around looking for the Boss which he kinda ducked outa sight, and we flush this here deviate running around in his embroidered longjohns, and work him over pretty good before we notice he's Boss, onney without his iron pants. Well, you can see that was a heavy downer which the onney way a guy could square it was to catch the bum taken his sheet-metal threads! So me and Horny and Pud come over this side and I seen you first, so now I gotta get outa here and report back, otherwise we're back in the soup."

Concluding his speech, Piggy reached for Magnan's thin arm. "Just come along nice, pal," he suggested, "and maybe it won't go too bad wit you. After all, ya bested old Boss in single combat, fair and square, right? He got no real beef—"

"Never mind that, my man," Magnan objected sharply, digging in his heels. "Why do you irrationally assume it was I who brast a spear on his lunch, rather than, perhaps, some more physical type?" He avoided Retief's eye while edging carefully into position to deliver a well-aimed kick to Piggy's crotch. On its arrival the latter released him and fell back with a howl.

"Ungentlemanly tactics, one admits," Magnan said, not without satisfaction, as Piggy writhed at his feet.

"That's quite appropriate, sir," Retief reassured him. "Piggy's an ungentleman."

"To be sure," Magnan cooed. "Shall we go?" He offered an arm to the wide-eyed Gaby.

Piggy had gotten to his feet and stood by grimacing in pain. "I infer yer off yer philosophical kick," he contributed. "Let's go. I can show you right where to find Pud, and Horny, too. I owe them bums a favor or two."

"I fail to grasp your meaning," Magnan dismissed the offer. "Milady and I are bound on personal affairs."

"I bet," Piggy snickered, then fell silent and ducked back as Magnan stooped to arm himself with a suitable jagged rock. "I din't mean nothing," Pig protested, and edged away. Once abreast the curve of the boulder, he turned and ran. Magnan hesitated, and Gaby snatched the stone from his hand and threw it with such accuracy that it impacted on the back of the fleeing man's head, knocking him flat. On his hands and knees, Piggy turned a protesting look on Magnan.

"No fair," he wailed. "Clobbering a unarmed man, which he's tryna scout the route up ahead."

"Then scout!" Magnan commanded. "Any signs of those rascals?" he queried as soon as Piggy had poked his lumpy nose around a bend, then jumped back.

"Cheese it!" he warned. "Old Boss is coming this way! Looks maddern's usual, too!" He shot a desperate look at Magnan, edging back, flat against the rock. "You done a bad tilt, mister, when you done unhorsed old Boss."

"It was him or oneself," Magnan pointed out. "One can hardly be held culpable."

"Who's this here 'One'?" Piggy demanded. "Two on One, hey? Or one on One, and One won; but which one? That's a little joke, see? Anyways, Boss ain't laughing." He looked around, ducked under the nearest shrub and out of sight. "Youse better duck out, too, pals," he called.

"Best we do as he suggests, Gaby dear," Magnan said, and thrusting the young lady ahead, eased into the cover of the dense foliage.

"You scared o' this bum?" Gaby inquired coldly.

"Of course not!" Magnan asserted. "I was merely responding to the Captain's well taken point that we are in fact, trespassing." From his point of vantage he peered out to see yet another burly fellow, clad in a grubby neck-to-toe garment, come striding along, only to lurch abruptly and fall headlong, uttering an oath of the coarsest kind as he did so.

"The wretch!" Magnan hissed to Gaby. "He uttered a curse that would make a longshoreman blush, in your presence!"

"Hush, Benzy," she cooed. "I guess I made a few hardcases blush in my time. It's only words. Besides he never knowed I was here."

" 'Only words,' indeed!" Magnan persisted, then shut up as two more wrestler-types came in to view, and halted at sight of Piggy.

"Horny!" the fallen man cried hoarsely. "Pud! Help me up at once. He done it again! Set upon me when I weren't looking! I was coming to warn youse!"

"Why, the unprincipled liar!" Magnan gasped. "Implying that it was *I* who tripped him!"

"Wasn't it, Benjy?" Gaby inquired encouragingly.

ACTUALLY, MISS GABY FELLED THE WRETCH, Voice spoke up.

"Hush!" Magnan barked. "That was unchivalric in the extreme!"

"Whattaya mean, 'unchivalric'?" Piggy demanded at the same moment that Horny and Pud uttered the same words.

"I never said—" the fallen man barked.

". . . who, me?" another contributed. Then the leader cut the dispute short with a yell. "Beat them bushes, you slobs!" At the same moment, he lunged directly toward Magnan's hiding place. For a moment, Magnan stared directly into the rage-contorted face, the red-rimmed eyes, noted the unshaven jowls, the pitted yellowed teeth, the undersized terminally filthy pink-and-yellow sport coat. "Good Lord!" he blurted. "It's

Dirty Eddie!" Then he backed away, barely evading the angry man's grab. He scrambled back on all fours, after a few yards got to his feet and ran directly into Retief.

"Easy, sir," Retief soothed. Magnan tried frantically to push past. "He's right behind me!" he yelped. "Quick, let me go!" Retief, still holding the Smeer intellect engaged, stepped aside and an unshaven, red-eyed face burst into view from the underbrush.

"I *seen* him!" Eddie yelled. "Lemme at him! It's the same tricky rascal I done brast my spear on!"

"First, let's have a little talk," Retief suggested gently, then grabbed Eddie's neck as he started past. Eddie made gurgling sounds.

"Leggo my neck, Mister!" he demanded loudly, if awkwardly.

Retief flipped the noisy fellow on his back, just as Horny and Pud came up. Horny sprang at Retief, rebounded from a stiff-arm, and wandered away, mumbling. Pud paused.

"Me, I never wanted no trouble," he explained to Posterity. "Heard old Boss kinda gurgling and that, so I come to see could a fella render aid. Humanitarian, see?" He was attempting to edge around Retief as he delivered his stirring appeal to the angel in us all.

"Touching in the extreme," Retief commended. "But as you see, the situation is well in hand."

"Hows come you're holding Boss by the Adam's apple?" Pud wondered aloud. "Hey, Horny!" he called as an afterthought. "Ain't no time fer you to be going off like that! This here feller's choking Boss!"

"No shielding offen *my* hull-plates," Horny pointed out. "Anyways, got no way to climb over that there slabite wall I run inta."

Pud craned his neck to look, over, past, and through Retief, who stood quietly, holding Boss down with one hand; with the other, he grabbed the open-mouthed Lout's shoulder and spun him around to face in the direction from which he had come; he gave him a slight push, which sent him headfirst ten feet into the dense foliage, where he threshed about noisily.

"That way, Pud," Retief directed the confused fellow. "Keep going. You'd better hurry." Then he returned his attention to the squirming mind-entity struggling against his impalpable restraint.

"Never seen no automatic deck-loader," Pud informed the ever-watchful spirits of air and water. "Can't blame a feller fer tryna get clear o' the machinery," he further informed his critics.

"I'll get you swabs for this!" Boss Eddie, AKA Looie Segundo announced, his voice somewhat blurred by the pressure of the rocky ground against his mouth. Retief cut off the flow of rhetoric by applying another few dozen foot-pounds of pressure.

"Before you start planning your revenge," he told the struggling chieftain, "let's talk about where you've been keeping yourself."

"Retief!" Magnan yelped, fairly dancing with excitement. "We mustn't linger here! I was bravely carrying on alone—then you interposed your presence between me and Dirty Eddie. Lucky for the scamp; I was about to take a just and dispassionate revenge for the upset he's caused me—*and* dear Gaby. Gaby! Gaby! Where *is* she? She was just here; I was shielding her with my body—but—"

"Easy, Benji," Gaby soothed as she emerged from behind a giant whum-whum tree. "I seen how you and yer friend here throwed old Horny and Pud fer a three-yard loss. Old Eddie, too," she added, glancing down at the now-quiescent Boss as she stepped daintily over him.

"I hope you'll excuse me, Ben," Retief said solemnly, "for interfering. We need him in a single unwashed piece for questioning. He's been the one behind most of the nonsense we've encountered here."

"Yes, he *was* rather quick to appear just after we'd

met Nudine," Magnan babbled. Gaby gave his arm a demanding tug.

"Nudine?" she echoed. "You been hanging around with that exhibitionist again?"

"Not for some time, my dear," Magnan improvised. "Anyway, she was Retief's friend. I was merely a bystander."

"You one o' them voyeurs?" Gaby demanded.

"Oh, that's an early French explorer on North America," Magnan suggested hopefully. "No I, Gaby! I've never explored that or any other world."

"Don't go weaseling on me, Ben Magnan!" Gaby objected. "Them Frogs you was talking about was *voyageurs*. Voyeurs is like Peeping Irvings!"

"You wrong me deeply, my dear," Magnan huffed. "It was just that I couldn't quite believe you'd accuse me of voyeurism."

"Aw, Benny," Gaby cooed.

"I must decline further to discuss the baggage," Magnan declared loftily. "I have this Eddie person to deal with." Magnan paused, looking expectantly at Retief.

"When last I saw you, Jim," he stated, "you were about to investigate a most uninviting excavation. Now, abruptly, some hours later, you pop up here—not that I'm ungrateful for your assistance in laying by the heels this uncouth fellow, Dirty Eddie, Looie Segundo, Boss, or Sir Farbelow, as you prefer."

"The hole led back into the cave where we had lunch," Retief told him. "Colonel Underknuckle and Counselor Overbore were still there, still arguing. They seem to disagree as to which one has priority in the deal with someone called Wiggly."

"Good Lord!" Magnan gasped. "No wonder matters are in a state of anarchy here: double-dealing of the highest level—or almost. The Captain has referred to his pet Worm as Wiggly! Surely His Excellency isn't actually implicated?"

"Not in writing," Retief reassured his supervisor. "I

had no idea the situation might be deteriorating here."
As they spoke, Eddie had carefully shifted position.
When he was ready to make his try, Retief stepped on
his ankle, then released him.

"Nothing I couldn't have dealt with myself, of course,"
Magnan pointed out stiffly, his eye on Gaby. "Still,
your advent was well-timed. Now, what's to be done
with Eddie?"

"Don't trouble yerselfs none, gents," Eddie urged,
rising cautiously. "Hang loose. Ta." And he was gone
into the underbrush, though not before Gaby had delivered a vigorous kick to his departing derriere.

"Quick!" Magnan blurted. "We'll have to go after
him!"

"No need," Retief suggested. "We know where he's
going."

"Do we indeed?" Magnan challenged. "I, for one,
find the comings and goings of this chameleon-like scamp
quite baffling."

"That's because you haven't yet seen the Domes,"
Retief pointed out. "Up close, I mean. We saw them
from a distance, just after we met Nudine, you'll recall."

"That dame again!" Gaby objected. She turned to
confront Magnan. "You must've spent a lot of time with
her, eh, Benny?"

"Only a few minutes, actually," Magnan stammered.
"Then our party divided. But as for the Domes—I
simply assumed—" he broke off, looking puzzled.

"Go ahead, sir," Retief urged.

"Well," Magnan resumed hesitantly, "everything was
so halcyon—or it seemed so at the moment—that a
cluster of golden domes in the distance just seemed to
fit."

Gaby spat. "Halcyon, ey?" she burst out. "It so happens I know what that means: 'Peaceful and calm!' So
you and this dame were peaceful and calm, were you? I
bet—" She was interrupted by a hoarse yell, accompanied by a crashing of underbrush suggesting the charge

of a rhino; instead, Dirty Eddie burst into view, on the reverse tack.

"I *seen* 'em!" he yelled, then came to a halt and made an effort to compose himself.

"*Big* ones!" he stated loudly. "Oh boy, oh boy, oh boy!"

"Could you perhaps clarify that a trifle, sir?" Magnan suggested tentatively.

"I'm tryna tell youse, ain't I?" Eddie demanded. "Go ahead, you're so smart, *you* tell it!"

"I haven't the least idea," Magnan said coldly, "what you're talking about. Now get yourself together, man, and explain why you came bursting in here, shouting in that unseemly fashion!"

"I guess you'd yell some, too, Dude, you seen what *I* seen!"

"What I *saw*, I presume you mean," Magnan corrected tartly.

"How do I know what *you* seen?" Eddie demanded.

"Aw, shut up, Ed," Gaby suggested. "Soon's you say what's scared you so bad."

"Me, scared?" Eddie scoffed. "Nid-nuts! Takes more'n a fire-breathing dragon to scare Dirty Eddie Magoon!"

"You seen the dragon?" Gaby gasped.

"Dern near got stepped on," Eddie confirmed, almost contentedly. "Two hundred foot long if it was a inch," he amplified. "Snorting and smoking, don't know why it never set the woods afire."

" 'If it was an inch,' you said," Retief pointed out. "That seems to be precisely the point at issue."

"Now don't go talking like one o' them dipplemacks back Zanny-du," Eddie protested. "I heard enough o' that jabber to last me. That Mister Overbore, now, smooth as blurb flops and mean as two fire-toads in a bucket. Crooked, too. Never done what he said, open up the front without no trouble. Don't know how the sucker figgered to work it, withouten *my* help! Heard old Worm had him, serve him right."

"Are you suggesting, sir," Magnan demanded haughtily, "that Counselor Overbore had engaged in some sort of trafficking with undesirable local elements in the person of yourself?"

" 'Suggesting,' my left hind *gabichy*," Eddie started, but Magnan *shush*!ed him instantly.

"A lady is present, I'll remind you!" he snapped.

"Whereat?" Eddie wondered aloud, glancing at, over and around Gaby. "You mean this broad here?" he muttered. Magnan stepped in and delivered a ringing *slap*! to the unshaven jaw of the bigger man, then turned protectively to Gaby, as Eddie wandered dazedly off into the underbrush, shaking his abused cranium.

"Come, my dear," Magnan soothed. "We'll just get along to the cottage, if you will be so good as to lead the way."

"Right down this here path, Benny," she cooed. "You was wonderful, Sweetie. Not many fellers would've socked old Eddie, which he done time for killing old Moose with his bare hands, like he done that time. Kind of sissy, slapping him," she added, "but I guess that's cause yer a gentleman and all."

"This seems to be an established path we're on," Magnan observed. "Quite well-worn, actually. Even a number of stumps where trees have been rudely cleared away. I thought we were going to a secret hideaway."

"Sure, onney everybody's in on the secret," Gaby reassured him casually. "Onney they're scared, is all. Not like us."

"Not like us at all," Magnan agreed reedily. "Scared of what, might one ask?"

"The Spectre is all," Gaby told him.

"I see," Magnan replied automatically.

"Knowed *you* wouldn't be skeert none," Gaby told him.

"Remarkable what the ignorant will believe," Magnan ruminated. " 'Spectre,' indeed."

"Oh, you know all about old Spectre, eh, Benny?" Gaby cooed and fell back to take his arm as usual.

"Never could understand," she remarked, "why it likes to tear fellers' heads off. Why's that, Honey?"

"Why, as to that," Magnan heard his voice saying, "that's to ensure he'll hear no more nonsense from them. 'Tears their heads off,' did you say? And it's to be found in this direction?"

"Eager to get there, hey, Benny?" Gaby deduced happily, edging behind him. Magnan advanced without enthusiasm, and reached out to pluck a pink and yellow thread from a thorny shrub. "It appears that Eddie has been here before us," he commented. "Curious he'd take precisely this route."

"Only path around here," Gaby pointed out. "So what? The sucker come back plenty fast." She forged ahead of Magnan. "Cain't wait to see that there rose-covered cottage and all," she remarked.

"But—but what about this Spectre?" Magnan wanted to know. "And poor Eddie was babbling about a dragon."

"You don't pay no mind to a crud-bum like Dirty Eddie Magoon, do you sweetie?" Gaby scoffed. "You a big-shot Embassy johnny like you said, and all. Fergit him."

"Mr. Magoon is quite beside the point," Magnan stated stiffly. "It was the dragon—and the Spectre—regarding which I was requiring."

"Sure, what I meant. Old Eddie's hung up on this here dragon o' his. Seen it first swimming in a gin bottle, they say—just a baby. Growed some since. Last time he had one o' his fits, it was fifty foot high and a hunnert yards long, and breathed out fire and smoke." She paused to sniff. "Smell anything burning, Benjy?" she asked.

He shook his head impatiently. "You're saying this dragon Mr. Magoon claims to have seen is a figment of his imagination?" he demanded.

"Sure, what else would it be?" Gaby snapped back. "You don't think he'd be talking about somebody *else*'s hangup, do you? Fifty foot high, blowing flames—" As her indignant voice trailed off, a sharp odor of scorched vegetation was wafted to Magnan's nostrils, accompanied by a *chuff*ling sound as a twenty-foot tongue of fire and smoke spurted out among the tree-tops, setting them crackling. Magnan stopped dead. "Gaby," he called, and pointed. "L-like that?" he inquired.

"Yep, zackly like that," she agreed. "Silly, ain't it?"

"Preposterous," Magnan mumbled in automatic agreement, staring through the folliage for a glimpse of the source of the conflagration. "Rather like the Woomy," he commented, gamely resisting a powerful impulse to flee the scene without further investigation. The Woomy, after all, had been merely a machine.

Gaby retreated to his side and clutched his arm. "Benny," she appealed in a strained voice. "If'n that dragon o' Ed's is onney a loose-nation like you said, what's making that far?"

"Why, as to that," Magnan started glibly. "It's merely an exhaust from an engine of some sort, I shouldn't wonder."

"Un," Gaby replied, sounding relieved. "What's a 'injum'?"

" 'Indian,' you mean, I suppose, my dear," Magnan corrected automatically. "They were the autocthonous population of an ancient planet called, naturally enough, India, as I recall. Or, not actually India, but the early explorers *thought* it was India, you see, and naturally referred to the inhabitants as 'Indians.' Meanwhile, the true Indians carried on, calling themselves 'Indians' as well, which occasions some confusion among young scholars in their astrography classes." As he spoke, the snorting sounds became louder.

"What's all that stuff got to do with this here far?" Gaby inquired in a tone in impatience, at the same time tugging at him as if to drag him back down-trail. "And that noise, too," she added. "Benny," she continued, "seems to me like sometimes you sorta lose the thread, if you know what I mean. But I guess that's cause you got so much important stuff on yer mind, you can't hardly get inneressted in stuff like this imaginary dragon and all."

"Pray release me, child," Magnan requested soberly, disengaging his arm from her determined clutch. "I must investigate this. Wait here, please." And he strode away, directly toward the source of the sound and the flame. Gaby uttered an only half-stifled shriek.

"You got no call to go off a-heroing and leave me here alone!" she wailed. "Sitch a thang as being *too* durn brave!"

Without pausing, Magnan spoke over his shoulder: "You really must take more care with your diction, Gabrielle," he nagged. " '*Such* a *thing*,' not 'sitch a thang.' And do be calm! I shan't be a moment."

Pushing ahead along the somewhat overgrown trail, Magnan noted that both the snorting and the volume of noxious gases was increasing. On an immense whickey tree just ahead, he saw one of the omnipresent reward posters.

"A primitive internal-combustion engine," he advised himself. "Just like the Woomy: Quite harmless. But it's really quite shocking that anyone would introduce such equipment to this pristine, unspoilt environment. Breaking ground for an industrial development, most likely." Just then a falling tree *ker-rash!*ed through the foliage and impacted close enough to send forest litter flying into his eyes, momentarily blinding him.

"Here, you assassin!" he yelled, shaking a fist in the direction of the louder-than-ever noises. "I could have been crushed! I shall have a word to say to your supervisor!"

As if in response to the threat, the blunt snout of a Mark XX Bolo thrust up above the fallen log, advanced over the obstacle, thrusting aside lesser trees like dry reeds. Magnan stood frozen, unable to decide in which direction to flee. Then Gaby screeched in his ear, grabbed his arm and pulled him to one side.

"Good lord, girl!" he yelped. "I told you to wait!" he

gabbled as he struggled to retain his feet. The giant machine canted downward and came on, strewing flying debris before it, to pass the awe-struck twosome at a distance of less than six feet and blundered on, heedlessly.

"Gaby, my child," Magnan managed at last, over the din. "You might have been killed! Why didn't you remain in safety as I suggested?"

"Figgered you'd get in trouble, bein' so brave and all," she told him. "Sure enough, here you were, holding yer ground whilst the dragon come at you! Never seen the like!"

"I was, ah, merely considering my strategy," Magnan explained, staring at the passing behemoth. " 'The dragon,' you say," he queried. "Do you realize what that means?"

"Sure, tole you it was just an old dragon," Gaby replied. "We're loose-nation, what else'd be that big and that noisy?"

"A Bolo Mark XX model WV/I, that's what!" Magnan snapped. "Actually what's known as a Continental Seige Unit, with the addition of an earth-moving blade, supposedly to convert it for agricultural use. But it still has its armor and firepower intact. Its presence here is an egregious violation of Chapter Nine, Sub-section five, paragraph two of the Charter!"

"Looks dangerous, too, fer a loose-nation," Gaby shouted in Magnan's ear, while the Bolo threshed in the dense growth, toppling trees left and right, including the one with the poster.

"Guess I shouldn'ta said that," Gaby reproved herself, "jest make you hotter'n ever to tackle it barehanded. Nope, Benjy," she added sadly. "I guess maybe you and me ain't made fer each other like I thought. I couldn't never get use to havin to stop and fall over ever cliff we come to. I guess I better go now—do it quick, you know. Bye, Benny. You were one tough hombre." And she was gone. Magnan dithered, croaked, "Gaby! Come back!" then blundered on down the trail still visible as a beaten path in the humus, though the deep tracks of the mighty Bolo had been imprinted across it.

"The cottage!" Magnan exclaimed to himself. "Perhaps she'll go there—so I'd best press on." The big war-machine was moving steadily farther away, off at an angle into deep woods.

"Disgraceful!" Magnan snorted, observing its trail of destruction. "I shall definitely bring this to the attention of the authorities!" Then, musing on the scene of the proposed denouement, a question presented itself: what authorities? For that he had no answer. Dismissing the matter from his thoughts, he hurried on, searching the wilderness ahead for the first glimpse of the rose-covered cottage where, he found himself hoping against his will, Gaby would be waiting. Quite abruptly, the trail widened into a grassy clearing with a tidy garden plot, the superstructure of a primitive well, complete with wooden bucket, and, at the far side, a modest but neat house of roughhewn logs, a reward poster stuck to the side. Magnan stopped short. "Good heavens!" he exclaimed. "Unpretentious in the extreme, and no roses in sight; still perhaps. . . ." His speculation was abruptly interrupted by the appearance of a man from the cottage; an elderly fellow with a bald head and an unsteady gait, who, aided by a gnarled cane, made his way along a red-brick path across the lawn to the garden-path.

The path of devastation left by the dozer, Magnan noted, passed close by the side of the clearing. He stepped out onto the brick path across the close-cropped lawn and hailed the old man:

"Here, sir! Are you responsible for this outrageous destruction?" he yelled, and motioned in the direction of the dozer's trail. The man halted, looking at Magnan without obvious approval.

"Who're you, feller?" the oldster returned. "And mind my herbaceous borders. Destruction? You're a fine one to talk to me about destruction!" The old fellow's appearance seemed familiar, Magnan thought.

"Would you deny the destructive effect of a rampaging Bolo?" Magnan demanded. "If it should turn this way I fear it will pay scant heed to your borders, herbaceous or otherwise!"

"You fellers come in here and start tearing things up," the old man grumped, "and then you come complaining to *me!*"

"I, sir," Magnan stated loftily, "am Career Minister Benjamin O. Magnan, Counselor for Trivial Affairs to the Terran Embassy to Goldblatt's Other World!"

"I guess that makes you a big shot," the old fellow remarked indifferently. "But I think I've got you outshot. Name's Sol Goldblatt." He approached Magnan and held out a work-gnarled hand. "You really from that there Embassy? Heard about that," he said when he had clasped Magnan's limp fingers and nearly pinched them off. Magnan jerked his hand back, wincing. "That's ridiculous!" he snapped. "I met Captain Goldblatt only today, a man in his prime. Besides which," he added confusedly, "his death nearly two centuries ago is a matter of record!"

"Then I guess you better amend the record, Mr. Magnan," Sol commented casually.

"I tried to contact you Embassy fellers," he went on, "right after I heard about you setting up shop here," he added. "Run into all kinds o' trash done invaded the place. Nice little planet when I first come," he went on. "Strange kind o' place, lots o' bugs; and I useta hear these like voices and all, but I still liked it a lot. Then the first bunch o' strangers showed up—clobbered in accidental, I guess—and started messing things up. Now a feller can't hardly weed the garden without some hard case coming along to stick his nose in. I get tired o' running 'em off; jest so they'd leave me be. But now they got that there infernal machine making passes just to rile me. Now *you* show up. A embassy's spose to look

out for a feller's rights and all, ain't it? What are you
boys doing about this?"

Magnan sank down on a rustic bench beside the
walk, fanning himself with his hand. "A moment, please,
sir," he pled. "I'm quite overwhelmed." He peered
curiously at the oldster's seamed face. "I thought you
were younger," he offered lamely. "Am I to understand, sir," he hurried on in a voice with a tendency to
break, "that I am indeed in the presence of the fabled
explorer, Captain Goldblatt, himself? Not a descen-
dant, or. . . ." his question petered out.

"Spikking descendents," his host came back. "What's
to descend, with no females? Or not hardly no females,
less you count them hard cases hangs out with them
hoodlums."

"B-but!" Magnan exclaimed, jumping up, "haven't
you seen—only moments ago—a young lady clad in a
most impractical long frock, who was preceeding me by
only a few moments? Oh, Gaby!" he raised his voice
slightly to call, meanwhile scanning the clearing anxiously.

"Over here, Benny," her reply came, from behind a
large clump of flowering, cactus-like plants. "Jest fixing
my face. Hang on."

"Thank Goodness!" Magnan gobbled. "I feared the
worst!"

"Jest ducked down when I seen Dirty Eddie sneaking around yonder," she explained, pointing across the
clearing toward a small out-building. "Reckon the skunk's
in the john. Go roust him, Benny. Serve the sucker
right." Magnan responded with a shocked gasp.

"Pardon me, ma'am," the elderly fellow interjected
hesitantly, peering curiously at her. "You're the first gal
I seen up close since last time I topped off at Rim
Station Nine, here a couple years ago."

"Rim Station Nine," Magnan intoned sternly, "was
closed down and converted to a museum over a century
ago, during the Apollo Demi-millenium celebration.

You really must abandon this habit of prevaricating, sir. It's hardly creditable, and furthermore it won't work."

" 'Prevarication,' " the old man repeated. "Means 'lying,' don't it? Guess you better watch yer manners, feller, or I'll get riled, and no telling what might happen." He turned and hobbled away.

"Who's that?" Gaby wanted to know.

"I'm the owner of this place, that's who, miss," was the grumpy reply. "Who're you?"

"I'm Gabrielle, ah. I use to know pa's name but I fergot."

"And are you, Miss Ah, in any way responsible for this persecution?" he demanded. "If so I insist that you desist at once!"

"Sir!" Magnan barked. "That is an insane suggestion! There is a crowd of ruffians intruding in these otherwise pleasant environs, and it is *they* who are causing all the trouble. Their ringleader seems to be a scamp going by the alias Dirty Eddie Magoon at the moment, the same who was seen skulking nearby but a moment agone! I suggest you lay him by the heels, and inquire of *him* as to responsibility for the numerous outrages we, and presumably yourself have suffered in recent days!"

"Oh, that's jest old Special Ed," the old man dismissed the idea. "I keep him around to do odd jobs. Use to, anyway, till he started getting big ideas."

"Some of them, sir," Magnan butted in, "are bigger than you think! Why, on one occasion I was actually assaulted by a fellow twice my size, encased in steel armor of antique design! Unhorsed the rascal, too," he added contentedly. "Had a curious hallucination," he went on, "that inside that armor was Sid Overbore. Transparent wish-fulfillment," he concluded with a sigh.

"You was wonderful, Benny," Gaby breathed, "but don't go bragging it up too much."

"I merely made reference to the incident *en passant*," Magnan objected. "I was citing an instance of the baroque with which I've been beset here."

"Sure, honey," Gaby soothed, stroking his forearm. "You—all of us—been in some fancy scrapes ever since we passed over."

" 'Passed over'? You say?" Magnan queried. "I know that term as a euphemism for death."

"One thang about bein' dead," Gaby mumbled. "You don't hafta worry about dying."

"So Hemingway said," Magnan observed tartly. " 'He who pays today is quiet for tomorrow.' But of course he had a pathological fear of death which eventually killed him."

"Ain't seen him," Gaby commented. "He musta been before my time. But anyways, what you got to do, you got to expect the unexpected. Like them nondeterminate polynomial complete problems you hear about. You got to do a Worst Case Analysis. Remember Ramsey's theory, Benjy: 'total disorder is impossible.' "

"I've read very little in cosmology and the like, my dear," Magnan pointed out. "May one ask when you acquired such apparent familiarity with the jargon in the Intermediate Physics?"

"Ain't jargon," Gaby objected. "Tole you this here is a sample of a nondeterminate polynomial complex problem!"

"Wave functions were never a hobby of mine," Magnan objected. "Can't we simply resolve our problems rationally?"

"The little lady's right," the old fellow contributed. "Rationality is a quirk o' the human mind. Be rational all you like, but that don't make the world conform to you. I oughta know."

"And precisely why, sir" Magnan challenged sharply, "should you, as you say, know of these matters?"

"Guess I can answer that," the elderly space'n answered promptly. "I come here, this place was a wasteland; jungle, desert, worms and gnats and worse. Big river. No folks. Started hearing these voices. That was a bad time, I'll jest be fair with ya." He paused, looking

solemn. "Guess it was my own fault, partly, anyways,"
he continued. "Had it made, but I got the big head:
going to be a big benefactor. Taken in this wounded
critter and named it Wiggly and started teaching it
tricks. First thing I knew, it was taking over, messing
everything up. Voices in my head got worse'n ever; a
ship come along and didn't know the ropes and got lost
and finely clobbered in—served 'em right. Bunch o'
no-goods, but they had a couple passengers aboard.
Some spoiled kid and his guardian or tutor or whatever—
good fellow, Prince William, the kid called him. Never
lasted long, though. Tried to take on the roughnecks
man-to-man, and they ganged up on him. Too bad." Sol
stared past Magnan. "Oh-oh—" he remarked. "Here's
another one. Big sucker, too."

"Heavens," Magnan gasped, turning. "You finally
came!"

"That's right, sir," Retief agreed. "I'm Retief," he
told the old man, who thrust out a toil-hardened hand.

"Call me Sol, ex-Merchant Navy of Terra," he supplied. "And I seen *you* before! On the wanted bill and
all!"

"Honored Captain," Retief said.

Magnan frowned at Retief. "Where in the world have
you been?" he yapped. "I've been set upon, chased by
a Bolo, wandered lost in this dismal forest—and what
were *you* doing while I was suffering, may I inquire?"

"Sure, go ahead," Retief replied easily.

"I just *did*," Magnan snapped. "That is, it's understood that when one says 'May I ask?', one *is* in fact,
asking! It's like 'I would like to take this opportunity to
thank you,' which means 'thanks.' "

"Trouble with you diplomatic Johnnies," Sol put in.
"Too many words, and most of 'em useless. What about
this here convict, Mr. Magnan? You going to arrest the
sucker, or what?"

"Why, Captain," Magnan demanded coldly of the
officer, "do you uniformly employ the unfortunate term

'Johnnies' with reference to dedicated bureaucrats? As for arresting my colleague, Mr. Retief—why it's an outrage! Art exceeded his instructions! Common sense was never Art's strong suit!"

"Leave it be, Benny," Gaby urged. "Coulda been a lot worse."

"But I was inquiring, or inquiring if I might inquire," Magnan regained his train of thought, "as to the recent whereabouts of my colleague, Mr. Retief."

"I was with you until half an hour ago, Ben," Retief reminded him. "Then you took off on your own to chase down Miss Gaby, here."

"You *did*, Benjy?" the lady gurgled. "How romantic—all except finding this old coot living in *our* rose-covered cottage."

"Reckon the place is mine," Sol corrected, "seeing I built it. Whattaya mean 'old coot'?"

"With your own hands?" Magnan demanded. "Including cutting all the lumber, and milling the woodwork?"

"Not exactly, Mister Ah," Sol corrected. "You see, Zanny-du ain't like most places, where a feller's got to go through a lot of intermediate steps. This was a unspoiled paradise, a blank slate, you might say; and my bein' the first Terry along, I shaped it nearer to my heart's desire, like the poem says."

"You know Keats?" Magnan asked in a tone of Mild Surprise (12-x).

"Nope. Prince William. He was full of it. Matter of fact, it was him named the place Zanny-du. Funny kind of name, but to me it's still 'Goldblatt's Other World,' like I called it in my report, just before I hit atmosphere."

"And where is this Prince William now?" Magnan wanted to know. He turned to Retief. "Didn't that objectionable child who called himself 'Sobby' refer to a Price William?"

"His tutor," Retief agreed.

"Pore feller was grabbed," the old man responded hesitantly to Magnan's question.

"Grabbed by whom?" Magnan persisted.

"By Old Wiggly, whattaya think?" was the impatient reply. "Tole you he got big ideas. I tole the damn fool to stay clear o' the Domes."

"Ah, the Domes," Magnan echoed, nodding as if wisely. "Tell us about the Domes."

"Tell ya nothing, wise guy," the old fellow snapped. "Go away. Lemme be. Got no time for no more damn fools."

"You've seen other damned fools here recently?" Magnan demanded hotly. "What cheek!" he added, for the benefit of any member of the Galactic press corps who might be within earshot.

"One swab called himself Colonel somebody, said he was a crack representative o' the Council, or Consul, or Consel, never did figger out which one. He was a talker, but never said nothing, only he was gonna get even. Pretty down on old Smeer, though. Claimed Smeer owed him some."

"Retief!" Magnan exclaimed, clutching at the latter's arm. "That reminds me: some time ago you said Smeer was Captain Goldblatt! I wondered at the time—but now it appears the Captain is a Terran after all."

"Well," Goldblatt put in, "only in a way—I mean old Smeer *was* me in a way for a time—I was using his nervous system, you see, to keep tabs on things. Tried to get him into that Terry Embassy, to get some info on what them boys was up to—but things kind of went awry, you might say—he run into this Mr. Overbore, and *he* wanted to talk deal, all right—only he thought Smeer was the local Overlord or like that—feller was in a big hurry to sell out the Terries—me included, even if he didn't know it—and get hisself set fer life—had a idea I could put my Smeer's hands on the local treasury—I strung him along some, greedy feller—that kind's easy to deal with, promise you anything—"

"Mr. Overbore!" Magnan yelped in belated indignation. "Why, I'd heard rumors but I could scarce credit them! Sidney Overbore is a Counselor of Embassy of Terra, His Excellency's most trusted advisor—and reliable rumor has it he's being groomed for Ambassadorial rank in the near future! I can't credit the charge that he deliberately set out to betray Terran interests."

"You really *are* a selfless sort of fellow, ain't ya, Benny?" Gaby cooed. "Wouldn't have no interest in a cave full of cut emeralds and them red ones—rubies—and such? No interest in the gold, neither, right?"

"What gold?" Magnan gobbled.

"*You* know," Gaby stated off-handedly. "The gold under the mountain, that the dragon guards."

"Oh, *that* gold," Magnan mumbled. "Nonsense!" he added as his brain resumed partial function.

"What rubbish," he expanded. "That's a silly fairy-tale! There's no dragon and no gold—and even if there were, I don't see what connection this fantasy might have with allegations of malfeasance in high places!"

"Naw, you got it wrong, feller," Sol put in. "No alligators, and anyway them crocs like the low ground. This here's a regular fire-breathing dragon."

"Eddie was babbling about a dragon!" Magnan improvised. "And all the while it was only a dozer!"

"Relax, feller," Sol urged. "Old Dragon won't bother nobody less they go poking their snoot in over the Domes, yonder."

"What about these Domes?" Magnan demanded. "What have they to do with alleged dragon of yours?"

"Tole you it ain't no alligator," the oldster snapped. "Ain't *mine*, neither."

"Tell us about the Domes, Captain," Retief suggested gently.

Sol looked keenly at him. "Thought all you fellers knew about them Domes," he grunted. "Where you been, stranger?"

"In the last few hours, just about everywhere," Retief told him.

"Before that," Magnan put in sharply, "we'd only

been around the Galaxy. Naive, you might say. But to
return to the Domes . . ."

"Nothing much to 'em," Sol stated dismissingly. "Kind
of fade out when you get up close. My idea," he went
on, "is they're kind of an optical illusion, generated by
the multi-dimensional intersection of incompatible wave
functions."

"Heavens," Magnan purred sarcastically, "why didn't
I think of that?"

"Might be because you ain't been marooned in a
crazy house fer a couple years, talking to yerself," Sol
guessed. "After a time you get to seeing things."

"As to that," Magnan started—

"Was saying," the old fellow went on, ignoring
Magnan's interruption, "first you see things, then you
hear 'em. Pretty soon they're back-sassing you. Bad fer
the nerves. All I wanted was a nice quiet place where a
feller could have a shot o' the good stuff, and some
plain, wholesome eats. Like a nice *gefeltefisch*, you
know, or *Boeuf Bourgignon*, maybe, and prolly a plate
of *consomme au Beurre Blanc* on the side."

"Rather elegant tastes you have, Captain," Magnan
remarked. "Considering your chosen profession as a
Merchant Astronaut."

"That some kind o' crack, mister?" Sol demanded
belligerently.

"Why, I merely meant—that is, I didn't mean,"
Magnan gobbled.

"He was trying to say it's hard to see where a deep-
space sailor'd get to know about fancy eats and such,"
Gaby clarified.

"Always carried a good liberry aboard," Sol growled.
"Over ten thousand tapes—the Five Hunnert Foot Shelf,
you know—lots o' time to view about wave mechanics
and *haute cuisine* and that."

"You've referred several times, sir," Magnan said
carefully, "to 'a couple of years'; are you unaware that

just over two centuries have elapsed since Sardon's discovery?"

"Never been discovered," Sol corrected curtly. "Been right here all along. Two hunnert years, you say? Must be a little distortion along the temporal axis, I guess. I ain't no two hunnert and sixty years of age."

"I'm sure we can sort that out later," Magnan brushed the objections aside. "Right now, it's imperative I know more about your 'arrangement' with Counselor Over-bore."

"Sucker never done what he said," Sol carped. "Tried to cheat me. I fooled him, though."

" 'When thieves fall out,' " Magnan muttered. "No wonder matters are in a state of chaos in this potentially idyllic world."

"Gonna pertend like I never heard that," Sol informed the circumambient air, at the same moment reaching out as if to snap off a whithered leaf from a flowering arbutus beside him. Retief caught his wrist. Sol attempted to pull free, then began angrily:

"You got no call to go jerking me around, right on my own land," he said, with a considerable volume of spit.

"You're a liar, Captain," Retief told him. "And a vindictive one at that." He looked toward the neat cottage across the lawn. "Why are the windows barred?" he asked, almost casually. As if in reply the glass in one of the small, barred openings burst outward with an astonishingly loud *crash*!

"Give you an idea," Sol grunted. "What I got to contend with: got a crazy man trapped in there. Busted out half my windows."

"Tell us about him," Magnan suggested, edging close to and partly behind Retief.

"Thinks he's some kind of king or like that," the old fellow stated contemptuously. "Trieda take over here. Right here—on my own planet, which I found it first!" Goldblatt paused to look indignant. "He's the one set up that rickety town yonder," he continued, nodding in a vaguely easterly direction. "Pretty soon the tramp traders started calling here."

"Traitors?" Magnan yelped. "Traitors to whom, may I ask?"

"Naw," Sol replied. " 'Traders.' Mostly ex-Navy swabbies got hold of a condemned space-hull and cruise around, seeing what they can do the natives out of, and selling the stuff to suckers someplace else. Space scum. Place is lousy with 'em now. Messed up my clean set-up, too. Can't get a nice plate o' chicken soup, nor no bagels and lox, just all this fancy stuff. Almost got me liking some of it. Them blurb-flops ain't half bad, I guess.

"Set up some kinda ancient ruins over Worm's cave, too," he went on. "Looks like a bank or like that. Useta be a swell-looking place: purty neon arch and colored pictures, a neat little fountain with red and yeller water coming out, and spotlights all around. Looked swell at night, I'll tell you. Then he messed it up: nothing there now but plain grass and some old trees and them plain white pillars. Useta have some great items with Old Wiggly, not a bad sorta critter fore he started tryna tell me what to do."

"But he didn't give up," Retief corrected. "In fact, your former pal has kept you penned up here for the better part of a couple of centuries, while he amused himself interfering with the stray Terrans who happened along."

"Once you'd found and registered this world," Magnan contributed, "it was off-listed and then became a challenge to the curious, the drifters, the easy-fortune hunters and the like, who've been seeking it out, and are never heard from again." He assumed a solemn expression (741-w) and added: "Thus, Captain, your irresponsibility in not fully reporting the unusual characteristics of your 'Other World' has caused a great deal of mischief, not the least being the diversion of my colleague and myself from our duties for an extended period."

"You wanta go back to that jack-built town?" Sol responded in a tone of skepticism, an approximation of the classic 13, and a b, Magnan thought.

"Your 13-b needs work, Captain," he pointed out. "It's curious how you laymen assume that you can deploy classic diplomatic subtleties, on the basis of a casual observation of some junior clerk's technique, perhaps. The fine nuances are lacking."

" 'Junior clerk' nothing!" Sol retorted. "I got that snooty look direct from a big shot name of Sid Overbore, time he come snooping around here looking to double-cross me when I was out. Only I wasn't out." He spat on the ground.

"But as to your question," Magnan resumed, "leaving aside for the moment the unlikelihood that Counselor Overbore would have confided precious diplomatic techniques to one of your stripe, I suppose the answer is yes: we *do* desire to return to town."

"Nothin easier," the captain told him, and turned and stamped off along the path toward the cottage.

"Here!" Magnan called after him. "You offered to guide us back to civilization! You can't just walk away. . .!"

"Easy, Ben," Retief suggested, and started along the path, following the irascible captain. Magnan fell in at the rear, still grumbling.

Close to the rose-trellissed front door, Sol looked back. "Maybe you better tell your side-kick to cut the chatter," he told Retief. "Guy gets on my nerves." He used a large, crudely-made key to open the door, and stepped inside.

Magnan hurried past Retief and without pausing, entered the dimly-lit interior. At once there was a meaty *smack*!, and sounds of struggle. Magnan staggered back to the entry, and grabbed at Retief for support. "Heavens!" he gasped. "We were assaulted in the dark!"

"Wait here, Ben," Retief advised and stepped inside. In the inadequate light from a single foliage-obscured window he saw the elderly captain trying furiously to close with a tall, solidly-built man dressed in a gray polyon shipsuit of antique cut, who held him at arm's length with a fist to the chest.

"Relax, Captain," the bigger man urged in an unexcited tone. "I didn't kick you; you walked into the table."

"Guess I know when I been assaulted!" Sol gasped, gamely continuing to throw his futile lefts and rights. "Snuck up on me in the dark, you with all yer fancy talk about ethics and such!" He fell back, breathing heavily.

The big man turned to Retief, offered his hand. "I'm William of Righolm," he said. "Have we met before, sir?"

"I think not, Your Highness," Retief responded, gripping William's hand firmly. "But I know of you, of course. Prince Sobhain sends his greetings. He's well."

"I left him in charge of an objectionable but sturdy lout," William confided. "After suggesting a few useful tricks which I hope he used well."

"He did," Retief reassured the nobleman. "In fact, he'd been making life hell for his 'keepers.' I urged him to take it easy."

"Headstrong lad," William replied, not without satisfaction. "Useful trait, considering the role in great affairs that awaits him."

" 'Role in great affairs'?" Magnan repeated with a rising inflection. "I found him a distinctly scruffy and undisciplined sort of ragamuffin."

"Mr. Magnan would be the first to accord His Highness all that protocol demands," Retief put in, "if he knew that he was a prince imperial, and heir presumptive to an ancient throne."

"What's that, Jim?" Magnan blurted. "Why I thought that 'Prince Sobhain' talk was just a joke, in poor taste at that! Why didn't you tell me? Now I fear I've unwittingly committed *lese majeste* of the grossest sort. His Highness will never forgive me."

"On the contrary, sir," Prince William said. "In fact—if you're a Mr. Magnan, he found you most amusing. Cheered him up no end."

"Well, as to that," Magnan improvised, "I fancy my sense of humor, though subtle, is one of my finest and least appreciated qualities. Pray express my satisfaction to His Highness—but how do you know what the boy thinks?"

"He told me, sir," the courtly tutor informed the dumbfounded Magnan, who gobbled, "B-but how? When? If you've been imprisoned here—"

"He wasn't," Retief tipped off his supervisor. "He posted himself here to guard the nexus-point, if I'm not mistaken."

"One has one's duty," Prince William pointed out quietly. "The captain had vengefully loosed his charming pet to rove freely; I felt it necessary to confine it."

"Here?" Magnan demanded, looking about the small room with an Air of Incredulity (41-v). "I see no puppy-dog nor pussycat. Here, kitty, kitty. . . ."

"Haply, sir," the grim-faced prince told Magnan, "the captain's pet is, as I said, confined; nor is the creature a lap dog."

"The place is hardly big enough to share with a pet sheep, like Little Mary's," Magnan sniffed. "And I see no cage for a hamster! Now, just what do you have to say to that, sir?"

"Nothing, mister," Sol told Magnan. "It's no skin off my sitzfleisch. Willy here had no call to go tryna trap *my* critter."

"Your creature, Captain," the prince stated firmly, "was in process of devastating the countryside."

"Old Wiggly don't mean no harm," Sol commented indifferently. "It's just he got to have some self-expression and all; felt a little frustrated, locked into *my* paradigm."

"What's this?" Magnan demanded, approaching what appeared to be a plain closet door. Before Prince William could reach him, he had opened it to reveal the

polished surface of a mirror. Pausing only to adjust the
lie of a lapel, he turned away.

"Curious place for a looking-glass—" he remarked,
then, as something in the reflective surface caught the
corner of his eye, he spun quickly to face it.

"Uh, Retief," he said quietly, then screamed. An
immense yellow eye was glaring balefully at him through
his reflection. A callussed eyelid came down like a
wrinkled roller shade, then snapped up again.

"It—it blinked!" Magnan shrieked. Then just as Retief
pulled him aside, the narrow yellow-green tongue flicked
out—*through* the reflective surface—and the space
Magnan had occupied an instant before. Retief slammed
the door.

"What—how?" Magnan yelped. "That—*thing* tried to
eat me!"

"Better you should stand clear o' the portal," the
elderly space-captain remarked. "It might be giving
out. He got his tongue through that time. Can't tell
when he might get his alignment right and bust through!"

"Why on Earth," Magnan demanded, "do you keep
such a menace in your closet?"

"Ain't *on* Earth," Sol reminded him. "Ain't been
there in years. Fact is, I built the closet around the
portal here after the Voice told me to, and the house
around the closet. Thought it best to stay close, ya
know. Couldn't let the critter run loose, once I seen
what he was doing."

"Most idealistic on your part, boss," Magnan approved.

"Ideals, schmideals," Sol replied carelessly. "I had
my own plan about how things outa be. Old Worm was
tryna mess it up."

"Perhaps," Magnan mused, "that accounts for the
curiously mixed nature of the place: a halcyon idyl on
the one hand; a thief-infested wilderness on the other."

"Them pirates done that," Sol supplied. "Messed up
my parks and gardens and all and Old Worm helped
'em do it. Jest for fun. Rascal likes trouble 'mongst us

Terries, it turned out. His idea of getting even. I raised him from a caterpillar that long." He indicated two inches with his thumb and forefinger. "Course, after I started hearing the Voice, it come along and helped me out at first, there, when I had the busted leg and all. Nice feller, back then."

I AM STILL A NICE FELLOW, the almost forgotten Voice spoke up suddenly. IT IS YOUR OWN CHARACTER FLAWS WHICH HAVE LED TO THE PRESENT UNFORTUNATE CONTRETEMPS.

"Likes to use them big words," Sol muttered. "Just to bug me. Knows I talk plain."

"Jim," Magnan managed in a stricken voice. "Does this mean that the voice which we took for a superior and friendly intellect actually emanates from that dreadful monster? Did you notice the deciduous teeth, some loose in their sockets, with a reserve row ready to take their place? Horrid!"

"So it appears, Ben," Retief confirmed quietly.

"But—what about Junior?" Magnan yelped. "He was decidedly cheeky to the Voice—so he must be an even more formidable monster!"

NOT REALLY, Junior corrected. I'M FOR-(WHAT HE SAID) BUT I'M NO MONSTER. GETTING OLDER, I GUESS, BUT STILL A FINE FIGURE OF A MAN. THE NERVE O' THAT WORM, CALL-ING ME 'JUNIOR'!

Magnan stared at Sol. "Was that—you?" he gasped. "I can scarce credit the concept of apparent omni-science in the first instance, quite aside from conceiving the phenomenon as emanating from a mere tramp captain!"

WATCH YOUR LANGUAGE, MISTER MAGNAN, Junior cau-tioned. WHO YOU CALLING 'MERE'? I'M A LICENSED DEEP-SPACE SKIPPER, AND THERE'S NOTHING 'MERE' ABOUT ME; AND I DON'T PLAN TO TAKE A LOT OF SPACEWASH FROM BUREAUCRATS!

"Mind your tone, my man," Magnan cautioned. "There are, or is, I should say, a number of matters which you've not yet explained satisfactorily; matters, I might add, which promise to make yours one of the most colorful trials in Corps history."

"Now you're talking trials?" Sol scoffed. "Maybe you're forgetting, Mister, you're on *my* turf."

"Your 'turf,' as you call it," Magnan reminded the now irate spaceman, "is in fact the sovereign world registered as CNGC-4, or in your local vernacular, 'Zanny-du.' "

"I found it before you did," Sol muttered. "Guess I got a few rights. Found the whole system," he added, "six planets; left the other five in the public domain. Some thanks I get."

"I for one, have little for which to be thankful, sir," Magnan intoned, "in the experiences which have befallen me here on this cryptic planet—all as a result of *your* meddling, I believe, with the natural order of things!"

"All I done was fix things up a little," Sol protested. "It was them mutineers and then Prince Willy, here, messed things up. Plus that Overbore fella. And Old Worm o' course."

"From the single horrifying glance I obtained," Magnan stated, "it appears your Worm is merely an overgrown specimen of the autocthonous Zanadoers."

"There you go with the twelve-buck words again," Sol complained. "What's a 'auto-thon' or what you said?"

"An autocthone," Magnan announced didactically, "is a mentational species indiginous to its environment."

" 'Indigent,' " Sol muttered. "That's 'broke,' ain't it? Bankrupt? Hell, Worm ain't got no bank to rupt."

"You're confusing 'indigenous' with 'indigent,' " Magnan corrected tartly.

"Whatsamatter?" Sol inquired of the cosmic All, "ain't they got enough words, they gotta use the same one twice? How about 'guglimp,' or 'intransbigural.' Heck, I can make up words don't sound like no other word, as fast as I can talk."

"Lexicogeny," Magnan commented in a lofty tone,

"is not a matter of on-the-spot improvisation. The vocabulary in common use is a product of millenia of linguistic evolution, with roots traceable to the Neolithic."

"You made that lexicogeny up," Sol responded. "I bet."

"Why, actually," Magnan responded with only a trace of Righteous Indignation (112-a), " 'lexicogeny' *is*, as it happens, a neologism; but a legitimate one, firmly based on classical roots."

"Calling something 'a legitimate neologism' don't clarify matters none," Sol told Magnan crisply. "Talk plain, mister. Try it sometime. You might be surprised how it helps."

" 'Talking plain,' as you so crudely put it," Magnan rebutted, "is the prerogative of the layman. Subtle nuances can hardly be expressed for the record in blunt Standard."

"What record?" Sol demanded suspiciously. "You guys taking notes, or what?"

Before Magnan could frame an indignant reply, the closet door burst open and Dirty Eddie staggered through and fell heavily. He seemed unaware of his surroundings as he rolled over, sat up and shook his head. Magnan stepped forward to close the door.

"Dern near got me that time," the newcomer announced blurrily. Then he looked around, his eyes holding on Sol. "How'd *you* get here, Boss?" he muttered. "Thought you was over to the Domes and all." He twisted to look over his shoulder at the closet door. "Prolly got *them* two," he added indifferently.

CHAPTER EIGHT

"Mister Segundo!" Sol barked. "I tole you and I tole you to stay clear o' here. What 'two' you talking about?"

"Old Nudine and her new boyfriend, some clown they call 'Small,' " Dirty Eddie supplied. "Got what's coming to 'em, nosing around and all. Caught 'em at the temple."

"Why, they're our friends!" Magnan wailed. "Our former associates, that is," he amended. "Perhaps it's not too late," he whimpered, as Retief brushed past him and wrenched the closet door open. Small stepped through, carrying Nudine in his arms.

"Thanks, Retief," the big fellow muttered. "Pore gal got knocked down by that overgrowed 'pillar, yonder." He put her gently on the narrow cot at one side of the tidy room.

"Had us quite a time since you fellers disappeared," Small remarked.

"*We* disappeared?" Magnan yelped. "It was *you* who were suddenly among the absent. Where did you go? What happened? We were together in the cave—"

"Right," Small agreed. "Then old Smeer and his boys come along."

"Those lowlifes are still bugging people?" Sol yelped. "I thought I'd dealt with that crowd once and for all when I fenced 'em in!"

"Not quite, Sol," Retief told the old fellow. "The situation here on Sardon isn't quite as simple as it appeared at first. Each time you've meddled with the Basic Postulate, you thereby altered the very phenomenon you were attempting to employ. Heisenberg's Uncertainty Principle at work on the mega-scale."

"Who's this Heisenberg?" Sol demanded. "Sounds like a wise guy to me!"

"Not a wise guy, Captain," Magnan corrected. "A wise *man*."

"Sounds like a cop-out to me," Sol returned. "I guess I can say what goes on my own—I mean, finder's keepers and all—without this Heisenberg butting in. He should butt out already!"

"Professor Doktor Heisenberg has never left Terra, Captain," Retief soothed the ruffled skipper. "In fact, he's buried there. His principle of uncertainty was a purely theoretical concept, at the macroscopic level."

"Retief!" Magnan spoke up sharply, pointing out the window. "Those yellow clouds: they look like something painted by N. C. Wyeth! And in that connection, it's clear what the city reminded me of: an Impressionist painting, as if one had constructed buildings to match Pissaro's sketchy technique. Even the cottage here—it's straight out of Monet!" He paused to blink at the landscape. "That bistro—the Cloud Cuckoo Club: the bar at the *Folies Bergere* circa 1880 to the life! Even Nudine, or Jacinthe, Manet's *Dinner on the Grass*. Someone has evoked in substance the fantasies of the great artists!"

"There's the guy," Sol accused, pointing at Prince William. "I trieda keep it homey, ya know, but as soon as *he* come along, things started to go to pot. That town o' his! Looks like it was stuck together outa slabs o' wet cardboard!"

The prince nodded affably. "When I discovered that my fancies took on form here," he told them casually, "I naturally did my best to make that form as pleasing to the eye as possible. A pity the captain here had such abominable taste; I was forced to re-do practically everything he'd blotted on the landscape."

"Where'd them knights with the iron suits come from?" Sol challenged. "*They* don't add nothing to the scenery."

"Sir Farbelow was no invention of mine, sir," the prince replied. "He seems to have arisen from some suppressed romantic streak in the blackguard Overbore, perhaps aided by Prince Sobhain's boyish fantasies."

"Sir!" Magnan burst out. "I must protest! Mr. Overbore is a fully accredited Terran diplomat and Counselor to the Terran Mission and my personal chief! One can hardly stand by and hear him slandered repeatedly in this fashion!"

"Calmly, Ben," Retief counseled. "I'm afraid His Highness is right."

"But—" Magnan objected. "How would a mere Second Secretary know of such matters, even if they had in fact transpired?"

"The boys had a rather unguarded conversation in my presence," Retief told him. "They didn't know I was there."

"He's right, Mister Magnan," Small put in. "Me and Nudine here caught some o' that—reason we went to hide out in the back o' the cave. That didn't work out good, like you know. Anyways, we come back and everybody was gone. Never left no note, neither."

"That," Magnan pointed out, "is a quadruple negative."

"Chaucer used 'em all the time," Sol commented. "I had plenty time to scan my tape liberry that I fetched outa the wreckage," he explained. " 'Who never yet no villayne ne said unto maner wight.' Four: count 'em."

"That is hardly the matter at issue here," Magnan

reminded the captain sharply. In an aside to Retief, he whispered, "Apparently the old fellow is paranoiac. He seems to think he's Captain Goldblatt."

"You're calling *me* nuts already?" the old boy yelled. "Mr, I'd be nuts if I didn't get a little uptight, I guess, with you folks comin around here trespassing, and giving *me* a hard time, and all the rest of what's happened! On top o' that now I got that tractor making close passes just to scare me. Works, too."

"Just *who* is operating that machine in that careless fashion?" Magnan demanded. "Very nearly crushed me!"

"That was old Eddie here, doin that," Sol told him. "Come by here and trieda stiff me for protection money. Hah! I shuld pay *that* loser! Looks like he run into Worm with that Mark XX o' his. Too bad he survived! But maybe I could fix that!"

Eddie, still on the floor, recoiled, scrabbling backward away from his irate host. "I done nothing!" he croaked. "Just tryna clear out a road, is all. Damn dragon come along an turnt my rig over, nearly squashed me!"

"And a good thing, too, you lowlife!" Sol yelled. Magnan caught his arm.

"Pray withold your just and dispassionate vengeance, Captain," he pled. "I fear your unfocused retaliatory measures have complicated matters considerably. That baroque incident involving a rhinocerous, for example, I suspect," he added, addressing Retief.

"Sorry, sir," Retief replied. "I don't remember a rhinocerous."

"Whattaya mean 'dispassionate'?" Sol demanded. "And don't be too sure about 'just.' These mugs don't worry about the details; why should I?"

"Because, Sol," Magnan reminded the officer, "you are a duly licensed master of a deep-space vessel, and as such a representative of Terran law and order here in this remote reach of the Arm."

"Big deal," Sol dismissed the idea. "Besides, my ticket

prolly lapsed some time ago. I been here a while, you know."

"In addition to which," Magnan continued his appeal, "when the scope of your discoveries and your heroic stand here versus the forces of anarchy become generally known, you will doubtless be recognized as a Hero of Terra. Schoolchildren will seek to emulate you; you must set them a good example."

" 'Emulate'?" Sol echoed. "Ain't that where they cut off a guy's—?"

"Hardly, Captain," Magnan cut him off quickly. "There are ladies present, sir, must I remind you?"

"Skip that," Sol grunted. "I didn't invite 'em. I should throw maybe a tea-party for a bunch a bums? Let's get back to what business you boys have got, trespassing."

"We are attempting, Captain," Magnan stated tartly, "to get to the bottom of the series of unlikely events which have unfolded here, to the detriment of the dignity of the Terran Mission to Zanny-du—or to Goldblatt's Other World, if you prefer."

"Nothin to me," Sol dismissed the matter. "What's important is I had a nice set-up here for my retirement years, and that ship-load o' trouble-makers comes along and nothing's been peaceful since."

"I understood you to say earlier that it was Worm, your former pet, which was at the root of the problem, Sol," Magnan put in promptly.

"You ain't been listening good, Mr. Ah," Sol snapped. "That's only part o' the picture. It was that Boreover that really messed things up—planting that nexus box and all."

"Still on that tack, eh?" Magnan objected. "But it *was* your Worm, or Wiggly you caged here."

"Yeah, that's right," Sol confirmed promptly. "Trieda oust me and take over. But I fooled him." He paused to chuckle. "I picked up a couple of tricks from the sucker, and then I traced him. That's how I got to lock him up, in the Recess there."

"For a while," Magnan told the old man, "we thought *you* were Worm—"

"What, me?" Sol interrupted. "You're on a bum lay, feller. I ain't no worm!"

"Mr. Magnan said, 'for a while,' " Retief pointed out. "But then something you said told us the truth."

"Sure, I told you the truth, the whole truth and nothing but the truth!"

"Well, Jim," Magnan prompted, "what *is* the truth?"

2

DON'T FORGET, Junior's long-silent voice spoke up suddenly. I DID TRY TO HELP YOU—GAVE YOU VALUABLE HINTS AND ALL; THOUGH IT SEEMS ONLY MR. RETIEF HERE WAS SHARP ENOUGH TO PICK UP ON THEM.

"Good lord," Magnan gasped. "I was quite persuaded Junior was Worm's rebellious offspring."

"In a sense, he was," Retief commented. "Worm learned from the captain and then it became the teacher: combining its natural endowments with the Terra worldview, it took over the relationship and shaped the captain's energies to its own needs."

"I see!" Magnan exclaimed. "It reprogrammed the captain to a degree, but was not, luckily, able to subvert him completely. Thus the captain retained sufficient control to enable him to rap and pen up the ravening monster! Well done, Captain!" Magnan reached for Sol's hand and shook it enthusiastically. Sol disengaged himself from Magnan's grip and backed away, wiping his hand on his pantsleg.

"Never ravened none, far's I know," he objected. "Old Wiggly is all right, boys. Just got a little carried away for a while is all. Thing's quiet down, I figger to have a nice talk with him, get him straightened out."

"Perish forbid!" Magnan blurted. "Pray leave well enough alone!"

"So who's in a hurry, already?" the captain protested.

"Got plenty time, now you fellers come in and give yerselves up and all."

"Came *in*?" Magnan yelped. "Gave ourselves *up*? Are you *quite* mad?"

"Naw, I'm cool," Sol soothed. "But if I don't havta be on my guard against three sets o' buttinskies, I can maybe relax a while and reason with him. I know him, remember. Raised him from that big." Once again he indicated two inches with a blunt thumb and forefinger.

" 'Reason'?" Magnan echoed. "One doesn't reason with an ambulatory appetite!"

"I like it," Sol commented. "I guess you got guts after all, Mr. Magnan, making up a alliterative nickname for a critter which it could gulp you down in a gulp, if you know what I mean—only he wouldn't—he's a pussycat, when you know him. Anyway, he's locked up safe."

"Are you right sure about that, Cap?" Small asked earnestly. "Nudie and me come cross-country from the cave maybe a couple day's walk, and come up on that door from behind. What's to keep old Worm from going the other way?"

"It's beyond your comprehension, I fear, my good fellow," Sol replied. "No offense—it's beyond *my* comprehension, too. Has to do with the polarity of the paradigm, or something of the sort."

"That why you stick to yer cabin so close?" Small suggested. "Feared he'll be waiting right outside yer clearing?"

"One may as well play it safe," Sol pointed out. "He's accepted as an aspect of his paradigm that the door constitutes an impassable barrier; I'm content to leave it at that."

"Looks to me," Small commented judiciously, "like he's got you penned up as much as you got him—and in a smaller space, too—course," he added mildly, "I guess it's all in how you look at it."

"And I assure you, Space'n Small," Sol stated firmly, "that I am very careful indeed about how I look at it."

"So we're all trapped here together?" Magnan mourned. "And that horrid great beast may well be lurking just outside?"

"Stand aside," Prince William spoke up suddenly. He drew his jeweled-hilted ceremonial sword from its black leather-and-gold filigree sheath, and took a step toward the closet door. "I for one will not be prisoned here, impotent, while my liege lord is in peril." Without further warning, he wrenched the door wide open, to reveal a view of a strip of velvety green lawn with a tiled path and a white-painted wrought-iron bench, all sun-dappled against a backdrop of black-green primeval forest. The only imperfection was a swarm of gnats around the bench.

"Retief!" Magnan burst out. "That's—I know that spot! It's— "

"You're right, Ben," Retief confirmed. "Over there—" he pointed off to the right— "You can barely see the Domes."

"Well, there ain't no worm hanging around here," Nudine stated. "This here's my own turf. I met you boys just yonder, by my pond," she pointed. "This is swell. Come on." She thrust past the prince and went to the bench beside the walk and sat down.

"Easy, Your Highness," Retief suggested as the by-passed William glowered at the girl. "I think young Sobby is quite all right."

"How can you know, sir?" William demanded. "What indeed do you know of my noble charge?"

"I know he's the heir presumptive to the throne of Fragonard," Retief told the prince. "He was kidnapped and you followed and managed to secure passage on the vessel on which he was being smuggled off-world. The ship crashed here on Goldblatt's Other World, in a lake, with no casualties. In the confusion, you found and released the lad, and together made your way clear of the wreck in a ship's skiff, and almost at once discovered indications that the world was not, after all, unpopulated. There was a rather disreputable-appearing structure visible across the lake, from which boisterous sounds emanated even though it was mid-morning. You made a cautious approach, unnoticed, and moored your skiff beneath the bistro, cautioned the boy to remain where he was, and found a side entrance. Inside you were astonished to find a scene that was familiar to you from your knowledge of ancient painting: the bar at the *Folies Bergere*, circa 1880, AD. You took a seat and soon found yourself in conversation with none other than Will Shakespeare, the Bard of Avon. Am I correct, so far?" Retief paused to inquire.

"I knew at once that I had lost my mind," Prince William confirmed. "On the bandstand, a youthful Arturo Tosconini conducted a pick-up combo in a preliminary version of a Giacomo Puccini piece from Tosca. The wine was an 1870 *Chateau Rothschilde*. I fled, of course. What man desires to confront his madness face-to-face?"

"That's what we've all been doing, like it or not!" Magnan declared. "Only it appears it's not really 'madness' in the sense of the loss of contact with reality. Rather, reality has lost contact with us—or me, at least."

"Aw, Benny," Gaby said soothingly, "don't go getting upset and all. This is all routine. I hear from the boys other places ain't like Zanny-du, but what I heard, they sound purty dull, nothing much ever changes."

"I'd hardly say nothing ever changes on a normal world, my child," Magnan corrected without heat. "But the changes are gradual and rational: evolutionary rather than revolutionary. Organisms come into existance, mature, age, and pass away—"

"That don't sound so good," Gaby put in. "I don't wanta age, so I don't. And I already passed over, like I told you. You, too, or you wouldn't be here." She hugged his arm in the possessive manner that had become habitual. Magnan disengaged himself hurriedly.

" 'I also,' you say? Do you suggest, my dear, that *I* am a dead man?"

"Well, I guess it's a matter of terminology," the girl hedged. "In a lot of ways we're more alive after we pass over than we was before, don't you think, Benny?"

"I'm sure I have no idea," Magnan huffed. "As for myself, I'm very much alive, thank you very much, and I have every intention of remaining so."

"Dern," Gaby commented contritely. "I done riled you again. I don't know if we can ever figger on getting along for the long haul."

"Again, your meaning escapes me, child," Magnan carped. "What is this 'long haul' to which you refer?"

"*You* know," Gaby urged, gazing soulfully into Magnan's eyes, a maneuver which had the effect of reducing the senior diplomat to babbling incoherency.

"I—ah, you say 'I know,' " he managed. "Let me assure you, miss, if I knew, I should hardly waste your time and my own by, ah, what did you say?"

"Getting married and all is a serious matter, Benny," she wheedled. "Don't go making jokes about it, puh-lee-us." She paused to dab at a moist eye.

"M-marriage!" Magnan yelled, then at once became solicitous as Gaby's sniffles gave way to a full-scale wail of despair. He patted the slender back which went with the shaply front which had somehow become plastered against him. "D-don't, for Heaven's sake, cry, child," he mumbled. "I didn't mean, I mean, I only meant— did you make reference to the holy state of matrimony?"

Her tear-stained face looked appealingly up at him. "Sure, Benny; I figgered—I mean, if a gent like you makes advances to a lady I got to figger yer intentions are honorable, right?"

"Of course, my dear," Magnan mumbled, deep in hypnosis. "Just as you say, child, so long as one doesn't become *too* serious."

"Take my advice, Mr. Ah," Sol put in, as if confidentially, "sheer off now, before it's too late. That gal's got you space-packed and coded Expedite."

Gaby's right cross was surprisingly effective. It caught the old fellow on the side of the jaw and sent him reeling back to—and through—the open closet door. Magnan stared after them in horror. "The dragon!" he yelped. "It will eat him for sure!"

"I doubt it, Ben," Retief said soothingly. "Worm has some big ideas, but he doesn't quite know what to do with them." As he spoke, Sol, who had tripped and fallen heavily, got to his feet, rubbing his jaw; then he spun and sprinted for the cover of the crape myrtles. Magnan yelled after him, "Wait, Sol! We need—"

Retief went to the shimmering veil before the woodland scene, paused only momentarily, and stepped through. Magnan uttered a strangled cry and would have followed, had Gaby not caught his arm and restrained him. Then the portal darkened as something huge and scaled moved in front of it.

"The dragon!" Magnan yipped.

"Durn Worm," Small muttered.

"Step aside," ordered Prince William. He advanced to the portal, drew his ceremonial sabre, and poked the monstrous obstruction. It responded by disappearing abruptly. Without delay, the gray-haired nobleman stepped through. Magnan's yelp of alarm was cut off abruptly as the prince spun, raised his jeweled sabre and hacked at a target out of sight beyond the door jamb. Again the view was blocked by an expanse of scaly hide; this time it seemed inert, Magnan thought, or at least not actively aggressive.

"He killed it!" Magnan yelped. "Good lord, he's slain the deity of these simple people!" Then the massive bulk blocking the doorway quivered, heaved, and slid aside. The prince was not to be seen, though Sol slipped back through the door.

"God!" Magnan wailed. "It's killed a prince of the blood!"

"Take it easy, already," Sol suggested quietly. "Remember, the opera ain't over till the fat lady sings."

" 'Sings?' " Magnan echoed in a tone of Stunned Incredulity at Gross Impropriety (1278-b).

"Easy, honey," Gaby urged.

"Never seen nothing," Small offered. "Maybe his Lordship's OK." He brushed past Magnan to pass through the narrow clear space opened when the monstrous form had shifted. Magnan yelped yet again, but shied away from following. He turned to the others.

"We have to *do* something!" he moaned. "Isn't there another way round?"

"Look!" Gaby said sharply and pointed. Magnan turned to see two immense yellow eyes, set in a complex pattern of tiny, vari-colored scales, staring, it seemed, directly at him.

"I know you, Ben Magnan," a rumbling voice said audibly, but without movement of the monstrous face. "I'm holding you *and* Retief responsible for this outrage."

"Me?" Magnan yipped. "Why, what ever did I do?"

"It's what you *failed* to do," the rumble replied stonily. "You omitted to restrain your subordinate when he set out to savage me."

"*He*, savage *you*?" Magnan gasped. "That's ridiculous! You're a thousand times his size, and you've those horrid bitey things, and claws, and—and . . ." Words failed the frail bureaucrat. "It isn't *fair!*" he lamented.

" 'Fair,' " the heavy voice repeated. "You an admitted diplomat, matter of fairness? Have you no respect for hallowed tradition? Remember Career Ambassador Pouncetrifle's wise dictum: 'Expediency; may she always be right, but right or wrong, expediency.' "

"Would you, Sir Worm," Magnan demanded with a show of spirit, stung by the harsh and, he was sure, undeserved rebuke, "—imply that I am remiss in my adherence to regulation, protocol, and tradition, as well as local policy? Outrageous! You can't prove it! I defy you to level such charges formally!"

"You forget Ambassador Grossblunder's adage, Ben," the deep voice came back sharply. " 'The implication is mightier than the affadavit.' "

"All right, break clean in the cinches, boys," Gaby admonished, thrusting between the verbal antagonists.

"Benny," she continued, "what about your sidekick, which he's in there with Worm, and nobody but old Small and the feller with the hat-pin to side him."

"Certainly, my dear," Magnan goggled, "I was on the way, was I not, when you restrained me. If the captain would kindly step aside. . . ."

Sol responded by executing a sardonic bow, and stepping aside—and through the mirror. For a moment his grin lingered, cheshire-cat like; then his rugged features rearranged themselves into an expression of horror, as he stared at something off-screen to the right. He held up his hands in instinctive defense and backed out of sight.

"Why, Benny," Gaby reproved. "You ain't going to let a little old gal keep you from your duty, are ya? Now you got the captain to rescue, too. Better hurry up."

"Precipitate action is not the diplomatic way," Magnan chided. "All in good time, my child." As he spoke, Magnan edged closer to the shimmering surface, poked it experimentally with a finger, leaned close and squinted sideways at it, and called through the reflected surface:

"Sol, perhaps you'd be so good as to explain to me the precise nature of this curious phenomenon you've so cleverly erected here in what seems otherwise to be an ordinary closet—"

Gaby interrupted the well-rounded period with a sharp rebuke. "—get going, Ben Magnan! If I wouldn't of seen you unhorse Sir Farbelow I'd be starting to wonder if you had all the *cojones* a feller oughta have to be sparking a gal half his age!"

"Your language!" Magnan gasped.

"I bet I'm the only one here talks Spash," Gaby cut him off. "And never you mind my furb-weed pickin language! Move yer butt, Ben Magnan! Yer friends are needing help! Now!"

Magnan experienced a momentary sense of deep relief that he had the option of a horrible death rather than endure further attack from such a quarter. He dived through. . . .

The immense Worm, scaled, bristly, and mindblowingly huge, lay like the Great Wall of Wubbadock, encircling the patch of smooth-cropped lawn. Dark trees loomed behind. The creature's head, raised high on its thick neck, was no larger, Magnan reflected wildly, than the Ambassador's formal limousine, a replica 1932 Dusenberg J; but against it hung Prince William, still gripping the hilt of the sword he had plunged fulllength into the monster's pale-scaled throat. Apparently little discomoded by the wound, it shook its head and threw the man off.

Retief stood near the behemoth, looking up at the underside of its jaw, ten feet overhead. Magnan lay where he had fallen, to his left he saw the circular mirror-bright surface of the Link. He made a convulsive lunge toward it, but Retief spoke quickly:

"Stand fast, Ben. I don't think things are as bad as they look."

"They *couldn't* be!" Magnan gasped. "What are you doing, do you mean to *dare* the monster to devour you?"

"Something like that," Retief agreed casually. "At the same time, I'm getting a good look at the bruise where I kicked Smeer one day."

"Whatever has kicking Chief Smeer," Magnan demanded, "a most undiplomatic ploy, by the way—to do with offering yourself as a sacrifice to this horrid great creature?"

"The chief was a pretty undiplomatic fellow himself," Retief reminded Magnan. "But I wasn't really sure what he was up to until I saw my boot-print on his adam's-apple just now."

"Have you taken leave of your senses, Jim?" Magnan wailed.

"Sure," Retief replied cheerfully. "We all have."

"Kicking Smeer was bad enough," Magnan went on doggedly, "but as for attacking this malevolent mountain of meat—pardon, no alliteration intended—if you had, in fact done so, isn't this a poor time to remind it of the incident?"

"By no means, sir," Retief replied. "He knows now his game's blown, and that it won't work anymore, now that we're on to him."

"On to him?" Magnan moaned. "Withdraw to my side at once!" he barked. Retief ignored him, and strolled around to a position directly beneath the gaping, ten-foot jaws.

"*Mister* Retief!" Magnan yelled. "I distinctly directed you to come here at once!"

Retief turned his head to look at him with a glance Magnan had seen only once before, on the occasion when a Groaci corporal had elbowed aside a senior Terran field marshall; the marshall, who had appeared on the point of apologizing, catching Retief's look had at once spilled the impudent non-com from the chair he had preempted and reclaimed the place himself.

"Good lord, Retief," Magnan objected. "I didn't mean, I only meant, I mean—"

"I understand, Ben," Retief replied. "You were concerned about my safety. But you needn't be. Smeer is going to be very nice from now on. Isn't that correct, Chief?" He addressed the final query to the fanged dragline bucket.

YOU'D BETTER BE! the long-silent Voice said sharply. OR I'LL BE FORCED TO—

"YOU WOULDN'T! Junior's comparatively weak voice responded.

"Sure, he would," Retief supplied. "He has a few points to make up with His Terran Excellency."

As Magnan stared in utter Amazement (331-a), Prince William, unhurt, came up beside Retief, and by standing on tip-toe, grasped the hilt of the sword still standing in the monster's neck. With a sharp jerk, he withdrew it; an immediate *hiss!* of escaping air was accompanied by the abrupt appearance of wrinkles in the scaly hide, which quickly became folds as the upreared torso collapsed in upon itself while the fearsome face, sagging grotesquely, assumed a look of drooling idiocy before collapsing in a heap of rubbery vinyl on the grass.

"R-Retief!" Magnan yelped. "It was only a—a sort of inflated dummy!"

"Very observant of you, sir," Retief commented. Then to the prince, "Nice timing, Your Highness."

"I'm sorry to say this whole farce is a result of the lad's rather impish idea of a joke," the prince said glumly. "I fear I've been lenient, but once I have him firmly in hand again, I'll do what I can to correct his thinking."

"Good idea," Retief commented. "You can start now." Even as he spoke, the crape myrtles parted and the boy's grubby face poked through.

"Aw, Willy," he said reproachfully. "You spoiled it! I was going to have some fun with that bunch of brigands when they got here—" he broke off abruptly as half a dozen unwashed louts garbed in soiled and ragged remnants of once-gaudy livery came crashing through the hedge, beyond the bench, their crude, home-made cutlasses drawn.

"Well, looky here," the apparent leader of the piratical crew remarked in a stagy tone. "A little snot-nosed brat and a couple old grandpas. Let's have some fun, boys."

"Do you want this one, Sir Retief?" William inquired gravely. "Or may I have him?"

"After you, milord," Retief responded. As the seven-foot thug gaped, Prince William walked over to him and without a word, reversed his sabre, and using the

finger-guard as brass knuckles, felled him with a blow.
He then carefully wiped the hilt on a linen handker-
chief. The next lout in line moved forward with an oath
just in time to be tripped by Retief's foot. As he came
to all fours, Retief looked down at him with an expression of Solicitous Concern for the Unfortunate (729-d)
and asked:

"Did it faw down go boom?"

"Jest wait—" the fellow started.

"Wait, heck!" Sobby supplied; the grubby boy pushed
forward, and laid the lout out with a well-directed kick
to the jaw.

"You—you kicked him while he was down!" Magnan
yelped from the sideline. "Good work!" he added, "Your
Highness."

Meantime, Sobhain advanced to the next ruffian, who
was now flexing his formidable shoulders and adjusting
what he hoped was a fierce look on his blunt features.
At the boy's hail, "Hey! You!" the big fellow turned to
hear what this audacious runt had to say and at once
received a kick in the calf of his burly leg with all the
force the child could impart to his worn boot, causing
the bulging muscle to spasm into a hard knot. The
victim leaned over with a yell to massage the agonizing
cramp and the boy kicked his other leg from under
him.

"Truss this rascal, Willy," the boy commanded his
princely tutor.

"Very well, Sobby," the elder nobleman replied
promptly. "Your sweep was a trifle slow; two hours of
exercise first thing in the morning."

"Sorry, sir," the princeling said repentently. "I didn't
mean to be cheeky, really," he amplified. "I was just
excited."

"Accepted, Your Royal Highness," William reassured
his young master. "You still need the exercise."

"Don't I know it," the boy agreed. "Locked up in
that storeroom I sort of let myself get out of shape."

"You didn't do badly, Sobhain," William commented, glancing at the two groaning thugs laid out on the grass. "But from now on I think you'd better let Lord Retief and myself handle the heavy work."

The boy prince turned to look interestedly at Retief. "Are you really Retief?" he demanded, not without a note of awe in his imperious voice. "I thought he was just a legend."

"I am indeed, he, Sobhain," Retief replied. "And I always believed *you* to be a legend."

"It appears," Prince William spoke up, "that each of my lords has spontaneously evoked the cosmos of his own profoundest yearnings. Both Northroyal's alternate destinies are realized here on this curiously malleable world. And I am somehow privileged to participate in both."

"Both, hell!" Sol interjected indignantly from beyond the gate. "I was here first, and it's *my* yearnings that count."

"So they do, Captain," William agreed soberly, "and you yourself can see the parlous state of affairs you've evoked."

"So now, *I'm* responsible already!" Sol yelled. "This bunch of bums comes along and messes up my set-up, which I just about had it running right—even had Wiggly bottled up and all; then you nosy diplomatic types got an oar in, and *fffft*! what's left is a good sample chaos! And now you blame *me*! I guess you boys better go now, before I blow my cool and let slip a few expressions like maybe 'incompetent crooks' and 'half-baked meddlers!' Good day, ladies and gents. Get outta my house at once, OK?"

"You're partially justified in your resentment, Captain," Magnan responded smoothly. "However, duty requires that *I* remain at my post, at least until certain matters are resolved to the satisfaction of Terran interests."

Sol advanced on them as if menacingly, then veered

aside and pushed back through the glittering portal. Then he turned and slammed the door in Magnan's startled face. For a moment Magnan could see the back of the hand-made panel; then it faded. He reached out, felt nothing palpable.

"Heavens!" the frail bureaucrat cried. "He's marooned us!"

"It's all right, Ben," Retief spoke up soothingly. "That silly Worm business is disposed of, and we know the way from here to the cabin."

"What?" Magnan yelped. "After days of wandering in this wilderness—how long *have* we been lost, Retief? I for one have no idea—and poor Gaby is on the other side of this confounded door!"

"We made a circle," Retief told him. "The cabin's just beyond the trees there. Notice the Domes are still in sight."

"Impossible!" Magnan gasped. "Come, let's be on our way before more of those ruffians come along. And though you've punctured this silly inflatable toy, but we know from experience that Worm is real, not a mere bladder! Those horrid shedding teeth!" he shuddered.

"An inflated neoprene bladder, plus your imagination, sir," Prince William interjected, "are quite sufficient to produce all the phenomena you've experienced. But you're quite right: the bladder was a mere imitation of the real Worm."

"Those teeth!" Magnan reminisced. "*That* was no balloon! But who could be responsible for the imitation?"

Prince William cleared his throat tactfully, but before he spoke, the boy Sobhain volunteered:

"I did it," he declared with pride. "Pretty good, eh? Scared the pants off old Boss and his hirelings, too. Wind blew it away, right after it helped me escape from that crummy room; I had it come poking around the windows and all. Willy shouldn't have popped him."

"Your Highness behaved irresponsibly," the gray-haired prince told his young charge.

"So we had not one, but two 'Worms' roaming the area," Magnan explained to himself. "No wonder things got confused."

I MUST ASK YOUR PARDON, SOL, the Voice spoke up. I HAD ASSUMED YOU WERE RESPONSIBLE FOR THE PRANK, AND IT WAS FOR THAT REASON I HAVE, I CONFESS, PERSECUTED YOU; WHEN I DISCOVERED THAT THE RENEGADE TERRY, ONE OVERBORE WAS ON THE MAKE, I COULD NOT RESIST THE OPPORTUNITY.

Sol slapped his forehead. "Oy!" he yelped. "Get that kid outa here, before I—" Prince William's outthrust foot tripped the enraged merchant mariner as he took his first step toward the boy prince, who stood his ground.

"I didn't mean the old coot any harm," he said sullenly. "Didn't even know him—except he looks a little like Boss."

"Not meaning harm, milord Prince," William told the lad, "is not sufficient for one who will one day administer an empire."

"Fat chance, Willy," Sobhain dismissed the rebuke. "We're all stuck here; back home they've probably forgotten all about me."

"By no means, milord," Retief told him. "In fact, you've come to be a legendary hero. The old story is told of how you were kidnapped from the hunting lodge at Steepcliff, and although the search went on for a hundred years, you were never found, nor was Prince William of Tallwood, your faithful tutor."

"I've only been gone for a few months," Sobhain objected. "What's this 'hundred years' stuff?"

"Time, it appears," Retief told the princeling, "is a matter of perception. On this strange world, all our perceptions are distorted."

"You mean—back in Fragonard everyone's a hundred years older?" The lad looked stricken. "Then my royal father and mother are long dead. I have to get back before my Empire falls into disarray! Why do we loiter here, William?" he turned to the older to demand. Then he whirled on Retief.

"Why should I believe you?" he almost shouted. "The great legendary worrier Earl, Retief, you claim to be. You have a knightly look, I grant, but—"

"I claim nothing, milord Prince," Retief corrected quietly. "I am Jame, Earl Retief. I know nothing of such a legend."

"It is told how, as a mere lad, you went alone to the heights of Bifrost Pass and yourself took alive the bandit Mal de Di; and later, how you—or Earl Retief—visited the Games at Northroyal incognito, and defeated the Champion; there were many who saw in him—or you— the returned emperor, and you did indeed unseat the false usurper Rolan." The boy paused to spit. "You turned him out, then disappeared as mysteriously as you had come—and *my* branch of the imperial House assumed the Lily throne. So, if you really are the fabled, and long-lost Earl, my cousin, I owe my throne to you." The boy turned to Prince William. "How say you, my lord Prince? Is this an imposter, or my benefactor?"

"He is none other than the true Retief," William said. "On that you may depend, Sobhain. But what now, sir?" He addressed the final words to Retief. "Will you resume the honors due you, or . . .?" He glanced at Sobhain, who returned his look keenly.

"Retief!" Magnan spoke up. "Does this mean that you actually, ah, are, or were in the line of succession to a throne, albeit a petty one?"

"No," Retief replied. "It's not so petty, sir," he added. "I recall that you yourself once called Fragonard the key to peace in the Eastern Arm."

"I—I only mean, I meant; I didn't mean," Magnan gobbled. "No offense, Your Imperial Highness," he went on, executing a clumsy curtsy before Sobhain, who watched in amazement.

"That's quite all right, Mr. Magnan," the boy said, almost concealing a snicker.

"Hey," Sol interjected. "If you guys are gonna start kissing each other's hands, I'm leaving." He set off in a determined fashion, but halted after two steps.

"*I* should leave already?" he inquired of the circumambient air. "It's *my* place; I'm staying. Now, clear outa here," he started and again paused. "Well," he ammended, "seein we're the other side o' the Portal, I guess there's no telling where we are. O' course, that don't matter, because the whole planet belongs to me, anyway."

REALLY, the Voice spoke up, I HAD THE IDEA IT BELONGED TO ITS AUTOCTHONOUS POPULATION.

"You think a bunch of Terries is gonna turn over a Class A world to a bunch of worms?" Sol inquired derisively.

"A moment, Captain," Magnan spoke up. "We are now entering the proper domain of the trained diplomat. Pray permit me a word."

"You already took maybe a couple dozen," Sol pointed out. "So go ahead, already. Who's counting?"

"It appears," Magnan stated soberly, "that this planet lacked a mentational species prior to the arrival of Captain S. Goldblatt, TMSS; accordingly, as is made clear in FSR One, 12-3, Chapter IX, sub-section 3-w, the Terran claim to the world cannot legitimately be challenged. Therefore, the question is merely that of the role to be assigned the local population which has attained trans-threshold status subsequent to, and due to the didactic efforts of Terran nationals."

" 'Nationals,' smashionals," Sol sneered. "*One* Terry, that's all, educated these schmendricks. Me." He gave Magnan a glance full of pride and defiance. "So what's yer fancy regulations got say about *that*?"

"Most conscientious of you to mention the point, Captain," Magnan replied smoothly. "Actually, Subsection Four, which deals with unauthorized technological transfer, is clear on the point: 'Any individual, Terran, or enjoying Civil status under Section Ten, who shall knowingly educate unsophisticated peoples, as defined under Section Nine, in such fashion as to enhance such population's capacity to wage hostilities against legitimate Terran interests shall be liable under Chapter One, Section One, to such penalties, not to exceed confinement for his lifetime plus ten years, as shall be prescribed by a duly constituted multi-species tribunal, as defined in FSR I, One, A-1.' "

Sol frowned at the frail diplomat as if incredulous. "You're coming in here, on my own turf and talking 'penalties'?" He tugged the loose collar of his well-worn tunic as if to relieve internal pressure. "This is *my* world, Mister Ah. What *I* say goes! I got no need for no space lawyers tryna get tough!" He advanced a step and was confronted by Retief, who said quietly, "Easy, Captain; if you're in charge as you say, then I presume you're responsible for the activities of Worm; the real Worm, not this silly bag of air."

"Well," Sol temporized, "don't get me wrong. I got maybe a few problem areas to clean up here. But I'm doing OK until you boys come along, so why don't you boys, and that crook Overbore and the rest of you just do a fast fade and leave me work it out. OK?"

"You speak, Captain," Magnan piped up, "as if a ravening monster were not at large, terrorizing the countryside! You've a great deal to answer for, sir! I suggest that if you would adopt a less truculent attitude, we may begin to evolve a solution to this contretemps!"

"There you go," Sol carped. "Talking them big words. 'Contretemps,' eh? Well, I got you on that one: I had plenty time I should view the Webber in my spare time, which I had nothing else but, for some time now. 'Contretemps,' that's a bum situation, which it should happen to somebody else!"

"Nonetheless," Magnan offered severely, "it has happened, indeed is happening to *us*. And all due to *your* irresponsibility, Captain."

Sol slapped his forehead again with enough force to rock his bullet-like head on its thick neck. "Enemies!" he yelled. "Woe! I maybe ain't got enough troubles I should have this schnook giving me a hard time?"

"Captain," Magnan said patiently, "in spite of your resort to obscure dialects, I happen to know that the appellation 'schnook' which you have applied to me is far from complimentary. I demand an immediate apology. You said 'schlimeil,' too," he added.

"Not me!" the captain blurted. " 'Schmendrick,' maybe. And let's see you make me apologize, Mr. Ah. I got rights, plenty of 'em! Now get outa here! I got no more time fer yuz!"

"Here?" Magnan echoed in a tone of Astonishment at a Logical Lapse By One's Verbal Opponent (281-Q). He waved a hand at the surrounding forest wall. "You're demanding I vacate the entire planet? I, a duly authorized First Secretary of Embassy of Terra, in the performance of his duties?"

"Secretary?" Sol hooted. "I don't see no typewriter, not even no dictation machine. What kind Secretary is that?"

"The title, sir," Magnan responded loftily, "is one of considerable dignity, as in 'Secretary of State,' and has nothing whatever to do with stenography."

"So now you're a big-shot politician, hey? So what're you doing out here in the boondocks of the boondocks, you should give a hard time to the sole owner this dizzy planet?"

"I emphatically did not lay claim to Cabinet rank," Magnan declared coldly. "I merely cited the ancient title of the foreign minister of an early historic state known, as I recall, as NICE DAY. That, in order to define the nonclerical nature of the title 'Secretary.' I am, as it happens, a close advisor to His Terran Excellency, Elmer Shortfall, Ambassador Extraordinary and

Minister Plenipotentiary to this benighted world. Are you satisfied, sir?"

Sol shrugged elaborately. "If *you're* satisfied you should be some kind bureaucrat, why should I complain about it? Just get lost, is all."

Retief came forward again to face the bull-necked spaceman squarely. "Mr. Magnan is merely trying to establish his *bona fides*, Captain," he explained. "He has a right to be here. Naturally, he's rather confused, as are we all, by the chaotic situation."

"*I* ain't confused!" Sol barked. "I built this here closet, and I guess I can say who's got business in it!"

Magnan peered over Retief's shoulder to interject. "We're no longer *in* your confounded closet, sir!" He came around his bigger colleague to expand on his thesis: "Clearly, we're out here in the woods, unconfined. Your house is perhaps some miles from here!"

"Then where *are* we at, huh?" Sol jeered. "We went inna closet, right? And we ain't come out, so *you* figger it, pal!"

"When you so rudely slammed the door in my face, sir," Magnan yelped, "the closet and presumably the room behind it disappeared! I saw them! I mean, I didn't see them! You know what I mean!"

"Don't tell me what I know, young feller," Sol grumbled.

"Well," Magnan faltered, "I was just. . . ."

"Sure you was, honey," Gaby agreed. "I guess we orter go now, since this *gentleman* don't want us."

"I heard the way you said, 'gentleman,'" Sol accused. "So get lost already! Scram! Dangle! Twenty-three skidoo!"

IT IS TIME TO RESOLVE THIS MATTER, the Voice spoke up, startling Magnan as usual.

"Don't *do* that!" he ordered. "Just when I was getting my thoughts in order, *you* pop up in that disconcerting fashion! Of course, the matter must be resolved, the question is; precisely *what* matter?"

"Trespassers on *my* claim," Sol supplied promptly.

"Getting back on the job at the Cuckoo," Small suggested. "Place is prolly looted and burned by now."

"Sending all these dreadful people away," Gaby offered, giving Magnan the Look. "So we can get back to *us*, Benny."

CLEARING ALL THESE ALIENS OFF ZANNY-DO, the Voice thundered, overwhelming lesser utterances.

"The matter requiring immediate effective action," Magnan stated loudly, "is the regularization of affairs here on U-748-A, to include the formalization of the *de facto* domination of the world by the indigenes known as the Zanny-doers, and recognition of the role of the Terran Mission in bringing this planet into the greater Galactic community. In addition," he went on, after a pause for breath, "to establish a rule of law and order here, to bring enlightenment to the native population, and to suppress the activities of the lawless element, as represented by Mr. Ed . . . (ward?) Magoon here."

As he paused again, dirty Eddie came up to him and said, almost quietly, "It ain't 'Egbert,' if that's what yer thinking about. 'Eddie' will do, good." Then he added, louder, "And whataya talking, 'lawless'? You said yerself we got no laws here, so what's to break?"

"It is to precisely that parlous situation that I refer, Mr. Magoon," Magnan quickly reassured the indignant hoodlum. "Now, what we have to do first, is decide just whose paradigm shall be paramount, and take steps to suppress all others. Actually," he added, to Retief, "I'm sure we've quite enough now to place before His Excellency the Terran AE and MP." Magnan looked triumphantly at the others. "So let's be off, Jim."

"Not quite yet, Ben, I suggest," Retief countered.

"Why ever not?" Magnan yelped. "Retief, it's not like you to drag your figurative feet at a moment like this! We must waste no time in placing this entire matter before the Ambassador!"

"I think, sir," Retief demurred, "we need one more item."

"And what, pray, might that be?" Magnan demanded. "Surely, the need to rectify this situation takes primacy over all other considerations!"

"*My* first, and indeed only priority, sir," Prince William spoke up, "is to restore my liege lord, Prince Sobhain cuchelaine ap Cool, to his people with all dispatch." He patted the boy reassuringly on the shoulder.

"It's *my* planet!" Sol reiterated hotly. "And you wanta turn it over to Worm to louse up for everybody. Damn animal!"

IGNORING THE PREJUDICIAL NATURE OF THE SENTIMENTS JUST EXPRESSED, the Voice cut in with a hint of indignation, I MERELY CITE PARAGRAPH THREE, SECTION A-1, OF THE PREAMBLE TO THE GROTIAN ACCORD, AS HOMOLOGATED ON WENDY, ALE THIRD, TWENTY-SIX-FIFTEEN.

"Groints!" Small exclaimed. "He's got us, right, Retief?"

"Not quite, Big," Retief replied quietly. "Actually the citation refers to natural life-forms only, genetically engineered forms being specifically excluded from the exercise of sovereign powers."

"Heavens!" Magnan gasped. "Do you mean that Worm is some sort of unnatural monster, and not just a sort of overgrown pillar?"

"Or not a pillar at all?" Eddie suggested. "Guess that leaves I and my boys in charge."

"Hardly, Mr. Voice," Magnan huffed. "Under no circumstances can one assent to the cession, by default, of a .999 Terroid world to a mere disembodied voice!"

NOR YET TO A BAND OF TERRAN FREE-BOOTERS, the Voice pointed out.

"Right!" Eddie agreed enthusiastically. "That Embassy crowd has got to go!"

"It was hardly the Terran Mission to which the Voice alluded," Magnan rebuked the saucy fellow.

"He's tryna pull yer laig, Mr. Magnan," Small told Magnan. "What I say is, we got to respect the Captain's prior claim and all, and allow fer Prince Willy's ideas,

as modified by us regler fellers: the concensus, you
might say—"

THE INVALID PRECEPT OF MOB RULE IS HARDLY GERMAINE,
the Voice put in. I PERCEIVE THAT I MUST NOW INVOKE
EMINENT DOMAIN, WITH ALL WHICH THAT IMPLIES. I SHALL
INFORM YOU OF MY DECISION PRESENTLY.

"Absurd!" Magnan gulped. "Why this matter would
tax the sagacity of a dozen Underground Deepthink
Teams! Surely you'd not propose we attempt to adjudi-
cate it quite on your own! And in the presence of totally
unauthorized personnel, too." His glance went disdainfully from Small to Eddie before coming tenderly to
rest on Gaby, dabbing at her eyes again—or still? Magnan
wondered.

IF I MAY BE PERMITTED A FURTHER WORD, the Voice cut
across the babble, I SUBMIT THAT JURISDICTION RESTS NOT
WITH THE VENAL PETTY OFFICIALS OF THE CDT, NOR THE
LAWLESS TRASH WHO'VE MADE MY PEACEFUL WORLD A HELL
THESE SEVERAL YEARS NOW, BUT INDEED WITH MYSELF—

"Yeah?" Small and Eddie challenged in unison. "So
what you got in mind?" Small demanded, while Eddie
blurted, "I hope you ain't figuring to ace I and my boys,
which I guess we got a few rights!"

VERY FEW, Voice agreed. ALL WAS ORDERLY HERE UN-
TIL YOU CAME. OR ALMOST SO. ONE MUST CONCEDE THAT
THE ADVENT OF YOUNG VICE-CONSUL OVERBORE WAS COIN-
CIDENT WITH THE INCEPTION OF A SERIES OF BIZARRE EVENTS
FROM THE REPERCUSSIONS OF WHICH POOR, SUFFERING
GOLDBLATT'S OTHER WORLD, OR SHOULD I SAY SARDON, IS
STILL REELING, FIGURATIVELY. AN EXPRESSION HAVING NO
REFERENCE TO THE PLANET'S AXIAL ROTATION, NOR ITS AN-
NUAL CIRCUIT OF THE STAR.

"You're simply complicating the issue!" Magnan
carped.

THAT, Voice informed him, IS A CONTRADICTION IN
TERMS. SINCE I AM ABLE TO COMMUNICATE WITH YOUR
SIMPLE MIND ONLY AT A CONCEPTUAL LEVEL, I SUBMIT THAT
IT IS YOURSELF, BENMAGNAN, WHO OBFUSCATES.

"Rhetoric aside," Magnan whispered, "let's stick to facts: one, Captain Goldblatt was here first; the first Terran, that is; he met a local, who, or which, used him in a most unprincipled manner. And what do you mean 'young Vice-Consul Overbore?' Mr. Overbore is a senior Career Minister, and Number Two man in the Terran Embassy to Sardon!"

EVEN SIDNEYOVERBORE WAS YOUNG ONCE, Voice reminded Magnan. All heads present nodded in agreement.

"You mean this Elmer feller was here before, when he was just a green hand," Small offered.

"He sure was!" Sol supplied. "Do I remember the young squirt! Come in the Place one night, full of ideas, he was. Started right in bossing; that's why we called him 'Boss.' Planted some kinda high-tech gadgets, too. Set up what he called *de facto* gubment. Had this Enforcer, and this here Emergency Crew—bunch o' young squirts. We never paid the sucker much mind, but them gadgets o' his bollixed up the paradigm—said he was just tryna measure the Vug flux and all. Full o' fancy talk, too, about the purity o' science and the sacred mission and stuff, but turned out he was on the make worser'n old Eddie here."

"Wait a *minute!*" Eddie protested, at the same moment that a man clad in a bramble-torn late mid-afternoon top informal dickey-suit stumbled into view along the path.

"I protest!" he barked, holding up a formerly manicured hand imperiously.

"Good Lord!" Magnan gasped. "Why, Mr. Overbore, sir! Pray take a seat; you look quite all in!"

"No seats here, Magnan!" the Counselor barked, looking around curiously. His gaze lingered on the collapsed bladder that had been one avator of the fearsome Worm.

"Damn scoundrel!" the Counselor muttered. "I suspected something of the sort all along, of course! That Sol imposter and his fairy-tales of over-educated cater-

pillars! Now, you fellows," he focused his remarks on
Magnan and Retief, "time to get busy here. Retief!" he
seemed belatedly to recognize his former colleague.
"What are *you* doing here? Thought you'd been kidnapped and done away with some time ago. In fact, I
heard a reward had been offered for your safe return,
my boy; you see how tenderly solicitous the Corps is of
even the humblest of its own!"

"I flunked humility at the Institute," Retief pointed
out.

"I saw several of those posters, sir," Magnan yelped.
"They said 'dead or alive.' "

"Poor Art," Overbore mourned. "He *did* have a tendency to get carried away. But enough of this yivshish,
we've work to do!"

"You tryna weasel outa that nice pile o' guck you
promised me if I laid the bandit Retief by the heels?"
Smeer demanded via the Captain, who recoiled, stepped
to the rear, and held a vociferous conversation with
himself.

"Lucky we know about old Cap's set-up with that
lousy cop," Small remarked. "Otherwise a feller'd think
he'd went off his gourd and all."

"Ben," Counselor Overbore's voice cut through the
small-talk like a machete, "candidly, I'm surprised to
find a diplomat of your seniority in the company of such
riff-raff—" Before he could complete the rebuke, Small's
arm, carelessly outflung, accidentally struck the senior
bureaucrat across the mouth. Small turned looking
solicitous.

"Geese, yer Worship," he exclaimed, miming Dismay at an Untoward Turn of Events, (945-d) overlain
with a classic 17-b (Astonishment at the Totally Unexpected). Overbore spluttered, spat a tooth fragment
and made gobbling sounds, among which the word
'assassin' was audible. Magnan leaped forward to soothe
the ruffled dignity of his Chief.

"Gosh, sir," he improvised unimaginatively. "I'm sure Mr. Small didn't mean—"

"What the oaf *meant*, Magnan," Overbore grated, "dwindles to insignificance in the light of what he *did*!" The Counselor paused to take dental census with the tip of his tongue.

"That implant set me back plenty, Ben," he announced, the while glaring balefully at Small.

"Now don't you go worrying, Mister Big Shot," Small advised. "The way I figure it, you got plenty in that coded account on Qumballoon to buy you a whole new jaw-bone."

"What's that?" Overbore barked. "Do you imply that I've feathered my nest in defiance of Corps regulation, local law, basic morality and common decency?"

"Naw, I just said you stole a bundle," Big corrected patiently.

"And you, Sol?" Overbore challenged. "Just what have *you* set aside for yourself, which allows you to join so readily in this defamation of a senior diplomat and Counselor of this embassy?"

"Ben," Overbore next addressed his junior. "Do you propose to stand idly by while this local dacoit slangs me in that fashion?"

"Actually, sir," Magnan replied in a rather lackluster 91-v (Prolonged Patience With One Who is Slow to Get it), "Chief Smeer's—or the Captain's charges are quite beside the point, however well-founded. As an officer of the CDT, it is my obligation to heed the evidence of my senses."

"Heed, is it?" Overbore snarled. "As for your alleged senses, Ben Magnan, they are, I submit a negligible factor in the present contretemps! I suggest, nay, I order you to disregard these fanciful allegations!"

"No, sir," Magnan replied doggedly.

"'No, sir,' you say, Ben?" Overbore barked in a harsh 172-b (Stunned Incredulity at Attack from an Unexpected Quarter). "Am I to understand that you are refusing a direct order given to you by your very own Deputy Chief of Mission?"

"That's right, I'm afraid, sir," Magnan confirmed as if incredulous of what he was hearing himself say. "After all, sir," he added, "that *was* you I unhorsed in single combat. What were you doing, riding with that bunch called, as I recall, the Rath?"

"Nonsense!" Overbore snapped. "I've never been astride a big black gelding in my life!"

"Tell him, honey," Gaby urged, pressing herself close to Magnan's side as she caressed his arm, which he gently disengaged in order to slip it about her slender waist.

"Can you deny, sir," Magnan challenged, "that it was this charming young lady whom you were terrorizing when we met on the field of Honor?"

" 'Field of Honor' indeed!" Overbore snorted. "Have you lost your mind, Ben?" he appealed with a feeble 310A (Inability to Credit Perfidy of Such Magnitude). Then he rallied. "Ben, I'm giving you one last chance to redeem yourself and to salvage your career; indeed, to emerge from this fiasco with a glowing recommendation for an accumulated bump in rank. What do you say to that, eh?" Overbore looked complacently at Retief. "As for you, a stretch in a Sardonic dungeon will be good for that stiff neck of yours. We'll see how long your arrogance lasts in durance vile."

"I doubt that, sir," Retief replied quietly. "I'm afraid you've distorted your paradigm a trifle too far for it to be retrieved now."

Overbore stepped back, and with a dramatic gesture barked: "Let this be deleted!"

I'M AFRAID NOT, SID, the small voice came back.

"You—you'd dare to attempt to defy *me*?" Overbore yelled. "Why, I invoked you and I can consign you to the Category of unrealized potentialities as easily as not!"

DON'T TRY IT, the Big Voice boomed out with sufficient

vigor to knock Overbore to his knees, in which position
he clasped his hands in a grotesque parody of a prayer-
ful attitude, his eyes fixed on Magnan. "I beseech you,
Ben," he wailed. "As one with whom you have fingered
the ceremonial kiki-stones—stop, before you soil your
conscience beyond repair! Remember the respect due a
Counselor of Embassy of Terra! Forget all this nonsense!"

"Sorry, sir," Magnan replied gloomily, "I confess it
hurts me, but not even a moral leper of the worst stripe
could stand by and see the rightful owners of this world
dispossessed, disenfranchised and displaced for the mere
personal gain of a greedy individual."

"Oh, you want graft," Overbore replied, on firmer
footing now. "Well, Ben, I'm sure something could be
arranged, such as an apartment duplicating those in the
New Waldorf Towers on Nouveau Nine, with your doxy
here, and a top-crust, solid platinum unlimited credit
card." His voice had segued to a confidential purr.
Magnan turned his back coldly.

"That does it," he announced to his biographers.
"Such venality is beyond belief."

At that point Sol spoke up: "What about *me*?" he
yelled. "When you two get through slicing up *my* world,
whataya got in mind I should get? Retire maybe on a
small pension in the Old Space'n's Home? Forget it!
Wiggly and me are gonna fight the lot o' youse to the
last!"

Magnan turned to Sol, registering Patience Overst-
ressed (17-w). "You mentioned, sir, that returning to
Zanny-du, the city, that is, would be a simple matter.
Kindly demonstrate its simplicity."

"Sure, Mr. Ah," Sol agreed. "All you got to do, you
got to come with me, over by the Spot." Without
awaiting assent, he went to the door and stepped outside; through the opening, the golden Domes were
visible in the distance.

"Retief!" Magnan yelped and grabbed his subordinate's arm. "Should we—?"

"Why not?" Retief replied and followed Sol, who led the small party, including the surly Eddie, along a woodland path to the clearing with the ruined fountain where Retief had found the nexus box. Sol went directly to the hinged tile and lifted it.

"I found this here gadget right after that louse, Sid, had it installed."

"I begin to perceive," Magnan gasped as One Beginning to Perceive (922-1), "the full enormity of your meddling here, sir!" He confronted Overbore, who shied, and abruptly became absorbed in a clump of flowering bum-bum vines twining about the base of the broken sculpture.

"Fascinating, eh, Ben?" he remarked in a tone of Utter Innocence (390-1).

"Not even an FSO-1 and Counselor of Embassy can really bring off a 390, sir," Magnan commented regretfully, "especially when you go for a mid-range. A 'b' or 'c' I might have bought."

"Intransigent to a degree," Overbore stated, as one dictating to a Court reported. "What's this about catching a cab back to town, out here in the woods? And who's responsible for breaking up this handsome Groaci copy of a Degas *Dancer?*"

"As to that, sir," Magnan began awkwardly, but was cut off by Sol, who had bustled over importantly to jostle the two diplomats aside.

"Now, like I said," he announced, "what you got to do, you got to like, scrunch down inside yer head and relax. Leave me do the work."

"What's this feller talking about, Benny?" Gaby demanded, almost climbing his arm. "I tell ya, I don't like this, messing around with Transfer point Sixteen and all. Why, I heard—"

"Not now, my dear," Magnan shut her off. He caught Retief's eye. "I say, Jim, do you suppose—"

"Don't do no supposing, Mister," Small suggested,

rather abruptly. "Ain't safe here in the stay-away zone. I just now figgered out—"

"All you guys are nuts," Dirty Eddie announced, coming up late. He was at once felled by a sweep of Prince William's arm. Sobhain was craning to see over Gaby's shoulder.

"What's in the box?" he inquired of his tutor, who shook his head. The boy fell silent.

"You got to like pick up the thread," Sol was announcing didactically. "I found out—"

"What is it, Jim?" Magnan inquired anxiously of his colleague. "I thought the nexus box was a Galactic Ultimate Top Secret device on the threshold of real-theoretical interface!"

"So it is, sir," Retief confirmed. "Remember Eisenstein's Dilemma? His rebuttal of Shrodinger's cat, if you recall."

"I guess I read something about that in *Unlikely*, a few issues back," Magnan acknowledged. "But what have essays in abstruse physics to do with the fact that we're stranded in the midst of a wilderness infested with hostile Bolos and non-inflatable Worms, plus a Spectre, I understand, to say nothing of these ubiquitous gnats, all the while being hunted by the Rath, as well as every idle cutthroat on the planet in expectation of a fabulous reward?"

"Well put, sir," Retief told his supervisor. "I think perhaps Sol knows something, so let's see what it is."

"Ha!" Sol barked. "I know stuff I don't even know I know. Now, get aligned, like I said."

DO AS SOL SUGGESTS, the Voice boomed out in the silence. I SHOWED HIM THE TECHNIQUE SOME TIME AGO.

I DARE YOU TO TRY IT! Junior's derisive voice came, as from a remote distance. YOU CAN DISSOLVE THE WHOLE SPACE/TIME/VUG INTERSECTION BACK INTO THE PRIMORIDAL YLEM. TAKE MY ADVICE, GET CLEAR OF THE CONCENTRA-TION, AND TAKE A HIKE. IT WILL TAKE A LITTLE LONGER. BUT YOU'LL GET SOMEWHERE. OR WOULD YOU LIKE SOME MORE GOLFBALLS TO DROWN IN, MR. RETIEF?"

"Go ahead, Sol," Retief prompted. At once he felt a diaphonous *touch* somewhere behind his eyes, crude by comparison with the delicate nuances of Voice's telepathic promptings, but clear enough. He *rotated* his attention in line with the prodding. His thoughts went to the shedding facades of the Terran Embassy, the now-deserted street before it, and—

"That's him!" a squeaky voice yelled. "Grab him quick!"

"—back there, you!" Small's voice snarled, at Retief's side. He became aware again of the surrounding forest, now aboil with unshaven louts, among whom he glimpsed Horny, Bimbo, Tiny, Tim, Gimpy, Hump, Chief Smeer, Deputy Chief Smudge, Buzzy and Constable Bob, all converging on him. He picked up the constable and using him as a flail, laid low the first ranks, at which the somewhat less eager recoiled. Small looked at Retief and grinned. Just then, Bill, the Marine guard, resplendent in fresh dress blues, burst into sight. He halted at the sight of the little group surrounded by their groaning attachees.

"On the way to tip you off, General," he told Retief. "Guess I missed the fun."

"There'll be more, Bill," Retief reassured the lad.

"Okay," Sol spoke up. "I didn't expect some kind of riot while I'm tryna get the old bug axes aligned. Let's try it again." He squeezed his eyes shut.

"Sir," Bill said diffidently to Retief. "Maybe you ought to report in now. Old Shorty's busting a gusset—oh, His Terran Excellency is eager to speak to you, sir, I mean."

"Just going, Bill," Retief replied, and after taking three steps along the path, emerged into a dimly lit strip littered with debris and lined with irregular pilings supporting, far above, the familiar peeling facades of Embassy Row.

"Hell," Sol remarked from close behind, "let's try that again, a little tighter, OK?" The oversized glass-walled elevator slid to a stop with a soft *whoosh*! and the entire party entered. Magnan paused to look back.

"Heavens!" he remarked. "In that fog, it's no wonder we became a trifle confused."

3

Five minutes later, on the carpet before the three-meter iridium desk, which was the Fortress Unvanquishable since far Sacnoth of His Terran Excellency, Magnan was stammering out his account of recent events.

"—actually, sir, it seems Sid Overbore was a member of a Secret Survey Party sent in here to Goldblatt's Other World—uh, excuse me, sir: to Sardon—"

"You mean this damned Spookworld, I assume, Ben," His Ex interjected. "Yes, yes, I know all that—"

"Not quite all, sir, if Your Excellency will forgive me."

"Get on with it, Ben," his leader urged, casting a glance at those waiting their turn. "I've still got to hear Retief's excuse, as well as the rest of this riff-raff you've dragged in here to my most private inner sanctum. Hate to be late to dinner," he added, without noticeable pleasure at the prospects for a peaceful afternoon.

"Well, anyway, sir," Magnan stammered on, "he—Sid, I mean, or, more properly, Counselor Overbore discovered some of the world's unusual properties, and conceived the plan of introducing certain elements into the local paradigm which would redound to his personal benefit—or, rather, one might say, it might not be incorrect to suggest that perhaps there are those who might, in light of the circumstances, tend to misinterpret, or, to put it another way—"

"Please do, Mr. Magnan," Shortfall boomed. "I'm sure I don't know what the devil you're talking about. Get on with it, man! I've already told you. I'm having *Chateaubriand avec Sauce Bearnaise* and Borovian Chocolate pie tonight, and I for one— "

"Please sir," Magnan begged. "Your blurb-flops can

wait. This is a matter of vital concern to the success of this Mission! You see—"

"I do *not* see, Ben," Shortfall barked; waving away the ever-present cloud of persistent gnats from his face.

"Well, after Mr. Overbore hatched his scheme," Magnan resumed, hardly less excitedly, "he needed a local intermediary, and he discovered that there were rumors among the locals of a super-pillar—"

"Rumors, Ben?" Shortfall exploded. "As for 'super-pillars,' I throw up my hands at such an epithet, mingling as it does racial prejudice of the grossest sort with superstitious dread of the unknown!"

"So," Magnan plunged ahead with a determination which was reminiscent of that of Admiral Farragut at Mobile, "he investigated on the sly, under cover of doing a wildlife survey, and he found this Standard-speaking local—"

"Nonsense, Ben," Shortfall interjected. "They all speak Standard of a sort."

"Not back then, they didn't, Your Excellency, sir," Magnan contradicted, exceeding Farragut's audacity.

"So, he found a pillar which had been taught by some marooned space'n, no doubt, to parrot a few earthly phrases," the AE and MP dismissed the matter.

"Hardly, sir, the creature actually communicated with him telepathically! Together, they worked out an arrangement whereby the peaceful, indeed inconspicuous local population, until then spending their time sleeping and moulting, were organized into disciplined mobs whose assignment it was to stir up the local Terry community, consisting as it did of the crews, and descendants thereof of a number of off-course vessels which had crashed here over the years. The latter found, to their great astonishment, that strange forces were at work here on Sardon—"

"Has no business here in the first place," His Excellency cut in. "Damned nuisance, these distressed spacemen. This TERRI organization is their idea of regularizing their state, I suppose."

"Probably, sir, something like that," Magnan whimpered. "But the point is, as I was saying—"

"Will you kindly come to this alleged point of yours, Ben Magnan!" the Chief of Mission yelled.

"The point, sir," Magnan intoned as impressively as one can intone while being humiliated in the presence of one's Maiden in Distress, who is tugging at one's arm and whispering urgently in one's ear.

"—tell the bag of wind to go blow himself out to sea, Benny!" Magnan shook off the tempting proposal, and resumed more or less where he had left off, "that Sid Overbore, in conclusion with an illegally educated local mobster, has transformed a once-peaceful world into a hotbed of intrigue, terrorism, and anarchy, and one in which the Terran Mission itself is menaced with disaster!"

"Heavy," Shortfall commented. At that moment, the door burst open and Bill, neatly shaved and uniformed, burst in, dragging by one upper arm the resisting bulk of Chief Smeer.

"Why," Shortfall cried, jumping to his feet with such haste as to knock over his hip-o-matic swivel, which threshed against the carpet, gribble-hide, hand-loomed, Chief of Mission, for the use of, like a stricken thing.

"Why, it's Foreign minister Blott," Shortfall continued his 7990a (Astonished Delight at an Unexpected Pleasure and Honor).

"Looky who I found tryna do a soft-shoe through the side-door," Bill announced proudly. "Hi, General, and Mister Magnan." He went on, "Big, you and Gabe here, lemme innerdooce His Excellency, the Terry Ambassador, Elmer Shortfall."

Shortfall was still on his feet, staring in amazement at the young Marine.

"Sergeant!" he barked. "What is the meaning of this outrage? Kindly release the Foreign Minister at once. Mr. Blott," he pressed on gamely, "pray accept my abject apologies for this unseemly occurence. I assure Your Excellency that it is not Terran policy to manhandle local dignitaries paying a call on the Terran legate!"

"Skip all that, Elmer," Smeer returned casually, gently massaging the member Bill had released. "What I wanna know, are you sticking with the deal Sid and me negotiated, or what?"

"Why, Mr. Minister," Shortfall responded eagerly, "I'm sure that any accommodation worked out with the planetary government by my Counselor during my brief indisposition following my rather informal reception at the port will be quite acceptable to Sector, and of course to me personally."

"We were gonna leave Sector out of this," Smeer corrected. "Just a quiet, little deal between beings-of-the-Galaxy, OK?"

"As to that, Mr. Minister," Elmer responded, "I can hardly negotiate a treaty establishing the basis of Terran-Sardonic relations for the next few millenia entirely on my own!"

"Say, Mr. Magnan," Bill spoke up in the momentary silence. "Ain't nobody gonna tell His Ex this heel is a renegade cop, and not no Foreign Minister, which there ain't one hereabouts?" Magnan shushed the lad.

"You don't get it, Elmer," Smeer announced. "This here got nothing to do with no treaty. Just the old handshake. Right?" The cheeky local bustled forward and offered His Excellency a callussed member, which the latter took in gingerly fashion and dropped at once, wiping his hand furtively on his issue striped pants.

"By all means, my dear Blott!" he agreed enthusiastically. "Those lintheads back at Sector prolly never heard o' good old Sardon anyway!"

"Is that for the record, sir?" Euphonia Furkle inquired, materializing at His Ex's elbow in a fashion quite unexplicable for a woman of her bulk.

"The record?" Shortfall yelled. "I've told you a thousand times, Miss Furkle, don't creep up on me like that! And forget the record, just for the moment, of course. I'm feeling my man, Furkie," he added in a confidential tone. "Let's keep this all quite informal for the moment," he cried in the tone of one proposing a late party.

"OK by me, Elmer," Smeer spoke up. "I guess maybe we got one or two little points here that kind of strain Terry ethics a little, not to say nothing about the old SAP."

"What old sap?" Shortfall challenged. "I trust you're not referring to me in that unseemly fashion!"

"The Strong Anthropic Principle, you know, Elmer," Smeer cajoled. "We agreed to relax it a little here and there to accommodate the local SSP and all, and that about wraps it up. OK if I put this here Retief unner arrest now?"

"What for?" Shortfall barked, more surprised than indignant. "What's the fellow been up to now?"

"Notta thing, sir," Magnan spoke up. "Like myself, Mr. Retief has been the victim of as baroque a chain of circumstances as have been recorded in Corps history."

"Oh, yes, there's the matter of Corps history," Shortfall acceded. "One dislikes to contemplate the footnote accorded to early Terry-Sardon relations will record. Riots, mayhem, the kidnapping of the Foreign Minister, to say nothing of rampant racism, isolationism, you should pardon the expression, war-mongering, inciting to riot and so on."

"I never done some o' that stuff, Elmer," Smeer Blott objected. "The war, now: that was old Boss's idea, and then the rest o' them wild Terries which the woods are full of 'em got big ideas, so nacherly I hadda protect my turf! Just hand over this Retief here, and we'll call it square."

"That's more generous of you, I'm sure, Mr. Minister," Shortfall gushed. "Of course, there are one or two trifling technicalities with which to deal."

"Under the rug, eh, Elmer?" Smeer proposed confidentially. "Like the part about the private girlie ranch for you and the double-sized *San Souci* onna beach at someplace Sid called *Beauticia*, and the string o' ponies, and the '31 Isotta Sedanca de ville replica, and the stock o' aged Lovenbroy red and black, and the rest o' the stuff Sid put in to keep you happy."

"Keep *me* happy?" the Ambassador yelled. "Preposterous! A thirty-one, you say, with full quadriphibian gear, concours condition, tump-leather throughout? Thoughtful fellow, Sid. By the way, where is he?"

"Right here," Overbore spoke up from his position flat on the carpet where Small's weight had been keeping him still and silent. "Get this Neanderthal off me, Your Ex, and I'll tell you about the best part."

His Excellency hastened forward to assist his Number Two to his feet, helped brush the leaf-mold and spidoid-webs from his travel-stained garments and helped him to a chair.

" 'The best part,' you say, Siddy," the Number One prompted. "And pray tell, just what concessions did you make in the course of your doubtless brilliant negotiation?"

"Well, I had to agree to overlook a few minor irregularities, of course," Sid informed his solicitous chief. "Naturally, I accepted the status quo, power-struggle-wise, but there's the question of old Worm still to be resolved, but I assured His Ex, the Foreign Minister, that Terra was a sophisticated enough Galactic power to take a reasonable stand on *that!*"

"On what, precisely, Sid?" his chief pled. "Do give me the substance of your quid pro quo, Sid, I'm all aquiver to get on the SWIFT gear and inform Sector of my brilliant coup."

"Back to that, eh?" Smeer spoke up with a new note of arrogance in his squeaky voice.

"The point is, of course, negotiable," Elmer hastened to reassure the Sardonic dignitary. "The girlie-ranch," he recalled, musingly. "I get to select—that is, I trust these homeless waifs are being well-cared for in the meantime?" The Great Man sat meditating for a moment then slapped the solid iridium desk with a sharp report.

"If *I'm* to get all these goodies," he said in a tone of Dawning Realization (2031-c), "what in heck is Sid setting up for *himself?*"

"Nothing much, sir," Overbore hastened to reassure his Chief; "only a modest residence right here on Sardon, so as to maintain surveillance of compliance with the terms of the treaty, of course."

"No girlie-ranch?" Shortfall insisted, "no '31 Isotta?"

"By the way, Sid," Smeer interjected, "is it OK if the red and green corundum crystals and the carbon ones and the element of atomic number 79 are cut and polished and stored in lock-boxes, or did you want the fun of mining 'em yerself from that patch of ground yer goodies-detector showed you?"

"Stored in a modest vault will do nicely," Sid dismissed the matter. "No need to quote the trifling details just now."

"You mean about being Emperor and having us build that palace and all," Smeer guessed.

"Enough!" Prince William spoke up suddenly. "If there's to be royalty, let it be the restoration of the true anointed, to wit milord Prince Sobhain, King of Fragonard and the Empire de Lys!"

"To be sure, of course, 'prince,' did you say?" Shortfall gobbled, straightening his tie. "Where precisely, is His Highness, and of course I didn't mean him when I characterized the present company as riff-raff."

"'Tis well he wasn't among those present and included in your insolence," William declared. "Else, he'd have rapped your skull before I could restrain him. But to proceed; I'm sure an escort of a squadron of Peace Enforcers to accompany His Highness home would seem adequately to emphasize *Corps* backing of his claim to the throne."

"Jest a fruffle-picking minute there, fellow," Chief

Smeer put in. "I guess before you go setting old Sid here up as Emperor of Sardon, us autocthones got a few words to say!"

"Reasonable enough," Shortfall agreed. "But I was under the impression, Mr. Minister, that it was you yourself who proposed the arrangement, which, though at variance with orthodox *Corps* policy is not, I suppose, entirely out of the question." Behind him, Miss Furkle rolled her eyes in expression of dazed incredulity, but dutifully recorded the statement. Shortfall turned in time to catch the tail-end of the expression. "Furkie!" he yelped. "It hardly behooves the clerical staff to assay sophisticated diplomatics such as that 987-y (Dazed Incredulity) not unmixed, unless I miss my guess with a touch of 71-a (Don't Look at Me: I Wash My Hands of the Affair)! And turn off that damned recorder."

"Sure, Chief," she agreed. "But are you really going to sit still fer Sid Overbore jumping you three grades of rank. Remember, you'll have to present credentials to *him*! But whatever you say, chief. On yer knees, too, if I know Sid."

"I heartily dislike the appellation 'chief,' Furkie, as you doubtless are well aware," the chief grumped. "As for bending the knee to Sid Overbore—" He turned in desperation to Magnan. "What about it, Ben? Is there any technicality I can air to weasel out of this one?"

"Fraid not, Mr. Ambassador," Magnan replied with a smarmy expression, edging closer to Sid, who was still dusting the evidences of his foray into wilderness from his frock coat.

"Well," Shortfall huffed. "Will no one rid me of this troublesome fellow?"

"Thomas Becket and King Henry," Magnan guessed. "Surely you don't mean me to assassinate Chief Smeer? Or was it Sid you had in mind?"

DON'T TROUBLE YOURSELVES, the silent Voice commanded, in a tone like Mount Rushmore. THE MATTER IS ACADEMIC. CHIEF SMEER IS, AFTER ALL A PILLAR AND AS

SUCH A LATECOMER TO MY NATIVE PLANET. THE ONLY PARTY
WITH WHOM A MEANINGFUL TREATY CAN BE JOINED IS
MYSELF.

"And who, pray, are *you*?" Shortfall and several others demanded in ragged unison.

ASK RETIEF, was the curt reply.

All eyes turned to the referenced diplomat.

"Yes, yes," Shortfall stammered. "What do you know
about this voice in the head, fellow? I'd feared I was
going bananas."

"Tell them, Gaby," Retief urged the girl, who stepped
forward and recited: "The pillars are latecomers to the
scene, Mr. Retief tole me, and Worm tole him," she
stated woodenly, "they have arrived only a few months
before Captain Goldblatt. Both were led and benignly
instructed by the resident intellect, a hive intelligence,
comprising several hundred billion individuals, intricately interconnected by telepathic linkages, analogously
to the interconnections of the hundred billion neurons
of the human brain, only more so. This Mind welcomed
the pillars, a party of malcontents from some place
called Kruntz, a few lights out-Arm, and taught them
how to manipulate the energies. Cap Goldblatt came
along and this Wiggly helped him out like he said, and
pretty soon Cap was busy revamping the landscape.
Not bad, either; nice woods and all like he read about
but never saw. Then more Terries arrived, and everything got messed up. But, Mind, or Voice, or Worm
like we been calling it, is a big-hearted fella, for a fella
with no heart—and no body, really—"

"Wait a minute!" Magnan objected. "There was no
native life-form here except for the pillars!"

"Just one, sir," Retief pointed out, brushing at a long
gnat.

"You mean . . .?" Magnan choked.

Retief nodded. Gaby resumed: "It was just a lot of
free-flying neurons—"

"Free-flying!" Magnan exclaimed. "Those confounded

gnats! Good lord! You mean all along they've been supplying the energy that keeps this madhouse running?"

"Enough, Ben," Shortfall ordained gravely. "At least we have a clear record there; not one of the little dacoits have we swatted, goaded almost to desperation as we were." As he spoke, the last few attendant gnats drifted away.

SORRY ABOUT THAT, Voice offered contritely, DIDN'T MEAN TO BE A PEST. BUT OF COURSE I HAD TO KEEP TABS ON JUST WHAT ALL YOU FOREIGNERS WERE UP TO. NOW THAT I SEE NOT ALL OF YOU—OR EVEN MOST OF YOU ARE OF THE STRIPE OF SIDOVERBORE AND BIMBO AND HIS ILK. NOW, CAPTAINSOLGOLDBLATT IS A REASONABLE FELLOW, AND I'M SURE HE AND I COULD CONCLUDE A MODUS VIVENDI, WHICH BENMAGNAN, A DECENT CHAP, COULD EMBODY IN A FORMAL AGREEMENT. SO LET IT BE DONE.

"Just arrange for a layman dead two centuries to negotiate on behalf of Terra, you suggest—" Shortfall started, halting abruptly as the old spaceman known to the other Terrans as Sol pushed forward.

"Not by a damn sight I'm not dead!" he declared vehemently. "Sure, I'll work out a deal with old Worm. Told you he wasn't a bad fellow," he told Magnan, who was dithering, uncertain whether to offer the old fellow a chair, or summon the Marine guard.

"Y-you mean . . . ?" he stuttered, "you're *really* the fabled Captain Goldblatt? Heavens, what an honor, sir!" He urged the old fellow to a chair, while Shortfall righted his hip-o-matic and settled himself in it, assuming his Benign (1-c) expression.

"As you were saying, sir?" he prompted. "Just sketch in the broad outline, and I'll have my staff fill in the details." He turned reluctantly to face the irrascible Sol. "Captain Goldblatt," he managed, "you'll be hailed as a living monument to the great deep of exploration! It's as if Christopher Columbus showed up alive and well in Cuba! You'll be hailed as a planetary hero!"

"Hero, schmero," Sol returned disdainfully. "I just want to get back to my retirement cottage, and see to the garden."

4

Half an hour later, with an impressive document indicted, signed, sealed with scarlet ribbon and a blob of CDT-issue wax, His Excellency turned his attention to Magnan and Retief, still standing by after the rest had been dismissed, except for Gaby, who lingered behind Magnan.

"In your case, Ben," Shortfall pontificated, "your very ineffectiveness redounds to your exoneration. You could have had nothing to do with this mess, from which I've so adriotly extricated us. You, Retief, are another matter: beginning with your unwarranted assault on my welcoming committee, you've repeatedly violated hallowed *Corps* policy by Doing Something where clearly, Creative Inaction was called for. I've been pondering an appropriate just and dispassionate response for Mother Terra to place in the record. I've found it, not, I admit without some hints from our new friend, Voice, and this is it." He fixed Retief with a steely, or possibly pot-metal gaze, and told the erring junior officer that Terra had decided that permanent assignment to his curious world as Consul-General would be in order. "You've made this mare's nest, Mr. Retief," he declared. "Now you lie in it!" He gave Retief a challenging look. Retief nodded casually. "Now you, Ben, I think it would be as well if I assigned you as a Special Supervising Consul just to more or less keep an eye on things. Dismissed."

5

Gaby attempted to sit in Shortfall's lap. "Why you're a sweetie after all!" she burbled. Then she hurried to Magnan. "Now that you're going to stay on, Benny, we can do something about loose-nating a nice ten-room house in Scarsdale, with a heated pool and a Olympic size tennis court, and a private bowling alley. It won't be much, but I'll make it home for ya!"

After a round of hand-shaking in the hall, Captain Goldblatt set off to see to his herbaceous borders, and Retief went alone along the empty corridor and out into the sunshine of the noisy street, hung with banners, alive with an eager crowd of Fragonards; looked eagerly along the street where a lead dire-beast had just appeared, brilliantly caparisoned. Retief's eyes went to a narrow window in an unremarkable facade across the way; something stirred behind the half-drawn shade, and light glinted from polished metal. He started determinedly across toward the inconspicuous door.

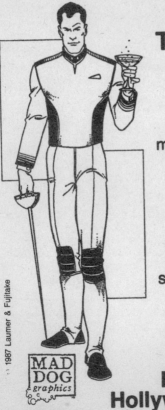

FRED SABERHAGEN

Fred Saberhagen needs very little introduction these days. His most famous creations—the awesome Berserkers—are known to SF readers around the world. He's reached the bestseller lists several times, most recently with his "Book of Swords" series, and his novels span the territory from hard science fiction to high fantasy. Quite understandably, Saberhagen's been labeled one of the best writers in the business.

These fine novels by Saberhagen are available from Baen Books:

PYRAMIDS
A fascinating new twist on the time-travel novel, introducing a great new series hero: Pilgrim, the Flying Dutchman of Time, whose only hope for returning home lies in subtly altering the history of our own timeline to more closely reflect his own. Fortunately for us, Pilgrim's timeline is a rather more pleasant one than ours, and so the changes are—or at least are supposed to be—for the better. Learn why the curse of the Pharaoh Khufu (builder of the Great Pyramid) had a special reality, in *Pyramids*. "Saberhagen's light, imaginative and enjoyable adventures speed along twisting paths to a climax that is even more surprising than the rest of the book."
—*Publishers Weekly*

AFTER THE FACT
This is the second novel featuring the great new series hero, Pilgrim—the Lost Traveller adrift in time and dimensionality. His current project: to rescue Abraham Lincoln from assassination, AFTER THE FACT!

THE FRANKENSTEIN PAPERS
At last—the truth about the sinister Dr. Frankenstein and his monster with a heart of gold, based on a history written by the monster himself! Find out what happened when the mad Doctor brought his creation to life, and why the monster has no scars.

THE "EMPIRE OF THE EAST" SERIES
THE BROKEN LANDS, Book I
A masterful blend of high technology and high sorcery; a unique adventure in a world on the brink of ultimate change; a world were magic rules—and science struggles to live again! "*Empire of the East* is one of the best science fiction fantasy epics—Saberhagen can be justly proud. Highly recommended."—*Science Fiction Review*. "A fine mix of fantasy and science fiction, action and speculation."—Roger Zelazny

THE BLACK MOUNTAINS, Book II
East meets West in bloody conflict on a world where magic rules, but technology is revolting! "*Empire of the East* is the work of a master!"—*Magazine of Fantasy and Science Fiction*

ARDNEH'S WORLD, Book III
The gripping climax of the "Empire of the East" series. "Ranks favorably with Tolkien. Exceptional in sheer unbridled zest and imaginative sweep."—*School Library Journal*

* * *

THE GOLDEN PEOPLE
Genetically perfect, super-human children are created by a dedicated scientist for the betterment of Mankind. As the children mature, however, they begin to wonder if Man *should* survive . . .

LOVE CONQUERS ALL
In a future where childbirth is outlawed and promiscuity required, one woman dares fight the system for the right to bear children.

MY BEST

Saberhagen presents his personal best, in *My Best*. One sure to please lovers of "hard" science fiction as well as high fantasy.

OCTAGON

Players scattered across the continent are engaged in a game called "Starweb." Each player has certain attributes, and can ally with or attack any of the others. But one player seems to have confused the reality of the world: a player with the attributes of machinelike precision and mechanical ruthlessness. His name is Octagon, and he's out for blood.

You can order all of Fred Saberhagen's books with this order form. Check your choices and send the combined cover price/s to: Baen Books, Dept. BA, 260 Fifth Avenue, New York, New York 10001.

PYRAMIDS • 320 pp. •
65609-0 • $3.50   _____
AFTER THE FACT • 320 pp. •
65391-1 • $3.95   _____
THE FRANKENSTEIN PAPERS •
288 pp. • 65550-7 • $3.50   _____
THE BROKEN LANDS • 224 pp. •
65380-6 • $2.95   _____
THE BLACK MOUNTAINS • 192 pp.
• 65390-3 • $2.75   _____
ARDNEH'S WORLD, Book III •
192 pp. • 65404-7 • $2.75   _____
THE GOLDEN PEOPLE • 272 pp. •
55904-4 • $3.50   _____
LOVE CONQUERS ALL • 288 pp. •
55953-2 • $2.95   _____
MY BEST • 320 pp. • 65645-7 •
$2.95   _____
OCTAGON • 288 pp. •
65353-9 • $2.95   _____

WILL *YOU* SURVIVE?

In addition to Dean Ing's powerful science fiction novels—*Systemic Shock, Wild Country, Blood of Eagles* and others—he has written cogently and inventively about the art of survival. **The Chernobyl Syndrome** is the result of his research into life after a possible nuclear exchange . . . because as our civilization gets bigger and better, we become more and more dependent on its products. What would *you* do if the machine stops—or blows up?

Some of the topics Dean Ing covers:
* How to *make* a getaway airplane
* Honing your "crisis skills"
* Fleeing the firestorm: escape tactics for city-dwellers
* How to build a homemade fallout meter
* Civil defense, American style
* "Microfarming"—survival in five acres
  And much, much more.

Also by Dean Ing, available through Baen Books:

ANASAZI
Why did the long-vanished Anasazi Indians retreat from their homes and gardens on the green mesa top to precarious cliffside cities? Were they afraid of someone—or some*thing*? "There's no evidence of warfare in the ruins of their earlier homes . . . but maybe the marauders they feared didn't wage war in the usual way," says Dean Ing. *Anasazi* postulates a race of alien beings who needed human bodies in order to survive on Earth—a race of aliens that *still* exists.

FIREFIGHT 2000
How do you integrate armies supplied with bayonets and ballistic missiles; citizens enjoying Volkswagens and Ferraris; cities drawing power from windmills and nuclear powerplants? Ing takes a look at these dichotomies, and more. This collection of fact and fiction serves as a metaphor for tomorrow: covering terror and hope, right guesses and wrong, high tech and thatched cottages.

Order Dean Ing's books listed above with this order form. Simply check your choices below and send the combined cover price/s to: Baen Books, Dept. BA, 260 Fifth Avenue, New York, New York 10001.

THE CHERNOBYL SYNDROME * 65345-8 *
  320 pp. * $3.50
ANASAZI * 65629-5 * 288 pp. * $2.95
FIREFIGHT 2000 * 65650-X * 252 pp. * $2.95